'I came for the hot Brit
the strong female main
was swept up in the che
It's a brilliant debut and

– LEONIE ᴍᴀᴄᴋ, ᴀᴜᴛʜᴏʀ ᴏғ *ɪɴ ɪᴛᴀʟʏ ғᴏʀ ʟᴏᴠᴇ*

'A feisty romance, perfect for fans of enemies to lovers'

– JENNIFER BIBBY, ᴀᴜᴛʜᴏʀ ᴏғ *Tʜᴇ Cᴏʀɴɪsʜ Hɪᴅᴇᴀᴡᴀʏ*

'Jen Smith has expertly crafted a love story for the ages, one that someone hundreds of years from now will dust off and see it for the treasure that it is. Nate and Laurel will dig their way into your heart and leave you breathless. The chemistry between these two pops of the pages. Laurel's heroine story of trying to save her family farm had me rooting for her from the very first page. A must read!'

– ALLY WIEGAND, ᴀᴜᴛʜᴏʀ ᴏғ *Fɪʀsᴛ Bᴀsᴇ*

'*Carbon Dating* is funny, sexy and emotional. I loved everything about the handsome Dr Nate Daley and was rooting for Laurel, her farm and her family from the start. This enemies to lovers romantic comedy had me hooked from the very first page. Archaeology has never been sexier!'

– HELEN HAWKINS, ᴀᴜᴛʜᴏʀ ᴏғ *A Cᴏɴᴄᴇʀᴛ ғᴏʀ Cʜʀɪsᴛᴍᴀs*

'A sharp-witted, enemies-to-lovers rural rumpus, that will have you wishing sexy Dr Daley would come and dig up your own garden, whilst you quaff Sauvignon Blanc with your newest fiery BFF, Laurel. I loved it and can't wait to unearth the next offering from Jen Smith.'

– SAMANTHA PENNINGTON, AUTHOR OF *DOUBLE BOOKED IN CORFU*

'A laugh-out-loud, forced proximity romance that also delivers on the swoons and spice. Blending the charm of a small-town setting, the excitement of an archaeological dig and some delicious enemies-to-lovers banter, *Carbon Dating* is guaranteed to have you smiling.'

– GEORGIA MOORE, AUTHOR OF *FOUR NIGHT STAND*

'Jen Smith's background in Medieval History shines through in her latest book. As a Field Archaeologist, I can confidently say *Carbon Dating* nails it – humour, heart, and just enough dirt to keep things real. If Bridget Jones swapped her diary for a trowel and studied with Indiana Jones, this would be her story! Packed with camaraderie, ancient secrets, and the unexpected drama of life on a dig, this rom-com is as unpredictable as C14 itself. At times, it felt like I was reliving the excitement and chaos of a month-long excavation.'

– NATASHA BILLSON, AWARD-WINNING ARCHAEOLOGIST, FILMMAKER & PRESENTER

CARBON

DATING

JEN SMITH

Serendipity, 51 Gower Street, London, WC1E 6HJ
info@serendipityfiction.com | www.serendipityfiction.com

Print ISBN 9781917163552
Ebook ISBN 9781917163569

Set in Times.
Cover design by Bailey McGinn.

Printed in India

Jen lives in the Midlands with her husband and two kids, but dreams of hot footing it down to the south of France to live in a chateau. With an MA in Medieval History, Jen's favourite castle is Caerphilly and her favourite monarch is King John (yes, yes, she knows). Jen loves writing about the trials and tribulations of falling in love, finding your person and overcoming everything that life throws at you, together. She writes for *you*, dear Reader, because everyone deserves a bit of escapism and a happily ever after.

For my HH, in spite of it all

CHAPTER ONE

LAUREL

Laurel Fletcher's life was not supposed to be like this.

She was supposed to be traveling the globe, making archaeological finds that would shock the world and challenge history. There was supposed to be academic renown, TV appearances, specialist books and grand exotic romances, before falling desperately in love with a sizzlingly hot French archaeologist who would look at her with the shining eyes of devotion.

Instead, she was shoulder-deep in a cow's arse.

'Robin! Robin, don't you dare hide from me,' Laurel called across the cowshed at her younger brother, who was trying to condense his six-foot frame to scoot behind the cattle without her seeing him.

'Robin!'

'Oh, hey Laurel, you okay?' Robin stood up from behind a cow and rubbed the back of his neck sheepishly.

'Do I look okay? Do I?' she said, bracing her free hand on the rump of the cow and pulling her arm out with a wet squelch. 'Why is it that *I* am checking the cows to see if they're pregnant? Why is it that they're late to milking? And, for the love of god, why is there cow shit all over the yard?'

The farmhand who was holding a bucket and towel for her backed away slowly.

'Look, Laurel, I overslept. Jack's being the golden child

and is out lambing. Dad's at old man Hibbert's.' Robin shuffled over. 'Nice shoes.'

He raised an eyebrow at her wellies and gave her the smile that had made a thousand hearts forgive him.

Well, not hers, and not today.

'I am not getting my shoes covered in cow shit, which I almost did because the yard is full of it.' She peeled off the arm length plastic glove and chucked it in the farmhand's bucket, along with her plastic apron.

Laurel knew that even if her clothes managed to escape whatever was coming out of the cow's behind, no matter how clean she got, she would still stink. All day. She would have to dry-clean her clothes and essentially decontaminate herself. Which is why Laurel did not do farm work anymore.

'Why is Dad at old man Hibbert's?'

Robin's face turned from contrite to accusatory, his Fletcher-grey eyes flashing with ire. Not for the first time, Laurel wondered how it was that her brothers had become typical Fletchers, and she was more like her mother.

'George Hibbert has been harassing the sheep up on the common with his quad bike again because he's pissed off that you're trying to buy those fifteen acres of land off his dad.'

Laurel rolled her eyes and pursed her lips because surely George Hibbert wasn't that petty?

'Can't you just fuck him and get it out the way? He's like a kid pulling your hair because he fancies you,' Robin grumbled.

'Fucked him two years ago,' she replied airily, 'and he was shit.' Laurel had been avoiding George Hibbert ever since, because he was ridiculously attached to what was the worst of one-night stands.

Robin grunted in distaste. Laurel had been enduring Robin's attention-seeking routine since he was old enough to speak and had been around this particular mulberry bush way too many times to be shocked. At least, not by Robin.

It was shit, and it had been a mistake. A couple of drinks

too many down the pub, and then an extremely quick and unsatisfactory fuck back at hers. But apparently, George didn't get the message that it was a one-night thing because he was still there when she woke up in the morning. He also thought that there was something nefarious keeping them from having this brilliant, sparkling, Grand Passion. That they were two halves of a whole, destined for each other. It was, however, the fact that he was as mature as a twenty-year-old which kept them apart. It's fine to act that way when you're actually twenty, but not when you're thirty-two.

'Can't you just leave it alone? Can't you just let them keep the fields?' Robin asked as he grabbed a rake leaning against the timber frame of the cowshed, purely to make it look like he was preparing to do some work. The farmhand disappeared quietly.

'I will tell you one last time, Robin.' She put her hands out and spoke slowly, as if placating a child. 'If we don't buy that land, it will be bought by developers, and there'll be five McMansions on there before you can blink.'

'And you're not going to develop it?' He scoffed, making a show of attempting to sweep the debris on the floor. She was, but not right now. Maybe in a few years with some tasteful, affordable, sustainable housing that employed local tradesmen.

Laurel glared at her brother.

'Fuck off, Robin,' she said under her breath as she left the cowshed.

'Love you too, sis,' he called after her. She flicked her middle finger up at him over her shoulder.

'Get someone to clear the yard, Robin, before we open,' Laurel yelled, because nothing said 'welcome' like a yard full of cow shit. The yard really had to scream 'welcome' at the top of its lungs, not just say it, because the cafe and farm shop were the only things that actually made a half-decent profit. They brought the customers in.

She ran through her mental checklist for today. There was

the meeting with the accountant about the viability of having a smidge more on their loan so they could buy Hibbert's land, the paperwork black hole of ridiculously complex Basic Farm Payments and Countryside Stewardship forms to check, the WI meeting in the conference centre, and she was showing a bride around at 11:30am.

All squeezed in this morning so she could revel in the arrival of the archaeologists in the afternoon.

Little Willow Farm was Laurel's life, and how she wished it wasn't. But who else was going to make sure that the farm that had been in the Fletcher family for generations didn't sink into the mire, like Hibbert's and so many other small farms? Certainly not Robin, who couldn't even be bothered to milk the cows at the right time. Jack, their older brother, could run the farm with both hands tied behind his back and blindfolded, but he couldn't get the farm to make actual money. Since their mother had died all those years ago, their dad had become increasingly reliant on Laurel to run the admin side of things and treated Jack more as a friend and colleague than a son. Robin, the favourite, the surprise, the flighty, beautiful boy, could do whatever the hell he liked.

Hence Fletcher's Farm had become Little Willow Farm (after many, MANY, hours of arguing), because it sounded fluffier and cuter and said 'come and visit our baby lambs and buy overpriced artisanal bread and organic, hand-reared meat'. It wasn't just the farm shop and cafe that Laurel had dragged her family kicking and screaming into accepting, oh no.

It was Little Willow Conference and Education Centre, Little Willow Petting Farm, Little Willow Bunk Houses, Little Willow Lake and Countryside Walks, and possibly Little Willow Maize and Sunflower Maze which could be planted on Hibbert's fields. If she could persuade the bank to just give her that extra bit of money.

It was a year ago, nearly to the day, that the gods of the earth took pity on Laurel, read her hidden thoughts and decided to smile upon her. One of the farmhands crashed through her office door brandishing a human bone. She'd been having them clear the little field at the top of the farm that was too sandy for grazing but could be perfect for the maize maze.

But not with an Anglo-Saxon burial to rival Sutton Hoo buried beneath the earth.

Laurel had eagerly put her archaeology degree into action and forbade anyone to enter that field without her (EVER AGAIN) until they'd had the police in. They could have been recent bones, although anyone with the most basic knowledge would have been able to see the harsh discolouration that signified ancient remains. She'd lobbied hard with the British Archaeology Society to have her old lecturer, Professor Rowlands, come to excavate the site and, after a year of meticulous planning, they were finally arriving today.

To the shit-filled yard.

Laurel smoothed her dress down over her thighs as she watched the two minibuses pull into the farmyard.

'Sylvie, I'm going to need you to find my brother, Robin.' She pulled her lips into that fixed, close-mouthed smile that did not bode well for anyone on the receiving end of it. 'Threaten him that I will chop his balls off if he does not clear this yard of cow manure in the next five minutes. Okay?'

Sylvie blanched. It could have been a reaction to Laurel's wrath, but it was more likely the fact that since she started two years ago, her assistant had had a massive crush on her little brother.

'Yeah, okay.'

Sylvie quickly pushed her clipboard into Laurel's hands and scampered off towards the cowshed, darting around piles of dung as she went.

Professor Rowlands was first out, and yes, he was exactly as a Professor of Archaeology should be. Tweed, threadbare blazer; too long, unkempt white hair; round glasses perched on his head; corduroy trousers that sagged at the knees. His battered satchel flopped open as he managed to put two feet securely on the ground, papers rustling dangerously in the light breeze.

'Professor Rowlands.' Laurel greeted him with a wide smile.

'Lauren, my dear girl, call me Ivor. How many times have I asked you?' About as many times as she had told him her name wasn't Lauren, but that didn't seem to stick, so neither would Ivor.

'Come on through to the café. You must need a cup of tea after the journey,' Laurel said, taking the elbow of her old professor.

'Yes, yes, but I think I've forgotten my...' he trailed off, patting his pockets, and headed back onto the bus, pushing through his dig team of wide-eyed undergrads and jaded postgrads.

A thin ribbon of jealousy tied itself around Laurel's chest, because in another life, this could have been (a younger) her. A PhD candidate poised to make exciting new discoveries, possibly running a dig team herself, a carefree version of Laurel who was focused on living her life exactly how she wanted to.

Being surrounded by twenty-somethings with their long, lean legs, designer beards and carefully curated well-worn t-shirts, with no responsibilities, made her feel frumpy and old.

Old. She was thirty-two, and there was absolutely no way she was going to relegate herself to 'old', but she wasn't young anymore. Well, not *that* young anyway.

Laurel self-consciously flipped through the paperwork on the clipboard that Sylvie had thrust at her. Her assistant may be partial to obscure French movies, ballet flats and short girlish skirts, but she certainly knew her way around a colour-coded spreadsheet. Laurel made a mental note to buy her a bottle of that cheap French wine she liked so much to say thanks.

'They were on my head, Lauren.' Professor Rowlands

chuckled like a cartoon character as he appeared again, and Laurel's hardened business heart melted just a little.

There were at least twenty people milling around the yard in little groups, sturdy travel backpacks leaning against the bus, palpable and infectious excitement quivering like a taut bowstring. A car pulled in and edged around the bus, looking for a parking space. Okay, Laurel needed to get this show on the road, so as not to disturb the rest of the business.

Sylvie appeared across the yard and shrugged helplessly, meaning that Robin either couldn't be found or, more than likely, he had fobbed her off with his lopsided grin and a touch to the arm that had her melting.

Laurel cleared her throat and raised her voice. 'If you could grab your bags, Sylvie will show you to your accommodation.' She gestured to Sylvie, weaving her way through the students with her hand up in the air like she was a tour guide trying to corral her group around the Acropolis.

'Actually.'

Laurel couldn't see the owner of that deep, warm-honey voice, dripping with authority.

'If you could have someone take my bags, I'd like to see the dig site.'

Someone to take his bags? This was not a hotel. She was not providing a concierge service here. In fact, Laurel had done the dig team a massive favour by letting them have the bunkhouse for a few months. Sure, the farm was getting paid for it, but it was a discounted rate and barely covered costs. Otherwise, they'd have to find their own accommodation in the tiny village of Little Houghton up the road. Or camp. For weeks. So yeah, a favour indeed.

'Oh, Lauren, you remember Dr Daley, don't you?' Professor Rowlands polished his glasses on the edge of his blazer.

The blood drained from Laurel's face. Daley?

How had she not known that he would be here? How had she not known that he even worked with Professor Rowlands?

She raked her eyes over the spreadsheet in her hands. Nope, DR NATHANIAL DALEY was not printed in neat Times New Roman on there.

Laurel couldn't believe she'd not seen him among the throng of wide-eyed, bright young things. He was taller than everyone, for a start, and completely ridiculous in dark blue suit trousers, a shirt and walking boots that he had obviously changed into on the bus. The students were parting for him like he was the Second Coming, eagerly awaiting the briefest touch of his archaeological genius.

Since when had that scruffy, sparkling eyed postgrad become a *Doctor*?

Nate was heading toward her and, like a proper person, she should just say, 'Hi, nice to see you again.' But no. She was caught off guard, hadn't planned for this, and therefore couldn't possibly make any decisions or hide her absolute mortification. So, she span on her heel and closed her eyes. Because, obviously, if she couldn't see him, he wasn't there.

'Is it Lauren?' Nate was talking, directly behind her.

Directly. Behind. Her.

Why did he have to be so close? Could he not invade her personal space?

'I thought it was Laurel?' He said to the back of her head.

Blinking a couple of times, Laurel pasted on a close-lipped smile and glanced down at the clipboard again for fortification.

'Yes,' she said as she turned. 'It's Laurel.'

Holy shit.

Ten years had been good to Nate Daley. His lankiness had filled out into the toned athleticism of someone who didn't work out but was always restlessly on the move. That black hair was nearly needing a trim, and waved casually over his forehead, with that speckle of grey at the temples that made men look distinguished.

Clothes were made for his body, shirt clinging neatly to a trim 'no Chinese takeaway has touched me' waist, and trousers that screamed 'Look! Look! I'm designer!'

Nate Daley had been attractive at twenty-two, when he hadn't quite grown into his arms and legs, and his Adam's apple had sat prominently in his throat.

Nate Daley at thirty-four was gorgeous. All he'd need was a waistcoat and Laurel would be a pile of goo on the floor. And she hated that.

She also hated the fact that she was faced with him after all these years, without any prior warning or any way to fortify or prepare herself.

The blood that had pooled in her feet rushed back up her body to set her face on fire. She was a literal beacon guiding ships home from sea.

'Uh, well, yeah.' Why wouldn't words come out? She took a breath. 'Laurel, yes, my name is Laurel.'

He was staring at her like she had made a wildly inappropriate joke in front of elderly parents.

'I thought your name was Lauren!' Professor Rowlands chipped in. Laurel smiled at the older man, silently thanking him for dragging her eyes from the dusting of stubble over Nate's jawline.

As long as she didn't look at him, she'd be fine, right?

'Sylvie, can you organise someone to take Dr Daley to the site?'

'Nate.' He corrected.

Laurel shot Nate a scathing look.

'Professor Rowlands and I will have that cup of tea.' She smiled kindly at her get out of jail free card, silently begging him to come and not make a fuss. She needed to interrogate him. There were a lot of 'why' and 'how' and 'what the fuck' questions circling her mind.

'Nathanial, join us!' Professor Rowlands said, all jovial exclamation marks. This man could obviously not read a room and Laurel didn't know why she expected him to.

Didn't Nate want to 'see the site'? Surely, he wouldn't want to join them. Would he? Laurel begged any god that would listen to make him *not* want to have tea with them, and clenched her jaw together tightly, her face blank and stoic. She desperately needed time to process the fact that Nate fucking Daley was standing in her farmyard, was going to be excavating her field, and would literally be in her home (well, not that she lived on the farm anymore, but whatever) for months and months. Maybe years, depending on the finds.

Nate narrowed his eyes at her, as if he was trying to read ancient Sumerian and hadn't got his dictionary, and his mouth twisted into his trademarked not-smile.

'Sure,' he said, tucking his hands into his pockets, cocking his head at her. 'The site can wait.'

NATE

Nate didn't really want tea, but he did want to see how red Laurel Fletcher could turn without exploding.

He knew from the paperwork that she was the same Laurel from university. She'd been an undergrad when he'd been a postgrad and had also been on the trip to the Wall (Hadrian's, not the Lord Commander's), but so had loads of people. As he followed Laurel and Ivor across the yard, sidestepping cow shit, he scoured his mind for any memory of Laurel Fletcher.

His best friend, Alex, had preened like a peacock when he found out Laurel had a massive crush on him. Alex had decided pretty quickly that she wasn't his type and Nate remembered a tearful Laurel escaping from the student union pub after Alex had let her down. Perhaps that had prompted the explosion of colour on her face. Perhaps it was something else? Dredging through his time at university, he really couldn't remember anything else about her at all. Although, at that time, he'd only had eyes for Lucia.

Okay, it was more than that – he'd revolved around Lucia.

He had inhabited her world, and he had been privileged to do so. That was, until she turned the warm light of her glow onto someone else, someone who would worship and venerate her as she needed. It was the age-old story. They grew up, they wanted different things. Lucia was destined for a nomadic Indiana Jones life of vibrant Hindu temples, sub-Saharan relics and First People religious icons, never staying in one place long enough to lay roots. Whereas he, Dr Nathanial Daley, wanted the exact opposite; a beautiful stable place that he could come home to every night, somewhere he could have a family, raise children. The excitement of travel and discovery was fun, but there was always that pull to somewhere he could safely say 'yes, I belong here'.

Lucia hadn't really got past twenty-four. She still worked for every opportunity, although she didn't have to grapple too much now. She was a much sought after, well-respected professional archaeologist who universities and conservationists begged to grace their dig sites with her divine light.

But here was Laurel Fletcher, sitting across from him in this kitschy cafe with duck egg blue wooden chairs and too many varieties of homemade chutney displayed on the crate shelves, looking like she wanted Moby Dick to come and swallow her whole. That *anything* would be preferable to sitting opposite him.

But why? He was nice, he was friendly, people liked him. So why was Laurel Fletcher's pretty mouth shrivelled up like a raisin? That intrigued him.

Nate jumped in as Ivor drew a breath, before the old professor could start another discourse on his gout. That's why Nate was here. Ivor couldn't possibly coordinate the dig, so he'd asked his dear friend and colleague, (and former student, 'taught him everything he knows') Dr Daley, to help an old man out.

'Are you the farm manager?' He frowned at the smell of cow dung.

Nate leaned back in his chair, hand resting on the table as Laurel bristled at his question.

'No. I am not the farm manager,' she said, voice quiet and dark. 'I am CEO of Little Willow Farm Holdings Limited, and Little Willow Farm is a subsidiary of the larger company. My older brother and my father are the farm managers.'

She tilted her head and pursed her lips, as if she was expecting some kind of challenge from him, some kind of put-down, some kind of 'there, there, aren't you a good girl'.

'A family business, then?' Nate asked.

'This farm has been in our family for generations.' So, yes. Again, there was that challenging look, like she was expecting him to say something derogatory.

'That's very...' he searched for the right word, 'admirable.'

Nate inched lower in his chair and closed his eyes briefly. 'Admirable' was definitely not the right word, because Laurel's eyebrow cocked so high it was nearly lost in her hairline.

'I don't work here out of duty,' she said, placing her teacup down in the mismatched saucer and drawing herself more upright, if that was even possible. 'I work here because I love this place. In fact, it's not work at all, it's my life.'

Nate took a long look at her, because that was awesome. Yeah, he loved his job. He loved the research, the excitement of discovering something new, the spread of dirt under his fingernails and the cool, crisp dewy morning air of a brand new dig site.

But it wasn't his life, and that was the problem with Lucia. She wanted it to be his life, just as it was hers. He'd tried. God, he'd tried. He'd lived out of a backpack for three years, trailing her around the globe, adventuring and discovering. But the tired ache in his chest wasn't soothed by Lucia's effervescence anymore, and he wanted to stop, to rest, to be home.

Purple jealousy bloomed in the pit of his stomach at the fact that Laurel had that – a ready-made home, embracing her with the warm arms of family – and just as jealous that she was obviously hell-bent on defending it.

His phone buzzed in his pocket and he shuffled to fish it out, grateful to have the excuse to turn away from her accusatory eyes. Why was she so combative? He had no idea. He hadn't done anything to her. Christ, he barely remembered her.

'Don't you need to get that?' she asked, tension evident around her mouth.

His phone read 'Alex Work', and it could be something that the British Archaeological Society needed, but more than likely, it was Alex just wanting a chat. Nate sent his best friend's call to voicemail and met her gaze frostily. If she wasn't going to be friendly, then neither was he.

'No.'

'Beautiful tea, Lauren, but we really must get on. I want to look at the site before that nice bus driver takes me back to the university,' Ivor said, clattering his cup on the table, ignoring the fact that the saucer was waiting right there.

Nate winced when he called her by the wrong name again, but Laurel just smiled benevolently at the old man.

'Perhaps you can find something exciting like last time you two were both on the same dig,' he said.

'The Pictish stylus,' she said quietly, glancing at Nate so quickly, he would have missed it if he wasn't already looking at her.

'Of course,' Nate said, leaning forward and tracing her face earnestly with his eyes. 'You found it.'

How could he have forgotten that it was Laurel who had carefully pushed the mud and dirt away from a five-inch-long bone stick, a soft point at one end and the other end squared off. He hadn't been there when she'd presented it to Ivor, but others said Ivor told her it was a lovely piece for holding together a cloak, but nothing of particular interest. Nate could imagine the disappointed slump of her shoulders, the crease between her eyebrows as she tried to explain something to their professor, the dismissal of a blithe 'yes, yes'. Her find had been photographed, catalogued, and put in the university's storage, with all the other finds, to be studied and assessed later. Finds didn't belong to the person who found them. They were university property to be studied and perhaps donated to a loving museum home.

What Laurel had lovingly excavated was the single most career-making find of his entire life. One that he could never hope to top. One that had literally made him. That single discovery had changed the centuries held view of the Picts being illiterate, changed the entire historiography. It was a massive deal.

First had been the lauded academic paper co-written with Alex, then the TV appearances. Lucia had been starry-eyed and proud. But that had been years ago now.

'Yes, I did.' Laurel tilted her head defiantly at him. Perhaps she was annoyed that he'd got recognition for the Pictish stylus and she hadn't? But she hadn't written the paper. He and Alex had.

'Well, hopefully, we can find something of equal, if not more, historical significance on your farm,' Nate said, leaning back in his chair again and watching her carefully.

Something about Laurel, maybe the way her full lip curved, or the sleekness of her neck, made him want to watch her, to study her. There was something hidden behind her bronze eyes, some blatant distaste for him. He knew himself, he was kind, he helped people out. So, what was it about him that made Laurel's lips tense together and her eyes become flat and distant?

They knew of each other in university, but they'd never had any interaction that could inspire this reaction from her, and certainly not ten years after they'd last seen each other.

'Hmm, yes.' Laurel folded her hands on the table and regarded him, clearly waiting for him to say something more. Her face was an attractive shade of fuchsia and she was obviously battling hard to not look down or away, anywhere but at him.

'Come on then please, Dr Daley. Let's get moving, get the

students up to the trenches.' The professor heaved himself up from the table, tipping an imaginary hat to Laurel.

This was precisely the reason that Nate had been drafted in to 'help' (i.e., run) the dig. The trenches had not yet been dug.

Nate checked his watch, precisely fifteen minutes until the plant machinery was due to arrive to dig said trenches. They'd already run the geophysics initial tests to see shadows of any finds under the earth, and he'd made the decision as to where the three trenches were going to be, which should be an excellent starting point. With any luck, this would turn into a full-fledged excavation of near enough the entire field, if the geophysics results were anything to go by. Which they should be.

There was hidden treasure in the fields, and all he had to do was find it.

'I'll need someone to direct the plant machinery,' Nate said, standing. Laurel's eyebrows climbed her forehead and she blinked at him, balancing her elbows on the table and linking her fingers together, waiting.

'Please.' Nate held back the eye roll, but couldn't stop his hands from flaring out, and his lips curving into a sarcastic little grin.

Laurel narrowed her eyes at him and was silent for two slow breaths. Nate could weather her little power play. Especially because the pink flush on her neck was deepening with every second he looked at her.

'Jack will be down from lambing shortly. He'll direct your plant.' Laurel stood, straightened the skirt of her dress, gave a fleeting smile to Ivor, a glare to Nate, and headed for the exit.

'Who's Jack?' Nate called after her, tucking his hands in his pockets and watching Laurel's dress swish around her thighs as she walked. God, she even walked authoritatively.

'My older brother,' she called over her shoulder, without stopping.

'Quite a girl that one, Nathanial. Quite a girl.' Ivor clapped Nate on his shoulder as he ambled past.

Yes, she was indeed.

LAUREL

Apparently, Nate fucking Daley, as well as becoming infinitely more attractive, had become infinitely more of an arrogant wanker as well.

Laurel fumed as she stormed up the stairs to the offices above the farm shop, and didn't everyone know it.

That condescending 'of course, *you* found it'.

That mocking smile when she pointedly refused to help until he'd said please (come on now, being polite is basic human behaviour).

And the insinuation that Laurel's little family farm business wasn't as worthy as his job.

Okay, fine, he didn't actually come right out and say it, but the way he probed for information, Laurel knew that's exactly what he thought – that Little Willow Farm and her life choices weren't sophisticated or exciting, and 'oh look at my suit'.

Well, fuck him.

'Sylvie,' Laurel called on her way past her assistant's office. 'Can you buzz Jack to make sure he's down in the farmyard to show the plant machinery where to go?'

'On it, boss,' Sylvie answered.

Laurel headed into her office and closed the door quietly behind her, leaning on it with her eyes closed.

This was not how today was supposed to go.

Professor Rowlands was supposed to be running the dig, probably with the aid of a post grad or two. Laurel had not banked on Nate Daley being here as well. How quickly did he turn from a gruff 'I need to get to the site' to 'oh yes, let's have afternoon tea'. What was that about? She wanted to pry open that nailed-shut box of dreams in the bottom drawer of her desk and let them out, bit by bit, just to see what it would feel like if she didn't have to run Little Willow Farm. Instead, her dreams of being on-site, helping out a little, being involved, drooped with her shoulders.

Laurel had helped with the funding, she'd lobbied for

Professor Rowlands and his team, she was putting them up, it was her fucking land. But no, with Nate I-don't-say-please Daley in charge, it was unlikely that she'd be able to enter her own field, let alone get her hands dirty. She certainly wasn't going to give him the satisfaction of asking.

No thank you. Her shoulders drooped.

Well, now that her afternoon plans of helping and coordinating with Professor Rowlands were scuppered, what was she supposed to do? Laurel had crammed as much as she could into this morning to ensure that she had some spare time this afternoon, and now she would be sitting at her desk watching the clock ticking. Sure, she could recheck the Single Farm Payment paperwork or have a look at the preliminary maize maze designs, but that had been planned for tomorrow and next week, and quite frankly, she didn't want to.

Laurel slumped at her desk and checked her phone.

Rebecca

> Yo bitch, how's the dig? Is it amazing? Are you filthy yet? Do you LOVE it?

It was her best friend and Jack's wife, Rebecca.

> I am not filthy. It is not amazing. I do NOT love it. Are you free?

Rebecca

> Oh my god, what's happened? I'm going into a meeting literally right now (I'm walking and typing), so text me back and then I'll call after.

Rebecca was Jack's true love, his one and only, the girl he first kissed when he was fourteen. He waited and pined and wrote terrible poetry until he was sixteen and Rebecca noticed him again. Rebecca had fallen hard for her brother and Laurel's heart grew every time she thought about their Grand Passion. Not that their life had been without ups and downs. It had been difficult when Rebecca went to university and Jack stayed on the farm. But what was Jack's loss was Laurel's gain.

By the time Rebecca had absolutely smashed her Legal Practice Certificate – to enable her to be the best lawyer that county had ever seen – and Laurel's BA was completed, and they both returned to the farm, Rebecca was no longer just her brother's girlfriend. They were fast, firm, best friends. Much to Jack's disappointment. He didn't like sharing, especially not when it came to Rebecca, but there were worse people to share her with than his sister.

And it was Rebecca. Not Becca, not Reba, not Becky, not Beck. REBECCA.

Thing was though, Rebecca didn't know what had happened with Nate Daley and Alex Woollard. Well, she obviously knew that Laurel had the most heart-wrenching, dry-mouthed, beetroot-red crush on Nate because twenty-year-old Laurel was about as subtle as two bricks smashing together. But Laurel had been too embarrassed to ever tell her, or anyone, what happened in the student union bar that afternoon ten years ago.

After, Laurel had taken a long, hard look at herself and resolved never to put herself on the line like that again. She'd protected herself and her heart by wrapping it in that magnificent iron ribbon in her chest, locked the ends together and swallowed the key.

Not that she'd completely given up. A Grand Passion was out there somewhere, but that iron ribbon was not being unwound unless she was absolutely sure. Tinder, and her favourite toys in the bedside drawer, helped. A lot.

Laurel wandered around her office, trailing her fingers across her large meeting table. She straightened the black and white photograph of the farmhouse from the 1860s and made sure all the ring binders on the shelves were neatly aligned.

The car park below was filling, and Laurel watched a mother try to navigate a pram around a massive pile of cow shit.

Could Robin do any less around the farm? Their father let him get away with anything, and he certainly didn't listen to Laurel. She'd have to get Jack to have a word with him, because this was less than acceptable.

'Sylvie,' Laurel called, unbuckling her sandals. 'Did you speak to Robin about the yard? The car park?'

Her assistant appeared in the doorway.

'Yes, I did. He promised he would do it.' Sylvie wrung her hands in front of her.

Laurel clicked her tongue.

'It's not your fault. It's my absolute dickhead of a little brother, don't worry.' She'd read enough management books to know that her highly strung temperament wasn't usually the most conducive for building a good working environment. 'I'm sorry for swearing,' she said, giving Sylvie what she hoped was a reassuring smile. 'Give me an hour, and then come and see me and give me an update on the social media campaign for the Pick Your Own.'

Laurel pulled socks over her beautifully manicured feet and shuffled them into her Hunters wellies.

'But, I...' Sylvie took a breath. 'That meeting is set for tomorrow. I haven't quite finished everything.'

Laurel regarded Sylvie and smiled kindly, because Sylvie had grown as an employee as well.

'Yes, you're quite right. Thanks for reminding me.'

Sylvie let out a breath and turned back to her office.

As Laurel headed outside to find Robin, or more likely, as CEO of Little Willow Farm Holdings Limited, shovel the shit herself, she reasoned that Nate Daley turning up was really just another management challenge. Another learning opportunity. Another way to help her grow as a person.

> I'm shovelling fucking shit out of the farmyard. My brother (not your husband) is an absolute wanker.

Rebecca wouldn't see this until after her meeting. It would make her laugh, hopefully to offset the worry that Laurel had probably caused with the ridiculously needy text she'd sent earlier.

Perhaps a bit of manual labour in her very nice summer work dress would do her good. If not, at least people would be able to park.

Yes, that would be the perfect end to Laurel's shitty day.

CHAPTER TWO

NATE

Little Willow Farm was really quite nice, Nate realised, as the farmhand that Ivor had commandeered led them up to the site. It was welcoming and homey, with well-tended flower beds and wooden signposts that pointed to 'Little Willow Petting Zoo', 'Little Willow Windmill' and 'The Secret Lake', although how a lake could be secret in a landscape with no hills, Nate failed to grasp. The name served a purpose though. It was cute.

The plant machinery was already up at the site and the breeze was full of buttercups and summer. His students were milling around and once again, no one had taken the initiative to even bring up the plans on any of their devices, and Nate knew they had the site maps because he had personally emailed them out. He had also uploaded them onto the Archaeology Department app that he'd remodelled from one of Lucia's digs in an attempt to drag the department into the twenty-first century.

Instead of scouting the fields, they were milling around like sheep. Waiting.

Ivor could deal with them, give them a pep talk, inspire them, promise them a life of discovering gold hoards or ancient Roman relics. Which, by the way, were very few and far between. Very. Nate would give them the cold, hard realities of working on a dig site.

There wouldn't be an awful lot for them to do today, but it would be good for the students to be there from the start, to see the entire process.

Bypassing Ivor holding court, Nate grabbed his plans from the masters student that he'd dumped them with earlier, and headed over to the men laughing by the plant machinery.

One of them was obviously in the middle of a story and Nate slowed his steps so as not to arrive mid-punch line.

'You know what Rebecca's like, there was nothing left of him once she'd finished.' They roared with laughter. Nate stopped a couple of feet away.

'I wouldn't want to get on the wrong side of your Rebecca. She's a force to be reckoned with, Jack.' The older man's accent was round and thick.

'No, neither would I.' Jack laughed, turning to Nate and pulling his threadbare t-shirt straight. 'You must be that fancy professor Laurel keeps banging on about. I'm Jack, Laurel's big brother.' His smile was warm and disarming, hand shoved out expectantly.

He didn't have the same glossy hair as Laurel. In fact, unless he was told, Nate wouldn't have put them as siblings. He grasped Jack's hand and gave it a hearty shake.

'No, I wish, I'm only a doctor. Nate Daley, nice to meet you.'

'You too,' Jack said. 'You've seen Laurel, yeah?' Nate nodded. 'She's so excited you're here, thinks it's "her time" or something like that.'

'What do you mean?'

Jack pushed a hand through his hair and surveyed the field before speaking.

'She's got a degree, like you,' he said.

Well, not *quite* like Nate, because he had a Masters and PhD, not just a degree, but he wasn't about to correct Jack.

'And she's always wanted to dig stuff up, so there we are.'

'Ah, right.' Nate made a mental note to involve Laurel, if only to see if he could figure out why she was so, well, her.

'You got the plans? I've finished lambing for the day, so I'll hang around and help if you like,' Jack said. It wasn't so much a question, more a 'I'll stay here to make sure you don't ruin my farm'.

'Yeah, okay, that would be great.'

It would also be great to have someone around who wasn't early twenties, i.e., his students. Yeah, he got on well with them, but still. They were *young*, and mildly annoying, especially in large numbers. The more buffers he could have around him the better and anyway, Jack seemed like a nice guy.

Nate could tell by the way that Jack surveyed the land, brushed his hand through the hedgerow, smoothed the collecting mud by the gate with his foot, that this was his life, this was his heart (apart from Rebecca?), this was Jack's archaeology and Nate respected that.

Jack was so different to Laurel, so at ease with where he was and what he was doing. Laurel was combative and prickly, as if everyone was challenging her. But either way, he was here to do a job and so what if she looked at him like he was the devil incarnate.

He was here to find the Anglo-Saxon hoard of the century.

Nate recognised his own crumpled plans in the hands of an older man.

'Ah, that's going to be tricky, what with the furrow,' the older man said. Nate opened his mouth to comment that it wasn't tricky at all, the terrain was smooth, but Jack nudged him and shook his head slightly.

'I see what you mean, Harold,' Jack sighed and looked at the plans pensively. 'You're right, very tricky.'

Okay, Nate would let this play out, but he *was* getting these trenches dug today, even if he had to drive that digger himself. Or go to the local B&Q and buy thirty shovels for the students to use. They'd love that.

'Well,' Harold said, narrowing his eyes at the sky. 'It just might be able to be done. If I can just about...' he trailed off, turning watery eyes on Nate. 'I can do it, I think, it won't be easy, but it'll be done. Give me an hour.'

Harold shoved his hands in his worn jeans and shuffled away.

'An hour?' Nate said, starting forward.

'Hang on a minute, mate.' Jack stopped him. 'You get what you're given with Harold, and he's the only plant machinery within thirty miles. He's a family friend. He'll do a good job, exactly how you want it. But he will definitely be an hour, he's very precise.'

'Oh, well then.' Nate sighed. 'I guess I should go and check out where I'm staying.'

He glanced at the students milling around. They could just do whatever twenty-somethings did. TikTok or whatever.

'I'll walk you down,' Jack said, meandering toward the gate.

Of course Nate had a little rented flat, but it was a good four hours away, way too far to commute daily. It made sense to stay at Little Willow Farm. It wasn't like he had any ties where he lived anyway – his mother didn't live there and his friends were scattered. His flat was somewhere to sleep. It wasn't home.

Little Willow Farm had definitely made sense, well, until he realised that he wouldn't be having the cosy little one bedroomed apartment he'd envisioned, but sharing with the students in cramped bunkhouses that were usually used for school residentials, corporate retreats, Airbnbs and the odd hen or stag party.

'Nice place you've got here,' Nate said, and he meant it. Little Willow Farm was all serene cows, hazy summer days and families making happy memories.

'Thanks, it's been in the family for generations,' Jack said proudly, echoing Laurel. He pointed to a cluster of three detached houses. 'That's mine and Rebecca's, Dad's in the middle and Robin's, our little brother, on the other side. Laurel could have one built, but she refuses to live on the farm. Something about "being too close".' He actually used air quotes.

It was obvious from the quiet passion that Jack loved this place because of course, to him, it was his home rather than a business.

''Course, it was called Fletcher's Farm until Laurel got her hands on it, and now it's all this.' Jack spread his arms wide.

'And you don't like it?'

There was an undercurrent of resentment to Jack's words, or was it resignation?

'Nah. I mean, yeah, it would be nice if we could just be a working farm and not have to worry about words like "commercial" and "viability" and "increasing our portfolio", but that's not how it works anymore. Farms are a business, and milking cows does not pay the rent anymore.' He looked at Nate. 'Laurel's done a really good job, she's dragged us onto social media. We have open-air cinemas here now.'

'I love an open-air cinema,' Nate said. 'Couple of beers, picnic, blanket. Girls love that shit.'

Hell, he loved that shit.

'Do they? Perhaps I should take Rebecca,' Jack mused, as if he had never thought of it before.

'Your wife?' Nate asked, hands in pockets as they strolled down through the farm, dodging children, prams, and some wandering ducks.

'Yeah, love of my life, man.' Jack really meant it; it was the open, warm smile and glint in his eye when he said her name, the unabashed vulnerability. Nate felt happy jealousy curl in his stomach.

'What the fuck?' Jack stopped mid-stride, his face frozen in a comical grimace.

Nate followed his gaze, and said a silent thanks to everything that was holy, because there was proper, prissy, strait-laced Laurel Fletcher, in her sundress and welly boots, literally shovelling shit. She had a large bucket with her, and she was working methodically, clearing up after what must have been quite a herd of cows, judging by the sweat shining on her forehead.

'Laurel, what're you doing?' Jack laughed at her. She whipped her head up furiously, strands of wavy brown hair flying in the light breeze.

'I'll tell you what I'm—' she hesitated and looked around, 'fucking doing,' she hissed. 'I'm cleaning up the yard after our twat of a little brother walked the cows through here for milking this morning.'

LAUREL

Laurel leaned on the shovel, cocked her hip out and narrowed her eyes at Jack because it was his fault for not being there to milk the cows.

Okay, he was lambing, but still.

'Sorry for swearing,' she said to Nate, because how unprofessional. He shrugged, trying to keep the amusement off his face, but he couldn't help the small twist of his lips.

Screw him. So she worked on a farm, and yeah, sometimes she had to shovel shit. What of it? She raised an eyebrow at Nate defiantly.

'So you are,' Jack said, trying not to laugh. Laurel glared at him.

'Yes, I fucking am, because one—' She tucked the shovel in her elbow so she could count on her fingers. 'None of the farmhands that *I* employ,' Laurel ignored Jack's eye roll, 'are anywhere to be found. Two, Robin has disappeared off the face of the earth, again, despite asking him on numerous occasions to clean this up. Three, Dad is probably day drinking with old man Hibbert by now, and four...' Laurel skittered off.

She didn't really want to blame Jack, he worked harder on this farm than anyone else (physically at least), and besides, it wasn't really his fault.

'Yeah?' Jack said, lifting his brows challengingly, smile dying.

Today had been shit; a hellishly busy morning just so she could spend the afternoon on site, which didn't even happen all thanks to the arrival of Nate Daley. Now, here she was, shovelling shit in front of him. Nate studied the horizon, mouth twisting and jaw working to hold in a smile. Laurel scowled at his stupidly perfect profile. Had his nose always been that straight?

'Well, you're hanging out with your new best friend, so who am I to interrupt you with, you know, actual work that's getting done?' Laurel finished off strong.

Jack and Nate exchanged an over-dramatic 'who me' glance before Jack fell about laughing and Nate finally released that smile that she remembered so well. Urgh.

'Oh, screw the both of you,' Laurel snapped, turning sharply.

The slightly too big wellies caught on the edge of the spade and oh shit, she was flailing and falling. The spade hit the ground with a clang and caught on her foot. She was going down and it was all Laurel could do not to put her hand in the bucket of shit she'd been scraping up, and she managed to twist her body to land on her bum.

Which squelched noisily into a massive pile of cow manure. She sat there, dazed, embarrassed, with an extremely warm arse. With Nate Daley puce and looking at her like he might explode from holding in a laugh.

Jack, on the other hand, was doubled over and roaring with laughter. He laughed just like their father, bellowing across the whole yard. If she was in a better mood, Laurel would have thought how nice it was to hear him laugh, that he should laugh more.

But not today, thank you very much, and not while she was sitting in a pile of cow poo.

'Jack!' She shouted, trying to lever herself up like a crab so she wasn't rolling in shit.

'Can I help?' Nate asked, a grin splitting his face as he leaned down to offer his hand to her. Laurel quickly assessed her situation. Jack was no help, he would continue to belly laugh until she rolled out of the muck, thus smearing it further over her dress.

'Fine,' she ground out, reaching for his hand.

Nate's warm, solid hand gripped her clammy one tightly and she cringed because yes, as well as sitting in shit, she had sweaty hands. He gave her a tug, and dragged her upright with a sucking noise as her rear came free from the warm gunky mess.

'There,' he said quietly.

She was a smidge too close to Nate Daley for comfort.

It was not fair that he smelled of hurricanes and danger, and she smelled like a farmyard. Had he grown, or had he always been this tall? Perhaps he'd got broader? He was certainly bigger. He tilted his head at her questioningly.

'Right, well, thanks.' Laurel took a step back and tried to twist to assess the damage. She'd lost more clothes than she would like to admit to cow manure. The dry cleaner was going to have their work cut out with this one. A non-committal noise came from Nate's throat as Jack finally pulled himself together.

'You can have some of Rebecca's clothes, Laurel,' he said.

'No, I've got clothes.' She shot an accusative look at Nate, because they were the clothes that she'd brought to change into for the dig: denim shorts and a tank top. Completely inappropriate for the office.

'Can you?' Laurel motioned helplessly to the half-cleared yard. 'And please, please tell Robin to go around the back to the milking shed. It's quicker and he just...' She wiped her forearm across her sweaty forehead and half turned her back on Nate, speaking quietly. 'He just pisses me off and won't listen to me.' She hated her thin and weedy voice.

It was true. Even though Laurel had practically raised the little shitbag after their mother had died, she was the last person on earth Robin would listen to.

'Yeah, I'll talk to him,' Jack said.

Laurel drooped. She was absolutely done with today, and she knew her older brother could see.

'Why don't you go and get changed, and then go home,' Jack said gently as Nate picked up the shovel.

'Jack, I—'

'And before you say you can't,' he interrupted. 'You absolutely can. As Managing Partner of this farm, I have decreed the rest of the day as "Laurel's Day Off".'

Jack wasn't really Managing Partner at all, he was Head of Farming and partner in the limited company. They were two separate things, but Laurel had given up telling him.

'Okay, fine. I've got nothing else to do anyway. I'm like a spare wheel this afternoon,' Laurel moaned.

God, she was pitiful today. Nate Daley had completely thrown her off her well-constructed path and it had turned her into some pathetic, whiny thing that she didn't recognise. What she needed was a large glass of white wine and to wallow in a veritable waterfall of rice pudding.

'Hey.' Jack put his arm over her shoulder, and Nate looked anywhere but at them. 'You alright?'

Laurel nodded. 'Yeah, I'm fine, Jack. I'm just having a moment.'

'That's alright, you're allowed to have a moment. You're not superwoman, yeah?' Laurel nodded again and tucked her head against her brother. 'I'll get this shit sorted and I'll mind the farm. I have been doing it since I was sixteen.'

And there it was.

The subtle dig that he knew better than her, that he could run the farm single-handedly and didn't need her at all. That he didn't approve of all the changes she'd made by diversifying and ensuring that they actually had a business, rather than yet another failing family farm that cost more than it made. He even still called it Fletcher's Farm when it had been rebranded as Little Willow Farm for about five years now.

Laurel sighed. There was a sliver of her that hated what

she'd done, prostituting her generations old family home with petting zoos and cafes and a windmill with a flower arch for wedding photographs. But if that's what it took so they still *had* their home, then that's what Laurel would do.

That's what she'd promised her mother she would do, and she would sacrifice her own hopes and dreams to do it.

'Look after the boys, Laurel,' her mother had said, lying there, pale and thin. 'Look after them.'

And she was doing her best.

NATE

Jack showed Nate to the bunkhouse after finding a farmhand, who had been hiding from Laurel, to sort the car park. Nate didn't blame him.

He was right. This 'bunkhouse' was not going to be the nicest place to live for the next few weeks. Or it could be months, depending. There was no timescale on things like this. Well, unless the university recalled him.

Nate had given the double room to a couple of postgrads who were thinking of moving in together (right, have fun with that), and the tiny apartment (which was essentially a bedroom and kitchen diner area connected to the main kitchen area) went to a couple who actually *did* live together. As the only senior member of staff, he could have demanded it, but it seemed a bit unfair. Especially when there were bunk beds available.

He'd always wanted bunk beds as a kid, but being an only child, had no one to share them with. Bunk beds at thirty-four? Sharing with a group of undergrads? No thanks. He'd have to rethink staying on the weekends.

The group of friends that he'd clung onto since university were scattered. Jess and Owen only lived about an hour and a half away, but he couldn't impose on them every weekend.

Paul was in France on a dig, so his house was free, but he shared with three people Nate didn't know, so that wouldn't work if he wanted his own space. That would be just swapping one shared place for another.

That left Alex. Now, Alex was great, his best friend since early undergraduate days, but Alex was... well, Alex. He was flighty, impulsive and (okay, he would say it) immature. Nate had grown up over the last ten years, carved out an academic career where he could still use his field skills but didn't have to be traipsing the globe, unless he wanted to. What he wanted in life had changed.

But Alex? Alex hadn't changed. Alex was living in a one bedroomed apartment in Oxford (which was fine, obviously), but he still behaved like he was twenty-two, and he really wasn't.

He had a good job at the British Archaeological Society, but Alex always seemed to want what everyone else had. He'd even asked Nate if it was okay if he asked Lucia out after they'd been broken up a year or so. Go for it pal, Nate had said. It really hadn't bothered him, he was done. Lucia's lustre had lost its shine, and anyway her and Alex were more suited anyway.

But still, come on man.

It wasn't that Alex was in desperate, world-changing love with Lucia, it was that she was everything that he wanted to be, and perhaps some of her shine would rub off on him.

So no, he couldn't be bothered with playing obscure Yes records until two in the morning, going to shitty gigs of 'the next best thing', and hanging out with Alex's friends who were all ten years younger than them.

No thanks. The shared bunkhouse it was. It wouldn't be that bad, would it? Perhaps a hotel on weekends.

Jack leaned in the doorway, assessing Nate.

'Hey,' he said. 'Fancy a beer later?'

'Yeah, okay. Is there a pub near?' Nate asked, hands in his pockets.

'About ten minutes' walk or so. Meet at six?'

'Sure.'

Jack knocked twice on the door frame, pushed off and disappeared into the farm.

Nate folded his clothes and hung up his shirts in the communal wardrobe area. It was nice enough, he supposed. It was clean, well-stocked with bare essentials and modern appliances, and had a cosy, rustic feel which tied in well with the rest of the farm.

And it was nice of them to let the dig use it at cost price or whatever. Nice of Laurel to let them have it, because as Jack had said, it was she who drove the commercial side of things.

He changed quickly into his dig jeans and a t-shirt and headed back out to the site. The trenches should be well under way by now and he needed to organise the students into teams and give them The Talk.

Ivor had done the exciting 'a find can change the course of history' talk, but Nate needed to make sure that they were doing proper archaeology; not contaminating the site with modern stuff, and not breaking finds with their grubby hands.

Nate retraced the well-worn track around the milking barn and down to the car park where a farm hand was dutifully clearing. It was busy now and Nate could see why. Little Willow Farm was beautiful and calm in the sun. Perfect for families, perfect for walks, just perfect.

He was halfway across the yard when Laurel stepped out of the admin building. She'd changed out of her knee length button-up dress into cut off jean shorts, a tank top and walking boots. Office Laurel was attractive, with full lips, lashes that dusted her cheeks and eyes that nearly saw your secrets, but Relaxed Laurel was something else. She was carefree, unburdened and, well, friendly. Office Laurel hadn't been friendly, at least not to him, but Relaxed Laurel looked like she could melt your troubles if she smiled at you.

Nate stumbled. His eyes had been on her.

'Oh, hey.' Laurel adjusted the bag on her shoulder awkwardly.

'Hey, uh.' Why was he self-conscious? Why were words difficult? 'Thanks for the bunkhouse, it's great,' he said.

'Yeah, that's okay,' she said, taking in his clothes.

'I'm going up to the site,' he said, as if he needed to explain to her. She nodded, looking at him as if expecting him to say more.

Nate drew in a breath. This wasn't Relaxed Laurel. This was Dig Laurel. She was wearing dig clothes.

That's why she had nothing to do, she'd been expecting to be up at the site this afternoon.

'Do you want to come up?' he asked. 'To the dig, I mean.'

Laurel's eyes hardened and the muscle in her jaw worked.

'No. That's your thing, your job, isn't it?'

It wasn't really a question.

'Yeah, but it's your farm, you can come up if you want.' He shoved his hands in his pockets and searched the horizon to avoid her eyes.

Laurel sniffed and raised that eyebrow.

'You're always welcome.' Nate tested a small smile on her. 'Jack said you—'

'Jack said what?' Laurel interrupted.

'Just that you were interested, so I thought maybe, if you wanted to come up, you could.'

She took everything he said as a challenge.

'We'll see.' She gave him a tight smile. 'Okay, well, see you.'

'Yeah, bye.' He watched Laurel walk to her car before realising that he was staring at her legs, again. The last thing he wanted was to be caught looking at Laurel Fletcher's legs.

As Nate headed up to the dig site, following the gravelled path past the pens of baby lambs, rabbits and tortoises (ah, the petting zoo), he tried to pinpoint what he had done to offend her.

It must be something from their time at university. Surely it couldn't have been just today? Laurel had turned daisy-white when she'd seen him, turned her back and then bloomed into a beautiful crimson tulip when she'd finally faced him again. It must have been something from before, and something bad enough for Laurel to still remember it all these years later.

Laurel was attractive, there was absolutely no denying that. For Christ's sake, he'd stumbled when he'd seen her.

There had been no one, really, since Lucia. Sure, there had been women, but no one that he wanted to introduce to his friends, and certainly no one he wanted to take home to his mother. No one that sparked anything in him. No one who had intrigued him.

But Laurel certainly did. Perhaps when he cracked her open, he'd find that she wasn't as interesting as she seemed.

He'd find out Laurel's deal from Jack tonight.

CHAPTER THREE

LAUREL

Laurel's little flat in Lower Houghton was her haven. It was a few minutes' drive from Little Willow Farm and that time in her little car was the most beautiful decompression time ever. It signified the end of the farm working day and the beginning of Laurel's time. She never brought work home. If she needed to, she would go in early and finish late, but her flat was a work free zone. She needed at least some respite.

The flat was clean whites and greys, glass and marble, sharp edges and straight lines. It was a world away from the warm, pastel-coloured farm, with its artfully distressed signs, soft curves and fuzzy ducklings. No, this was modern and cool, her books neatly stacked on the floating shelves beside her TV, her sofa standing on industrial style metal legs.

Laurel had rinsed the worst of the cow muck off her dress in the farmyard, and rubbed copious amounts of Vanish into it, praying that most of the staining would come out before she sent it to the dry cleaners.

The first large glass of white wine barely touched the sides. Laurel curled up on the sofa and was well into her second when Rebecca called.

'Why hasn't my husband shut up about Nate Daley, and why has Nate Daley turned my best friend into a moping weirdo?' She didn't even say hi.

'I'm not moping.' Laurel pouted, pulling the blanket tighter around her.

'You are moping, I can feel it. And why, for the love of god, is Jack ironing a shirt?' She could hear the beep of the oven timer as Rebecca put tea on for the kids.

'Apparently, they're going for drinks tonight.' Laurel tried not to sound bitter. 'Jack and Nate,' she clarified.

Rebecca fell silent.

'How has Nate Daley turned my life upside down, and I haven't even seen him in ten years?'

'Yeah well, join the club,' Laurel muttered, swallowing another mouthful of sauvignon blanc.

'Are you still there? Do you want to come over?'

'No, I'm at home. I left early. Couldn't go up to the site because he was there.' Laurel left out the part where Nate had actually invited her to the dig site at any time. On her own land. Laurel was not about to give him the satisfaction.

'You left early? That's like me leaving a pair of heels in the shop,' Rebecca said. 'It doesn't happen.'

'I've had a shitty day. The meeting with the accountant was less than good, the wedding I showed around wasn't biting, and I fell on my arse in cow shit in front of Nate fucking Daley, so yeah, I left early.' Laurel took a large gulp of wine. 'Jack forced me to go,' she admitted.

'Say that last bit again?' Rebecca said, closing the fridge and glugging post-work wine into her own glass.

'Jack forced me to go.'

'No, no, about falling in cow shit.' The grin in Rebecca's voice was evident.

'I'm sure Jack will fill you in. It was mortifying! And then Nate Daley in his stupid perfect shirt with his stupid perfect hair was all like "oh let me help", and my arse literally suctioned out of the shit.' Laurel took a breath. 'Don't you dare laugh.'

Rebecca swallowed loudly down the phone. 'I'm not laughing, I promise. Suctioned?'

'Suctioned, squelch, suction.' Laurel rolled her eyes and

held the phone away from her ear as her best friend roared with laughter, exactly the same as Jack had done.

Rebecca caught her breath. 'In front of Mr Perfect Hair?'

'In front of Nate fucking Daley,' Laurel said, which set Rebecca off into further howls. Talk about a supportive best friend.

'Oh, come on Laurel. That is absolutely hilarious, it's the kind of stuff that only happens in films.'

Laurel allowed herself a little smile. 'I suppose he won't forget me in a hurry.'

'Is he still hot? I can't wait to see him, check out who my husband and my best friend are both into,' Rebecca said. 'Hang on.' She held the phone away from her face while she shouted, 'Lila, Micah! You'd better be putting those toys away! Okay, Laurel, go.'

'Stop giving my niece and nephew a hard time.' Laurel smiled. 'And yes, he is still hot. But never tell him that. In fact, don't even talk to him. I can't have my brother and my best friend swooning over him.'

'Why, because only you're allowed to swoon over him?' Rebecca teased.

'Fuck off, Rebecca. He was a dick then, he's a dick now, and that's it. End of.'

'Mmm hmm, I remember what you were like, Laurel, all moon-eyed and swoony. *Ooooh Nathanial.*' And like she was five, Rebecca made smoochy kissy sounds down the phone. 'Not that you ever talked to him.'

The fact that Rebecca knew Laurel so well, all her secrets and fears, her embarrassing moments and her deepest desires, was fine. Until now, when she was taking the piss relentlessly about a crush Laurel had had ten frigging years ago.

'No, thank you,' Laurel said. 'Hey, I've got to go, I'll talk to you later.'

'Oh, Laurel, before you go, Fletcher family dinner at your dad's on Sunday, I'm cooking, two o'clock.'

'Alright, I'll bring rice pudding.' She could feel Rebecca rolling her eyes down the phone. 'It's Dad's favourite, so shut up.'

'Didn't say anything! Okay, talk to you later, love you,' Rebecca said, before ending the call.

Laurel flicked idly through Netflix. So what if Nate Daley had aged like a fine wine, and smelt like choppy seas and thunderstorms? So what if he was befriending her brother? So what if he was going to be in her back yard for the next few months.

It's not like she would see him all the time, was it? Perhaps just in passing. Now and again.

Only when she had to inspect the farm and happen upon the site, and possibly catch a glimpse of him in those jeans that hugged his arse just right (yes, she'd seen, oh boy, she had seen), and that faded salmon dig top that makes his skin warm and seductive, and that stubble on his jawline, rugged and daring. Perhaps his hair would fall, unkempt, over his forehead and his brown eyes would look at her and really see *her*. Not the her that was pimping the family farm out, the middle sister, the boring, business one, the one that had to sort everything out.

Perhaps he would see her as Laurel Helena Fletcher, person in her own right.

Who was she kidding? This was Nate Daley she was thinking about, of course he wouldn't. He was a cold-hearted, weaselly coward ten years ago, and there was nothing to suggest that he had changed at all.

Except his eyes had changed, hadn't they? They weren't the bright light of youthful exuberance anymore. They'd lost their sparkle, become wary, careful, thoughtful.

What was she doing? Why was she thinking about Nate Daley's eyes? Screw this, Laurel needed another glass of wine.

NATE

Harold had dug the trenches exactly how Nate wanted them. Exactly. To the millimetre, as shown on the plans he had provided, so all that posturing and 'oh it can't be done' had been worth it.

The students were in varying states of filthiness. They quietly scraped, dusted and blew at the earth, uncovering its hidden secrets, the things that it had kept cocooned and warm for centuries until it was ready to give them up to his curious eyes.

Nate breathed in the scent of freshly turned dirt and the aniseed tang of cow parsley hidden by hedgerows. It was lush and verdant out here, so quintessentially English. He was surprised that the maypole wasn't out.

Running a dig wasn't messing around in the dirt all day, stealing back human treasures from the earth, but Nate wished it was. He gathered his paperwork from the put-up table. The summer breeze was a little too breezy, and no matter how he angled his laptop, he couldn't see a damn thing with the glare bouncing off the screen. They hadn't been granted enough funding for a dig tent – a large tent with flappy walls, electricity and lighting – so he was making do.

Or not, as the case may be.

'I'm going to head down to the farm. You've got my number if anything interesting comes up, or if you have any questions,' he called.

Anwar, a masters student, waved but the rest ignored him, intent on their own little patches of earth. He took a longing look at them, sighed, and closed the gate behind him.

Paperwork. Great.

Nate was the most senior staff member. He was running the dig. Ivor was supposed to be, but let's face it, he was months from retirement.

Nate headed to the cafe. It had free WiFi, large tables, coffee on demand and was much more spacious and comfortable than the bunkhouse. In fact, the bunkhouse didn't even have a desk. It had a miniature two-person table, already covered with stuff that couldn't go anywhere else; a camera, books, notepads, a skull called Dave (Nate had no idea who had brought that). So, the cafe it was.

He negotiated his way around a couple of prams, smiled wanly as a toddler tried to hand him a green lorry, and ignored the looks and whispers of a couple of mums. Nate wasn't delusional. He was the only eligible guy in the cafe, and these ladies looked like they would whisper about anything with a pulse. Nevertheless, he made sure to give them a little smile. Well, he did have a pulse.

'Coffee, decaf, black,' he said to the waitress hovering near the large table he spread his papers over. The laptop swung open, and Nate settled down to work.

Three decaf coffees later and Nate's quiet haven was becoming more and more like a child's play area. The kids had multiplied somehow, and the cafe was busy with parents with prams. A couple of grandparents doted on cute pudgy kids, and those who were child-free looked on adoringly.

He'd managed to get halfway through the weekly report due to the university, had planned out the report due to his funders, ordered more materials and catalogued the few noteworthy finds that had come to the surface. It wasn't unusual to find a lot of early 20th century debris in the first layer – bottle caps, drinks cans, coins – but he was a bit concerned. They hadn't even found any Victorian junk yet. Geophysics had said that there should be finds here, and Nate trusted geophysics more than he trusted most people. He just had to be patient.

Nate pushed the heels of his hands into his eyes. Sleep was an issue on those fucking bunk beds, and the noise in the cafe was giving him a headache.

'Ahem.'

Nate dragged his hands down his face slowly and looked up at the woman who had sidled up to his table.

He straightened up in surprise when he saw it was Laurel

before him, in a pretty green sundress, arms crossed over her chest.

'Oh, hey,' he said.

Laurel surveyed his mess of paperwork, and her lips curved up in what could have been a smile, if her eyes weren't blazing with annoyance. 'Hi. You've been here for nearly an hour and a half.'

So? Nate shrugged and shook his head; she must be driving at something. Why did she care where he was?

'An hour and a half. In peak time,' she added meaningfully, raising her eyebrows. Nate looked around. Huh, yeah, it was busy.

Laurel sighed. 'You can't work here. The cafe needs the table. You'll have to find somewhere else.'

He didn't have the patience for this.

'Where, Laurel? You know full well that there's nowhere in the bunkhouse I can work,' he said, leaning back in his chair.

'There's a dressing table in the apartment. That should be big enough for your...' she surveyed his table again, 'work.'

'I'm not in the apartment. I gave it to a couple of masters students who live together,' he said, checking his coffee. He let a tiny self-satisfied smile curve his lips at her surprise.

'Oh.' She bit that full bottom lip, thinking, narrowing her eyes as she weighed up her options.

If she didn't give him somewhere to work, then he would take up this very same table each and every day. Just to piss her off.

'Come with me,' she said, taking a couple of steps away from the table.

Nate flipped his laptop shut and scrabbled for his papers, clumping them together messily. Two pens were in the mix somewhere and Nate scooped it all up to his chest. He scowled as he pressed the work to his chest and scraped the chair back.

Nate had taken three steps after Laurel before those pens started making themselves known.

Oh no.

They were rolling between his laptop and notebook, and no matter how hard he clenched the papers to him, they were starting to slide. The noise of the cafe was overwhelming and everything was slipping. She was walking too fast and blatantly choosing the most tortuous route. He hoisted the laptop against his chest again.

As if in slow motion, a sticky handed child with a snotty face trundled into his path and oh god. Nate swerved and twisted to avoid the corner of a table and it was happening. He clutched the papers to his hips as the laptop slid dangerously low. It was all falling, he was losing his grip and instinctively grabbed the computer as the papers exploded out of his arms, showering down in a rain of print and scrawl.

'Fuck,' he said loudly, dropping to the floor to collect his work.

Laurel whirled around, her face flashing from shock to fury.

'Sorry everyone.' She smiled brightly at the reproving looks from mothers and the elderly. 'What are you doing?' She whisper-shouted at him, lips pulled back into a not-smile.

'You could help,' Nate muttered aggressively, stretching under a table to retrieve scribbled notes.

'You could be less clumsy,' she hissed back, all pretense of a smile disappearing as she knelt in front of him, shoving papers into a pile.

'It was your fault for rushing me,' Nate snapped. He was close enough to see the flecks of gold in her annoying whiskey eyes. How did she smell so fresh when it was sweltering in this goddamned cafe? 'Couldn't wait to get me alone?'

Laurel's lips curled. 'Don't flatter yourself.'

'Why else are you rushing me out of here?' Nate knew full well why she was rushing him, but his frustration was bubbling in his stomach and he couldn't help himself.

'You're pathetic, you know that? Pathetic.' She scowled, those full pink lips pulled in tight.

'The only thing pathetic,' Nate scoffed, 'was that weak ass, *pathetic* come back.'

Her eyes flashed with anger, and a fleeting sense of satisfaction warmed his throat.

'Get your stuff, *Doctor* Daley,' Laurel said dangerously. She pushed back on her heels and stood, hands on her hips as she frowned down at him. She was an angry teapot and didn't have half the gravitas she thought she did.

Nate was furious, both with her and himself. Laurel had rushed him with her prissy, uptight eyebrow, commanding him to move from her precious table; she had thrown him, and he'd allowed himself to be thrown. Nate kept his eyes on hers, realising that the longer he glared at her, the redder she would get.

This was his power play, and he knew it was petty, but he would not let her win. That rosy pink blush flickered up her neck, skittered across her jaw and it was headlights on full beam by the time it reached her cheeks. Nate smirked.

'Urgh,' Laurel rolled her eyes and spun on her heel, sweeping her way across the room.

Nate smiled to himself. He was going to make her wait. He made sure his papers were poker straight, secured the two pens in his pocket, and straightened his slightly crumpled shirt before following her across the cafe.

LAUREL

How had Nate fucking Daley thought it was a good idea to sit in a busy cafe for an hour and a half, taking up a six-person table? Did he not have eyes? Was he incapable of seeing how busy it was?

He was following her up the stairs and Laurel refused to either speed up or slow down, regardless of the fact that he was probably eye level with her arse. She was going to have to put him somewhere because he was absolutely right; the bunkhouse wasn't geared for office work.

But what annoyed her more was that her mind went blank at any moment of conflict, no matter how trivial. Laurel could be commanding, snarky, and use that eyebrow to its best effect, but a snappy rejoinder? A withering comeback on the hoof? Nope, not her. Her mind didn't work that way.

Laurel led Nate along the pastel peach corridor, past the tiny kitchenette area, and stepped into Sylvie's office.

'Can I put Dr Daley in here with you please?'

Sylvie looked up from her computer screen and glanced at the man standing behind her, a smile stretching her face. 'Of course, but...' she trailed off, wincing apologetically as she gestured to the spare desk in the room.

Nate made an annoying self-satisfied 'hmm' noise behind her.

Why was he standing so close? Hadn't he heard of personal space? She could feel the heat of his chest behind her and his stupid seashore at dusk smell was way too enveloping.

The desk was covered. Absolutely, soul-destroyingly covered with papers, printed spreadsheets, invoices, remittances and notes, the sheer magnitude of which Laurel's mind could not even begin to fathom.

'What. Is. That.'

In through the nose, out through the mouth.

'It's Barbara, she's organising, she'll be back in a minute, she's just popped to the loo,' Sylvie said, eyes flicking between Laurel and Nate.

As if summoned from the fiery depths of disorganised hell, Barbara, the part-time accountant, excused her way into the office, pushing past Nate appreciatively and giving Laurel a wide berth.

'Oh hello, Laurel.' Barbara pushed her glasses up her nose.

'Hey, Barbara,' Laurel said. 'What you doing?' She pointed at the paper-covered desk.

'Oh, you know, just a bit of sorting,' Barbara said cheerily.

Sorting? If Barbara wasn't the best payroll clerk and office accountant Laurel had ever had the fortune of finding, who had been at PWC for years before deciding to ease into retirement with a part-time job on a farm, she would have lost her shit.

Lost. Her. Shit.

How Barbara could work in that mess was beyond Laurel.

'Okay, Barbara, okay.' Laurel forced a smile on her face, her eyebrow itching to rise. 'Carry on!'

Laurel whirled and crashed straight into Nate's chest. He was obviously made of some sort of military grade metal, because he didn't even flinch as Laurel ricocheted off him. In fact, he put his arm out to steady her, gripping the top of her arm to stop her swaying too far back on her heels.

That smirk, again.

'After you,' she said, pointedly, indicating that he should get out of her way.

'Okay.' He shot a beautiful smile at Sylvie, who was watching them with wide-eyed interest

She closed the door behind her, because if she couldn't see Barbara's overly laden desk of hideous mess, then surely it didn't exist. Laurel avoided his eyes, and her shoulders dropped resignedly. There was nowhere else to put him, other than her office. The conference centre was in use, the cafe was a definite no, and the bunkhouse just didn't have the space.

'Come with me.' Like an obedient puppy he was quick on her heels.

It was strangely intimate, letting him into her office. It was the space where she spent the most time, besides her haven of a flat, and she was disturbingly concerned as to what he thought. She flattened herself against the wall as Nate entered, broad shoulders taking up too much space in the room. He glanced around, taking in the pastel paint, the pictures on the wall, the rustic shelving, all designed to help her be in 'Little Willow Farm mode'.

Before she could direct him to the conference table, he'd put his laptop on her desk and was heading to her ergonomic, perfectly aligned for her spine, cream chair.

'Uh, no.' Laurel pushed off the wall and pointed to the conference table.

A flash of surprise passed over his face.

'Oh.' He glanced around the room. 'This is your office?'

'Yes, and that,' she pointed, 'is my desk.'

Did he think that he would get his own office? She'd worked so hard for the dig and provided so much for them. What more could they possibly want?

'I see.'

He took a long look at her before grabbing his stuff and throwing it haphazardly on the conference table.

Laurel sat behind her desk, tapping at the keyboard to bring her computer to life. She clicked through her emails and tried to focus on the latest online issue of Farming UK.

There was absolutely no need to look across the room at Nate Daley.

'Is this you?'

Laurel dragged her eyes from the screen to Nate.

He was leaning back in his chair, pointing up at a photograph of her, Jack and Robin outside of the farmhouse, Robin's pudgy arms around her leg and Jack's arm thrown carelessly over her shoulder. They looked happy, but it had been taken a few months after their mother had died. Laurel had been trying to hold things together and quite frankly, she had not been equipped. Their dad did his best, but three kids and a time-consuming farm? That's hard.

'No, it's three urchins who wandered onto the farm and Dad thought it was a good idea to snap a photo.' She looked back to her computer.

Sarcasm she could do.

'I was just asking,' he said, defensively. It was silent for a beat. 'You don't like me much, do you?'

'It doesn't matter whether I like you or not.' Laurel

tapped on her keyboard, writing an email mainly comprised of skdhfoossdfjjdooshciiso so she didn't have to look at him.

'If we're going to be sharing an office, then we might as well get along,' he said, linking his fingers together on his stomach and turning those blue eyes earnestly on her.

She cut her eyes towards him.

'Firstly, you're in my office. We are not "sharing". Secondly,' Laurel took a breath, because she wasn't exactly sure what 'secondly' was. 'I don't not like you, I don't know you. I never knew you.'

Could she sound any more bitter?

Nate cocked his head and frowned at her.

'So, get to know me.' His voice was low.

Laurel's stomach tightened and she flicked her eyes towards him briefly to see if he was kidding. He was relaxed and languid in that uncomfortable hard chair, one long leg stretched out. The only thing that hinted at him being uncomfortable was a tightness around his jaw.

'Hmm.' The noise came from her throat, and she swallowed, not trusting herself to speak. Nate Daley still had the ability to make her stomach flutter.

Nate scoffed, and shuffled his chair under the table, shaking his head slightly.

Perhaps she was being immature and petty in not immediately jumping on his offer of friendship, but she needed time to rearrange her thoughts. The kind of doom that you feel at age twenty, when everything is big and dramatic, stays with you and shapes your interactions with other people, your relationships. That kind of crushing embarrassment moulds who you are as a person.

Thing is though, he was in her space, in her home and he wasn't leaving any time soon.

Nate was right. It would make it easier on everyone if she could put what had happened before in a bucket, lower it into a well and seal the top, with only whispers to be heard now and again.

Laurel would think about that another time. Right now, she had to get through the next few hours of Nate Daley sitting close enough that she could see the angle of the stubble on his chin.

CHAPTER FOUR

NATE

Nate was going to have to find some kind of coping mechanism if he was going to sit in Laurel's office every day. His evening run in the dusky heat through the winding lanes on the way to Lower Houghton was helping erase her non-committal 'hmm' from his mind. Because that 'hmm', coupled with the glare of her whiskey eyes when she realised that the only place he could work was in her office, had been haunting him. Haunting him in a good way.

When she'd bitten her lip in thought, he'd wondered what it would taste like and how easy it would have been to back her up against the wall and see for himself.

Nate frowned, his running shoes beating the uneven road.

What a weird thing for her to say, that she never knew him. Of course she hadn't, they had barely said hi to each other. So, no, she wasn't likely to know his deepest darkest secrets. Nate cringed as he remembered that he had literally invited her to curl up in his lap with that 'get to know me' comment. Why had he even said that? It was to annoy her, to see if she snapped at the line, to see if he could win.

Nate increased his pace, wiping the sweat across his forehead as the lane widened into Little Houghton town.

It wasn't big, obviously, but the little high street included two barber shops – although how many barber shops one tiny place needed Nate was unsure – an estate agent, opticians, a couple of cafes, a little Sainsbury's. He'd explore it properly one weekend. It wasn't like he didn't have time.

Jack had taken him to the Dog & Gun, the pub at the end of the high street, and they did nice on-tap ale. Local brewery, so Jack had informed him. Nate had never felt so welcome and embraced as he had when he'd walked into that pub with Jack. The eldest Fletcher child was like some kind of local celebrity. Jack knew absolutely everyone, remembered their kids' names, had a kind word for every single person. If there was a mayor for Little Houghton, it would have been Jack. He was so unassuming, calm and relaxed. So comfortable in himself. So different from Laurel. Nate stopped abruptly. Jack had been such good company, he hadn't even thought to ask about Laurel.

Stretching out his quads, he watched the orange pinks of the sun filter through the buildings and skitter across the uneven road. There were definitely worse places to be spending a few months, especially in the summer.

He ignored the initial buzz of his smartwatch, probably belligerently telling him to MOVE, but couldn't ignore the second. Nate retrieved his phone from his shoulder pouch.

'Alex,' he greeted.

'Yo, Nathanial, have you been avoiding me?' Alex was in the pub, the telltale clink of glasses and low hubbub giving him away. What was that terrible music playing?

'I've been busy, Alex.' He held back a sigh.

Nate had to be in the mood to deal with Alex and over the past few years that mood had been less and less forthcoming. Perhaps he had been avoiding Alex, just a smidgen.

'But it's work related, that's why I've been calling. Don't you listen to your messages?'

No, he didn't. That unmoving notification on his phone didn't bother him one little bit.

'Jane is my British Archaeology Society liaison, not you,' Nate replied.

'If you'd listened to your messages, then you'd know

that I've managed to swing it so that I'm your liaison.' Alex took a loud swallow. 'How cool is that? Getting the band back together.'

'You didn't.' Nate grinned. 'Why didn't you tell me you were doing that?' Alex must have begged and pleaded and brown-nosed so hard it was painful, because Nate's dig was well above Alex's pay grade. 'That's amazing, Alex. Congratulations.'

'I fucking tried to tell you, man, but you weren't answering your phone,' Alex said, trying to sound nonchalant, but Nate knew him well enough to hear the hurt in his voice. He resolved to be a better friend, i.e., answer the phone and perhaps instigate a conversation with Alex once in a while.

'That's excellent, Alex. I'm looking forward to it.'

The Pictish Stylus was the last time they'd properly worked together, collaborating on the paper, and it had been fun. Alex had been insightful and eager, bringing more to the table every time they met. Sure, he'd been assistant liaison on a couple of digs, but never head liaison.

'Oh, and you'll never guess what.'

'What?' Alex drawled.

'Do you remember Laurel Fletcher from uni? A couple of years below?' When Alex was silent, he prompted, 'She came to the Wall with us?'

'Brown hair, nice arse?'

Nate frowned. She did have a nice arse, but Alex didn't need to say it.

'It's her farm,' Nate said.

Alex hesitated just that little bit too long. 'What, where the dig is?'

Nate laughed at his friend. 'You can't lie for shit, Alex. You knew it was!'

'Yeah, alright, I knew,' Alex conceded. 'She still got a nice arse? Or has it sagged with age?'

'Don't be a dick, Alex. We've just got through the layer of Victorian debris,' he said, launching into a detailed report of the site. He was so relieved to have found the crap that the Victorians had left – coinage, buttons, stoneware, kitchenalia – all finds in their own right, documented, noted and set aside so someone else could deal with them. Because the interesting stuff, the stuff that Geophysics had promised, was below.

Alex cut him off after a few minutes. 'You know, I've got your weekly reports, I don't need a verbatim transcript from you at 7:30pm on a Friday night. Why aren't you in the pub?'

'Because, Alex, I don't have a social life, unless I want to hang out with twenty-somethings and unlike you, I can't cope with that shit.'

Nate started the long walk home, vaguely wondering how far his signal would reach.

'Why don't you take her out, Laurel?' Alex probed.

Nate smiled down the phone at his best friend.

'Yeah, no, she's a bit prickly. You remember her, she had that crush on you, right?'

Alex slurped his drink. 'Yeah, I remember her, but barely.'

That was fair, Nate barely remembered her either.

'Anyway, when you coming to visit?'

'Couple of weeks. I'll stay with you? We can make a night of it.'

It had been a while, but usually Alex stayed on-site with Nate and they would have an epic night out in the local area. It usually included many, many shots, traffic cones and a lot of very loud, very bad singing. Nate couldn't cope with the hangxiety and horrendous hangovers anymore. Perhaps just a couple of drinks and in bed at a time that would enable him to be a functioning human the next day.

'Yeah, I don't know if you can this time, Al,' Nate said, wincing.

'What?' Alex choked on his drink. 'What do you mean, you don't know?'

'I'm staying in this bunkhouse. There are no beds spare and no sofa, there's literally no room. There's a pub with rooms, though?' Nate said, hopefully. It would be nice to have a bit of respite from the students.

'You're staying in a bunkhouse? Nate Daley? In a bunkhouse?' Alex guffawed, and Nate rolled his eyes, jumping onto the grass verge as a four-by-four swerved past him.

'Yeah, alright. Have a look at the pub. There's a restaurant, I think. Let's have dinner. We're not twenty anymore,' Nate said, hoping Alex felt the same way. Fat chance of that.

'A bit of stomach lining wouldn't go amiss. I'll email you when I'm coming,' he said. 'Alex, signing off.'

Nate smiled as he pressed the red button to end the call. Alex had started using that little phrase way before Nate had met him. It made him smile, because Alex was such a funny, weird little man sometimes.

LAUREL

Nate beat her to the office that morning, and she hated that. She felt it gave him the upper hand. In what, she had no idea. But his eyes were on her as soon as she walked through the door. Which was annoying because the five minutes she normally took at her desk to orientate herself, make sure her makeup was alright, have a glass of ice water and prep herself for the day felt strangely pressurised.

'Morning,' she said, turning her computer on. 'You're here early.'

'Catches the worm.'

Laurel looked at him, because that was a saying that her grandmother used to rock out.

'Besides, I live close.' Nate tried a smile on her.

Laurel would have bet anything that he was wondering whether she'd decided to take him up on his 'get to know him' offer. Start again, afresh, ignore what happened ten years ago.

As it was, she'd deliberately not obsessed over Nate's

offer of friendship, of putting a decade-old hurt to bed. If she'd let herself think about it, then she would have spent all night visualising what being friends with Nate Daley meant, running through different conversations in her head, and ultimately not sleeping because she didn't know him well enough to accurately predict his answers. So, like any self-respecting Fletcher, she'd ignored it. Well, until this morning on her drive to work.

Nate pushed himself up from his table, and grabbed a mug from his desk, looking dangerously edible and flashing that little trail of hair that paved the way into his jeans.

'Here, I made you a cup of tea.' He put it on the edge of her desk and looked at her, challenging her to snap at him, to be rude, to give him the excuse to have the upper hand.

'I don't drink tea,' she said. 'Well, I do sometimes, but not first thing in the morning.'

He looked taken aback, and she wasn't surprised; who didn't drink tea in the morning? Laurel had to be in the mood for hot drinks, and people who drank tea when it was promising to be a disgustingly hot British summer day? Yeah, they were weird.

'Oh, alright.'

He was like a wounded puppy, his bottom lip popping out in a small pout as he reached for the poor neglected cup.

It wasn't that Nate had been right about starting again, or whatever. It was more that Laurel had realised that she was thirty-two and had absolutely no need to behave like she was twenty. Again. She could let him have a space in her office and she could be accommodating. But they didn't have to be best friends.

'But it was very kind of you to think of me. Thank you.'

Why so formal? Oh, that's right, because she wasn't sure how to do 'getting to know you'. Wasn't sure how to behave around him without the crippling fear of embarrassment dictating her every move. Or perhaps it was because she had literally no idea how to converse with anyone outside of her family, her business acquaintances and her Tinder dates.

Nate glanced at her as he sat down, now with two cups of tea to slurp from, and she smiled a little at him. Not a sarcastic one, not one that didn't reach her eyes, but a proper one, a 'yes, we can cohabit this space for a little bit' smile.

Nate looked at her, narrowing his eyes slightly, his mouth curving on one side in what could have been intrigue, or confusion. Or possibly wind.

The moment stretched as they watched each other, and Laurel's mouth lost all ability to produce saliva. Her lips parted because breathing through her nose just wasn't cutting it.

One thing was for certain, and that was that Nate Daley was, and there was simply no way other way of putting it, sexy. Sexy as hell.

Laurel would have to be very careful, very careful indeed.

NATE

Nate was confused. What type of weirdo didn't like tea in the morning? The weirdo that he was sharing an office with, obviously.

What else was wrong with her? Perhaps she peeled her face off at night to let the demon inside her get some airtime. Perhaps she kept the bones of baby lambs and bunnies to boil up, make a nice stock base for risotto.

These were the things Nate was thinking about as he typed and deleted, typed and deleted. Full sentences were not his friend and it was because he was distracted by the ridiculous 'thank you for thinking of me'. What even was that? Was that her version of nice?

Regardless, he'd spotted her chest flush, watched the way her legs had uncrossed and crossed again under the desk.

Trying to put thoughts aside of what he would do if he got his hands on Laurel Fletcher's legs, because that was never going to happen, Nate clicked open the third email from Alex with 'OPEN ME YOU PRICK' in the subject line.

Ah, okay. He could deal with this. Alex was coming next week, and that was okay. The dig just wouldn't be as far along as he had originally planned for with Jane. As well as next week, Alex was coming in a month's time. He'd already booked rooms at the Dog & Gun in town. It would be nice to see Alex, nice to spend some time with him. Nate would just have to get in the mood, and that would be fine. He could do that.

'What's wrong?' Laurel asked, tapping away at her computer, not even looking at him.

He leaned back in his chair and stretched a leg out. 'What makes you think something's wrong?'

She cut her eyes to him, before looking back at her screen and deleting whatever she had just typed.

'You sound like The Little Train Who Could.'

What the hell was she going on about?

'You're huffing, sighing, expelling breath loudly,' she said, turning to face him.

He crossed his arms over his chest.

'Oh, so now I'm not allowed to breathe?'

Laurel stilled. She looked hurt.

'I was just asking,' she said quietly, lips pinching together.

'Sorry, it's just...' He pulled a hand through his hair, giving her an apologetic smile. 'Do you remember Alex, my best friend from university? He went to Hadrian's Wall as well.'

'Alex Woollard?' Laurel wheeled her chair away from her desk and assessed him. 'Yes, I remember Alex Woollard,' she said crisply, her face blank.

'Al is my liaison at the British Archaeology Society and he's visiting next week.' Laurel's eyebrows shot up, her blank mask falling off her face. 'I just thought I'd have more time, you know?'

'Alex Woollard? Is coming here? To my farm?' she squawked, hands flat on the desk.

'Yeah...' he drew the word out, confused.

Should he have told her, cleared it with her that he was having visitors to the farm? No, of course not. It might be her farm, but it was his dig, and it was up to him who he had on site.

'But he can't stay here,' she spluttered, 'there isn't space.'

'He's booked a room at the Dog & Gun.' Nate cocked his head to the side, confused. Yeah, Alex could be a bit of a dick, but what the fuck was going on to make her react like this.

'What's with you? What's all this?' He pointed vaguely at her.

Laurel looked down at her desk, blinking furiously, wringing her fingers together. When she finally looked up at him, it was with defeat.

'Alex Woollard is coming to my farm,' she murmured, resigned.

'Is that a problem?' Perhaps if he pushed her, then he'd finally understand what was going on in that messy mind of hers.

'Is that a problem?' Laurel repeated. 'No, Alex Woollard being here, on my farm, is not a problem at all.'

Nate kept looking at her, utterly and completely confused. What had happened? Who was this scared little girl? She'd gone pale, he suspected clammy as well, considering that she kept wiping her hands on her skirt, and obviously had some issue with her hair because she kept touching it.

She noticed him looking at her.

'What?'

'What?' He was incredulous. 'What's happening over there?'

'What's happening over here?'

Why was Laurel Fletcher repeating everything he said? Was she having some kind of breakdown? She sucked in a breath like she had just come up for air, and rolled her shoulders back, visibly pulling herself together.

'Nothing, I'm fine. I'm fine. Of course I'm fine. I'm fine with everything.'

She pulled a smile from the depths of her soul and plastered it on her face.

Nate took a considered look at her, not believing her one bit. 'Alright then.'

If that's the game she wanted to play, then that was fine. If she wanted to pretend that the mere mention of Alex causing her to hyperventilate was 'nothing', then who was he to argue? If she was upset by Nate being here because of her crush on Alex, then having Alex himself here may just tip her over the edge.

Nate glanced up at the photograph of the three dirty kneed kids in front of the old farmhouse again. How had her brothers Jack and Robin turned out so calm and laid back, relaxed and friendly, and Laurel had turned out to be this highly strung, twitchy, authoritarian? He looked again at Robin's arms wrapped around fourteen-year-old Laurel's leg, and Jack's protective arm over his sister's shoulder. They were smiling, but it wasn't the carefree, unfiltered smile of childhood. No, they were forced smiles with tired, worn eyes.

Laurel's chair wheeled back, and she stood abruptly.

'I'm going to the kitchen. Do you want a cup of tea? Of course not, you've got a cup, well you've got two cups,' she rambled.

'Yeah.' He nodded, gesturing at the pair of cups on the table. 'No more, thanks.'

Laurel shot finger guns at him. Finger guns. 'Okay, yeah, good. Uh, okay, I'm going. Yeah.'

Nate stared after her in disbelief. What the *hell* just happened?

Laurel was so prim one moment and the next she's shooting finger guns? She was the vanguard, there to protect her family at any cost, but she was also a fuzzy bumblebee just trying to make it to the next flower. Full of contradictions.

Nate found himself grinning as the door closed behind her. She was a breath of fresh buttercup air in his staid and boring little life.

Sharing an office with Laurel Fletcher was going to be interesting.

CHAPTER FIVE

LAUREL

The end of the week couldn't come quick enough for Laurel. The bank had said that they would have to further consider her application for more funding for Hibbert's fields, which would result in her stressing until the answer came through. It was the worst part, being in limbo. She could deal with a 'no', so long as she knew.

Laurel strapped the large bowl of rice pudding into the front passenger seat of the car. She was aware that strapping a large bowl of homemade rice pudding into the front passenger seat of a car was not something that was done regularly by people, but she really did not want it all over the upholstery if it tilted a little too far as she was driving the lanes to the farm.

Hopefully, she wouldn't have to see Nate today. He'd be off doing whatever he did on the weekends. Hiking, saving puppies from burning buildings, reading to sick children. Urgh. It had turned into a game, seeing who could get to her office first. Nate would spend an hour or two ensconced in her office before the lure of the dig called, flashing his obnoxious but thoroughly delightful thighs in shorts and those Timberland boots that all the students seemed to wear like some kind of uniform.

Except on Thursday, when he spent all day reviewing his notes and making sure his funding reports were all present and correct, ready for submission on Friday. Which was horrific because it meant that her office smelled of thunderstorms and autumn nights all frigging day. The flexing of his forearms against his rolled-up shirt sleeves as he typed was immensely distracting.

Discovering that Alex Woollard was Nate's British Archaeological Society liaison was like thinking you've made a massive archaeological discovery, only to realise that it was actually a cesspit. It still needed dealing with, assessing, studying, but it wasn't remotely fun.

Alex Woollard was the cesspit.

But of course, she couldn't make a fuss, she had to let it run over her like a Mongol horde. Because she'd put Alex's part in what had happened behind her. It was not colouring her view anymore. She was being the bigger person and that included giving Cesspit Alex a fair crack at the whip. He could have changed in the last ten years, could have become less of a dick.

Doubtful, but it could have happened.

Regardless, he wasn't here for another week or so, and today was Sunday. Fletcher Family Sunday Lunch.

There were things to discuss after the roast lamb, and Laurel went over her spiel in the car. It was an uphill struggle trying to get her family to do anything that was in the best interest of the business. They always did in the end, but each time it was a battle. It had been a struggle to open the cafe, open the conference centre, make the lake pretty enough for country walks, and it had been a fight of the most epic proportions to change the name from Fletcher's Farm to Little Willow Farm.

Laurel was tired. Tired of having to butt heads with her family to get anything done, tired of having to be the bad guy all the time so the farm could make money, and certainly tired of getting absolutely no thanks for any of it.

If this was a normal job, she would have quit.

Laurel bit back that thought. There were times when she felt she was martyring herself, that she was a glutton for punishment, but she really couldn't see herself doing anything else. Of course, she'd dreamed of using her archaeology degree on a dig site making exotic discoveries, dreamed of living in the south of France running her own vineyard. But everyone had pipe dreams, no one did exactly what they wanted to do, lived their life beholden to no one, did they?

She would never quit. It was her life, her family legacy. Laurel would do anything she had to do, be anyone she had to be, to keep her farm alive, especially in this political and economic climate where farming was way, way, way down on the government's list of priorities.

Parking on the plot that would be forever reserved for her house, Laurel unstrapped the rice pudding and balanced it on the top of the car while she sorted her bag out. The three houses sat snugly together and she headed for the old, wisteria-covered farmhouse in the middle where she grew up. The thatch nearly needed replacing, but the whitewash was fresh and crisp. Robin's tiled roof house on the right looked cold and uninviting. He had insisted on having it built when he was eighteen, much to Laurel's chagrin. He could barely look after himself, let alone a house. She had steadfastly refused to deal with anything to do with it. If he was old enough to live by himself, he was old enough to deal with the bills and insurance and cooking and cleaning and washing his own goddamned bedclothes. Although she suspected her father did more than just help out now and again.

Not that Robin *lived* there. He was mostly in his childhood room at the old farmhouse and used his own house for parties, girls and, well, more girls.

Rebecca and Jack's was much more inviting, with neatly trimmed hedgerows and wildflowers that Jack had cultivated so it matched the garden that their mother had planted next door all those years ago.

'Hey, I'm here,' Laurel called as she opened the door to her dad's house. Like all old farmhouses, the front door opened into the main room. If you were coming from the farm, you went around the back, via the mud room.

'Laurel, my girl!'

Rebecca appeared from the kitchen, looking the perfect wife in a breton top and jeans. Designer, but not pretentious.

'Where do you want this?' Laurel said, holding out her offering. 'Don't say in the bin. You know it's Dad's favourite.'

It was her mother's recipe, although Laurel couldn't quite get it right.

Rebecca rolled her eyes good naturedly.

'Give it to me. Here, this is for you.' She held out a large wine glass to Laurel, who swapped it for rice pudding.

'Where are my favourite niece and nephew?' Laurel called, and was rewarded by a thunder of feet on the stairs.

'Laurel, Laurel,' six-year-old Lila shouted as she raced down the stairs. 'We're showing him your room! He's seen Daddy's!'

She laughed, setting her glass down on the mantelpiece. 'Showing who?'

The question died on her lips as little Lila, the image of Rebecca, appeared from stairwell, tugging a very abashed Nate by the hand. Micah, the image of Jack, appeared behind them, his hand tight in Nate's other.

Nate Daley. In her childhood house. For Fletcher Family Sunday Dinner.

What. The. Fuck.

Nate curved his lips apologetically, his eyebrows creasing slightly and goddamn it, she found him hot even when she was annoyed by him literally going through her childhood stuff.

Good lord, her dolls. The pink floral wallpaper. The My Little Ponies that she would never throw away because she'd brushed their manes with her mum when she was dying.

Laurel pushed down a cringe.

'And where are my cuddles?' She crouched and opened her arms.

The kids rushed her, Nate forgotten, and she stumbled backwards a little. 'Gosh, you guys are super strong. Must be all the vegetables your mum feeds you.' She planted a kiss on each of their heads. 'But...' Lowering her voice to a whisper because Rebecca had supersonic hearing, Laurel reached into her handbag and withdrew two chocolate bars. 'Shh, don't tell Mum and Dad.'

Micah squeaked in delight. Lila gave Laurel a long-suffering look borrowed straight from Rebecca. As if summoned like a creature from the deep, Rebecca called from the kitchen, 'Don't you eat that, kids. In fact, bring it to me. Now.'

You didn't argue with that tone, and the kids shuffled off, leaving Laurel with Nate. Deliberately not meeting his eyes, she reached for her wine. Only when she'd fortified herself with a gulp did she smile at him, keeping a blush down by sheer force of will.

'What?'

Why was he looking at her like that? All soft around his stupid blue eyes. It was the first time she'd seen him in casual clothes. Dig clothes didn't count; they were messy clothes, and he'd been dressed up (kind of) when he'd arrived. Her eyes wandered of their own accord over his chest; the duck egg blue shirt accentuating the muscular curve of his shoulders, sleeves rolled up to show sun-browned forearms.

So annoying.

He was watching her when she dragged her traitorous eyes up to his face again. Not that his face was any less annoying. 'Nothing, just,' he hesitated, 'you're really good with them.' He gestured to the kitchen, meaning Lila and Micah.

'Yeah, 'course I am,' she said, crossing her arms and tilting her head. 'I helped the twins come out of Rebecca's vagina.'

Nate had the good grace to cough slightly and he looked away, pink embarrassment shining on his neck.

'It's just...' he obviously didn't know when to quit, 'you're so different at work.'

Laurel raised an eyebrow. This could go one of two ways. She could be insulted and ruin family dinner, or she could shrug, sip her wine and think 'fuck you Nate Daley, you don't get a rise out of me'.

'Work is work. This isn't work.'

Laurel settled for something in the middle. Nate narrowed his eyes at her, dropping his chin slightly in what she was coming to know as his 'thinking stance'. Although what there was to think about, she had no idea. This wasn't work, so of course she wouldn't behave like she was at work.

'Do you have a drink?' she asked, politely.

Nate glanced around the well-worn and loved living room. 'Somewhere,' he muttered.

'I'll get you one.' Any excuse to go and see her 'best friend' and thank her for the heads up that Nate fucking Daley was joining them for Fletcher Family Sunday Dinner.

'Oh and,' he said, and she turned back to look at him. 'I'm sorry about your mum.'

Huh. The kids must have told him about the Grandma Helena they'd never met. He rubbed the back of his neck awkwardly.

'Okay.' She nodded, a little taken aback at his oddly intimate comment.

NATE

Nate groaned internally. Was it weird that he brought up her dead mother? Or would it have been weird if he *didn't* bring it up, given that he had just been in her childhood bedroom with the picture of her mum on the bedside table and My Little Ponies standing neatly on the shelves.

But when he'd seen the picture of the woman who was an older version of Laurel, he'd had to ask the twins who she was. They told him that Grandma Helena had died when Daddy (Jack) was sixteen, which would have made Laurel fourteen and Robin around four.

It all fell into place.

Laurel must have taken on her mother's role in looking after Robin, ensuring they had clean clothes, making meals.

Jack would have been on the farm with his dad and Robin, well, Robin would only have hazy memories of his mum. Laurel would have been the only mother figure he would have ever known.

Farming is a hard life, long hours, no holiday, no break. People did it because they loved it, because it was in their blood, and certainly not because it made a lot of money.

The passion and drive to make the farm a success made sense. Really, Laurel and Jack were an excellent team.

Of course, Bill, their father, was still around and it was easy to see where the boys got their Fletcher looks from, but Jack obviously did most of the heavy lifting around the place now. Besides, Bill had two gorgeous little monster grandchildren to enjoy.

Nate felt like a pink fluffy cushion on a tractor (i.e. completely useless) standing in the living room by himself, so he followed Laurel into the kitchen, all cream painted wood and scuffed slate floors. It was a huge room, taking up the entire rear of the house. French doors to the garden stood open by the laid dining table, and the kitchen area filled the other side of the room.

Laurel was hissing at Rebecca in one corner, no doubt about having him there. The kids were shrieking outside as Robin squirted them with a water pistol, Jack and Bill looking on indulgently with bottles of beer in their hands.

'Sorry, I just...' Nate started, gesturing to where the Fletcher men stood.

Rebecca turned a smile on him that must have made teenage Jack's heart skitter.

'Nate, here you are.' She pulled the bottle of beer that Laurel had clenched in her hands and handed it to him.

'I'm going t—' Rebecca became distracted by something. 'Robin, no, don't,' she called, as though Robin could hear her from the other end of the carefully curated wild garden.

Rebecca dashed out of the back door.

'Jack asked me the other day,' he blurted. 'I assumed

someone would have mentioned it.' Perhaps *he* should have mentioned it.

He had really, really, wanted to be involved in a proper big, cosy, family dinner and didn't want Laurel to put an abrupt end to that dream. The bunkhouse was awful and lonely on the weekends. The students had their own lives and he didn't fancy hanging out with them. Not that he'd expected to be invited to spend the weekend with his students. Besides, Jack had told him that Rebecca's lamb gave life meaning, so he couldn't pass up that.

'Yeah, well, Fletchers aren't known for their communication,' she muttered, lifting saucepan lids off to check whatever was bubbling away on the hob.

No shit.

He thought he'd been getting on a somewhat friendly keel with Laurel, but maybe not. Nate scowled at her. Laurel Fletcher was hard frigging work sometimes.

Rebecca reappeared, dusting her hands together.

'Can someone get the extra chair from the cupboard under the stairs please,' she said, peeling back the tin foil on the resting lamb.

Nate's mouth watered. Jack was absolutely right. If it tasted half as good as it smelled, then it would indeed give his life at Little Willow Farm meaning. It had been so long since he'd had a home cooked, family meal and certainly not with a tight-knit, loving family like this.

'Yep.' Laurel brushed past him and he dumped his beer on the side, following her through to the cupboard under the stairs.

'I'll help,' he said.

'I can do it, I know where it is,' Laurel threw over her shoulder. Yes, he knew that she didn't need any help, that she was self-sufficient, but still. He wanted to help.

'I know, I'm just helping.' He grinned as she flitted her eyes at him.

It wasn't so much a cupboard under the stairs but next to the stairs, and it was packed to the literal rafters with boxes, including an ancient version of Monopoly, and small pieces of furniture that were obviously too precious to throw away but weren't quite right in the house. Laurel reached up to take down a box that rested on the seat of a dining chair, which in turn had its front legs precariously balanced on the arm of a comfy chair and its back legs on a higher small cupboard.

Laurel edged the box forward and it tilted dangerously, starting to fall. She stretched to her full height with a grunt, smacking her hands flat against it as it teetered on the edge of the seat. The thin fabric of her top rose up around her waist, showing a delicious strip of milky skin above her skirt.

'Are you just going to stand there? You could help,' she said, trying to look over her shoulder but afraid that everything would fall if she moved too much.

'Thought you didn't need help,' he couldn't stop himself saying.

'Shut up, Nate, and just help me,' Laurel snapped. 'It's going to fall.'

Nate stepped towards her. Sure, he didn't have to press his chest to her back and follow the line of her arms with his as he reached for the box above her. He didn't have to take slightly too long in securing the box in his hands, but why not? She was attractive, and she was obviously attracted to him by the way her eyes had skimmed over his chest earlier, so why not flirt a little?

Laurel's breath hitched in her throat, and the tips of her ears turned pink. She held herself entirely still as he pressed against her, making awkward and difficult work of gripping the box. He traced her pinking neck with his eyes and grinned at the hitch in her breath. What would her skin taste like? How would her legs feel wrapped around his waist?

The tension ratcheted up intensely.

'Okay, have you got it?' she asked, lifting her hands and shuffling away from him as best she could in the tight space.

'Yeah,' he said, lifting the box and setting it down somewhere less precarious. His voice was rough.

Laurel let out a breath and her throat bobbed in a swallow. 'Okay.'

Grabbing the legs of the chair, Laurel angled herself towards the door. Nate took hold of the other side.

'I've got it,' she said, still flushed.

'I know, one of the legs is caught.' Nate tilted the chair this way and that, but it wasn't shifting.

'Can you just,' she started, 'if you pull it towards you,'

Nate frowned. She was wrong.

'No, it needs to go backward.'

'I can see where it is, Nate, you need to pull it towards you, then twist it left.'

She was agitated but whether it was because of the chair, or because the air was still thick with the memory of her back against his chest, he didn't know.

'No,' he argued, 'it's just, hold on.'

The frustration fizzed up in her face like a shaken bottle of pop, and she pulled the chair as hard as she could, Nate pulling in the other direction. The wood creaked and cracked, and Nate stumbled backward as the backrest of the chair came off in one devastating popping, crunching sound.

Laurel fell against the door frame, mouth open.

'What have you done?' she hissed at him, shooting her eyes around to see if anyone was coming.

'What have I done? You're the one who wouldn't listen, this wouldn't have happened if you had just done what I said.'

'If *you* had done what *I* had said, then we wouldn't be in this mess.'

Nate sighed and looked around the cramped cupboard for a solution. 'Is there another one?'

'No,' she sighed. 'Give it to me, perhaps we can put it back together.'

Between them, they managed to balance the spindles back in their holes. It was rickety, but it would pass muster. If people were careful with it.

'Come on guys, it's on the table,' Rebecca called.

Laurel assessed their work.

'It'll hold until I find some wood glue after lunch,' she said as he reached to pick it up. 'Just be careful with it.'

Nate glared at her. He wasn't an idiot, and it wasn't like he didn't know what to do with a wooden chair that could fall apart at any minute.

'What?' he said, as Laurel's lips pressed together, mirth crinkling her eyes.

'You look like you're carrying a baby duck,' she said, letting that smile split her face. Nate watched the pulse jump against her neck for two heartbeats.

'Well, I happen to think baby ducks are cute and deserve a lot of gentle carrying,' he said flippantly, leading her back into the heart of the family. He glanced over his shoulder to check that Laurel was following and caught her assessing his arse.

Nate raised an amused eyebrow at her, and she scowled back.

LAUREL

Rebecca had outdone herself. Really, the lamb was one of the best, the roast potatoes were crispy and fluffy, the carrots and parsnips just the right side of honey glazed. Nate had seconds. Not just a bit extra, but actually two dinners. How in the name of all that was holy did he keep himself looking like that if he could eat two dinners without batting an eyelid? When he had pressed up against her to rescue the box from on top of the chair, she felt every inch of him.

Every. Single. Inch.

Her mouth had run dry. It had been a while since she had been that close to a man, and certainly a man with a body like that.

The plates had been cleared, the kids sent to play outside, disappointed because Nate had remained at the table. Robin had moaned at the rice pudding but helped himself to an extra-large second serving.

Laurel sat on the broken chair, not leaning back, not daring to put any weight against the precariously balanced wood. Nate laid his arm behind her, holding the chair in place. She got why, and it was a sound decision to ensure that the chair didn't explode. But he was close, and he smelled so good, and if she did happen to lean any further back, then his skin would be on hers. Again. And she did not need her traitorous body to react as it had in the cupboard again, certainly not in front of her family.

Laurel kept her elbows on the table.

'Rebecca.' Dad leaned back in his chair, folding his hands over his belly. 'That was so good. Nearly as good as Helena's.' He tilted his wine glass towards her in celebration.

'Thanks, Bill.' Rebecca smiled, settling into Jack's side.

'So, Nate, tell us about what you've found in our field,' Bill said, turning shrewd eyes on their guest.

'Actually,' Laurel said, placing a hand on his thigh to stop him from talking.

Oh god, why had she done that? Because it was so tempting to run her palm up and down the length of his leg, his very warm, very muscular leg. This was definitely not the right place, or time, or pretty much anything. Suggestive amusement flitted across Nate's face when she glanced at him to see if he, what? Noticed? Minded? Thought it was really, very weird? Or all of the above. Laurel snatched her hand back and cleared her throat. 'Before Nate gets into that, I've got something I want to discuss.'

Robin groaned.

'We're having a nice dinner, and you have to go and ruin it every time,' he grumbled.

Laurel shot him a look but carried on regardless.

'I want to discuss what could happen if the dig team find what I hope they will find.'

Jack's shoulders visibly sagged, and Dad sighed softly. 'Okay, Laurel, what scheme have you got this time?'

She bristled at that, because her 'schemes' were what had saved this place. When she'd come back from university,

Fletcher's Farm wasn't even covering costs. It was a dying farm, and her 'schemes' had turned it around. Sometimes she really wished her family would just see how hard she worked. Just because it wasn't physical work, she wasn't up at the crack of dawn milking, and wasn't checking the sheep on the common every day, didn't mean that what she was doing wasn't work. Because it was. Damned hard work. Laurel pushed that well-worn argument way down into her stomach.

'So, if it is,' she glanced at Nate, 'an Anglo-Saxon burial, then English Heritage is going to want to be involved.' She didn't miss the apprehensive glance between Jack and their father. 'That would mean that we could get funding from them to build a visitor centre, and we would become a Protected Heritage Site. Meaning,' she took a breath, because this was her trump card, 'that we wouldn't have to do anymore. We wouldn't have to scrimp and borrow funds for Hibbert's fields, we wouldn't have to pray that we have a good Pick Your Own season or that we get five weddings in the summer. We would have English Heritage funding, and English Heritage visitors.'

Jack and Dad looked at each other again, unspoken words passing between them. Dad had Jack helping on the farm way before their mother had died, they all had, but it was Jack who had really taken to it. It was Jack who had done the milking when their dad had been grieving and couldn't get out of bed, and Jack who had negotiated the sale of cattle to ensure that they could afford the electricity throughout the winter that year.

Whilst the farm would go to the three of them equally when Dad died, they all knew it would be Jack managing it.

'What's the likelihood of finding a burial like that? Big enough that English Heritage would be interested?' Dad asked.

'Well, Bill,' Nate said. 'It's looking promising, but we won't know for certain until deeper trenches are dug. We've found coins, we've found metal, a possible shield boss, but no bones yet.'

'For what it's worth,' Rebecca said, as family solicitor,

'English Heritage are a national charity, it would be a massive deal for Little Willow to be associated with them. Free advertising, practically guaranteeing visitors.' She took a sip of her wine. 'Everyone could relax a bit.'

The unspoken words were 'Laurel could relax a bit'.

She looked down at her hands folded neatly on the table.

'Well,' Bill said, 'let's hope it is then.' He tilted his glass to Nate, smiling, but not convinced.

'Jack?' Laurel asked. Jack gave a brusque nod.

'Robin?'

Robin sat back in his chair, fingers linked behind his head.

'So, you're saying you'll stop with all this shit around our home if there's some old bones in that field?'

'It's not shit,' Laurel mumbled, pursing her lips. 'But essentially, yeah.'

'And you're not saying this because you fancy him?' Robin nodded to Nate, sarcastic grin on his face.

It fell silent, and she could feel her family's eyes crawling over her skin. Nate lifted his wine glass and took a sip, studiously ignoring this family bicker. Laurel's face flushed, hard. Out of the corner of her eye she could see the tips of Nate's ears turn scarlet. Embarrassed, either for her, or for him. Whichever, it clearly indicated that any attraction that Laurel may, or may not, feel towards him was completely and utterly unrequited. Besides, it was just a hangover from university, surely.

Jack lurched forward, because knowing Rebecca, she had just booted him in the shin. 'Who wouldn't fancy him? I mean, look at him. Even I fancy him.'

Rebecca snorted her wine, Bill chuckled, and Robin glared.

'You're a dick, Robin,' Laurel said, grabbing her wine and pushing the chair away from the table as hard as she dared. She'd made it to the back door to check on the kids when she heard Nate clear his throat.

'What is it you do on the farm, Robin?'

Laurel turned and leaned on the door frame, uncertain

how this would unfold. Nate was looking earnestly at Robin, leaning forward, genuinely interested.

'What?' Robin said, petulant scowl on his face.

'I mean, I know what Laurel does, and I know what Jack and Bill do, but what's your role? What's your job here?' Nate leaned back in his seat and lay his arm across the back of Laurel's empty, rickety chair, tensing as he pushed down to make sure the back was as secure as it was going to be.

'I do loads, and I don't have to explain myself to you.'

If Robin pouted any harder, he would be mistaken for a trout. Oh, could they do trout fishing in the lake?

'Robin,' the three adult kids jumped at Bill's harsh voice, 'Nate is our guest.'

'But he—'

'Asked your role on the farm, and I don't think it's an unreasonable question. You were late milking the other day when Jack asked you to cover for him because he was lambing on the common. Laurel had to check for pregnancies. The pig shelter needs re-felting, the henhouse needs a good clean and the fencing around the Pick Your Own needs looking at.' The room was still. Dad pointed at Robin across the table, angling his face so his good eye held Robin's gaze. 'These are *all* your jobs, Robin.'

Against the door frame, Laurel was speechless. Their father didn't often shout, wasn't often firm, not really since their mother had died, and certainly never with the favourite, the surprise, the get-away-with-anything, baby of the family.

Rebecca's mouth dropped open, volleying between the eldest and youngest Fletcher men. Jack watched the tablecloth intently.

'I'm sorry, I didn't mean to...' Nate coughed slightly to hide his discomfort.

'Not at all, Nate.' Bill turned to the archaeologist. 'Not at all.'

CHAPTER SIX

NATE

The week after Fletcher family dinner, and that heated moment in the cupboard under the stairs, saw a thawing between him and Laurel. In fact, it was actually quite warm, and there was the distinct promise of friendship. With perhaps a bit of flirting thrown in for good measure. Just a bit, not a lot.

He had turned it into a game, seeing if he could get the right drink for Laurel in the morning. He was there early because he hated being in the bunkhouse when the students roused themselves from their slumber and scurried messily around for food and clothes that weren't too filthy. Whether they had discovered Simon and his laundrette in town was anyone's guess. Today, he sat with two cups of peppermint tea in front of him, having received a grin and a head shake from Laurel.

Nate glanced across the office at her, engrossed in whatever was on her computer screen, a slight frown crinkling her forehead.

'Do you know anything about trout?' Laurel asked, tilting her head at him speculatively.

Nate frowned. 'I know how to cook trout, but beyond that…' He trailed off. 'Why?'

'I don't know, you just look like the kind of guy who would know about trout fishing.' She grinned at him. Was she winding him up?

'I consider fishing to be one of the most mind-numbingly

boring things to do.' He stretched his arms above his head, watching Laurel scan his chest. 'Second only to golf.'

Her eyes came back to his. 'Did your dad never take you fishing?'

He shook his head. 'God, no. Did yours?' he challenged.

'No, Jack always wanted to, but Dad was too busy on the farm.' She leaned back in her chair, uncrossing her legs under her desk. 'I took Robin once. It did not go well.'

Laurel breathed out a little self-conscious laugh, like she'd just overshared. Nate's stomach lurched. She'd given him a glimpse, a tiny sliver of her life and he greedily shoved it in his pocket for further analysis later.

'My dad went out for cigarettes when I was about ten, and never came home.'

'Oh.' She tucked her hair behind her ear.

'It was a long time ago. I'm over it.'

Nate wasn't sure why he felt the need to tell her that, but he did.

It was her turn to say something and he waited patiently. She was probably imagining how she would have coped with her father wandering off and never coming back.

'Well,' she raised one shoulder, 'his loss. Is it just you?'

'Just me and my mum,' he said. Nate couldn't help but glance wistfully at the picture of the Fletcher children on the wall.

'She must be really special.' Laurel's voice was honey quiet, her golden eyes searching his face for something.

'Yeah, she is,' he said softly.

Laurel's throat bobbed in a swallow. He let his eyes wander over her lips to the sleekness of her neck and across her collarbone, exactly how he could trace her skin with his mouth. She would taste of buttercups and jasmine, and her breath would catch in her throat.

Laurel's phone vibrated angrily on her desk, jerking him out of his reverie. His eyes flicked quickly up to hers. She was flushed, those full lips parted, her eyes a wanton dark gold. Her phone vibrated again and she grabbed it, tapping at it forcefully.

'Sylvie, hi,' she breathed.

Nate turned back to his paperwork, satisfied. So, it hadn't been a one off, the way Laurel's body had stilled against his in the cupboard at Bill's house.

Laurel Fletcher was attracted to him.

'Mmm hmm, sure, I'll ask him'

Nate glanced at her, but she was studiously typing with her phone propped under her chin.

'Can you forward me the details for the next outdoor cinema? I just want to double check the food provision.'

Nate looked at the list of finds in front of him, tuning out Laurel's work chatter. They were getting deeper, and now he knew there weren't any significant Victorian discoveries, he was close to getting Hector back in to say it would be difficult to dig deeper trenches, but then do it amazingly right.

'Nate, do you want to?' Laurel interrupted.

'Huh?' He was way too invested in assessing how deep his next trenches needed to go.

'Robin's organising some kind of night out tonight at the Dog & Gun with the students and the farm workers. Sylvie was asking if you wanted to go?' Laurel said. 'It's probably because Robin's got his eye on one of your students and Sylvie is always up for a night out. I don't know who's going, or anything,' she gabbled.

'Oh right.'

It would be interesting to see Casual Laurel, Social Laurel. 'Are you going?

She shrugged and turned her eyes to her computer.

'I don't know, I suppose I should, you know, show willing and all.'

A smile tugged at his lips. 'I'll go if you go,' he said, narrowing his eyes at her.

She regarded him carefully. 'Is that a challenge, Dr Daley?'

Nate laughed. 'No, no. I'd rather be with you, than against you.'

'Hmm.' She made a show of considering his statement, then shrugged casually. 'Okay, yeah, alright.'

'Good.'

That was settled. Him and Laurel, a group of pent up twenty-somethings and alcohol. What could possibly go wrong?

Nate ran a hand through his hair. It was too long for his liking. He'd like to have it cut before they went out, but there was no time.

As always, Nate ignored the first buzz of his smartwatch but fished his phone out of his pocket on the second and answered his masters student. 'Anwar?'

Anwar didn't even say hello, but gasped, 'You need to come, now, right now.'

The urgency in his voice was palpable.

He shot to his feet, chair clattering overturned on the floor. 'What have you found? What is it, Anwar?'

'Metal. Old, old metal with a coloured stone. Dr Daley, it's old. You need to come, now.'

'Don't touch anything. I'll be right there.' Nate was already halfway out of the door before he glanced back at Laurel standing behind her desk, eyes pleading. 'Come on then,' he said, anxiously waving his hand at her.

Nate had never seen Laurel move so fast as she flew from behind the desk, grabbed the green wellies by the door and hurried after him down the corridor.

'What is it?' she asked breathlessly. She was striding fast to keep up with him as he flew down the stairs.

'Metal, a coloured stone. Old,' he said, mind racing. It could be a brooch, a necklace. He hoped it wouldn't be a one off, that it could signify the preliminary finds of a burial site or a horde. If it was either of those, it would make his career, so much more than the flash in the pan Pictish Stylus. It would mean years of work, years of funding for the university. He would be secure and safe in exciting discoveries for the rest of his life.

Nate tapped his fingers on his leg restlessly by the back door whilst Laurel fiddled with the buckles on her funny shoes, before sliding her feet into those green wellies.

Laurel darted off in the complete opposite direction to the dig site. God give him strength.

'Where are you going?' he called.

'Come *on*, do you want to get there or not?' she threw over her shoulder at him. Frustrated, he jogged after her, around the back of the building and into a parking area.

For tractors.

Laurel was climbing up into a little green one, the skirt of her dress flying dangerously up her legs. She settled in the seat and the old engine rumbled into life as she turned the key.

Nate stopped for a second, because this was a weird picture. Prim and proper Laurel in a pale blue sundress and wellies, in the little green tractor. Huh.

'Get in, it's quicker this way,' she grinned, hair flying around her face in the breeze. Startled into life, he ran to the passenger side and climbed in.

Of course Laurel Fletcher could drive a tractor.

LAUREL

Laurel put the tractor in gear and took the milking route up to the dig site. Okay, they could have run it, but she wanted to show off. Nate had looked dumbfounded when she'd climbed into the old Massey Ferguson and cranked the engine into life. She suppressed a smile as he looked around for a seatbelt. This little tractor was way too old for such luxuries.

'What do you think it is?'

Laurel kept her eyes on the rutted track and rested her hand on the juddery gearstick.

Nate hesitated. 'I don't want to guess. I don't have all the information.'

'But it could be—'

Nate put his hand over hers to cut her off. She held her breath, not moving.

'Laurel, don't guess,' he said, leaning closer so she could hear him over the engine. She glanced at him. His face was closer than expected, excitement shining in his eyes. 'I've learned not to expect too much, you can't be disappointed then.'

'That's sad,' she said, swallowing hard because he still had his hand on hers and he was still looking at her with soft, sea blue eyes. 'You get to expect things, Nate, everyone does.'

Nate sat back in his seat, taking his hand away from hers. Good lord, if she was breathless and hot just from him touching her hand, she'd pretty much explode if he ever touched her anywhere else. With anything else.

No, no. This was not the time to be delving into those thoughts. Besides, apart from a bit of harmless flirting, how could she even know if he liked her in that way?

She forced the old tractor into first gear and slowed at the side gate to the dig site. He jumped down eagerly and jogged toward the gate, before turning back.

'Just because I'm not expecting anything, doesn't mean I'm not excited!' He grinned, and Laurel's stomach lurched. He was beautiful, the sun shining behind him, face flushed and eager. Nate Daley lived for this.

'Come on!' he called, because Laurel had hesitated, trying to ignore an unfamiliar feeling of fullness. He wanted to share this. With her.

'I'm coming, I'm coming,' she said, trotting over to him as best she could in her wellies.

Nate pushed the gate open and motioned for her go first.

'Dr Daley!' A scraggly student waved frantically from a trench about waist deep. People were crammed around, trying to catch a glimpse of what had been uncovered. They parted like the frigging Red Sea for the shining archaeological light of Dr Nate Daley, and he jumped down into the trench effortlessly. The students jostled around her, smelling of dirt and sweat. Also, how were they all so tall?

'Guys, move,' Nate commanded, giving them the frustrated look Rebecca saved for Robin when he was being immature. 'Laurel, jump down.'

Jump down? Uh, no thanks.

Laurel wasn't short, but she wasn't going to jump three feet into a trench, and certainly not in front of twenty-five students who were watching avidly. But she did want to see, so she sat down and dangled her legs over the edge of the trench. Unceremoniously, she slid into the hole in the earth. Great. That would be another dress for the dry cleaners.

Nate was already on his knees, carefully brushing at the earth.

'Laurel, look.'

She knelt next to him on the soft gardener's pad the students used to protect their knees, angling herself closer to him so she wasn't getting in his light. His summer rain and hot nights smell mingled with the dry earth. This was what she was supposed to be doing, uncovering hidden treasures buried for centuries. On her farm, here in the dirt.

Laurel's heart thudded painfully in her chest. The last time she'd felt this adventure, this nervousness, was when the earth had given her the Pictish Stylus. But what if it was a bit of tin? What if it was some ridiculous piece of awful Victoriana that had been buried extra deep? Could her little soul take the disappointment?

She reached out and covered his hand to stop him dusting. Nate looked up at her quickly.

'What if it isn't?' she breathed.

His hair had fallen slightly over his forehead, his eyes were more grey than blue.

'Then it isn't,' he said quietly, 'and we keep looking.'

Laurel nodded and rested her hands on her thighs, trying

to keep out of his way. But she wanted to see, she wanted to catch a glimpse of whatever it was.

Nate bent forward and blew gently at the dirt. It was there, a curved edge of dull metal, a tinge of dirty red just below it. He brushed at the earth painstakingly for four long, long minutes, and Laurel tried not to breathe. His deft fingers worked the earth, slowly clearing away time.

'Anwar,' he said without looking up, holding his hand out to him. Anwar placed a round-edged palette knife in Nate's hand. 'Laurel, can you see?' he whispered.

She edged closer, put her hand on his shoulder and leaned against him. Definitely just to stay out of his light.

The dull curve of metal had become a full circle with a raised edge and something defiantly red in its middle. Nate looked over his shoulder and gave her two very small nods. He wiggled the palette knife in the earth below the edge and levered it up, careful to make sure he was moving the earth below the item, not catching the possibly precious metal itself. Nate must have been able to feel her heart beating as she leaned against him, and she tried not to breathe so closely to Nate's ear.

This. Was. Everything.

It was more than the Pictish Stylus. This would change her life, her family's life, everything. If only Nate would confirm what she thought, what she knew, deep in her bones.

Nate ran his thumb tenderly around the edge of the piece, across the small mound of red in the middle. The corners of his mouth lifted in a smile and he turned to her, closer than they should be, chest rising as he caught his breath. She tucked her hair behind her ears.

'It's a brooch, Laurel. Could signify a burial.' He turned to her with shining eyes. 'It is. We've found it.'

His face split into a grin and tears sprang unbidden to her eyes. A cheer went up from the students and she flung her arms around his neck, hugging him tightly because she couldn't speak, she didn't have the words. Nate hugged her back, one arm tight around her waist, the other buried in her hair. He laughed, tears were flowing down her face, the students were clapping and cheering, and it was magnificent.

Nate pulled back, because regardless of how good she felt with his arms around her, he couldn't just hug her forever.

'Hey, hey, don't cry,' he said, pushing tears away from her cheeks with dirty fingers. All she could do was nod and sit back on her heels.

Nate pushed himself to his feet.

'This is trench one now,' he called to the students. 'Bring me a finds box and get the tarpaulin.' His hand rested on her shoulder, and she looked up at him, dazed. 'Are you okay?'

She nodded as the students burst into action around them.

'First round is on me tonight!' he called, and a little cheer went around the students. 'Anwar.' Nate motioned to the find and Anwar fell on it eagerly with his fine brush. 'Hey, I have to...' He motioned around them.

'Yeah, yeah, go,' Laurel said, smiling up at him. Anwar was crouching, dusting the metal. Nate climbed effortlessly out of the trench, digging his mobile from his pocket.

Laurel watched Anwar silently, making sure her hair was securely tucked behind her ears. It was everything that had been sitting in the periphery of her mind ever since the moment that human bone had been waved around in her office. This find, this site, would change her life, change her family's life. It could be more, it could be a burial, it could be a horde. Whatever it was, there was something here on her farm, and it was something amazing.

Anwar shuffled around in the trench, and she was in the way. Like a baby gazelle, she flailed herself out of the trench and stood for a moment, soaking in the buttercup excitement. Everyone else had something to do, and she was a spare part here. Nate was smiling and gesturing on the phone, probably to Cesspit Alex and besides, she had to get the tractor back. Her smile faded and purple jealousy bloomed hazily in her stomach. She wanted this life, this excitement, not to have to retreat into her office and look at spreadsheets and reports and social media campaigns. Laurel's shoulders drooped as she headed back towards the side gate.

'Laurel.' She looked over her shoulder at Nate jogging toward her, his face still split in that grin.

He crushed her to him in another hug, that hand tangling in her hair again at the nape of her neck. This was a different hug from the one in the trench. This was thought about, unobserved. Intimate. He whispered, hot breath in her ear.

'We did it, Laurel. We did it.'

Whatever they'd done, being pressed against Nate's body made heat rush to her core. His stubble scraped against the soft part of her neck and she bit her lip. Good lord, he smelled good. What was that noise? Did a *whimper* just escape her throat? How frigging embarrassing.

Nate pulled back, frowning at her. 'Are you okay?'

With his hand still wrapped in her hair at the nape of her neck, his arm wrapped around her waist and his lips inches from hers, she was anything but okay.

'Mmm hmm.'

Her hands rested on his chest, and they were still hip to hip. Well, her hips to the top of his thighs, his hips to the bottom of her stomach. His hips and *everything* else.

Nate's eyes dropped to her mouth, and his hand tightened on her waist. They were still for a long moment, his chest rising and falling under her hands. If she lifted her head slightly, leaned up on her tiptoes, their lips would be together. Kissing. In the middle of the field. Kissing Nate Daley was not on the agenda for today, no matter how delicious he smelled, no matter how his fingers brushed against the soft skin at the back of her neck.

Nate shook his head slightly and dropped his hands. He took a little step back from her and blew out a sharp exhale, like he'd been holding his breath.

She jerked a thumb over her shoulder. 'I should get the tractor back.'

Nate cleared his throat. Whatever *that* had been, he was obviously embarrassed because a rosy flush was tinting the tips of his ears. It was just the excitement of finding gold, that was it. No need to read anything else into it.

'You'll be at the pub later, yeah?' he asked, rubbing at the back of his neck.

'Yeah, of course.' She grinned. 'And first round is on me, not you.'

NATE

It was there. They'd found it.

The earth had given up its delights and Nate and his team had found them. The atmosphere was warm with achievement and hot with anticipation. There were grins and laughter, high fives and hugs between the students, but Nate had spent his afternoon on the phone with the university, with Alex, demanding more funding for a dig tent.

If there was going to be something more than the brooch Anwar had uncovered and he had edged from the earth, then he was going to get all the funding he could. The more finds the better, for him, for Laurel and for Little Willow Farm.

Nate couldn't help the smile that crossed his face. Laurel had cried. She'd had tears running down her face. It had been the right decision to involve her in this. He hadn't meant for them to have a moment, but she had been windswept and flushed and it had been a while since he'd had an incredibly attractive woman in his arms.

He watched the sun sag like a limp balloon in the sky. It was hazy and quiet on Little Willow Farm, the only sounds the gentle lowing of the cows. It was muggy though, a thunderstorm threatening. He'd have to make sure that the tarpaulins were tacked down hard, especially over that all-important trench.

Nate, extremely disappointingly, had Anwar clean up the piece and it was exactly as he suspected. A round golden torque, a ridge of twisted metal around the edge. Two thin strips of gold crossed over the front and in the exact middle, an oval garnet of the deepest red he had ever seen. The back had two small rings for a pin to secure to a cloak. It was magnificent; detailed, lustrous and big. It signified someone important, someone rich.

A niggle of worry had started in the back of Nate's mind as soon as Laurel climbed back into the battered tractor.

Because what if that was it? What if that was the only find?

He couldn't spend the next months, years, whatever, on a dig that didn't find anything. Besides that, Laurel would be devastated, and he didn't want to watch the excitement drain from her face day after disappointing day.

'Dr Daley.' Anwar came up behind him, clapping his hand on Nate's shoulder. 'Good day, good find. It's going to be a good site, I can feel it.'

'It's a great start, Anwar,' he allowed.

'Oh, come on man, let yourself enjoy it.' Anwar rolled his eyes.

He was right, Nate should enjoy the moment, rather than thinking what if, what if, what if. What he had said to Laurel earlier had been true though, no expectations lead to no disappointment.

'Let's head to the car park. The minibus will be here soon,' Anwar said.

They took the short walk across the car park and headed towards Robin, lounging against the farm gate, smiling lopsidedly at some female students and pointing leisurely at his house. What a dick.

Robin opened his mouth as soon as Nate was in earshot. 'Hey man, heard you found some jewellery.'

Yep, definitely a dick.

'Yeah, we did,' Nate replied, checking his phone. The

minibus trundled into the car park, saving him from any more conversation.

'Sweet,' Robin said. 'Ladies, after you.' He ushered the students on the bus.

Nate rolled his eyes. Of course he wanted to celebrate, but did he really want to spend the evening with a group of kids? Even Anwar was nearly ten years younger than him. Jack's company would have been welcome, but he hadn't come because Rebecca had expressly forbidden him from cancelling one of their rare date nights, while Bill watched the kids.

Regardless, he sat on the bus and watched as the hedgerows and crop-filled fields rolled past for the ten minutes it took to get into Little Houghton.

'Dr Daley, are you okay?' Anwar said, slurping back a can of Fosters.

'Yeah, why?' he answered, frowning.

'Your leg hasn't stopped tapping.' Anwar frowned back at him. 'It's annoying.'

So was Anwar when he'd had a few swigs of beer.

It was still hot when they arrived and piled into the Dog & Gun, and Nate glanced around to see if Laurel had arrived. Not yet.

'Robin Fletcher,' the middle-aged barmaid called. 'Your sister phoned and opened a tab. She's been very clear. One drink each.'

A cheer went up and Robin leaned on the bar, giving her a wink.

Drinks were handed round, and Nate spilled outside with the rest of the dig team to the picnic benches in front of the pub, basking in the last of the day's sun. He pushed his hand through his hair impatiently. Not for the first time, Nate wished he'd had time for a haircut. It was too long and unruly. He could at least look neat.

'Dr Daley, do you think we could be moved into trench one?' A couple of students had cornered him, one batting her eyes eagerly. 'I mean, I just really want to find something, you know? Something important.'

He did know, so he smiled benevolently at the girls, making some non-committal noises because he had absolutely no intention of reallocating trenches.

Where was Laurel? He pursed his lips in annoyance. This was her celebration as well, and she was missing it, and she was the only one that he could have a decent conversation with. Robin was here enjoying himself when he had done precisely nothing to contribute to the dig. All he had done is book a minibus, which was easy because it was his mate's dad who ran the local taxi company. Apparently, Robin Fletcher could coax a loving hug from a scorpion if he so wished.

Nate tuned out the two girls babbling on about how excited they were and what they were going to do with their pretty, young lives, and glanced down the road, wondering which direction Laurel would come from. She lived in Little Houghton, but he didn't know where exactly. Nate took another sip of his beer and looked in the other direction.

There she was, walking down the dusky, hazy main road.

'Excuse me, ladies,' he said, moving to stand at the edge of the pub forecourt.

Laurel was in turned up jeans, flat sandals and what looked like the softest, most comfortable white t-shirt he had ever seen. This was Casual Laurel, wavy hair loose down her back, shoulder bag diagonal across her chest. Nate raised his hand to her and she waved back.

'Hey, you're late,' he said once she was in earshot, smiling. Her cheeks had a glow to them. 'Drink?'

'Yeah, and I'm not late. I'm perfectly on time,' Laurel commented, but her mouth curved up at the corners. 'Robin,' she called. 'Drink?'

Robin called back that he was alright and indicated his full pint. Laurel turned to him expectantly.

'Come on.' He let her go first into the pub, guiding her

with a hand to the small of her back. He was right, it was the softest t-shirt he had ever felt.

Most of the older locals had congregated inside, away from the noise and effervescence of his students and Robin with his friends outside, but there was a group who had taken the remaining picnic table.

'What would you like?' he asked, resting an elbow on the slightly damp bar. 'Wine?'

'Pint please, lager, not that treacly stuff.' She gestured vaguely at his half-drunk pint and he grinned, signalling for the barmaid. It both amused and annoyed him that he got her drink wrong every single time.

'You look nice,' he observed, cutting his eyes to hers before ordering at the bar. A blush flowed across her collarbone and up her neck.

'Oh, thanks,' she muttered, grabbing her pint and taking a long draught as soon as the barmaid put it in front of her. 'I needed that,' she said, wiping her mouth with the back of her hand and looking up at him with those big whiskey eyes. He knew Laurel was pretty, but a realisation smacked him hard in the chest.

Laurel Fletcher was beautiful.

CHAPTER SEVEN

LAUREL

Laurel hoped the lager would calm her nerves. Why was she so nervous?

She was, indeed, late because she had changed her outfit about twelve thousand times; different shoes, different top, different trousers, dress, skirt, shorts. And hair. Why did it take so long to do her hair?

In the end, she'd decided fuck it, don't try so hard, don't worry about it. It's not like she was looking to pull Nate Daley, or anyone for that matter, was it?

But when he had ambled halfway onto the pavement, pint in hand, and watched her walking down the road, she knew exactly why it had taken so long.

'Let me pay the tab, Angela,' she said to the barmaid who handed her a bill that was way more than one drink each. Either that, or Angela was screwing her over, but she couldn't argue, not today, not when they'd found something magical and beautiful under her field.

'I haven't stopped smiling,' she said to Nate. 'It's so exciting.

His eyes sparkled and he drained his pint, picking up a new one.

'It is exciting, you're right.'

He leaned closer and she held his eyes for a beat. How did he always smell good? Like fireworks and colourful dreams.

'Don't you have to celebrate with your team? You know, good leadership and all that?' Laurel said.

Nate pulled a hand through his hair and glanced out the window.

'I suppose I should, shouldn't I?' He scrunched up his nose.

'You really should.' She nodded.

'Come on then,' Nate put his hand out, 'after you.'

Laurel let him usher her out, his warm hand nearly burning through her thin t-shirt.

Nate Daley was so damned attractive. But they worked together, so she had to keep it in her pants. Besides, he was just being friendly and probably like this with all women around his age. Let's face it, there wasn't much choice was there? The students were too young and the only other person was a very married Rebecca. Perhaps he just found it hilarious making her blush.

The students were sprawled on three of the four picnic benches, overflowing onto the low wall, looking like a music festival advert in their pork pie hats, skinny jeans and unironic t-shirts. Laurel perched on the wall behind them, Nate sitting next to her. She waved at a couple of locals sitting on the remaining table. If she kept everyone onside it could only help with development.

'Laurel!' Came a cheer from Robin's friends, who had congregated near a clump of female students.

'Boys.' She tilted her glass to them in greeting.

'You get on well with Robin's friends?' Nate asked.

'Half of them grew up on the farm running around playing lost boys and pirates. The amount of skinned knees I've patched up and sleepovers I've refereed.' She angled her body to him. 'But enough about me, you know practically everything there is to know, and I've got to ask.' Her face was hot, but she'd started now. Her mouth wouldn't stop moving and the words were just escaping from her brain. 'Where's Lucia?'

Nate nearly spat out his beer and Laurel clapped him on

the back, because that's what you were supposed to do when someone was choking, wasn't it?

'Uh, she's in Goa, or Colombia, or Moldova, I don't know.'

'Oh.' Laurel studied her drink. 'So, you're not still together then?'

Oh god, why had she asked this? It was literally like turning on a very big flashing neon sign that said LAUREL FLETCHER WANTS TO HAVE SEX WITH YOU. But it was a desperate, burning need to know whether he was attached or not, which had first planted itself precisely at the time Nate had stepped into her line of sight all those weeks ago.

She glanced up at him to check that he had heard, because he was taking too long to answer. Nate glanced around.

'No, we're not. There's no one,' he said.

She nodded and dragged her eyes away to a group of female students dancing to tinny music from a phone in the middle of the patio area.

'You?' He nudged her with his shoulder.

Laurel's stomach flopped around like a tantruming child because this thing between them, whatever it was, wasn't just her. Perhaps he had a neon sign as well.

No, he was just making conversation.

'In case you haven't noticed, it's hardly bursting with eligible bachelors around here.' She grinned. 'Besides, I grew up with everyone here, and I am definitely not into the incestuous small town relationship thing.'

Especially after her one night stand with George Hibbert, and his utter inability to let it go.

Nate nodded contemplatively, his nearly-too-long hair flopping over his forehead. Well, that was all different kinds of sexy.

'Laurel,' Robin called sharply and she snapped her eyes to him. He nodded to a newcomer stalking down the road, obviously displeased with the brisk business of the pub.

George Hibbert. How frigging wonderful.

She hadn't seen George Hibbert since she'd put in the

expression of interest for his fields. Obviously, there was an issue because, despite her father discussing the matter with Old Man Hibbert, George was still harrying the sheep on the common, like a petty fourteen-year-old.

'Who's that?' Nate asked, following her eyes.

'George Hibbert,' Laurel said, giving Nate a wan smile. She didn't need to bring up the fact that she and George had seen each other naked. Once. Two years ago.

'Oh, you're buying his fields?' Nate asked, gulping his beer.

'Trying to, if the bank gives me the money.' She rolled her eyes. 'I'm still waiting on them.'

'But you won't have to if you can get English Heritage sponsorship?' Nate pushed.

Laurel sighed. 'No, I won't have to, but I will still want to. Hibbert has to sell. His farm is dying. If he doesn't sell to me, he'll sell to developers and they'll put five disgustingly big "country cottages" on the land and ruin it for everyone.'

This was the argument she had repeated again and again to her family, to the bank, to pretty much anyone who would listen.

Nate narrowed his eyes at her.

'So you're saving it, really?'

'Yes!' she exclaimed, turning to face him properly. She tapped him excitedly on the shoulder. Huh, those shoulders were more toned than she thought. 'Why does no one else see that? It's definitely saving the land, definitely. Keeping it undeveloped and grazed by Little Willow Farm, or let out for grazing. The maize maze. A tasteful, affordable, sustainable, local development.'

'Can you afford that?' Nate asked, his eyebrows wiggling together.

'Well, no. Not really.' She let her hand drop into her lap, deflated. 'But can we afford not to? That's the question. Can Little Houghton afford for us not to?'

The frown on Nate's face deepened.

'You're not a saviour, Laurel. You shouldn't take all this on yourself.'

'But if not me, who? The farm would die, the town would be turned into some kind of hipster foodstall with Londoners coming for their "quaint countryside breaks", which is great, don't get me wrong, it brings in money and tourists.' Laurel looked up and down the tiny high street. 'But that's not what people here want, they want to farm and they want to live a quiet life. They don't want to be gentrified.'

Laurel looked back at Nate, throat a little tight. It was the first time that she'd actually, really, honestly articulated that before. Her need to save Little Houghton, to keep it hers. To keep it theirs. If she couldn't save her mother, then she could save the family, the farm and the village she loved. Or at least, she could give it her best shot.

'Anyway, enough.' She swallowed her emotion. 'This is supposed to be a celebration.' Laurel forced a smile to her lips and stood up. 'I'm going to the toilet.'

Nate nodded and she turned to head into the pub. He caught her hand to stop her.

'You're doing a great job, Laurel,' he said.

She smiled. 'Thanks, Nate.'

NATE

The atmosphere was charged between him and Laurel. He knew it and she knew it.

Nate ran a hand through his hair. She had been buttercups and summer when she'd leaned against him in the trench earlier. Sure, he didn't have to hug her that tightly but shit, she smelled so good and she was so excited. And he'd wanted to.

When she'd asked about Lucia, looking up at him from underneath her lashes, brave but flushed and shy, he'd nearly choked on his beer. He did choke on his beer. God, he'd wanted to kiss her there and then, in front of everyone, sat on the low wall in the pub garden.

Kiss her until she was breathless and desperate.

Nate turned his face up to the dusky sky and ignored the single vibration on his smartwatch. It was probably Alex. Today was a good day. The amazing find and very slim possibility, not expectation, of more.

And her. Laurel Fletcher.

'Yo, Nate,' Robin called. 'Where's Laurel?'

Robin had done well for himself, his arm slung around one of the female students, holding court with his mates.

'She's inside,' Nate called back, gesturing to the pub.

Robin's eyes flitted over to the local's table and he stood up quickly.

'By herself? Jesus, Nate,' he said, winding his way through the melee.

'What? She's a grown up,' Nate said, standing. What was Robin's problem?

'Yeah, but George fucking Hibbert isn't, Nate,' Robin said pointedly, frowning at him. Nate glanced over, and yeah, George Hibbert wasn't there, but his half-drunk pint sat on the table.

'He's not going to follow her into the toilet, Robin,' he said, rolling his eyes, because surely not.

'Who fucking knows?' Robin's jaw was tense. 'How long has she been gone?'

Nate didn't have time to answer because Laurel's voice cut through the air.

'George, I'm not talking to you about this right now.'

'That's right,' he slurred. 'Laurel Fletcher, too good for the likes of me.'

He was too close behind her, trailing across the pub patio. George Hibbert's face was blurred and his ruddy, dirty blond hair was cropped short against his head. Nate took two steps toward them. Laurel's eyes were fixed on the ground, shoulders curving in as she hurried over to them.

'George, no,' she said, not looking around at him.

'Don't fucking "George no" me,' he said loudly.

George Hibbert grabbed Laurel's arm and jerked her backwards sharply. Grabbed her. No.

Nate moved quickly, reaching her before Robin, and pushed George violently, hands smacking flat in the middle of his chest. George Hibbert stumbled back, confused and sneering. Nate put an arm protectively around Laurel's shoulders and she tucked herself into him.

Robin launched himself at George, his swinging fist connecting with George's jaw with a thud.

'Don't you ever fucking touch my sister,' he yelled. 'Don't even think my sister's name, you fucking bastard.'

George Hibbert stumbled again and spat disgusting blood onto the ground. It looked like he was about to take a running jump towards Robin, but spotted Robin's band of feral boys like greyhounds barely restrained, begging for a fight, just behind him.

'You Fletchers think you own the fucking town, and you don't,' he said, red eyes flicking between Robin and Laurel.

Who the fuck did this guy think he was? Laurel was shaking under his arm and he squeezed her tightly.

'You should go home,' Nate said, voice low and harsh.

'I'll take him, come on boy.' One of the older men from the local's table ambled over and ushered George Hibbert away, shooting Laurel a dirty look. What was the deal with these fucking people?

'Fucking Fletcher bitch. You'll get what's coming to you, you better watch yourself,' Hibbert shouted as he stumbled away.

'Are you okay?' he asked her.

She didn't seem to be physically hurt, but she was scared and shaken. She nodded.

'Robin, you absolute idiot, what did you do that for?' Laurel smacked him half-heartedly on the shoulder.

'No one grabs my sister,' he said vehemently, glancing at Nate. Anyone with that kind of protective instinct over their sister deserved some respect.

'Are you alright?' she asked. 'How's your hand?'

Robin grinned. 'It's alright, Laurel. Besides, girls love the hero look.'

Nate rolled his eyes.

'Okay,' Robin said, and meandered off back to his table, his boys following.

The chatter started up again and Nate led Laurel over to their little perch on the low wall.

'Are you sure you're okay?' he asked, a little reluctant to let her go.

'I'm sure,' she said, with a resigned close-lipped smile.

She wasn't.

'Anwar,' Nate called, fishing his credit card out of his wallet. 'Get us a couple of brandies, doubles, and one for Robin. Oh, and get one for yourself as well.'

'Brandy?' Laurel's mouth turned down in a grimace as Anwar obediently trotted off.

Nate smiled briefly. 'Yeah, it'll settle your nerves.'

Laurel looked down at her hands. He had the sudden urge to follow George Hibbert, grab him like he had Laurel and force him to grovel. She reached out and put a small hand on his larger one, folding her fingers around his.

'Thank you. You didn't have to, but thank you,' she said, looking up at him with those big whiskey eyes.

'I did have to,' he said, heart thumping in his chest. Her throat bobbed in a swallow. 'People don't get to treat you like that, Laurel. You shouldn't have to put up with it.'

The brandies arrived, and Laurel coughed after throwing hers back in one long gulp.

'Urgh, how do people do that?'

'Well, they don't normally do it with brandy, that's for starters.' Nate laughed, sipping his drink.

Laurel laughed as well.

'Anyway, tell me about your mum, she must be amazing to have raised you by herself,' Laurel said, touching his arm lightly.

'She is.' So, he told her about his mum.

Nate told her about the time she'd cried when he passed his judo white belt grading aged six, how she had saved for months so he could have a bouncy castle party in the local town hall and how no one, ever, could make a tuna and cheese toastie like hers.

He let his knee rest against her thigh, her hand lightly touching his arm. This was heading somewhere, he knew it, and he wanted it.

'Oh, I love this song!' Laurel's face lit up when some god awful, soft indie rock came on.

'Come on then, let's dance,' Nate said, taking her hand and pulling her up to join the students waving their arms around and sashaying drunkenly to the music.

He twirled her under his arm and she laughed up at the darkening sky, and then he pulled her close, wrapping his arm around her back. She was slightly soft around the edges and he wondered what it would be like to kiss her, but then pushed it quickly out of his mind. They had to spend every day together, and a one night stand would not be good for their working relationship. Besides, it's not like he was in love with her.

'How did you get all these muscles?' Laurel said, squeezing his shoulder and sliding her hand down his bicep.

'How did your skin get to be so soft?' he murmured, letting his hand slip under her top. She pressed herself tighter against him.

The sound of the minibus rumbled closer and the students cheered drunkenly, getting ready to leave.

Laurel bit her lip and looked up at him, heat and desire in her eyes. 'Do you want to come b—'

The trill voice of one of the female students interrupted her. 'Dr Daley, Anwar's throwing up behind the wall!'

Laurel shook her head with a smile and stepped back from him. Was she going to ask him back to hers? Would he have gone? Damn right he would have gone.

'I don't have to deal with that, do I?' he asked, hopefully.

'You really do,' she replied with a grin, taking a couple of steps towards the pavement. 'See you on Monday.'

He took a step after her.

'You're not walking home by yourself, are you?'

'I live above the Post Office, it's fifty metres away,' she called.

'Text me when you get home.' Why the hell had that come out of his mouth? But what if George Hibbert was somewhere around?

He watched her walk for a few seconds, before attempting to manhandle Anwar onto the bus.

LAUREL

Laurel's mouth felt like she'd stuffed ten thousand crackers into it. She reached for the pint of water Drunk Laurel had put on the bedside table. She was a good one sometimes, Drunk Laurel. But she hadn't been all that drunk, had she? She'd taken off her makeup, she wasn't sleeping in her clothes, she'd plugged her phone in to charge, so those were all wins. But Drunk Laurel had forgotten to draw the curtains and she hissed like a vampire as she turned over into the blinding, warm sun.

She sat up gingerly. Okay, good. No spinning, no pounding. Drink the water, take two paracetamol, just to be on the safe side, and everything would be right with the world.

Laurel drained her water and checked her phone.

Rebecca

How was your night out? I need you today, can we go for a walk?

She texted back quickly.

Rebecca

Meet you there in half an hour.

What had happened to make calm, collected, stare-down-hardened-criminals Rebecca needy? Laurel frowned at the phone, concerned. She was never needy, never insecure, always on top of things.

Laurel dragged herself out of bed. Walking had always been their saving grace, a way of keeping their sanity and getting away from, well, everything.

Laurel considered texting Jack. See, that was the problem when your best friend was your brother's wife; split loyalties. Laurel had learned the hard way that the best thing to do was to keep way, way, way out of their relationship and never, ever mention it to Jack. Ever.

Quick shower and brush of teeth, and Laurel was out of the door with big sunglasses covering her face. Surely, the unfeasibly hot British summer had to give way to furious storm clouds at some point.

When she arrived at the start of the footpath, Rebecca was already wearing out the path, pacing back and forth in her expensive trainers.

'Hey,' she waved.

'Oh, Laurel, there you are,' Rebecca said, hugging her tightly. 'You look kind of alright for going out last night.'

'Yeah, I know!' Laurel was as surprised as Rebecca. 'There was only one brandy, and that was Nate Daley's fault.'

'Brandy?' Rebecca scrunched up her nose.

'Don't ask.' This wasn't about her; this was about her best friend.

Rebecca linked her arm through Laurel's and they started along the footpath. There were picnickers, a family playing cricket, dogs chasing balls, kites flying. It was a quintessential British summer day, but Laurel didn't see any of it, because her friend marched her unrelentingly along the pathway to the hill.

'Come on, don't be a baby, the twins walk up this hill,' she said when Laurel started to moan.

They could have easily sat on the bench at the bottom and talked, but no. Rebecca obviously needed to burn some energy, work something out in her mind by making her legs hurt.

'Fine, but I'm stopping halfway up,' Laurel huffed. Rebecca strode ahead.

It wasn't a big hill but still, bigger than she wanted this particular Saturday morning. Laurel was red faced and puffy when she collapsed on the bench at the top.

'Are you going to tell me what's going on? Or are you just going to punish me for the rest of the day?' Laurel said, turning her back to the sun and pushing her sunglasses into her hair. Rebecca twisted her fingers in her lap and avoided Laurel's eyes. 'Did something happen last night? What's Jack done? You know he's a complete idiot sometimes.'

Rebecca shrugged and looked over Little Houghton.

'He wants another baby,' she said, deflated.

'Oh.' Laurel blew out a breath. 'I thought you guys were done after the twins?'

'Yeah, so did I,' Rebecca muttered. 'It's not like I don't like babies, or kids. I do. I love them, and I love Lila and Micah. I just,' she shook her head. 'I just don't know if I can have another. I mean, I'm mid-thirties—' She stopped abruptly and cut her eyes to Laurel. 'Sorry.'

'Don't be sorry, Rebecca,' she said. 'This is about what you want, not me. Besides, mid-thirties isn't late to have kids anymore. There are plenty of first-time parents in their late thirties, forties, fifties.'

Rebecca looked to the sky for divine inspiration.

'But it's classed as a geriatric pregnancy.'

Laurel bristled.

'Well, perhaps they need to rethink the name for it,' she said indignantly. 'There is nothing wrong with having a baby at your age, or older.'

Laurel put her hand over Rebecca's, bringing her back to earth.

'But it has to be what you want, and it doesn't seem like it is?'

'I'm so selfish, aren't I?' Rebecca's chin wobbled. 'It's supposed to be a joint decision, equal weight. Me and Jack together.'

'But it's not like Jack has to be pregnant, is it?' Laurel said softly.

Rebecca had been so big, so tremendously uncomfortable and had been prescribed multiple bouts of bed rest throughout her pregnancy with the twins. Some women glowed and enjoyed their pregnancies. Rebecca, however, had been a whale, and the birth? Well, let's just say it was traumatic for all involved.

'Jack was so excited. He said it would be amazing for the twins to have a little brother or sister,' there was a catch in Rebecca's throat, 'and I feel so guilty, so bad, because it would be.' Rebecca turned to face Laurel, her eyes shining with tears, pleading for understanding. 'I really don't want to have another baby.'

'Oh Rebecca,' Laurel said, reaching for her.

'You remember before?' Rebecca continued.

Laurel remembered the bleeding, the sleepless nights. Then, when the twins were born, Rebecca's utter exhaustion. Now she looked back at it, she suspected that Rebecca had some post-natal depression, and Laurel bitterly regretted not spotting it in her friend at the time.

'It will be like that but worse, because I'll already have the twins to deal with,' Rebecca whispered through choking sobs. 'I already miss out on so much of them with work. The nanny takes them to swimming, drama club, school. I do as much as I can, but I'm on track for partner and work is important to me. It's important to the family, because, no offense, we can't live on Jack's wages.'

'None taken at all.' There wasn't much money to go around.

Farming was a tough life. You didn't just marry the farmer, you married the land, the way of life. Jack couldn't take time off to take the kids to school, take them to their clubs in the evening. Jack didn't get weekends to himself, he didn't get holidays. Sure, there was more help now that Laurel had managed to hire some farmhands, but Jack was Jack. He didn't know any other way of life. Rebecca and him had argued endlessly over it when the twins were babies, but nothing changed. It had been a rough couple of years for them.

Rebecca pulled back from Laurel and wiped her face.

'If I have another child, I'll be off for six months to a year, and then there's the night feeds and the sleeping. And what if I have twins again?' She shook her head. 'The kids are in school now and I thought this would be time for me, and time for Jack and I to be a couple again, now the twins are older.'

'Did you tell him this last night?' Laurel asked, holding Rebecca's hand tightly.

'I was too shocked, I thought he was on the same page as me. We hadn't discussed it explicitly, but how would it work? That he would carry on living his life and then there's me, giving up everything, accommodating everyone, doing everything.' Rebecca was getting angry now, her tears turning from sorrow to rage. 'Again? Does he even understand and appreciate what I did with Lila and Micah? What I still do?'

'You need to have a conversation with him, Rebecca,' Laurel pressed.

'I'm being so selfish.' Her shoulders slumped.

Laurel took a breath. 'Rebecca, you are an incredible mother, an incredible wife. Lila and Micah are the luckiest children in the world to have you,' she said.

Rebecca nodded, sniffing.

'You *both* have to want another baby, and it seems that you don't.'

'I don't, Laurel. I really don't.' Rebecca shuddered, saying it so bluntly out loud.

'Then you have to talk to Jack about it, you have to explain. He'll understand, won't he?' He would have to understand, otherwise Laurel would beat it into him.

'I don't know,' Rebecca shrugged. 'He was so excited last night.'

'He didn't want to start trying last night, did he?' Laurel asked, trying to lighten the mood. 'Oh god, I don't know why I asked that, please don't tell me. I do not want to think about my brother having sex.'

Rebecca snorted a laugh. 'I've got my period so no sexy times, thank you very much.'

Laurel looked at her best friend earnestly.

'Rebecca, you don't have to have another baby if you don't want one. You are not being selfish,' Laurel said. 'You are allowed the life you want right now. If you change your mind in a few years, then you change your mind.'

'If I do change my mind, which I won't, I would be too old anyway,' Rebecca said, grumpily.

'You won't be, but if you are then there are other options. Adoption, fostering, surrogacy.' Laurel shrugged. 'Besides, maybe you'll get to be the best aunt in the world.'

Rebecca raised an eyebrow at her.

'Robin may knock up some girl from town.'

Rebecca laughed out loud.

CHAPTER EIGHT

NATE

Nate forced one foot in front of the other up the little hill on the outskirts of Lower Houghton. He really wasn't in the mood for running, but he could not stand to be in the bunkhouse. Anwar was not a delight to be around, and he was monopolising both the bathroom and the tiny sofa in the living area with his hangover.

Besides, running would burn off some of his frustration and disappointment.

Nate slowed to a walk on the second buzz of his smartwatch and wiped the sweat off his face with the bottom of his t-shirt. He glanced around quickly to check no one was nearby and pulled his running top off. God, the slight breeze on his bare skin was so good. His watch buzzed again and he yanked his phone out of his arm pouch.

'Paul, mate, how are you? How's France?' Nate asked, grinning down the phone at his old friend.

'Nathanial, my man! Good to hear your voice,' Paul said exuberantly.

It had been months since they'd talked. Text and email just wasn't the same.

'France is amazing, it's perfect. It's hot and sunny, and there are finds galore. I'll be on this site at least another year.'

'That's fantastic, Paul, really good.' Nate continued a slow walk up the hill. 'Funding extended?'

'Yep, funding extended,' Paul hesitated. 'Actually, that's the reason I've called.'

Hmm.

'Oh yeah?'

'Yeah, I'm looking for a university partnership and of course you, Dr Daley, are my first and best choice,' Paul said.

Nate stood still, blinking in surprise. 'You want me in France? Looking for Cathar treasure?'

'Yeah.'

Nate was silent for a moment. Everyone knew that there wasn't really any lost Cathar treasure buried amongst the mountains of the Languedoc in the south of France. But it was a magical place, romantic with a hint of supernatural religious mythology. And it was the south of France.

'Listen, don't say anything now. I'm going to send you the documentation, the site location, everything we've found so far. You know the drill,' Paul said. 'You must get loads of promotional packages begging you to come on site.'

It was true, he'd received a multitude of offers in the first few years after the Pictish Stylus paper, but recently they'd waned.

Paul carried on, 'I'm coming back for Jess and Owen's summer barbecue. You'll be there, right? We can talk more then?'

'Yeah, I'm going.' There was no harm in having a chat. 'Okay, yeah, let's have a conversation.'

There was no harm in keeping all options open.

'Heard the news?' Paul said cagily. Nate waited for him to continue. 'Have you read the recent email Jess sent round? You know how she likes to be super organised?'

'No, it's on my list of things to read.' Once he'd fished it out of his 'Social' folder in his gmail account.

Paul paused dramatically.

'Lucia's coming.'

'Oh right, I didn't know she was even in Britain,' Nate said.

Why Paul, and everyone else for that matter, felt they had to pussy foot around him when Lucia's name came up he would never know. They'd broken up years ago, there had been other women for him and he wasn't as naive to think that there hadn't been other men and women for her. It's not like he was pining after her, waiting for her to drop everything and realise that she wanted a settled life with Nate.

No, he had gotten over her a long, long time ago.

'Yeah, she's coming back from Egypt for a whirlwind tour, which includes Jess and Owen's barbecue,' Paul said. Nate rolled his eyes.

'Good, well, it will be nice to see her.'

It was the truth, it would be nice to see how her life was going, even if she was going to behave like she was gracing them with her presence.

'Oh, and…' Paul hesitated.

'Yeah?' Nate prompted.

'I'm bringing Angeline.' Nate could hear the smile on Paul's face. 'She's French.'

Nate grinned. 'Angeline, eh? How long have you been seeing her then? Must be serious to bring her all this way.'

'A few months. Nate, man, she's amazing,' Paul gushed. 'I can't wait for you to meet her, she's perfect. You'll love her.'

'I'm sure I will. You deserve it, Paul. I'm chuffed for you.'

It had been way too long since Paul had a girlfriend. He was such a nice guy, sweet, kind and absolutely adoring of any girl he was seeing. Which often meant that he got his soft little heart squashed and shredded. Hopefully, this Angeline would be better.

'Yeah, me too.'

Nate caught a stream of French from a female voice at the other end of the line.

'Look mate, I've got to go. Look out for that email, yeah?'

'Will do. See you, Paul,' Nate said, hanging up the phone.

Nate stuffed his phone back into his arm pouch and started up a slow run again, not bothering to put his top back on.

He had a vague idea of what Paul was working on from the email updates he'd glanced through. It wasn't that he wasn't interested in his friends' lives. He really was. If Nate really analysed why he didn't want to pore over Jess's emails with photos of smiling family games, their boy, Benji, on horseback, paddling in the sea on holiday, then he wouldn't like himself very much. It was hard not to give in to the jealousy that swelled in his stomach. Nate adored Benji and every time he called him Uncle Nate, his tough little heart melted. He adored seeing his friends as well, but he didn't need his inability to settle down and start a family rubbed in his face with every single email. He knew that wasn't their intention, of course. But still.

He pushed on, pumping his legs harder as the hill took a steeper curve upwards. The burn in his thighs was a welcome punishment for being a jealous fuck.

Nate crested the top of the slope and looked over Lower Houghton. It was pretty, with its small winding streets, lazy rambling roses and beautiful old buildings. Yeah, it was a bit ramshackle and could use some love, but what place wasn't in need of some attention? That's what Laurel was trying to do, wasn't it? To not exactly gentrify the place, but to just make it nicer. Keep it the same, just a bit better.

'Oh, hey Nate.'

He whipped his head around at the female voice. People didn't know him here. Not people who would be on the top of Lower Houghton hill, anyway.

'Oh,' he said. 'Hey Rebecca, Laurel.'

They were sitting on the bench, Laurel's arm around Rebecca's shoulders. Rebecca's face was puffy and red, like she'd been crying. Oh god. What had he walked into?

'Hi,' Laurel said. Her sunglasses were propped on top of her head and she looked tired, but he didn't miss her eyes as they flitted over his chest and down his stomach. Nate grabbed his t-shirt from where he'd tucked it in his shorts, wiped his face, and pulled it over his head. By the time he'd done that,

Rebecca had disentangled herself from Laurel and had pasted a smile on her face.

'Out for a run?' Laurel asked, her face flushing ever so slightly. Did she remember flirting with him, sending those ridiculous messages last night? Or was there something else going on?

'Yep.' He grinned.

Rebecca looked at Laurel oddly. 'I haven't asked, how was last night?'

'Yeah, it was really good,' Nate said. 'Oh, except for George Hibbert.'

'George Hibbert? What did that little twat do?' Rebecca sighed, looking at Laurel expectantly.

Laurel rolled her eyes.

'Oh, he's just a dick. You know what he's like,' she brushed it away, shooting him a pointed look. Alright, if she didn't want to talk about it, he certainly wasn't going to go into it.

He stretched out his calf.

'Oh, and thanks Laurel,' he said, with an impish grin.

She exchanged a confused look with Rebecca. 'For what?'

He was amused. 'Those pictures last night.'

Rebecca's wide eyes flicked between Laurel and Nate and her jaw dropped just a little.

Laurel turned pale. 'What pictures?'

Oh, so she didn't remember? Nate feigned shock.

'Those pictures you sent when you got home, Laurel.' He winked.

Laurel was unnaturally still. She obviously did not remember. Nate smiled, enjoying her discomfort way too much.

'Oh, yeah, okay,' she said quietly.

Nate tapped on his smartwatch.

'Anyway, I've got to get back. See you on Monday.'

He took off down the hill, smiling at her horrified face.

LAUREL

'You. Sent. Him. Pictures.' Rebecca said, jabbing her in the shoulder with each word. 'You never send me pictures,' she grumbled.

'I didn't send him naked pictures.'

Did she?

Oh god, please no. Drunk Laurel could be kind of an exhibitionist.

'But before that, I need to know what happened with George Hibbert. Now, please.' Rebecca wasn't asking. It was a demand wearing the skin coat of politeness. Laurel quickly told her about George Hibbert being drunk and gobby, Nate pushing and Jack punching him.

Rebecca grinned. 'So, Nate came to your rescue, knight in shining armour style?'

'I didn't need a knight in shining armour,' she lied. 'George would have gone after a bit. Besides, Robin and the boys were there too.'

But it had been nice, being pressed against his side, the evident concern in his eyes and of course, the restrained shove he'd given George Hibbert. She'd been his first priority, not beating the shit out of George, like Robin.

'Mmm hmm,' Rebecca said knowingly. Laurel glared at her. 'Right, pictures now please.'

Laurel pulled her phone out and scrolled to the brand new WhatsApp chat she had started last night with Nate Smug Bastard Daley. Rebecca pushed closer so she could live vicariously through Laurel's embarrassment.

Picture 1: her key in the street-level front door.

Picture 2: halfway up the stairs to her first-floor flat.

Picture 3: her key in the front door to her flat. Nothing but originality there.

Picture 4: a pint of water on the kitchen sideboard.

Picture 5: a slightly blurry mirror selfie of her with her

pyjamas on, makeup off, and a toothbrush sticking out of her mouth.

Nate

So you got home alright then?

Picture 6: a selfie of her pretending to be asleep and trying not to smile.

I'm asleep now.

Right. Good, Laurel. Urgh.

Picture from Nate: Anwar sat on the bathroom floor, hugging the toilet.

Nate

Really enjoyed tonight with you. See you Monday.

'Really, Laurel? What are you, five?' Rebecca said, cringing at her.

'I was a bit drunk, alright? He asked me to let him know when I got home.' She raised a shoulder despondently. 'So, I did.'

'Evidently.' Rebecca laughed as Laurel scrolled through the pictures again.

How. Frigging. Embarrassing.

'It's awful, isn't it?' Laurel asked.

Rebecca considered. 'He didn't seem to think so. Seems like he thought it was funny?'

'Hmm, maybe.'

'It's a good thing you weren't wearing that Boux Avenue pyjama set that I got you for Christmas that year.' Rebecca giggled.

Laurel shuddered.

'Christ, yes. That does not leave much to the imagination.'

'Neither did Nate today, running with no t-shirt on.' Rebecca fanned her face. 'Oof.'

There was no denying it. Nate Daley was hot.

Extremely. Beautifully. Hot.

That little path of dark hair that she'd glimpsed in the office led all the way up to his belly button and there was a dark dusting across his toned chest. And his legs? Well, Laurel fully enjoyed that view. She wondered what his skin would taste like, all hot and delicious from running.

'Did you see him being all embarrassed that he wasn't wearing a top? Bless him,' Rebecca said, breaking her out of his reverie.

'What?'

If there was one thing Nate Daley wasn't, it was embarrassed by anything. He was always flaunting his obnoxious body in her office.

'Why else do you think he went all red and put it on as soon as he saw us?' Rebecca gave her the 'you're stupid' look. 'Perhaps it was because you were literally drooling.'

'Shut up,' Laurel said, grinning. 'He is hot though, isn't he?'

Rebecca grinned back. 'Mmm hmm.'

Laurel looked over Lower Houghton and bit her lip.

'I nearly asked him back to mine last night. I was fully prepared to jump his bones.'

Rebecca squealed. 'Laurel, you dog! Why didn't you?'

Laurel pointed to the picture of Anwar hugging the toilet and rolled her eyes. 'Anwar throwing up is why. One of the girls screeched for Nate and he had to go.'

Rebecca's brow furrowed in thought and she opened her mouth, obviously thought better of whatever she was going to say, and snapped it shut again.

'What? I know that look,' Laurel said.

'Maybe,' Rebecca started and then sighed. 'Laurel, don't

take this the wrong way, but do you think you could just have a one night stand with him?'

The breeze ruffled her hair.

'What do you mean?' she asked, warily.

Rebecca turned to face her, squinting into the sun.

'I know you, Laurel Fletcher. I see how you watch him, how you're awkward and weird around him.' Rebecca hesitated. 'You like him, much more than a one night stand.'

Laurel glanced away from Rebecca because once again, her all-seeing, all-knowing best-friend-slash-sister-in-law was right. The last few weeks in the same office, spending last night with him. Yeah, she wanted him for a whole lot longer than one night, and if he didn't, sharing her office with him would be horrendous.

Rebecca pushed on. 'What if he doesn't feel the same? What if you're just a quick shag for him?'

Laurel looked at her hands, because that would be shit. Sure, they'd probably have a night of wanton, rampant, all-night sex, but how would she feel when he left afterwards? You knew what you were getting with Tinder dates. Thank you for your service, off you pop. Perhaps a second time around the mulberry bush, but perhaps not. No ties, no expectations.

What had Nate said? That he didn't allow himself to expect things, so why would she be any different?

Rebecca was still talking.

'I'm just warning you to be careful. I just don't want you to be hurt.' Laurel could hear the unspoken words that Rebecca would have to pick up the pieces. That was unfair of her. She would never ask Rebecca to take on her emotional baggage, but that wouldn't stop her best friend from trying, from being there while she cried into a vat of rice pudding.

Laurel perked up. 'Did you see him with his t-shirt off?'

Rebecca tipped her head back and laughed at the sky. 'Yes, I most certainly did!'

'Don't worry, I won't tell Jack you said that.' Laurel shouldered her friend lightly.

Rebecca's eyes darkened a little. 'Seriously, I love you and I don't want you to get hurt, okay?'

'Yeah, I know.' She was so lucky to have Rebecca. 'But you have to talk to Jack.'

Rebecca nodded despondently.

Laurel pressed Rebecca's hands to make her look at her.

'Then you call me, yeah?'

'Yeah, I will,' Rebecca said. 'Love you.'

'Love you too.'

NATE

Nate didn't spend any time in the office on Monday morning. With Alex visiting, he needed the site to be immaculate. Although Alex was his oldest and best friend, it didn't mean that he'd get any special treatment, in fact, the complete opposite. He squinted at his costs spreadsheet under the picnic umbrella put up on site and desperately hoped Alex wouldn't pick up on anything wrong with it. If he did, it would be another week's delay in processing the funding application for the site tent and other bits he needed, because Alex would make him resubmit the whole thing. It wasn't that Alex was a jobsworth or a stickler for getting stuff right, it was that he liked to break Nate's balls. Alex thought taking him down a peg or two was funny.

Paul had sent the information about the Cathar site he was working on, and it looked amazing. A mature dig of a small, long forgotten stronghold, a huddle of burned bones and, wonderfully, some English coins from Simon de Montfort's 'crusade' to wipe out the Cathar religion. Nothing that was earth shattering, history changing, but a nice addition to the well-known canon of Cathar history. And, of course, the beautiful rolling hills and lazy sun of the south of France. It was tempting, especially as autumn and winter were coming up. An archaeological site in England in the winter? Not fun. Nate wondered idly if the university would let him have a secondment for a few months.

Thing was though, he wasn't sure he wanted to leave Little Willow Farm. The site really was very promising. Regardless of what he had told Laurel, he was sure that there was more under the earth. There was an unaccounted for human femur, so there must be something. There had to be.

Anwar, now hangover free, could deal with the site with minimal supervision, so he didn't have to be there. But he had gold and dirt in his eyes, just like the students.

'Dr Daley, have you thought anymore about moving me to trench one?' Nate's thoughts were interrupted by the same girl who had asked him this exact question on Friday. She was furiously batting her spidery eyelashes, her top low enough to show the lace of her bra.

'Yes,' he lied. 'No moving at the moment. I'll revisit it in two weeks.'

She pouted and gave him what he could only imagine were doe eyes. Whilst he wasn't quite old enough to be her father, he wasn't far off from a legal, but teenaged, father, and seriously? Just no.

'Okay, Dr Daley, remember me when you do.' She sauntered off, shaking her ass.

'Nope,' he muttered, staring at his laptop screen.

Nate breathed a sigh of relief as the sun went in and the screen came fully into focus. Ten more minutes of work on this budget sheet and he should be done and able to spend the rest of the day in the earth.

'Nate.'

Well, it would be ten minutes if he wasn't interrupted all the time.

'Oh, hey Jack, you alright?' Nate hit ctrl+s.

Jack leaned against the makeshift table. He was always leaning against something. 'You want to go for a drink tonight?'

'I can't, I've got my friend Alex coming to visit the site

tomorrow and everything has to be ready.' Nate launched into a whole explanation as to why he was hosting the British Archaeological Society liaison. 'Why don't you meet us tomorrow in the pub before closing?'

The other man shook his head.

'Nah, I can't be that late. I've got milking in the morning,' his shoulders slumped. Jack was completely defeated.

'Are you alright, mate?' Nate asked gently. 'Has something happened with Rebecca?'

Jack turned his shrewd eyes onto Nate. 'Rebecca? Why do you say that?'

Nate's stomach dropped.

'Oh, no reason, just that I saw her and Laurel when I was out running on Saturday and it looked like Rebecca had been crying?'

Had he just thrust himself into some kind of family drama that he had no business, and no desire, to be in the middle of?

'She was with Laurel?' Jack asked, eyes flinty hard and jaw clenched.

'Yeah,' Nate said slowly. 'I feel like I've done something wrong here, Jack. Is everything okay?'

Jack sighed and pinned his gaze on Nate. 'Yeah, just a little disagreement with my wife that I didn't really want my little sister weighing in on.'

Nate took pity on him. 'Listen, I can be done with this paperwork and all prepared for Alex by six, seven at the latest. I can have one beer.'

Jack's face lit up like a child who got extra dessert.

'Do you mind? Won't be long, just want to get out of the house,' he said.

''Course not.' Nate nodded. Jack was a good guy and was turning into a good friend. He sauntered away after extracting a promise from Nate to text him when he was ready.

Watching Jack go, he had a sinking feeling that he had just put his size ten feet into a massive pile of family shit. He texted Laurel.

> Uh, I may have just done something wrong. I've just seen Jack.

Laurel

Oh, are you here today?

> Yeah, I'm on site.

Nate watched the three dots fade in and out across the WhatsApp message showing she was typing.

Laurel

Oh, okay.

That was a short message after such a long interval.

Laurel

What have you done?

> I told Jack that I saw you with Rebecca on Saturday, and that she was upset. That's it. But I feel weird about it.

He could almost see Laurel rolling her eyes in frustration. There was a pause before she texted back.

Laurel

Okay. I'll sort it.

Sort what? What had he walked blindly into? He didn't want to know, but it was a bruise he couldn't stop pushing.

Have I done something wrong?

I don't know, have you?

Well. That meant that he had definitely done something wrong. He scrolled to her number and pressed the green button. She made him wait for four rings before she answered, when she blatantly had the phone in her hand. They were adult enough to have a conversation, surely.

'Nate,' she said, her voice clipped.

'Laurel,' he replied. She was silent. 'I think I've walked into a family minefield and I want to make sure I don't do it again.'

Laurel sighed down the phone. He waited. Not everyone appreciated his forthright approach. Lucia certainly hadn't, but it was so much easier, rather than second guessing everything all the time. Just ask.

'Look, I've got a lot on my plate at the moment. I didn't know you were on site, Alex Woollard is coming tomorrow, and...' she hesitated. 'Jack and Rebecca are working through some stuff. Sometimes Jack doesn't like the fact that his little sister is his wife's best friend.'

Exactly what Jack had said. They'd obviously been there before.

'Don't worry, I'll handle it,' she said.

'Okay, um, sorry,' he said eventually, although what he was sorry for, he had absolutely no idea.

'Okay,' she said. 'Oh, and Nate?'

'Yeah?'

'Thanks for calling,' she said.

'Okay, see you later.' He grinned and ended the call.

He could one hundred percent stay out of family politics.

CHAPTER NINE

LAUREL

Laurel stared at the phone in her hand. That was weird. Not that he'd called. That was a socially acceptable thing, telephoning someone. Wasn't it?

She sighed. Why did he have to say to Jack that he'd seen them on Saturday and that Rebecca was upset? She couldn't blame him though, not really. It's not like he knew the intricacies of the family relationships. At least he'd had the forethought to tell her about it.

> Rebecca, Nate has told Jack that he saw us on Saturday and that you were upset. Did you talk to Jack?

There was no blue tick, so Rebecca was probably being very important in a meeting somewhere.

'Laurel.' Sylvie knocked on her office door. 'You've got that call with the bank in half an hour, I've just emailed you those spreadsheets.'

'Okay, thanks,' Laurel said, clicking on her email. Sylvie hovered, tapping the folder in her hands nervously. 'Are you alright, Sylvie?'

'Yeah, can I?' she motioned at the empty chair in front of Laurel's desk.

'Sure, of course.'

Sylvie scurried into her office and sat down in front of Laurel's desk.

'Um, it's, well,' she stuttered.

'It's okay, Sylvie,' Laurel said, coming around and leaning on the front of the desk.

Sylvie looked at her anxiously.

'I want to go do a Business Management degree, I've got all the information here, it's expensive though, and I was hoping…' she trailed off, watching Laurel pleadingly.

Well, that was unexpected.

'Oh! Right, okay, yes, give me the information, let's have a look,' Laurel held her hand out for the folder and slid the tidy colour coded pages out, flicking through them quickly. Her eyes landed on the fee at the bottom of the last page. Wow. That was a lot.

'I think I'd be good at it.' Sylvie swallowed and wiped her hands on her thighs. 'And it would be super beneficial for the farm, I could take a lot of work off of your hands, and I would only be out one day a week.'

Laurel's mind whirred quickly. It was nearly unbelievable that she'd found the amazingly talented Sylvie in this little place anyway, but a Sylvie with business degree superpowers? Yes please. If Sylvie did this with the help of the farm, she'd be guaranteed to stay at least until the end of the degree which, part time, could be years.

'I think it's a fantastic idea, really good,' she said.

Sylvie's shoulders sagged in relief. Was she really that scary that Sylvie was nervous asking her? But it was a lot of money. She'd have to see if there were instalment options and whether they could cover Sylvie when she was out that one day a week.

'I'll have to look through it and see if it's feasible money-wise, but I think it's a really, really good idea.'

Sylvie grinned. 'Thanks Laurel. I want to move my career on, but I love it here, so I thought this would be the best of both worlds?'

'Yeah, I agree.' Laurel smiled back at her.

'The application deadline is next month, I've highlighted the date for you on the front sheet,' Sylvie said. She would fly through this business course.

'You're an asset, Sylvie, you really are.'

Sylvie beamed and stood up.

'Laurel, thank you so much, I knew you'd be supportive.' She headed to the door. 'I won't let you, or Little Willow, down.'

'I know you won't, Sylvie,' Laurel said.

Sylvie let out a squeal and skipped away. Well, that was a management win in Laurel's book. It was a no-brainer really. If she could make it work financially, then Sylvie would be on that course. Laurel smiled to herself as she sat down behind her desk and added 'Sylvie – Course' to the bottom of her to do list. Everything else was on her computer, but she liked the satisfaction of drawing a nice biro line through items as she completed them.

Her phone buzzed.

Rebecca

Ah fuck. Sorry, you'll have to deal with Jack being a dick now.

Don't worry, I can cope with Jack being arsey for a few days. Did you talk to him?

Rebecca

Kind of. We'll talk again.

Talk later?

Rebecca

Yes please.

Oh, have you seen the Sexy Doctor today?

Laurel's grin quickly turned into a scowl.

> **Not today, but he called.**

Rebecca
> **As in, on the phone? Like a telephone call?**

> **Yes, as in a telephone call.**

Rebecca
> **Huh. Weird.**

It was kind of nice that he had wanted to talk to her, although she'd been unable to keep her annoyance tamped down. Really, he had no obligation to tell her where he was going to be, but a bit of courtesy wouldn't go amiss. Laurel realised that and, like a proper grown up, had moved past it. She hadn't lied, she did have a lot to do at the moment.

The meeting with the bank today would be her yes or no as to whether she'd receive the extra funding to buy Hibberts fields and consequently, whether she could save that little part of Lower Houghton from being overdeveloped by big building companies.

To: Nate
> **Hey, I know you're probably busy, but when you get a moment, can you let me know the plans for Alex Woollard tomorrow please?**

Because that was another thing playing on her mind. Alex. Surely he couldn't still be as big of a douche as he was ten years ago?

Nate
> **I'll drop by now?**

I have a meeting. An hour?

Cafe?

Sure.

He's not still a dick is he?

Oh god, she'd pressed send before her mind had caught up. How unprofessional was that? Considering Alex was still Nate's best friend as well. Christ. She watched those dots move back and forth across the screen.

Nate

You'll have to tell me what your issue is with Alex sometime.

Ha. Like he didn't know. She scowled at the phone. Why had she even said that? It was a written invitation to bring to the surface everything that she had worked so hard to push all the way down.

Whatever. She didn't have the head space to think about Nate Daley right now.

Laurel checked her makeup and opened the secure meeting website with the bank. She pasted on a smile as her business manager joined the meeting.

NATE

Laurel looked both flustered and resigned when she sat down at his table, plopping a teapot and mismatched cup and saucer down in front of her.

'So, you do drink tea,' he said.

Laurel nodded slowly.

'I do drink tea, and I drink peppermint tea. Just not when it's boiling hot in my office,' she said, sitting back in her chair and sighing.

'How was your meeting?'

She was wan and deflated.

'Are you okay?'

'Oh, yeah, it was fine,' Laurel said, pulling her lips into a tight smile. 'Fine,' she repeated, pouring a tiny drop of tea into her cup to see if it had steeped long enough. Apparently not.

'Hey, if something is going on, you can talk to me about it if you want,' he said, leaning towards her across the table. 'I'm sorry about talking to Jack as well, didn't mean to put my foot in it.'

It was an unthinking movement. He reached across the table to graze her arm with his fingertips. Laurel's eyes rested where his skin touched hers, before flicking her eyes up to his. There was a swirling warmth in the pit of his stomach and a definite tightening of his trousers because the way her teeth sank into her bottom lip made all sort of dirty, *filthy*, things flash through his mind.

But this was Laurel, they were getting on, and he didn't want to ruin that for a quick roll in the hay. He leaned back in his chair, picking up his coffee cup with both hands. No touching.

'Yeah, don't worry about it, you weren't to know.' She flashed him a tight smile. 'It's just money stuff. There's never enough is there?'

'No, there isn't,' he said.

'Tell me about the site. Any finds? Do you think Alex will be happy? Is there anything I can do?' Her brow creased anxiously and he frowned. He didn't want her to worry about stuff like that.

'Site is going well, we've got a few more finds, there's definitely more under there. I'm having Harold back to expand the trenches soon,' he said, sipping his coffee.

Laurel nodded and poured her tea. She looked up at him, as if wondering how much to tell him. With Rebecca and Jack's minefield relationship, he was pretty sure Laurel wouldn't want to burden them with whatever was going on, and she probably needed someone to vent to. He raised his eyebrows, waiting.

'I need this to work,' she started. 'I need Alex to be impressed, I need his recommendations for funding.'

'Is the farm in trouble?'

'No, no, nothing like that,' she said with a smile. 'It's just not as financially healthy as I would like it to be, and that funding would be very welcome.'

Nate nodded for her to continue.

'It's like all businesses, I suppose. You never get all the money you ask for, and there's always unexpected costs. We're not developing the site field, we're not getting as much income from the bunkhouses this year because we've given them to the dig at cost.' She shook her head slightly. 'It's just tighter than I would like.'

He didn't have any sage advice about running a business or a farm, so he wisely kept quiet.

'Anyway,' she said, swallowing. 'Tell me about Alex tomorrow, what can I do to help?'

'Alex is arriving about eleven. I'll show him the site, we'll have lunch here and then we'll head up to your office, if you don't mind, so we can go through some details?'

Laurel set her teacup daintily back in the saucer. 'Yeah, of course. I'll make myself scarce tomorrow afternoon.'

'No, it's okay, you should be there as well.'

Laurel's nose turned up. 'Okay, if you think so?'

'Yeah, why not?' Nate shrugged at her.

'You guys still close?' she asked, her face neutral.

Nate sipped his drink. 'Not as much as we used to be. But yeah, I suppose.'

'Oh.' Her eyes flicked around the cafe before she sighed. 'I mean, he was a bit of a dick when we were at university.'

'I get what you mean, but he's a good guy underneath. He really is,' Nate said, unsure why he was defending Alex. Habit probably. 'You should definitely meet him. You're the face of Little Willow Farm after all.'

She nearly choked on her tea.

'Oh god, am I? I'm pretty sure that's my dad. Or Jack. It's not me, is it?'

'Of course it's you.' That much was obvious. Well, it was to him anyway. 'You're the lifeblood of this place. Absolutely nothing would get done without you.'

A smile lit up her face. Not a little 'yeah whatever' smile, but a big, radiant, amazing smile and his breath caught in his throat. She was glowing, beaming, and it was him who had made her so happy.

'Oh, I wanted to run something past you,' Laurel said, interrupting his thoughts.

'Oh yeah?' He would give her literally anything she wanted to see that smile again.

'I've been thinking about asking Robin if the dig could use his house. He's got a three-bedroomed house just sitting there that he uses probably once a week, maybe less.' She was looking at him earnestly, and he had to concentrate hard on her words, not the movement of her mouth. 'He usually stays with my dad, and if you guys are going to be here longer, then it might be best if you have some more space?'

Good god yes. Yes please. A bedroom, even in a shared house, would be better than the hell he was currently living in.

'Only if you're sure? I wouldn't want to kick Robin out of his house?' Nate said.

'I mean, how long are you going to be here for?' She traced the rim of her teacup with her finger. 'Would it be worth it?'

Was she asking because of the house, or was she asking because of him?

'Certainly another couple of months or so, maybe longer.

It would be worth it,' he said, watching her pulse jump haphazardly in her neck.

'Oh right, okay.' Laurel glanced away, and then smiled back at him. 'Well, then it would probably be worth being somewhere more comfortable then.'

He wasn't entirely sure they were still talking about Robin's house, but he grinned.

'Then it's a deal. Let me know when you want us to move.'

LAUREL

Cesspit Alex was on her farm. She hadn't talked to him yet, but she'd seen Nate greet him at the car park and lead him up to the site.

So, Nate was going to be around for at least another couple of months, possibly longer. Longer would be good, because it would mean that they had found something substantial. Longer would also be good because she'd get to ogle his obnoxious legs for a little longer. And that was it. Thank the lord that Nate had been called to deal with Anwar that night at the pub, before she'd finished her sentence and invited him home with her. She wasn't sure which would have been more mortifying, being turned down or having a one night stand and having to see him every day because honestly, he hadn't given her any indication that he was the least bit interested in her. Yeah, she'd caught lust in his eyes (she thought), but everyone felt a little fruity after a couple of drinks, didn't they?

He was just being a good, supportive friend, showing an interest in the farm. Getting to know her. That was it, and that was all it would ever be. It would probably be best for Laurel to squash those pesky feelings once and for all. Done and dusted, so her heart didn't get trampled.

Jack had avoided her this morning, and Laurel was

absolutely fine with that. Rebecca said last night that he'd gone to the pub and then went straight to bed when he got home, out again at 4:30am for morning milking. It wasn't just Laurel he was avoiding, it seemed.

They were arguing, and Jack was being as pig-headed as ever. She hoped he'd see reason soon enough, or at least demonstrate some basic understanding of Rebecca's position.

Nate

We're heading up to the office now. You around? Alex wants to meet you. Again. You know what I mean.

Yeah, I'm here. See you in a minute.

She tucked her hair behind her ears. She needed Cesspit Alex. It wasn't just Nate and the dig who would benefit from Alex's funding recommendation, but Little Willow Farm as well.

The British Archaeological Society had big dick energy; if they said 'Little Willow Farm is a site worthy of investment', English Heritage, the university, third sector bodies and other private funders would be falling all over themselves to throw money at the dig and the farm. With the BAS standing firmly behind the dig, Little Willow would be eligible to receive compensation for the loss of their field from English Heritage. They'd be eligible for development grants, for eco-tourism grants, historical preservation grants.

But only if BAS say 'we endorse this site'.

That compensation alone would make all kinds of things run smoother, her dreams be less anxiety filled and monthly meetings with the bank not so fraught. Laurel hadn't been granted the funding for Hibbert's fields, so who knows where she was going to pull that money out from. It was a massive set back if she was going to stop the gentrification of Lower

Houghton because she, and let's face it, the rest of the town as well, didn't want holiday McMansions for rich Londoners on their doorstep.

Impressing Cesspit Alex today was a massive deal. He was the gatekeeper for everything.

She took a last glance around the office to check that everything was in its place. Nate's flipchart was propped expectantly by the wall, and his laptop was stacked neatly on top of piles of papers, tabbed with different neon colours.

'So, this is where the magic happens, is it?' She heard him before she saw him and steeled herself.

Alex Woollard strode into her office, Nate closing the door after them both.

He was still handsome and solid even though his blond hair was thinning slightly and streaked with grey. His broad shoulders and rugby player legs hinted at exercise, and his carefully cultivated stubble suggested someone vainly chasing youth.

Laurel moved around to the front of her desk. 'Alex, hi.' She held her hand out to him and he pumped it in an effusive handshake.

'Ah yes, Laurel Fletcher,' he said, eyes flitting over her. 'I remember you.'

Of course he did.

'I remember you too,' she said, a smile not quite reaching her eyes.

He scrunched up his nose.

'Smells of shit in here,' he said, looking around. 'Can you close the window?'

His question hung heavily in the air. Laurel glanced at Nate, who coughed and headed to the conference table. Alex swung around, hungrily absorbing everything in her office. He was too big for this room, took up too much space. His jacket was ever so slightly too tight across the shoulders.

'So, Alex,' she started, 'what do you think of the site?'

'Well, could be better, I suppose,' he said, tucking his

hands in his jeans pocket and rocking back on his heels. 'Of course, more finds would be beneficial, Nate, wouldn't it? And you know, it being somewhere not as backwater-y as this shithole?'

How. Fucking. Rude.

Laurel clenched her jaw and glanced at Nate, who was watching their exchange with wide eyes.

'It's promising, though?' she pushed.

Alex blew out an exasperated breath and shrugged.

'Sure, why not.' He smiled like a viper.

'I'd be happy to give you a tour of the rest of the farm if you'd like, show you how we could accommodate more visitors, why we'd be perfect for investment.' Because without his recommendation for funding, she wouldn't be able to buy Hibbert's fields and her vision for Lower Houghton would be shattered and broken.

'Nah, I've seen all I need to,' he said, his eyes raking down her.

Laurel willed herself not to cringe. She was not having a good reaction to Alex Woollard.

Alex turned his back and stretched out in one of the conference chairs, making himself at home. In her office. On her farm. In her life.

She clenched her jaw.

Alex linked his fingers behind his thinning hair.

'Mine is black coffee, four sugars,' he called vaguely in her direction.

Laurel's eyes widened in anger and heat rose in her face, blood throbbing in her temples, threatening to spill out in a tirade of 'get it your fucking self'.

Nate caught her eye and she couldn't tell whether he was pleading with her or warning her. Either way it was inappropriate, and confirmed that Alex Woollard was the same self-centred, arrogant fuck he had been ten years ago.

'I'll go, I need a coffee. Peppermint tea?' he asked her as he passed.

She nodded abruptly. It was a peace offering, it was an apology, a reminder that not everyone was as much of a dick as Cesspit Alex.

Laurel tried a different tack.

'Nate tells me this is your first senior liaison position. Congratulations,' she said, perching on the edge of her desk.

'Oh yeah,' he glanced over at her. 'My first official position, but I've run lead on loads of sites, so none of this is new to me,' he said, dismissively, tapping away on his phone.

Mmm hmm, neither was being a douche, obviously.

Alex threw the device on the table and swivelled in his chair to look at her with narrowed eyes.

'So, you and the good doctor, then? Just like old times?' He smirked.

Laurel's heart plummeted.

'What?'

Alex scoffed.

'Come on, don't tell me that you don't still want to jump his bones?'

'What business is my personal life of yours?' Laurel was frosty. How goddamned unprofessional. Exactly what had Nate told him?

'Oh none, none at all,' he said. 'But if you want my advice…' She did not want his advice. 'I wouldn't bother.' Alex picked at his short nails. 'I mean, you're not exactly his type, are you?'

She knew he was winding her up, but she couldn't help herself.

'Oh?'

'Don't take this the wrong way,' he said, conspiratorially, leaning towards her, 'but you're just a small town girl. You work on a farm.'

Laurel crossed her arms across her chest, fighting to keep her eyebrows down. 'What's wrong with that?'

'Well, Nate's a big picture kind of guy. He's after exciting, exotic, unusual.' Alex was describing Lucia. 'You know, and that's just not you, is it?' She did know, and it wasn't her.

'I mean, you'd be a great little diversion.'

Her jaw dropped.

Alex whipped a hand to his mouth mockingly. 'Oops, sorry, can't say stuff like that, can I?'

Laurel cleared her throat. What was even happening here? It was all so surreal.

'I'm just saying, you're not really…' he looked around for inspiration, 'his type.'

Alex gave her a condescending, closed-lipped smile.

'He goes for stunningly attractive, intelligent women.'

What. The. Fuck.

This was a horrifying repeat of the last conversation she and Alex had had ten years ago. Except last time, Alex was sitting opposite her in the student union bar. He had been disgustingly, shatteringly harsh. So had Nate for sending Alex to talk to her, rather than having the guts to talk to her himself. But she and Nate had put things behind them and started getting to know each other. Alex didn't seem inclined to do the same.

But Laurel wasn't twenty anymore, and she didn't have to put up with Alex's shit. She did, however, have to get him onside for his financial recommendation. She ground her teeth.

'I think it's so admirable how far you go for your friend, admirable that you look out for him so much, after all this time,' she said, laying it on thick. 'I mean, what an amazing person you must be to be constantly thinking of Nate and his life.' She shook her head slightly. 'I don't know how you do it, you must love him very much.'

Laurel pushed up from the desk and turned to grab some papers and her phone, her heart a military march in her ears. Didn't matter what papers, just some papers, anything.

Alex made some kind of throaty, choking, coughing sound. 'I'm not gay, you know,' he said, wide eyed and shocked.

'Oh.' Laurel looked at him with feigned surprise. 'I would never presume to know you that well,' she said with a smile.

'I like women,' he said scathingly. 'I'm just looking out for my friend.'

What a fragile little man Alex Woollard was.

'Just doing what any good friend would do,' Laurel commented and headed for the door, turning back to Alex before opening it. 'I'll be around if you want that tour, or if you need anything else. I really want to make this work.'

Laurel gave him a genuine smile. She desperately needed his recommendation, but he also needed to know that he couldn't get away with saying things like that. It wasn't the fifties, they weren't twenty, and there was no tolerance for that in the workplace. Although, she was just as bad as him, goading and baiting him, being petty and immature.

Little Willow Farm needed this funding, and Laurel hoped to God that she hadn't fucked it up.

CHAPTER TEN

NATE

Nate balanced the two coffee cups in one hand, the peppermint tea in the other and started what felt like an excruciatingly long walk back to Laurel's office. He'd left them alone long enough and Alex could be… irritating? Annoying? Vindictive? All of the above?

That wasn't fair. Alex had always been a good friend, even if his tendency to be a bit of a pompous dick hadn't diminished over the years.

He was five paces away when the door swung open and Laurel bustled out, arms brimming with papers.

'Woah,' he said, as she nearly careened into him. 'You alright? Where are you going?'

She was flustered, pale-faced and a little shaken. She was not calm, collected Manager Laurel. What the fuck had happened?

'Uh, I've got to, um,' she started, eyes flicking down the corridor.

'What's going on? Are you okay?' He took a step towards her.

She tucked her hair behind her ears. 'Nothing. I'm fine.'

The smile she had plastered on her face was not convincing.

'Laurel, what—' he started, but she held her hand up to interrupt him.

'Look, I've told Alex I'll show him around. Give him whatever he needs.' She sighed and her shoulders dropped in defeat. 'I need this funding, Nate.'

'Yeah, okay,' he said, still confused. 'I'll do what I can.'

Laurel nodded and hugged her papers to her chest before hurrying along the corridor.

'Do you want your tea?' he called, but her heels clattered as she headed down the stairs. What the hell was that?

Alex was playing some childishly loud, colourful game on his phone when Nate lowered the cups to the conference table.

'So, old man, let's see what you've got,' Alex said, putting his phone on the table. Nate looked at him carefully, considering his friend.

'What did you say to Laurel?' he asked neutrally.

'Nothing, you know how women can get.' Alex waved his hand dismissively. 'They're sensitive, take things all the wrong way.'

Nate scratched his forehead in disbelief. How could Alex possibly have offended her in the five minutes Nate had been out of the office? How was Alex not able to be left alone with a woman without pissing her off?

'She's alright looking. I'd bang her, but—'

'Alex! Come on man, don't talk like that,' Nate interrupted. Alex scoffed. 'Like what?'

'Like women are a piece of meat there for your pleasure. It's not the *lads lads lads* culture of the nineties anymore, mate. I've got to work here, be around Laurel all the time. Don't piss her off. And for god's sake, grow up a little bit. Be a professional.'

Alex rolled his eyes and swung his head like a toddler who hadn't got their own way.

'Alright, whatever, Nate,' he said. 'But, and don't take offense here, she's not very…' he cast around for the right word, 'exciting, is she? I mean, she's a bit drab.'

Nate flinched. Laurel wasn't drab. She was beautiful. Sure, she was highly strung and had an awful lot on her plate. In fact, he admired her for what she'd built at the farm and for the saving of Lower Houghton, especially because she was up against literally everybody.

'You've got her wrong, Alex.' Nate shuffled his papers.

'What? You want to shag her?'

Nate placed his hands flat on the table. His jaw clenched and he narrowed his eyes at Alex. Had he not heard a word he said? They were too old for this shit. There was silence in the office as they looked at each other, some kind of power shift happening. Alex must have got the hint, because he pulled his chair closer to the desk and reached for some papers.

'Do you want to show me what you've got then, old man?'

Nate spread the papers out and launched into his pre-prepared spiel about what they'd already found, his well-calculated assumptions for what else was there and how the British Archaeological Society could help. Alex nodded and made the right noises in all the right places. This was important to the site. If Alex threw the considerable weight of the British Archaeological Society behind the dig, the funders at the presentation he'd have to give would be practically throwing money at them.

If they had the funding, then they could stay on site indefinitely and explore the extremely promising Little Willow Farm site. The Fletchers, well, Laurel, would be able to relax a bit as well, which she could most definitely do with. They were friends now, weren't they? They'd had a fun time together at the pub, and she was good to talk to. She was obviously fully invested in the site as well.

Alex was looking at him expectantly.

'What?' he asked.

'Aren't you listening?' he snapped. No, he quite obviously hadn't been.

'Sorry man, my mind was elsewhere,' he said, leaning forward to study the finds list.

Alex rearranged some papers in front of him.

'In between Laurel Fletcher's legs I bet,' he said under his breath.

'For fuck's sake, Alex,' Nate said, louder than he would

have liked. 'What the fuck is wrong with you? She's my friend, stop talking about her like that.'

'She's your "friend" is she?' Alex actually used air quotes. 'Man, the woman has got "fuck me" written all over her face.'

It was a gut reaction. Nate's fist flung out and connected with Alex's cheekbone before his mind could catch up and say, no Nate, this is not a good idea.

'What the fuck, Nate?' Alex was incredulous. 'What the fuck is wrong with you?' He dabbed at his cheek with his fingertips, checking to see if the skin was broken. Which it wasn't, obviously, because it was more of a bop than a full-blown punch, but still. He'd have a bruise.

'I'm sorry, Alex, but I told you not to talk like that,' Nate started, eyebrows high. He was sorry that he'd punched his friend, but not really sorry. Not at all. 'It was an unthinking reaction.'

'Whatever,' Alex sneered. 'Plain to see where your loyalties lie, with some woman you've known a matter of months, instead of your best friend who you have known for what? Ten years? Twelve? Fuck you, man.'

'Alex.' Nate ran his hand through his hair. 'Do you want some ice for that?'

'No, I don't want fucking ice.' He pushed the chair back violently. 'I'm getting off this shit-filled farm.'

Nate held out the packet of papers he'd prepared for Alex. He shoved his phone back in his pocket and stuffed the packet into his battered satchel.

Fuck. He'd fucked this up. Big time.

'Let's talk at dinner, yeah?' Nate winced, olive branch well and truly held out.

'Whatever,' Alex said, petulant to the last.

Nate couldn't blame him. He had punched him in the face. So, there was that.

Alex stormed out of the office, the door shaking on its hinges as it whacked the wall where Alex had thrown it open.

Fuck. Fuck. Fuck.

What a massive fucking mess. If Alex hadn't have behaved like a Neanderthal, kept pushing and pushing after Nate had told him again and again to give it a rest, he wouldn't have exploded like that.

But there was no excuse. He only hoped he could salvage the friendship.

Alex was vindictive and stubborn, and he could choose to punish Nate, and by proxy, Laurel and Little Willow Farm. He could be unnecessarily harsh and fail to recommend the dig for funding. Nate knew his proposal was good, the finds were good, it was a significant site, and a boon for Alex to be involved with. He'd done enough of these to know what should be recommended for funding.

Nate didn't want to think about what he'd have to do if Alex declined to throw the British Archaeological Society weight behind the dig. He'd have to report him for unprofessional behaviour, sexist comments, failing to carry out his professional duty, and would have to request another liaison. That would signal the end of Alex's career in the Society, and Nate really did not want to be responsible for that.

He also did not relish telling Laurel what had happened. God, what a mess.

Alex may call himself his 'best friend', but Nate finally recognised that, over the course of ten years, Alex had become someone Nate no longer wanted, or needed, in a friend.

LAUREL

The weather was turning, she could smell it as she trudged across the farmyard.

Laurel had been walking the grounds, ostensibly checking that everything was running smoothly, but really to clear her mind. The soft swaying of the wheat fields reminded her of simpler times before her mother had died, when it was carefree and fun and she didn't have to deal with all of this, well, shit. There had been no accounts, no Countryside Stewardship Schemes forms, no professional development to worry about, no panicking about whether they'd make the wages run or not.

There was a school in the conference centre, the cafe was busy, the petting zoo was holding its own and the plants in the farm shop needed replenishing. Today was a good day for Little Willow Farm, except for the fact that her stomach curdled like sour milk at the thought of Alex in her office.

Oh. But he wasn't in her office. There he was, striding angrily across the car park to his little banger of a Golf. He wrenched open the door and threw his old satchel onto the passenger seat before forcing his big frame into the little car.

Alex was leaving way too early.

Nate appeared at the door to the admin building and watched Alex's car pull out of the car park. His hair was dishevelled as if he'd brushed it with his fingers. He sighed deeply and looked at his shoes. Laurel frowned. Something had happened.

Nate glanced around the farmyard, his eyes settling on Laurel, and he started over to her.

'Hey,' she said when he was in earshot. 'What's going on? Where's Alex gone?'

'Laurel, I've fucked up, but I'll fix it,' he said earnestly, mouth tight.

She narrowed her eyes at him. 'What do you mean, you've fucked up?'

'Alex and I have had a bit of a...' he hesitated, 'disagreement.'

Her mouth pinched.

'A disagreement? About what?' Because if it was about the funding recommendation, then she would not be impressed.

Not. At. All.

He rubbed the back of his neck sheepishly.

'Uh.' A disbelieving little smile flickered across his face. 'Well, it was about you, actually.'

Laurel paled. Because surely to God, they weren't having a conversation about what happened ten years ago.

'Well, not *you* you. It was women in general, and you happened to be the closest one.' He sighed. 'Alex is, well, he behaves like a fifteen-year-old boy sometimes, and I just, I couldn't cope with it anymore.'

'Right...' she drew out the word, waiting.

'He made a couple of rude, sexist comments and we're friends, right?' he gestured between the two of them.

Friends, yes. Laurel swallowed and nodded.

'So, I kind of bopped him on the nose.' He squeezed his eyes shut and screwed up his face.

Bopped him on the nose? *Bopped* him? What was that? Laurel's eyes widened as recognition dawned. He hadn't 'bopped' Alex at all. He had punched him. Punched the BAS liaison. Punched the person who very possibly held the future of Little Willow Farm in his hands.

'Nate! You *punched* him? You punched Alex?'

Her stomach dropped, and she scrubbed at her face with both hands. This was the worst possible outcome. It would have been preferable for them to have had a good laugh about what had happened ten years ago, for her to be a laughing stock. But this? Ruining the chances of the site getting BAS recommendation for funding? This didn't just affect her, this was the family, the farm, the village. Nate had ruined everything.

Nate gripped the top of her arms and stepped closer. 'I'll fix it, Laurel, I promise.'

'You'll fix it? God Nate, don't fucking bother!' Laurel wrenched herself away and took a few steps back from him. 'You *know*, Nate, you know how important this is to me, and you've fucked it right up! He's never going to recommend the site for funding now, is he? Never.'

'Laurel, please. I know Alex. Let me talk to him, deal with him.'

'What, like you dealt with him today?' Laurel scoffed. 'You just said we were friends, Nate, and I cannot trust you not to ruin this, not anymore.'

Laurel wilted like a dying sunflower. She had been completely mistaken in Nate. Completely. She thought he understood what she was trying to do at Lower Houghton. But to mess this up for her just showed that he didn't give a fuck.

'Laurel, please,' he said again. 'I'm sorry, I'm so sorry. I'll talk to him. The site deserves recommendation, and if he doesn't give it then I will be having a very strong conversation with the BAS.'

What was she supposed to do? She could let him try and fix it, or she could try and fix it herself. But could she even do that? Alex probably wouldn't even listen to her and she didn't have any sway with the BAS. But she'd have to try.

'I don't know, Nate—' she started, wrapping her arms around herself.

'No,' he interrupted. 'This is my mess. Please, please let deal with it.'

'What are you doing, Laurel? You're in the way,' Jack called, ushering a pig past her with a large stick.

For fuck's sake. First Nate absolutely ruining the farm's chances of funding recommendation, and now her stroppy big brother on at her as well. Great.

'Oh, sorry, Jack.'

He was still in a mood with her, even though his and Rebecca's marriage was literally nothing to do with her.

'Are you alright?' She couldn't help herself asking.

'Yeah, I'm fine, Laurel, just fine.' Okay, so that meant he wasn't fine. 'Nate, hey man.'

'Hey, Jack,' he said.

'I was just asking, Jack. No need to bite my head off.' She crossed her arms across her chest.

'I'm sorry. I'm just tired.' He took a breath and stopped,

letting the pig wander slightly. 'Thanks, Nate, for the other night at the pub. Good chat.'

Oh, so it was Nate who had been to the pub with Jack. Were they now the bestest of friends? And had Jack opened up about him and Rebecca's child discussions? That would actually be quite good for Jack, having someone to talk to, rather than just their dad. Or even worse, Robin.

'I enjoyed it. Thanks for inviting me,' Nate said.

Laurel sighed at the dark bags under her brother's eyes.

'You need a break, Jack. Why don't I see if I can find cover for the weekend? I'll have the kids, and you and Rebecca can go away somewhere nice?' she suggested, knowing full well that it would never happen.

'Who would you get to cover?' He kicked at a couple of dandelions. She must remember to have the gardeners go around and tidy up.

She shrugged. 'Robin, Dad, me? Everyone would muck in.'

That drew a smile from Jack. 'You? Really?'

'What?' Laurel feigned hurt. 'Just because I don't, doesn't mean I can't milk as well as the rest of you.' Although she wouldn't, unless it was the very bottom of the last resort pile.

'I'll think about it,' Jack said, giving her a half-hearted smile. He glanced around the farm. 'Look, I know I give you a hard time, but I'm grateful that Rebecca has you for a friend,' he mumbled, colour chasing up his neck.

Like their father, Jack was never good at expressing his feelings. Whatever Nate had said to Jack at the pub must have worked, must have made her brother revisit his long-held beliefs, have a little self-introspection.

Begrudgingly, Nate was good.

'I love you too, big brother,' she said.

'Yep,' he said. 'I've got to get this pig back, the vet's coming to check her udders.'

Laurel craned her neck to have a look. Yep, the telltale red swelling of mastitis.

'Okay, see you later.' And just like that, all was forgiven.

'See you later,' Jack said to both of them.

She turned back to Nate and took a long look at him. Laurel was so tired of having to do everything and maybe Nate would be better at dealing with it.

'Two days. Two days and then I'll have to dig the farm out of whatever hole you've managed to land us in.'

'I promise, Laurel. I promise you won't have to.'

NATE

Nate hated Laurel being upset with him. His chest ballooned hopefully every time he saw her, but she wouldn't, or couldn't, smile. He had to fix this, but sitting in the restaurant at the end of Lower Houghton High Street by himself with a bottle of chilled white wine was not a good look for Nate.

Alex was late.

Not particularly late, but late, nonetheless. He hadn't replied to Nate's text asking if he wanted to meet in the pub for one beforehand, so Nate had gone straight to the restaurant.

Eventually, Alex did turn up, fifteen minutes late. It was a deliberate power play, making him wait to show how displeased Alex was that he was no longer top billing for Nate, no longer able to get away with whatever he liked. There is no way in hell Alex should have been saying those things about anyone, especially not in a professional environment. If he told the British Archaeological Society, Alex would be fully reprimanded and an investigation would be started. Alex had to give his dig, and therefore Little Willow Farm, a fair crack at the whip. Also, if he fixed it, then Laurel wouldn't be mad at him anymore.

The question was, would his friendship with him ever be repaired? Did Nate really want it to be repaired? Yeah, sure, he obviously still wanted Alex in his life, but they'd grown apart over the last few years. The thing was, Nate wasn't twenty anymore and didn't want the lifestyle that Alex peddled. If that was good for Alex, then brilliant. But it wasn't good for him, and that was fine.

'Nate,' Alex said, dropping into the chair opposite. He'd already had at least two pints.

'Hey, wasn't sure you were coming,' Nate said, signalling the waiter to bring another glass.

'Of course I came,' Alex said, snatching the glass from the waiter and slopping wine nearly to the brim. 'Wouldn't miss dinner with my best friend, even if he did punch me in the face.'

Nate sighed. Alex was always so combative and antagonistic.

'Yeah, about that,' he said. 'I'm sorry I punched you.'

'I'm sorry you punched me as well.'

Okay, Alex was still being a douche.

'But you get why, yeah?' Nate pushed.

Alex took a long drink of wine.

'Whatever man, it's done now.'

So, he wasn't going to accept any responsibility for his words, then.

'Okay, done.' Nate smiled tightly. Knowing Alex, it would be far from done. Alex never let anything go. He may profess to have forgotten things, but it would surface again years and years down the line, like how he had written the celebrated opening of their joint Pictish Stylus paper. In fact, the whole thing had initially been Alex's idea, which was something Alex never let him forget.

'Shall we order?' Alex called the waiter over.

Then followed the most excruciating dinner he had ever had with Alex. He had tried. God, he had tried to fall back into that easy pattern of the two of them. But Alex's jokes, his stories, his anecdotes were immature and ridiculous, involving people he didn't know and didn't care to know. Nate's own stories were met with boredom and sometimes outright derision.

In the end, Nate sat back, enjoyed his seafood linguine and

let Alex talk about whatever he wanted, giving appropriate responses when required. He could not wait for it to end.

'So, Lucia's coming back for Jess and Owen's barbeque,' Alex said, draining his glass.

'Yeah, so Paul tells me,' Nate replied, sipping his wine.

Alex looked surprised.

'Oh, you speak to Paul?' Was there a hint of jealousy there?

'Now and again.' Nate shrugged.

'Lucia,' Alex started, a predatory grin crossing his face. 'Now there's a *real* woman. Exciting, sexy, adventurous.'

'Yeah, she's all those things,' Nate said neutrally. He wasn't going to be baited into comparing Laurel with Lucia.

'You know,' Alex said, drumming his fingers on the table. 'I've always had a bit of a soft spot for Lucia.'

'A bit? Alex,' Nate laughed, 'you drooled over her every time you saw her when we were together.' He didn't mention that Alex had tried it on with Lucia as soon as they'd broken up and she had turned him down hard and fast.

'No, I didn't. Whatever, Nate.' Alex looked out the window. 'God, this really is a one-horse town.'

'I don't know, I quite like it,' Nate said, following his gaze. It was the homeliness, the couple of cottages that still had their thatch, the slightly ramshackle shops, the little church in the middle of town, the farm, the site.

'Hmm,' Alex pondered.

'Do you speak to Paul at all?' Nate inquired.

Alex shook his head.

'Not really, he's in Spain or something isn't he? France?'

'France,' Nate confirmed.

'I speak to Lucia all the time, we're meeting up before Jess and Owen's barbeque, you know, see how things go with the two of us,' he said nonchalantly.

Ah, so that's why he brought her up, an attempt to rub Nate's face in the fact that he'll be spending time with Lucia. Well, crack on, pal.

'That's great, Alex. Really good,' Nate said genuinely. 'If that's what you want, I hope it works out for you.'

'Well, just keeping it casual, you know?' Alex said, 'No pressure, no labels, keeping it loose.' Which meant that Lucia probably had no idea about his plans for them.

'Sounds great, Alex,' Nate said. 'Look man, I've got an early morning start, I'm going to see if the taxi is free to take me back to the farm. Dinner has been great.'

Alex looked at him like he'd grown two extra heads. 'You're not coming to the pub? It's still an hour before closing?'

'Nah, don't fancy it.' Nate stood, sliding his chair under the table. He placed some notes on the table to cover his half. 'I don't expect I'll see you tomorrow. You're not scheduled to come to the farm are you?'

It wasn't really a question.

Alex eyed the notes warily. Nate had always paid for both of their meals when they'd been out the previous few times, and Alex was probably expecting a free ride again tonight. Nate had stopped at the little Sainsbury's cash point to ensure he had enough cash to make a quick getaway if he needed to.

'No, I'm not,' Alex said, eyebrows raised at Nate, obviously waiting for an invite.

'Alright, so I'll hear from you about the funding recommendations, probably in a week or so?' Nate asked, pointedly.

'Oh that.' Alex waved his hand dismissively. 'I don't know if I'll have had enough time by then to go through everything.'

Nate raised one eyebrow.

'I'm sure you will have. I mean, the society are going to want to know what happened today, aren't they?'

Nate let that statement hang in the air. Even in Alex's inebriated state, he should realise what Nate was getting at. If he was going to drag things out and make it difficult for Nate's dig, then his unprofessional behaviour would be brought up. Christ, was he really blackmailing one of his oldest friends? No, just reminding him to do his job.

Alex's face hardened. 'Yeah, they're going to want to know that one of their employees was physically assaulted.'

Nate considered his friend. God, he wasn't very smart sometimes, was he? Nate leaned on the back of the chair.

'They're probably going to want to know the context of that as well. They're going to want to know about the professionalism of their staff, their objectivity, their ability to do their job.'

'Are you seriously choosing that girl over me? Do you seriously think I'm unprofessional? That I lack objectivity and am unable to do my job? All because of a couple of little comments, just banter between friends?' Alex drained his glass.

'I told you I didn't want to hear it.'

'You're pathetic, you know that? You've gotten old, you're flagging, you're sinking into obscurity.' Alex's words slurred together.

'I'm not twenty anymore, Alex, and I'm happy with that.' He put his hands in his pockets. 'I'm happy with my life, my choices.'

'Whatever, man.' Alex smirked. 'You do you.'

'See you at Jess and Owen's barbeque, Alex,' Nate said, shrugging on his jacket. 'Look after yourself.'

Nate drew out his phone and scrolled to the taxi number but changed his mind. It was a nice night. The long walk would be good for him. He glanced up at the flat above the Post Office as he passed. A glimmer of light showed through the crack in the curtains and he wondered what Laurel was doing. Was it too late to knock on her door and tell her he'd sorted everything out with Alex? Yes, it was too late. It wasn't like he was hitting her up for a one night stand.

But also, had he sorted everything out with Alex? Alex was mercurial and could never be trusted not to cut off his nose to spite his face. But Nate wouldn't hesitate to cop to an assault charge for the chance to explain to the BAS why he did it in the first place.

CHAPTER ELEVEN

LAUREL

After the drama of Alex's visit, the rest of the week had been nice and quiet. Laurel told Sylvie that the farm would sponsor her to do the course she wanted and she would find the money somewhere, somehow. She reworked the budget with Barbara and if everything went well this year, meaning no wedding cancellations and a half decent Pick Your Own season, then the farm would be more or less on an even keel.

Nate had promised her he'd fixed it with Alex. That funding, when it came through, would ensure that the farm was as far away from the edge of the abyss as they could be. Which wasn't particularly far.

But, what if she didn't get the funding for Hibbert's fields? If developers bought the land, she could lobby against them, she would petition, she would bring injunctions. Whatever it took, because she was not going to let her mother's little slice of heaven become a tourist resort.

Nate had come and gone through her office, telling her he would let her know as soon as he had news about Alex and the BAS. Well, he had until Monday before she took things into her own hands. It had already gone on far too long.

Laurel spent Saturday morning with Rebecca and the twins, brunching raucously at a cafe two towns over, then braving the parental hell of soft play.

'So, have you managed to speak to Jack, properly?' she asked her sister-in-law.

Rebecca's eyes were on the ball pool.

'Yeah, he went for a drink with Nate, thought about things, and said that he should be a bit more accepting of how hard it was for me.'

'What?' Laurel spluttered on her disgusting soft play coffee. 'Nate convinced Jack to see another point of view?'

Rebecca grinned. 'Looks like Nate is the Fletcher Whisperer.'

Laurel smothered a smile.

'He still wants another one, but he's willing to have a proper conversation about it, and a proper look at the division of labour in our family.' Rebecca glanced at Laurel in disbelief. 'That's what he said, "division of labour in our family".'

'Fuck me, did he?' she said, louder than she should.

'Laurel,' Rebecca admonished.

'Sorry, sorry.' Laurel looked around and cringed at the other parents. 'Jack's got a new boyfriend. You should be careful about that,' she teased.

Rebecca smiled benevolently.

'It's good for him to have a non-farming friend, someone with a different, more enlightened opinion.'

Laurel took another sip of her coffee. She spent more time than she wanted to thinking about Nate and his different, more enlightened opinions. Well, less about that and more about his forearms pulling against his crumpled shirt, and his throat working in a swallow. Good job she didn't get the words out in the pub, because quite frankly she could never sleep with him and then have the torture of working with him every day.

Yes, best leave all that in the box.

Her phone buzzed and she pulled it out of her handbag.

Nate

Pub later? My round.

Huh, this was new. Perhaps he had heard something and this was his way of breaking the news to her gently, around a lot of people, and so she could drown her sorrows.

> **Do you have news from Alex?**

Nate

> You'll have to come to the pub to find out. ;)

> **You have news. Tell me.**

Nate

> Come to the pub! 7?

Surely, surely, it couldn't be bad news if he was making her wait like this?

> **Fine. But alcohol will only make me want to murder you more if it's not good news.**

Nate

> Duly noted.

'Who are you texting?' Rebecca asked, craning her neck to spy her phone.

'Nate. We're meeting for a drink later. He's got "news" about the BAS apparently.'

'Laurel,' Rebecca trailed off, tilting her head to the side.

'I know, I know! I'm not putting myself out there to be shot down.' Again.

Rebecca pursed her lips. 'I'm not saying you shouldn't put yourself out there, I'm just worried about you being hurt.' She took Laurel's hands over the table. 'I want you to be happy, that's all.'

'I know.' Laurel squeezed Rebecca's hands. 'If he's attracted to me, he can make the first move.'

Rebecca narrowed her eyes. 'Okay.'

'And if he's not, then he won't.' Laurel shrugged.

'You're giving a man an awful lot of credit. Men are stupid. They don't know what they want and half the time they don't know a good thing if it slapped them around the face.'

Laurel smiled. 'He's very highly educated. I'm sure he can make up his own mind.'

'The educated ones are the worst!' Rebecca grinned. 'They have absolutely no common sense.'

The spectre of Alex and the power he held over her niggled at her brain.

'What if it's bad news?'

'Tell me exactly? I'm not sure I follow,' Rebecca said, giving Laurel her full attention.

Laurel explained that the gold brooch that had been found was probably a part of something bigger, a burial perhaps. If the British Archaeological Society, aka Alex, said 'yes, Little Willow Farm dig site is of special historical importance', then English Heritage would want to be involved. English Heritage came with funding for the dig, and for the farm; compensation for losing their field to the dig site. There would be media interest, academic interest, there would be grants that the farm could apply for – all with that little piece of paper from Alex that said 'yes, this site is important'.

'If it is a burial site, can you imagine?' Laurel asked. 'We could have an immersive history area, a living museum, a gift shop, all of it funded, or part-funded, by grants or English Heritage. Think of the money it would bring into the farm. You could go on holiday, because we could afford a thousand farm hands to do Jack's job.'

Rebecca nodded slowly, her lawyer's brain working. 'If it's bad news, you'll deal with it, like you always do.'

Yeah, like she always did. Her stomach sank a little at that because just once it would be nice if everything went smoothly. It would be nice if she didn't have to deal with it like she always did. God, what she wouldn't give for a weekend off.

'But, more importantly than that...' Rebecca flicked her eyes over the ball pit. 'What are you going to wear tonight?'

Laurel scoffed. 'It's not a date, Rebecca.'

'No, but it's an opportunity to show Dr Daley what he's missing.'

Laurel chewed on her lip. She didn't want him to think she was trying too hard.

'I've got a beautiful silk top, classy, high neck, sleeveless. Perfect with jeans and sandals. You should—' Rebecca stopped mid flow. 'Lila! You throw balls at your brother once more and you will be going to bed without dessert tonight!'

'Rebecca, if it's see-through or super revealing, I'll kill you, okay?'

'You'll look chic, classy and absolutely perfect,' her sister-in-law winked at her. 'I promise.'

NATE

Laurel was not on time. Or perhaps he was just early? But no, she'd been late to the pub when they were celebrating the first significant find. She was always early in the office, so what was it about the pub? Also, she lived up the road.

Nate checked his watch, again, before sipping his half-drained pint. There was a pint of lager on the little round table for Laurel, but for all he knew she was in a random mood and wanted Malibu and orange, or an espresso martini or something. Not that they would serve espresso martinis in the Dog & Gun.

His leg bounced impatiently and he glanced out the window up the road to see if he could spot her. Ah, there she was, rushing across the forecourt, past the benches and a smattering of locals and students. She was slightly flustered as she bustled into the pub, quickly making her way over his table and giving him a grin.

'Hey, sorry I'm late. Got a bit caught up.' Laurel sat and gestured to the lager. 'Is that for me?'

'Go ahead,' he said, and she gulped back a large swig. 'How was your day?'

'Yeah, cut to the chase, Nate. You've got news and refused to tell me over the phone earlier. I've been worrying all day.' Laurel tugged at the collar of her silvery top. 'So put me out of my misery and just tell me that the BAS have declined to recommend the site for funding. Then I'll go home and drown my sorrows with a bottle of white wine and a frozen lasagne.'

Nate pressed his lips together and frowned, before sighing and taking a long gulp draw of his ale.

'You're actually killing me, Nate! Come on, let me have it.' Laurel pulled her hair over her shoulder and ran her fingers through it.

He debated whether to make her work for it, to keep her in suspense, but her big eyes were pleading and desperate.

'Alex has been an absolute nightmare to get hold of. I'm sorry it's taken this long. I called him again this morning, three times actually.'

'Yes?' She scowled at him. 'Nate, seriously, I'm going to lose my shit in a minute. Just tell me.'

'Okay, they've approved the site. They're recommending Little Willow for funding.' Nate grinned at her, but she just stared back. 'You alright? Did you hear me?'

Laurel snapped her mouth shut.

'Nate.' Her voice was quiet. 'You promise you're not messing with me? I don't think I could take it.'

His smile widened. 'I'm not messing with you, Laurel. Funding is pretty much all but guaranteed with the BAS endorsing the site.'

Her throat bobbed in a swallow, and she pressed her fingers to the corners of her eyes, blinking rapidly. Was she nearly crying? He'd wanted to see her face when he told her the good news, but this was not the reaction he'd expected.

'Laurel? Laurel, what's the matter?' He leaned over and touched her elbow lightly. 'Are you okay?'

'Oh god, I'm sorry.' She puffed out a breath and gave him a watery smile. 'I'm just so relieved.'

'Good, I thought you were upset for a minute then.' He leaned back in his chair, also relieved.

'It means I don't have to scrimp and save and worry. It means funding for the site is practically guaranteed, which means I could possibly, possibly scrape enough together to buy Hibberts' fields. It means I can relax for a few minutes.' Laurel's eyes sparkled.

'This calls for celebration! Angela,' he called across the pub to the barmaid. 'Champagne!'

Laurel laughed. 'You think they have champagne here?'

'Angela! Scratch the champagne! Prosecco instead!'

Angela scowled at him from the bar and he gave Laurel a wide grin.

She took a deep breath and placed her hands on flat on the table. It certainly seemed like a weight had been lifted from her shoulders. He should have realised she would have panicked, and he winced.

'Hey, I'm sorry for making you worry. I just wanted to tell you face-to-face.'

'Don't worry about it. Oh, thanks, Angela,' she said as Angela plopped a couple of red wine glasses and what passed for 'celebration sparkle' on the table. He grabbed the bottle to pour and she moved their existing drinks to the side.

'To Little Willow Farm,' he said, holding his glass up to her. 'And to you, for making it all happen.'

Her smile was infectious as she clinked her glass against his. He took a sip of his slightly warm prosecco and grimaced as it went down. It was *not* nice.

'It's a huge weight off my mind, Nate. Without this

funding,' she sighed. 'I just don't know how the farm would survive.'

He looked at her carefully. She was tired, and stressed, and no matter how much makeup she put on, she couldn't hide the exhaustion in her eyes. When did she ever do anything for herself?

'You need a break, Laurel. You were going on about Jack and Rebecca going away, but what about you?'

'God, I can't remember the last time I had a whole day off, let alone a break. It's so hard not to worry all the time.' She sipped her wine. 'The farm means so much to me, I can't let it fail.'

Nate leaned his chin on his hand. What must it be like to be so intrinsically linked to a place? Little Willow Farm was a part of Laurel Fletcher, just as she was part of it. But she still needed a break.

'Hey, my uni friends have an annual barbeque. It's next weekend. You should come.'

Well, that just popped out of his mouth.

Laurel looked taken aback. 'Come with you to your friends' barbeque?'

'Yeah, why not?' He was warming to the idea. 'Get out of Lower Houghton, away from the farm for a little bit? Socialise with people who don't talk about crop rotation and pig mastitis?'

She narrowed her eyes at him. 'I'll have you know, pig mastitis is quite common and can be very painful for the sow.'

'Okay, well, that's excellent dinner party conversation.' He raised an eyebrow at her. 'Come on, it will be fun.'

Laurel took a long look at him, and he could practically hear the cogs whirring in her mind.

'Will Alex be there?'

'Alex will be late, but he'll be there.' Nate shrugged. 'It'll be fine. Jess and Owen are so nice, and Paul will be there as well. Do you remember them from uni?'

'Vaguely. You guys didn't hang out with lowly undergrads.'

Was there a hint of bitterness in her tone? Or was it the bubbles from the nearly flat prosecco making her voice funny?

Now he'd said it out loud, he actually did want Laurel to come and meet his friends. Hanging out with Laurel was fun and would be even more fun if there wasn't the spectre of the farm, or her family, or the dig site hanging around.

Laurel flicked her hair over her shoulder and her throat bobbed as she took a sip of her prosecco. He swallowed, because he could not look away from her pulse beating hard in her neck, her pink lips glistening with sparkling drops of wine. If he reached out, he could drag his thumb over that bottom lip. Something hard and warm expanded in his chest, pushing the air out of his lungs.

Shakily, he blew out his breath. What was that? He couldn't reach over and touch her lip, that would be ridiculous. Wouldn't it?

'Okay, fine. I'll come.' Laurel narrowed her eyes at him. 'But you have to run interference between me and Alex.'

'Deal.' Nate lifted his glass in a toast.

Her phone buzzed on the table and she quickly swiped at it. It buzzed again immediately and again, she swiped at it.

'It's Robin, and I don't want to talk to him. He'll just be moaning about something or other, and I don't want to hear it.'

Laurel's phone was hot tonight, because it buzzed again.

'He really wants to talk to you,' Nate said.

'It's Jack. Jack never calls. Sorry,' she said, lifting the phone to her ear. 'Jack. What is it? I'm busy.'

Nate looked away to give her some privacy and took the opportunity to get himself together. Yes, Laurel was beautiful, and yeah, following her collarbone with his tongue, licking into the V at the base of her neck, nipping at the softness where her neck met her shoulder, would probably be amazing. But he couldn't, he wouldn't. Besides, who said she would even welcome that? A niggling thought in the back of his mind said that she would, that she nearly invited him back to hers that time. But copious amounts of alcohol had been involved, and people get flirty when they've had a bit to drink.

This attraction was passing, fleeting, and let's face it, who wouldn't be attracted to Laurel Fletcher? There wasn't a lot not to like.

Nate could hear Laurel hissing down the phone.

'What's happened? Can't it wait until tomorrow?' There was a pause and he could hear Jack's voice coming through the speaker. Jack was *not* happy. 'Okay, okay, Jack. I'm coming.'

Laurel put the phone back on the table and looked at him, wilting. 'I'm sorry, I've got to go.'

'Is everything alright?

'I don't know, but whatever it is, it's urgent. Do you want me to take you back?' She stood up from the table.

'Yeah, if you could.' She'd only had a quarter of a pint of lager and a few sips of prosecco.

Besides, he wanted to see what was so urgent that it destroyed Laurel's sparkle.

CHAPTER TWELVE

NATE

Laurel was quiet and jittery as they sped along the country lanes to the arm. He hoped it was something trivial and ridiculous that could wait for Laurel to deal with next week. Or even better, someone else could deal with it. She had too much on her shoulders already.

'It'll be okay,' he said, putting his hand on top of hers restlessly tapping the gear stick. 'Whatever it is, we'll deal with it.'

She cut her eyes quickly to him.

'It's probably boring work stuff. You don't have to hang around.'

'Look, if I can help, then I want to,' he said. 'You don't have to do everything by yourself.'

A sad smile flashed across her face. 'Okay.'

Laurel let out a low groan as they rounded the corner into Little Willow Farm.

There, scrawled across the kitschy, leaping sheep Little Willow Farm sign was 'Fletcher Bitch' in big, black, spray-painted letters.

'Laurel, I...' Nate started, but he didn't have the words.

Well, that was obviously about Laurel. If he had to guess, George Hibbert would be his first, and only, one. Nate's jaw tightened.

The headlights flashed over Robin, pointing towards the

admin building, mouth turned down. As the lights illuminated the wall, he could see the big black letters 'Fucking Fletcher Bitch'. Well, look at that. George Hibbert could use more than two words.

'Are you okay?' he asked, voice low.

Laurel nodded as she pulled the handbrake up, jaw tense. She was not okay.

Robin didn't even let them shut the car door before he was on at Laurel.

'Not enough that you're giving him my house, you're shagging him as well now.'

'Fuck you, Robin,' she snapped. 'We were having a drink in the pub.'

'There's more,' Robin said grimly. 'Come on.'

They followed Robin through the farm to the Pick Your Own. Laurel wrapped her arms around her waist. Whether she was cold in the summer night, or whether she was trying to fortify herself, Nate didn't know.

'There you are,' Jack snapped, striding towards them, taking in Nate just a step behind Laurel.

'Yes,' Laurel said. 'Here I am.'

'We've not touched anything, but look at what we've found,' he said pointing to the shed. They gathered around the doorway and Nate peeked over Laurel's shoulder.

'Shit,' she whispered. 'Shit, shit, shit.'

'What is it?' he asked Robin.

'That, my good doctor, is an empty bottle of industrial strength weed killer.' Robin clapped him on the back. 'It's been dumped into the water butts that waters the Pick Your Own fruit. It has been on for hours, ruining this year's crop, perhaps next years as well.'

'Oh fuck,' Nate said, the implication dawning on him.

'Give the man a gold star.' Robin shrugged. 'They must have just chucked the empty bottle in there after making sure the irrigation system was switched on.'

Laurel was crouching, head in her hands. The only sound

was the whirring of the irrigation system controls from the shed. The Fletcher men waited for her with bated breath. She stood up, pushing her hands through her hair.

'Right. Jack, call the police and tell David, the lazy shit, that if he doesn't come out right now, I'll lodge a formal complaint.'

Jack pulled his phone out and took a few steps away.

'Robin, turn off the irrigation at the mains and make sure the timer is turned off so it doesn't come on in the morning.'

'Yes, boss,' he said, jogging away.

She turned to Bill. 'Dad, call old man Hibbert. It was George. I know it was. Find out where he was tonight.'

'Laurel, it's gone ten,' Bill said.

'If you don't want to call him, I will,' she said darkly. 'And I guarantee you, he will not appreciate a call from me.'

'Okay, okay. I'll call him.' Bill squinted at his phone.

'I'm going to check the CCTV in the office.' She turned to him, deflated. 'You don't have to hang around here, Nate.'

He looked around at the Fletcher men busily doing her bidding and the farm that she had built.

'I'll come up with you.'

'Okay, but you don't have to.' Laurel's face was tight.

'Look, just let me help,' he said.

He was rewarded with a little nod, a yes, she was letting him in, letting him help her. He put his arm around her shoulders as they turned towards the admin building.

'Laurel, David's not happy, but he's coming,' Jack called. 'Nate, can I have a word?'

'Good,' she called back.

'I won't be a minute,' he said quietly to Laurel and jogged back over to Jack.

Jack was looking past him, watching Laurel head towards the admin building.

'What's up?' Nate said, expectantly.

Now was not the time for a catch up chat.

Jack took a breath and set his jaw, face illuminated by the artificial light coming from the shed.

'I like you, man, I do.' His voice was steel and flint. 'But if you hurt Laurel, then I will hold you down while Robin smashes your face in.'

'What are you talking about?' Hurting Laurel? They weren't going out. They were just friends.

'Don't be stupid. Can't you see the way she looks at you? And I certainly see the way you look at her.'

'What? Like she's my friend?' Nate snapped. What the fuck was Jack going on about?

'You can tell yourself that all you like, man,' Jack scoffed. 'You search her out all the time, you smile when she smiles. You look at her just a little bit too long.'

What? 'You don't know what you're talking about.'

'Whatever man. But I'm telling you, if you break her, I'll kill you.' Jack assessed him slowly, letting it sink in. 'If this is George Hibbert, and I think it is, she'll put on a brave face, but she'll be scared.'

Nate scrubbed a hand over his face.

'What's George Hibbert's thing with Laurel?'

Jack shrugged. 'He never got over her. It was only ever a one night stand for her and it was two years ago, but now he's got a massive chip on his shoulder. He's bitter and spiteful, and obviously a twat.' He glanced at his phone. 'I've got to go and see Rebecca. She wants an update. See you later, man.'

Jack jogged away with a wave over his shoulder and Nate headed for the admin building and Laurel.

Deal with one thing at a time, and Jack's wild assertions could be dealt with tomorrow.

LAUREL

She was numb.

A little from the chill in the night, but mainly from the fact that George Hibbert thought she was awful enough to try and destroy her business.

He may well have succeeded.

She'd have to draft an email to send to all the Pick Your Own bookings tomorrow. The insurance company would have to be called. The local policeman, David, was on his way, but he was useless so she'd have to escalate that. The graffiti would have to be cleaned, but not until evidence photographs had been taken and who knows when that would be?

This was a family farm and it had swear words tracked all over it in big black spray paint.

Tears pricked at Laurel's eyes and she swallowed heavily. She'd been so happy with the endorsement from the BAS and now this had happened.

She was scanning back through the digital CCTV when Nate came in and she glanced up, giving him a worried smile.

'Any luck?' he asked, perching next to her on the edge of her desk so he could see the screen too.

She shook her head silently, eyes glued to the screen.

After what seemed an age, there he was; George Hibbert scrabbling backwards through the different screens as she rewound to when he first arrived, bold as brass, climbing on the five-bar gate to spray paint the Little Willow Farm sign. He was wearing a black hoodie and black shorts, holdall slung across his chest, but she would recognise him anywhere.

'It's him, yeah? George Hibbert?' Nate asked, squinting at the figure running across the farmyard to the admin building.

She nodded slowly. That waste of space police officer David wouldn't do anything with this unless it was definitive that it was George. Laurel watched intently as he headed into another camera shot towards the irrigation shed. He crouched on the ground and opened the holdall, pulling out the weedkiller. Laurel stopped the playback and zoomed in on his bare calf as close as she could without distorting it too much.

'It's definitely him, that's his tattoo,' she said, tapping the screen.

'What is it? Looks like a red and green smudge from here,' Nate leaned towards the monitor.

'It's Vision, as in the comic book thing? Marvel, I think?'

She pressed play again, watching as George found the water butts and emptied the entire container of weedkiller into them, then headed to the irrigation controls, dropping the empty cannister on the floor.

He sauntered out of that shed and out of her farm like he was shit on a stick. Like he'd just pleasured a woman so well she'd never forget it. Well, newsflash, he needed a lot more practice before he allowed himself that amount of swagger.

Laurel put her head in her hands. This was deliberate sabotage because she didn't fancy George Hibbert.

What a fucking mess.

She felt a strong hand rubbing her back between her shoulder blades, but Nate didn't say anything and for that she was grateful.

After allowing herself a couple of shuddering sobs and a few deep breaths, Laurel straightened.

'I need to make a list.' Her voice was hoarse.

'Okay,' he said. 'What can I do?'

She gave him a little smile. 'Nothing, Nate. Why don't you go home, get some sleep, prep whoever it is for moving into Robin's house tomorrow.'

There really wasn't anything he could do.

'I'm just going up to check the site.' He hesitated. 'I know it doesn't seem like he's gone up there, but I just want to check, you know, make sure.'

Shit. She hadn't even thought about that. It was clear from the CCTV that he hadn't taken the winding road up to the archaeological dig site, but that's not to say that this was his first trip. That's not to say that he was the only one here. Perhaps he had recruited someone else into his scheme.

She gave Nate a slow, sad nod.

'I'll come back, I won't be long,' he said.

Another nod, because she didn't trust herself to speak.

Nate squeezed her shoulder and she swallowed, a lump in her throat forming at his kindness and watched as he left the room.

Pulling herself together, Laurel began her list. Telephone calls to the insurance company, drafting emails of apologies, stabbing George Hibbert, sending emails to be delivered at 8am on Monday morning to Sylvie to keep her updated. She'd sleep at Dad's tonight, because David was going to take a hell of a lot of coaching and hand holding to get him to do anything of substance. Who knew how long it took to report something like this? It wasn't your usual shoplifting or car theft, not that they had much of that in Lower Houghton.

This was industrial sabotage, and George Hibbert was damn well going to pay for it.

'Laurel.' Her father knocked on the door frame, interrupting her frenzied scribbling.

'Dad, it was definitely George, he's here clear as day on the CCTV.' She pointed to the computer screen. 'Did you speak to Old Man Hibbert?'

'Yeah,'

Her dad shuffled into her office and sat down. Her father looked defeated.

'He's coming in with George tomorrow at ten.'

Laurel stared at her father. 'With George?'

How was that a good idea? Jack and Robin better not see him. Hell, she certainly didn't want to see him.

'He didn't believe me at first, didn't think George would do something like that. I didn't say that I thought it was him, just asked where he had been.' Her dad passed a hand across his weathered face. 'He called me back and said that they'd be in.'

Laurel's eyebrows refused to sit down on her forehead.

'So, he didn't actually say that George had done it?'

'Not in so many words.' He leaned forward with his elbows on his knees. 'Look, Laurel, he's asked us not to do anything with the police until we've met with him.'

'No way,' she said, instantly. How could he even think about agreeing to something like that?

Her dad straightened.

'Hibbert is my friend. He's asked us a favour, we can do this for him.'

'Dad, I don't think industrial sabotage—' she started.

He held his hand up, face hard. 'Stop right there, Laurel.'

'Dad,' she started, leaning her head to the side.

How was he going to give George Hibbert a pass for something that could very well force their farm under? It's not him who had to deal with the insurance, the bank, the balance sheet. It's not him who had the constant worry of trying to pull the business together so they could live in the place her mother had so loved.

'Last I checked,' his voice was sharp, 'I get a say in how this business is run. It's my farm, it's my name on the deeds.'

That cut her, hard. The room was silent. She sat back in her chair.

'Fine,' she said. 'I'll meet with them tomorrow. But for insurance purposes, I need a police reference number.'

'Leave all that until after.'

He stood up, conversation closed.

She took a breath and steeled herself. 'No.'

Going against her father with all of his kindness and support, ignoring his definite insistence that he was right, that they should obey, was not an easy thing. Her heart stuttered nervously.

Her father turned back to her, eyes flinty hard, just like Jack's.

'What do you mean, no?'

'David is on his way. I'll have a police reference number, and I can choose whether or not to press charges after I've met with Hibbert tomorrow,' she said, trying to push down the desire to revert back to a scared seven-year-old who had just broken a greenhouse window.

'I'll have Jack call David, tell him not to come out.' He dismissed her comment with a wave of his hand.

Laurel persisted. 'He needs to come out now. He needs to see first-hand, take statements, photographs, evidence. Tomorrow will be too late.' She spread her hands wide and forced out a humourless smile. 'I need at least that as a bargaining chip for my meeting with Hibbert.'

Bill Fletcher let the weight of his grey eyes rest heavily on her.

'Fine,' he reluctantly agreed. His face softened a little. 'Are you going home or staying here tonight?'

'I'll go home.' Like she'd want to stay after that dressing down from her father.

Her dad hesitated with his hand on the door frame.

'You keep saying "I", Laurel. If anyone is an "I" on this farm, it's me. Not you.' He turned to pierce her with those grey eyes. 'You'd do well to remember that.'

NATE

There was no disturbance at the site. It was fine. Nate sighed in relief.

Fucking George Hibbert.

If he could go back and change the timeline, he would. Stop Robin from punching George Hibbert, calm things down, stop Hibbert from getting all wound up and thinking that this was a good idea.

The admin building glowed like a beacon in the dark farmyard as he strode across it, wanting to check on Laurel. Behind the barn were the farmhouses, no wonder the Fletcher's or the students hadn't seen or heard anything.

He was just about to open the door to the admin building when headlights flashed across the brickwork. Laurel appeared in the doorway a second later.

'It's David, the policeman,' she said. She was a wilted sunflower, defeated and faded.

'Laurel, what's all this?' he asked, gesturing to the black scrawl across the building.

'What do you think it is, David?' she snapped. 'Sorry, David. It was George Hibbert. We've got CCTV footage. He's also put weedkiller in our irrigation system for the Pick Your Own. It's industrial sabotage. I need a police reference number for my insurance claim.'

She was succinct and to the point.

Nate looked around, frowning. Were the Fletcher men really going to leave her to deal with this by herself? Where was the support?

Well, he would be her support. Nate put his arm around her shoulders.

'Irrigation system?' David said, confused. 'Pick Your Own?' Laurel stiffened under his touch, obviously angered at the incompetence.

She took a deep breath.

'I'll walk you through it, shall I? Then I'll show you the CCTV.'

He trailed after them around the farm as Laurel showed David the policeman what had happened, giving timelines as to when the Fletchers found things, what they have done to mitigate the weedkiller, the difficulties that it would then cause the business.

'I'll need to collect statements from your brothers and father, and…' He looked at Nate. 'Whoever you are.'

'Dr Nathanial Daley,' he said, holding his hand out.

'Ooh, a doctor, is it?' David said, offering a limp, dead fish handshake.

'Yes,' he said shortly, hoping that he exuded some kind of authority. There were some benefits of spending most of his life studying.

'You can come back tomorrow at midday and collect statements. That should give you or whoever enough time to write up the incident and allocate it a crime number. I'll need that when you come tomorrow,' Laurel said, leading them back to the farmyard and David's police Ford Focus.

He hesitated slightly as he opened the car door. 'I don't know if that's enough time.'

Laurel cut him off with a wave of her hand.

'It is enough time, David. We both know that. I need the crime number for our insurance claim. You, or whoever, bring it tomorrow when you attend to take statements. I'll make sure my family and Dr Daley here are ready.'

David wrung his hands, trying to appease her.

'Okay, Laurel. We'll see you tomorrow.'

The car door slammed behind him and they both watched as he executed a seven point turn in the large farmyard to turn his car so he could drive through the wide gates. Nate shook his head in disbelief.

Laurel turned to him. 'I'm going home now, I'm not staying here,' she said bitterly.

'Are you okay?' he asked.

It was a stupid question. Of course she wasn't okay.

'I've had a bit of a… disagreement with my father.' Laurel gave him a sad smile.

'Oh?' he said.

What could they possibly have disagreed about? This was a cut and dried issue. George Hibbert had graffitied their farm and dumped industrial strength weedkiller in their irrigation system to destroy their Pick Your Own crop. It was a criminal act, the police were called, end of story.

'Yeah.' She didn't go into details. 'Thank you though, for coming back with me. You didn't have to.'

'I'm sorry all of this happened.'

'Yeah, me too,' she said. 'I'll see you tomorrow.'

Laurel drove off into the night, headlights flashing across the spray paint and Nate trudged across the yard back to the bunkhouse. Well, the evening had turned out to be a bit of a bust really. What had started out as a fun celebration had quickly crashed and burned with George Hibbert. What a pathetic, self-absorbed, selfish little man.

And the big brother spiel from Jack? Really? He didn't look at Laurel too long, he looked at her just the right amount of time, like he would look at anyone. Didn't he? Of course he smiled when Laurel smiled, because her smile was infectious. What was he supposed to do; scowl when they were talking and when she smiled? Also, how did Laurel look at him? Like he was excavating her farm, sharing her office, and yes, like they were friends. Because that's what they were. Friends.

CHAPTER THIRTEEN

LAUREL

Makeup hadn't done a very good job at hiding the puffy purple smudges under her eyes, but that was the best she could do on three hours sleep. Her mind had been churning and whirling, skipping from George fucking Hibbert to how her father had dismissed everything she had done for the farm and the family for his 'friend' Old Man Hibbert. It wasn't even as if they were close.

Now, they were all sat around the conference table. Fletchers on one side, Hibberts on the other, her at the head but everyone focused on Bill Fletcher.

Everyone except George, who had his eyes firmly trained on the table, like a surly teenager. Pathetic.

'I don't condone anything that my son has done,' Old Man Hibbert said after viewing the CCTV three times, trying to find a sliver of evidence that it wasn't his son who had ruined their business. 'How can I make this right, Bill?'

Laurel bristled. There would be no agreement without her input.

'It's not about "making right", it's about how are we going to get through the next six months? The Pick Your Own income is essential to the farm business and without it we are in dire financial trouble.'

Hibbert glanced at her and frowned.

George snorted.

'You're not in financial trouble, you don't know what financial trouble is,' he spat. 'You're all the same, don't think of anyone else but yourselves. Fucking Fletcher bitch,' he said the last under his breath, but loud enough for everyone around the table to hear it.

Robin's chair flew back as he shot up, Jack soon after with a placating hand on his bulging arm. 'Don't you talk about my sister like that. Don't you fucking dare, Hibbert,' Robin shouted, the veins popping out in his neck.

'Jack, take him out,' Dad ordered, his voice strong and commanding.

Laurel straightened her papers in front of her, not letting this spectacle get to her. If it did, she'd lose control of this meeting, and that was the absolute last thing she wanted or needed.

Jack bustled a brimming Robin out. The door closed behind them, clicking loudly in the quiet room.

Her dad took a breath as if to start the meeting again, but Laurel jumped in.

'So, you've seen the CCTV, you've seen what he did.' She didn't even acknowledge George. He wasn't worth her time. 'I have a police reference number and David is coming to take statements at midday.' She spread her hands out. 'Tell me what you propose.'

Bill Fletcher ground his teeth audibly. George crossed his arms and stared at the table.

'Well,' Old Man Hibbert started, eyeing both Laurel and her dad carefully. 'What we wouldn't want is a protracted court case or anything like that, it just costs money.'

The silence stretched as Laurel waited.

'Besides, we can't be sure that it is actually George in the video,' Old Man Hibbert said quietly, not even believing his own words. 'And we don't really need to involve the police for a bit of graffiti do we?'

Laurel just looked at him, her eyes dead.

'It's industrial sabotage. Our Pick Your Own business has

been ruined for this year, perhaps into next. We will have loss of earnings, excessive damage to our reputation, not to talk about the unmeasurable impact on ancillary sales in the farm shop, the cafe, the petting zoo,' she said, pausing to let that sink in. She didn't dare look at her father, instead keeping her eyes on Old Man Hibbert's greying face. 'So, no. It's not just graffiti.'

Laurel's hands were sticky as she clasped them together on the table.

'What do you propose?' she repeated, enunciating each word.

The Hibbert men exchanged glances and George shrugged slightly. Colour her surprised that George Hibbert hadn't thought about the repercussions of his actions.

'What do you want? We haven't got any money,' George's voice was cold.

Laurel's eyebrow raised. How could he be annoyed with her, when it was him who had put his own family in this mess? She had anticipated this question.

Laurel spoke softly to Old Man Hibbert, not George.

'Look, I've had to report it to the police so I can get a reference number for the insurance, but if we can come to some sort of...' she cast around for the right word, 'arrangement, then I'm sure it's both in our interests to have as little police involvement as possible.'

'You've obviously got something in mind, what is it?' Old Man Hibbert said.

She glanced at her dad's stony face. He wasn't impressed with the way she was dealing with this, but she'd laid the granite hard facts out for them all. They needed money to get past these next few months. Money that had to come from somewhere. She was eighty percent sure it would come from the insurance, but when and how much would be a different matter. It would come from the BAS funding recommendation, but that wouldn't be for a few months. It wouldn't come from the Hibberts because they had very little money.

But they did have the development land.

The development land that she could let out for grazing, perhaps even back to Hibbert, although that would definitely stick in their throats. It was valuable, good quality grazing land. Even if she had to sell an acre, she'd have to bank that it wouldn't be enough to build a substantial property on.

'I—' she swallowed. 'We want your fields.'

George sat up suddenly.

'What? No. No way, no fucking way.'

'Watch your mouth, boy,' his father snapped. 'You're the reason we're in this mess, so you can damn well keep your mouth shut before you get us in any more trouble.'

Old Man Hibbert passed a hand across his face.

She carried on.

'I'm prepared to give you a grazing licence, guaranteed for five years at a good price and,' this was the big thing, 'I'm prepared for your cattle to fall under our umbrella, which means they will fall under our vet charges, our TB testing, but they will still be your cattle. They will have your marks, your breeding, you can choose if and when to sell them, but we will pay for their upkeep.'

They'd had a massive argument over this. Laurel on one side, and Jack and her father on the other, Robin sniping at both sides from the middle.

If Hibbert gave them the fields for free, then the money that she'd been able to wangle from the bank could go to covering the unknown loss of earnings from George Hibbert's escapades last night, before the insurance came through. The five-year guaranteed grazing licence and the living expenses for his cattle were massive sweetener that her father had suggested, once he'd got over how appalled he was that Laurel would even dream to ask for such a thing.

Hibbert was their *neighbour*, he'd known Hibbert for *fifty years*, George was just *acting out*.

Laurel wasn't having any of that bullshit.

Hibbert looked at her father across the table in disbelief. She held her breath, because her dad could ruin everything with something as simple as a slight huff. If Hibbert could see that he wasn't on board, then he would push back, hard.

'And in return, we won't press charges, we won't go to court, and I won't obtain a restraining order on this occasion,' she added.

Hibbert looked confused.

'Why would you need a restraining order, Laurel?' he asked slowly.

She stared at him in disbelief. 'Because George has been harassing me, and last night was another example of George's escalating behaviour. I don't want him anywhere near me. Ever.'

'Harassing you? You're fucking delusional,' George hissed, but she kept her eyes fixed on Old Man Hibbert. He closed his eyes in disappointment.

'How long do I have to think about it?'

'David's coming in,' she glanced at the clock above George's head, 'forty-five minutes.'

A look passed between her father and Hibbert.

'Come on Laurel, let's leave them to think,' her father said authoritatively, standing.

She blinked at him and raised an eyebrow.

What. The. Hell?

Leave them in her office when George Hibbert had literally *just* committed industrial sabotage.

She looked back to a defeated Hibbert. He nodded sadly. She took it as a show of good faith, an 'I won't look at your business shit and try and destroy you'.

Okay. She could give him that.

NATE

Nate had been for a run, packed up his stuff to move into Robin's house, checked the site and was now sitting on the grass, watching cows meander lazily around the field. He hadn't heard from Laurel yet today, and he was waiting to see what she needed him to do with the police.

He unfolded the papers that he'd had Sylvie print and looked over them again. Paul's dig was looking fantastic. The finds were solid and varied, not going to set the archaeological world on fire, but enhancing and adding to the existing knowledge base. The south of France was a beautiful place to spend a few months.

What would his university say? Would he even be allowed? Probably not, and besides, did he even want to? Leave Little Willow Farm, leave this dig?

His smartwatch vibrated, and again, and he shuffled his phone out of his pocket.

'Paul, just thinking about you,' Nate said, smiling down the phone at his old friend. 'How's Angeline?'

'She's perfect, mate, really good. Can't wait for you to meet her,' he said.

'Me too, mate, me too.' He was genuinely happy for Paul.

'Have you thought anymore about France?' Paul asked.

Nate held up the papers as if Paul could see him. The cows mooed in response.

'Yeah, I have, and it looks perfect, your dig looks amazing.'

'But?' Paul could obviously hear the hesitation in his voice.

'But I can't,' Nate said. 'I can't leave here. We've got an Anglo-Saxon burial, we've got gold. It's going to be big. I can't leave.'

Paul sighed. 'Okay, man, I get it.'

'I'm looking forward to seeing you next week, mate, and meeting your girl.' Nate smiled down the phone at him.

'Yeah, I'm excited for her to meet you all. Don't tell her any stupid uni stories, okay?'

Nate laughed. 'Do you remember Laurel Fletcher from uni? She was an undergrad while we were postgrads?

Paul was quiet for a moment. One thing about Paul was that he always gave everything his undivided attention. 'No, why?'

'She owns the farm that my site is on. I'm bringing her next weekend.' Nate picked at the grass beside him.

There was a beat of silence from Paul. 'As your date? You haven't brought anyone to meet us, ever.'

'No, just as friends. We're just friends.'

'Oh right, yeah.' The sarcasm poured down the phone line.

'We are, Paul,' Nate said. 'Anyway, I think something happened at uni. She hates Alex.'

'Everyone hates Alex. Alex is a dick.' Paul snorted. 'But I wouldn't be surprised if something happened. What did Alex say?'

'I've not asked him. I don't want to, I don't know…' Nate looked at the cows for the right phrase, 'wake the sleeping dog?'

Paul sighed heavily down the phone. 'I don't know why you put up with Alex anymore. He's always been a prick.'

Nate was quiet. He used to defend Alex to Paul, but he couldn't bring himself to do so anymore.

'You know Lucia is coming, right?' Paul asked. 'You should probably tell your girl.'

'She's not my girl, Paul.'

He hadn't told her anything about next weekend, had he? They would have talked more about it last night, but the shit hit the fan at the farm. He'd catch up with her this week and give her some more details. Not today, she had too much going on today.

'Have you called Jess?'

'I'll email her,' Nate said. Probably for the best. The conversation he was having with Paul about Laurel not being his girlfriend would be ten thousand times more pressurised with Jess.

'Can you do me a favour?' Paul asked.

'Yeah, man. Anything, you know that.'

'Can you watch out for Angeline, yeah? With Alex? He can be a bit creepy with women, and he doesn't know when to shut his mouth.'

Nate's shoulders slumped. Everyone had seen Alex for what he was a lot sooner than he had.

'Yeah, sure. Don't worry.'

He said his goodbyes to Paul and stared at his phone for a couple of seconds. He'd really dropped the ball on Alex. He'd been so blind to what Alex was really like. He'd ignored it. Perhaps he was the frog in the boiling water, and Alex just kept getting worse and worse, and he couldn't see it. Well, he saw it now. The way Alex had behaved over granting BAS endorsement to the Little Willow site was unprofessional and borderline negligent. His behaviour when he was on site had been beyond the pale. Perhaps it was time to admit to himself that Alex was never going to change.

Nate's phone buzzed in his hand. Laurel.

'Hey.'

'Hey, just calling to let you know that you won't be needing to give a statement to David about last night.' She was straight to business.

'Oh, okay,' he said. 'Everything alright?'

'Yes, fine thanks,' she said abruptly. There were other people there, he could tell.

'Good, um…' he trailed off.

Laurel was straight on him. 'What?'

'Is everything okay with Hibbert? With your dad?' he asked quietly, hoping not to be overheard by anyone.

'Kind of, and no,' she said. 'Look, Nate, I've got to go.'

'Okay, talk to you later,' he started to say, but she'd already hung up.

Huh. Rude.

Nate set his phone carefully on the grass next to him, putting Paul's papers underneath so they didn't blow away in the light breeze.

That was okay, he had stuff to do anyway, and she was busy and stressed.

He had the funding visit to put together, which he had been putting off for a while, but it was creeping closer. Alex needed chasing because he would have to attend to lend BAS's weight to the dig.

He hated this part of his job with a passion. He was an archaeologist, he was supposed to say things like 'this belongs in a museum', not 'could I have a couple of hundred thousand to support this dig of a possible Anglo-Saxon burial site'.

The schmoozing part of his job was the worst.

LAUREL

Well, of course, Old Man Hibbert took the deal.

He couldn't not take the deal, unless he wanted his son involved in an incredibly large, long and public legal battle. George never admitted it, but they all knew he'd done it. The jungle drums in Lower Houghton would be banging nice and loud and everyone in town would know within approximately three hours' time. David, the worst policeman she'd ever known, was also the worst gossip she had ever met.

Laurel was sitting in Rebecca's back garden, Jack putting the twins to bed.

'And he hasn't talked to you since?' Rebecca asked, placing a nice full glass of cold white wine in front of her.

Laurel shook her head sadly.

'No, not one word.'

'He'll come around though,' Rebecca said, sipping her own glass and propping her feet on the bottom rung of the kids' slide.

'We'll see, you know what he's like. It'll be like the Cold War now for ages,' Laurel groaned.

'Yeah, but your dad always comes around in the end,' Rebecca repeated.

Laurel scowled. He did come around in the end, but only after everyone had been made to feel the wrath of his disapproval. Half the time, she just apologised, even if she wasn't in the wrong, so everyone could move on.

Not this time though. She was not in the wrong this time.

George Hibbert could have ruined their business, and she was only doing what any good business person would do. Why couldn't her father see that? Why couldn't Jack see that? Jack, usually her supportive, level-headed brother, thought asking for Hibbert's fields was 'over the line'. Would they prefer to see awful, gentrified houses built on that land? Would they prefer the business to go under? For them to lose their home? Their mother's home? No, they wouldn't.

So why did she feel so guilty?

'I won't stay long, I'll have this then go,' Laurel said, resting her head on the back of the chair.

What. A. Day.

'Why don't you just stay here?' Rebecca asked. 'You've been cleaning the sign and the wall all afternoon.'

Laurel swivelled her head to look at her.

'No. I can't. I want to go home.'

If she stayed here, it would be work, work, work. She'd end up back in her office, prepping everything for when the insurance company opened in the morning, worrying over the 'what ifs' of financial forecasting when realistically, all she wanted to do was curl up on the sofa with a vat of wine and massage her hands, sore from scrubbing at the graffiti. It had been an extremely long day.

'Is Jack putting the kids to bed as part of his "sharing the responsibilities" thing?' Laurel asked.

'Yeah.' Rebecca grinned. 'Oh, and we've put the baby talk on the back burner as well.'

Laurel sat up.

'So, you've agreed, you're not having another?'

'We're not having another right now,' Rebecca said carefully, running her finger around the rim of her wine glass.

'But you're thinking about it?' Laurel probed.

'I told him that I'd consider it again in a year,' Rebecca

raised an eyebrow, 'if he still wants one. I've made him promise to go on an abroad holiday and then we'll have that conversation again.'

Laurel raised her glass to her friend. 'You've worked that really, really well.'

'Well, I want the twins to go somewhere with both of us, for longer than a couple of days, out of the country. You know, villa with a pool, by the beach. They'd absolutely love it.'

Talking about where Rebecca and Jack could take the twins on holiday was like slipping on a pair of comfy old slippers.

'The next time we go, you and Nate can come as well,' Rebecca teased.

'Ha, ha, very funny.' Laurel narrowed her eyes at her sister-in-law.

'How's it going with him?' Rebecca looked over her garden.

Laurel shrugged, but couldn't suppress a smile. 'It's fine.'

'Oh, don't give me that,' Rebecca crowed. 'You haven't told me anything about last night, and I want to know. Now. Tell me.'

'God, I haven't told you! The BAS are endorsing the site for funding!' Laurel grinned.

'Laurel, that's amazing. You must be so pleased. Congratulations!'

'I'm so relieved, Rebecca. You've got no idea.' She sipped her wine.

Rebecca rubbed her arm. 'You're doing a good job, Laurel. Good work.'

'Nate and I were celebrating in the pub, and then your stupid husband called and all hell broke loose, but…' Laurel shot a smile at Rebecca. 'Nate's invited me to a barbeque with his friends next weekend.'

'So, the top worked then? Not too try hard at all.' Rebecca wiggled her eyebrows.

'Uh, nothing like that. Just friends, Rebecca.'

They were just friends. Nothing had been said about

a date, nothing had changed between them. Just friends. That's it.

'You're meeting his friends? That's a big deal.' Rebecca leaned back in her seat. 'That *is* a big deal,' she repeated.

'No, it's not, it's just a barbeque,' Laurel said dismissively.

'You're blushing,' Rebecca said quietly. 'Laurel Fletcher, you are blushing. You really like him.'

'Yeah, so what if I do?' Laurel huffed, gulping at her wine and crossing her arms defensively. 'Anyway, I've got to go.'

'Oh Laurel, I'm only teasing. Don't be annoyed,' Rebecca whined, following her into the kitchen. Laurel deposited her glass on the side.

'I know,' she said, heading for the door. 'I just want to lie on the sofa and watch crap TV and eat crisps. And possibly have some more wine. But not too much, work tomorrow.'

'Okay, but text me if you're feeling bad about the whole, you know, thing,' Rebecca said, hugging her tightly.

That was why she loved Rebecca.

Rebecca knew that she was full on blaming herself for George Hibbert and didn't bring it up once. Laurel didn't want to talk about it, she didn't want to be reassured that it *wasn't* her fault. Her logical brain completely knew that she had no control over how George Hibbert behaved. George chose to vandalise her place of work and she dealt with it in a professional, businesslike manner, getting the best deal that she could. Despite her father.

'Love you,' Laurel called over her shoulder as she headed for her car.

She kept her eye out for Nate on her way through the farm but didn't spot him. She could call him, she supposed, or text him, apologise for how abrupt she'd been earlier. Her dad had been there, as had the Hibberts. They'd insisted on hearing her tell the policeman, and Nate, that statements were no longer needed.

Fine, as long as she got those damned fields.

CHAPTER FOURTEEN

NATE

Nate sat at Robin's kitchen table with his laptop, the smell of furniture polish and lemon antibacterial spray lingering in the air. Laurel must have got in some industrial cleaners because they were in Robin's house all day, and now it sparkled like a show home. He was sure that the students would make it less show home-y in no time. In fact, a few of them were sprawled across the sofa and onto the floor, glugging cheap beer, ringing for pizza and watching what can only be described as 'absolute shit' on TV.

At least he had a place to work and a bedroom that did not include other people.

He pressed send on the email to Jess to let her know he was bringing Laurel, closed his laptop and waited. It took approximately 45 seconds for his phone to ring excitedly. It was 'excitedly' because he knew full well it was Jess wanting the exact nature of his relationship with Laurel, and every tiny little intricate detail of their every interaction. Jess meant well, but she was a bit much sometimes.

This was just a barbeque with his friends, not a date. Laurel just needed to get away from Little Willow Farm and relax for a bit.

Jess usually only called once and left a long and rambling voicemail whining about why he never answered his phone or why he didn't return his calls, and when, for the love of god, was Benji going to see Uncle Nate again? True to form, after a couple of minutes, the voicemail symbol popped up on his phone. He'd listen to the first ten seconds and then delete it before he could feel even more guilty about not being a better friend.

So, when his phone vibrated again on Robin's kitchen table, he looked at the unknown number intrigued.

'Nate Daley,' he answered.

'Why, hello, Nate Daley.'

Nate's eyebrows sprang up.

Once, he'd have done anything for Lucia if she purred at him like this, put her full lips together and dipped her chin seductively, but he'd been immune to that now for a long while.

'Lucia, this is a surprise, how are you?' He sat back in his chair.

'I'm really good, Nate. How are you?' she said. He could practically feel her flipping her curls over her shoulder as she spoke.

'Yeah, good.' He waited, but she didn't say anything. 'Where are you now, what are you working on?'

'I've been in Huaca de Chena in Chile.' She pronounced it 'She-lay'. 'It's an Inca site.'

He rolled his eyes. Every archaeologist worth their salt knew of the pre-Colombian cemetery at the foot of the Chena mountain.

'And you? What mysteries are you unearthing?'

Nate used to think that Lucia's fondness for the dramatic was aspirational, but now it was just a bit pretentious.

'I'm on an Anglo-Saxon site,' he said, not wanting to tell her anymore. She almost never called him. There must be a reason for this.

She gave a small laugh into the silence.

'I'm really looking forward to seeing you next weekend. I'm around for a few days. Actually, I wondered if we might...' she was silent for a couple of beats, 'catch up, just the two of us?'

Oh, so it was a booty call. Hmm, this was new.

'I don't know, Lucia, I'm really busy. I'm not sure I can,' he said, ever the diplomat.

'Too busy to see me?' she asked, voice low and husky. He pursed his lips.

'Yeah, sorry Lucia.' He didn't sugar coat it. 'But I'll see you next weekend. You can meet Laurel.'

'You have a girlfriend?' Her voice was sharper than she probably would have wanted.

'She's a friend.' Nate huffed. 'Look, Lucia, I'm looking forward to seeing you. It'll be nice to catch up, but I really am too busy to see you after. I've got a funding visit to prep for.'

And he had no attraction to her whatsoever. There was no need or desire to see her after next weekend.

A few years ago, he would have jumped at the chance to spend a few more hours in her bed, bathing in the golden glow of her beauty and success, but not now. He'd got over that infatuation a long time ago.

'Okay, fine, well I don't know if I could have fit you in anyway,' she said airily.

'But didn't you—' He cut himself off. 'But didn't you call me' is what he was going to say, but whatever. 'Never mind. I know Alex is looking forward to seeing you.'

Yeah, he was planting that seed.

'Oh, Alex is always looking forward to seeing me,' Lucia said dismissively.

What was he supposed to say to that?

'Oh, okay.'

'But anyway, I suppose I'll meet your new lady love on the weekend,' she said provocatively.

'Lucia, she's not...' he trailed off. What did he care what Lucia thought?

'She's not what? She isn't your new love?' Lucia pushed.

'No, she isn't. Look, you've caught me at a busy time. I'll catch up with you on the weekend, see you at Jess and Owen's,' Nate said, ending the call.

He was pissed off. No, correct that, Lucia had pissed him off. Why did she think that he would drop everything for a couple of days' roll in the hay with her? Why did she think that he didn't have a basic knowledge of world-famous archaeological sites?

Nate would definitely have to warn Laurel that Lucia was going to be there next weekend, and that she thought they were more than friends. If she didn't want to come, then that would be fine. So why did his stomach drop a little at the thought?

'Nate?' He was jerked out of his reverie by the girl with the spidery eyelashes. 'Nate' was it now? What happened to 'Dr Daley'?

'Yeah,' he said, elbows on the table, eyebrows up.

The girl twirled a lock of hair around her finger.

'With this new house, surely it would be best if people shared? I mean, I'd be happy to share...' she trailed off, biting her lip suggestively. What the actual fuck?

'If you can find someone to share with you, then knock yourself out,' he said, grabbing up his laptop and heading upstairs, leaving her by the table.

He didn't want to deal with that shit.

LAUREL

It was Thursday and she hadn't seen or heard from Nate all week. Sylvie had given Robin's keys to one of the students she had been flirting with all summer, and she'd seen some of them moving stuff over to her brother's house from her office window, but no Nate.

Sure, she had been busy with the insurance company, who were taking their own sweet time despite her saying how urgent it was, dealing with the frosty weather from her father, and trying to sort out a social media campaign to close the

Pick Your Own while also trying to entice people to come to other parts of the farm. But a text or two to see how she was doing would have been nice.

Her phone buzzed on the arm of the sofa and fell down the side of the cushion. She put down the bowl of crisps and wiped her hands on her shorts before retrieving it.

sylvie

> Sorry to text you out of working hours, I'm just reminding you that I've got an induction tomorrow morning at the college, I'll be in by 1pm.

> Okay, enjoy! I want to hear all about it when you get back.

She really did not want to hear all about it, there were way too many things going on, but all the management magazines said that she should be a supportive boss. So, she would be. Fine.

Laurel scrolled to the chat between her and Nate and read through the messages.

Fuck this. She was thirty-two. It wasn't 1950. She could call him. Although he might just want to be out of the minefield of all this stuff with George Hibbert. Just a massive mess that he didn't want to be involved in.

But they were supposed to be going to this barbeque on Saturday, and she had absolutely no idea of any details at all. Unless he didn't want her to come anymore?

Well, only one way to find out.

> Hey, haven't seen you recently. Are we still on for Saturday? If you have to cancel, don't worry.

He was immediately online and those three dots flashed back and forth accusingly for way too long.

In the end, he called.

'Hey,' she said.

'Hey, sorry, look…' He sounded urgent and well, quite frankly, a bit weird.

Laurel's shoulders drooped. Was this the 'let's just be friends' speech? The 'I really like you, but as a friend' conversation?

'Yeah?' she said, warily.

'I've just had a call from Lucia. She's going to be there this Saturday and I wanted you to be prepared.' His words rushed together.

'Lucia? Your ex, Lucia?' On one hand her heart perked up at the fact it wasn't the 'we work together, so let's still get on' speech, but Lucia? Gorgeous, exotic, worldly ex-girlfriend Lucia? Just. Fucking. Great. 'Why would I have to be prepared?'

'Do you know more than one Lucia?' he asked, sarcasm popping through.

'No, just checking,' she said lightly.

'I told her you were coming with me, and she seems to think that we're together. I told her we're not, but she won't take no for an answer. Jess, as well,' he said, his words all mashing together, 'she will think we're together. I just want you to be prepared, there may be a lot of gushing and hinting.'

'Oh.' What was she supposed to say to that?

'My friends can be a bit much, and I completely get it if you don't want to come.'

Perhaps she shouldn't go. But now it was potentially being taken away from her, she realised how much she was looking forward to being off the farm, away from Lower Houghton, away from all the pressure and stress. Just being herself for an afternoon, and not Boss Laurel, Stressed Laurel, Farm Laurel, EVERYTHING Laurel.

'No, I was looking forward to it. But if you don't want me to, I can stay home. It's okay.'

'You should come, Laurel,' he said. 'Just don't say I didn't warn you.'

She laughed at that. She was big enough to look after herself.

'Right, well, okay. I'll see you on Saturday then,' he said. 'I'll pick you up at 11:30am?'

'Okay, see you then.' Laurel waited. The hesitation on the end of the line was like he wanted to say something more.

'Bye.'

He ended the call.

Uh, what did he mean, he'd pick her up? He didn't have a car here. She wasn't even sure that he could drive. Not her problem.

Now the agonising worry of what to wear. She dialled Rebecca who didn't answer, so she texted her instead.

> Rebecca, I need you. Come over, I'll get a pizza for us.

She smiled at the nostalgia because this was exactly what going on dates was like in uni – her and Rebecca deciding what to wear over pizza the night before and gossiping about whoever she was seeing the next night.

Her phone buzzed with two different messages.

Rebecca

> Forty minutes? I'm just bathing the kids.

Jack

> Are you taking my wife away from me again?

Lucia at university was next level. She didn't walk, she floated. She was ethereal, beautiful, intelligent. Perfect. Her and Nate had been the perfect couple, but they weren't together now, and he and Laurel were nothing more than friends. He had made that abundantly clear. So, it didn't matter that Lucia was there. Didn't matter at all. Besides, Laurel was moderately attractive, wasn't she? She was a successful (kind of, sometimes) businesswoman, and she was proud of herself for what she had built at Little Willow Farm. Just because she wasn't a world-famous archaeologist didn't mean that she was a failure.

No. She could do this. She could rub shoulders with Nate's successful friends.

Laurel ordered ham and mushroom pizza to be delivered from the pizza place around the corner and waited for Rebecca.

NATE

He checked his hair in the mirror. Again. Like it had changed in the thirty seconds since he'd checked it last. Those speckles of grey weren't going anywhere, no matter how he styled it, and he refused to dye it. Just For Men was just not for him. He was embracing aging gracefully. Well, mostly gracefully.

The hire car had arrived this morning to the farm. Robin had whistled and insisted on sitting in it, while Jack had eyed it appreciatively. If he didn't have his own Mercedes C Class convertible here, then he could at least hire one for the weekend.

His overnight bag was in the boot and he was sitting around

the corner from Laurel's flat, because of course he was ten minutes early. It would take about an hour and a half to get to Jess and Owen's house.

Top down or top up? Is top down too pretentious? Or did top up on a sunny day mean that he was one of *those* people who had their tops up on a sunny day? He hadn't sweated through his shirt, had he? And yes, he knew he had three extra shirts in his bag, just in case.

'Hello?' Laurel's voice cracked through the intercom after he pressed it.

'Hey, it's Nate.'

'I'll be down in a sec, just putting my shoes on.'

Nate took a couple of steps away from the door and assessed the lazy main road of Lower Houghton. He smiled. The greengrocer's wares outside on crates, the newspapers in the holder by the door of the newsagents, the smell of the bakery. He could definitely get used to it here.

The door opened and closed behind him, and he turned to face Laurel.

'Hey.' He smiled at her. 'You look nice.'

She was wearing a floral dress and some kind of casual high wedge sandal things. It was perfect. She'd fit right in.

'Thanks,' she said.

Nate frowned. 'Where's your bag?'

She looked at him like he was crazy and pointed at her handbag over one shoulder.

'No, no, your overnight bag.'

Laurel's face flattened in shock and surprise.

'Overnight?' she squeaked. 'You didn't tell me it was an overnight thing.'

Nate's stomach dropped. 'I'm sure I did. I mean, I did, didn't I? We all have a few drinks and crash at Jess and Owen's.'

'No, you didn't frigging tell me! Otherwise, I would have packed an overnight bag!' Laurel swivelled on those heels and unlocked her door. 'You'll have to help me,' she called over her shoulder.

Help her do what? Why would she need help packing? It was only one night. He followed her into the hallway.

'Stay here,' she urged and she charged up the stairs, reappearing a moment later with a bundle of clothes.

'This dress, or this one?' Laurel asked, holding up first a blue dress and then a yellow one with white flowers. 'Or shorts? These?' She waved a pair of forest green shorts in his face. 'With a white top?'

'Um,' he hesitated. He was crap at stuff like this.

She huffed.

'Look, it took me and Rebecca about two hours to decide that this was the dress I should wear today. I thought we'd be home by eight or so, but now, I've got perhaps an evening to change for, and clothes for tomorrow as well.' She actually looked rather concerned. 'It's hard, Nate. I don't want to look stupid.'

'You would never look stupid,' he said, raising an eyebrow. 'You're beautiful, Laurel.'

She stilled and jerked her eyes up to his. He held her gaze easily, because he wanted her to see it was the truth. Beautiful, accomplished and more than capable, Laurel probably wasn't told often enough that she was, and he wanted her to know. He was a great believer in upfront honesty.

The air between them was loaded with something tangibly warm. Her mouth opened and closed, but no sound came out. A flush flowed up her neck into her cheeks, and her eyes widened. Big, round, bronze eyes stared at him. Was that disbelief? Was she surprised? Objectively, she was pretty much perfect; brown hair that glowed red and gold in the sunlight, plump kissable pink lips, and a figure he knew would fit against his just right.

'It's the truth,' he said quietly, a frown crossing his brow.

Her throat bobbed in a swallow and she dropped her eyes.

'Nate,' she huffed out a laugh, shaking her head.

'Usually, when someone gives you a compliment,' his voice was low and he took a step closer, 'you say thank you.'

He swallowed and smiled to ease whatever this thickness was between them, but his stomach was fluttering at the way she caught her breath. Something flickered across her face, but he couldn't be sure what it was. Flustered, sure, and she obviously didn't know what to do, what to say. Laurel had not been complimented enough, and Nate felt a sudden anger at all the men who made her feel like this – shocked when told she was beautiful.

She was full of contradictions. Assertive and confident when it came to her farm, her family, but shy and tentative, bashful almost, when anything was about her personally. There was a softness, a vulnerability about her that he instinctively knew he couldn't crush.

'Thank you,' Laurel whispered.

'Okay.' He grinned. Progress. A tentative smile pulled at her mouth.

Nate randomly pointed to a dress in the pile. 'Take that one if we change in the evening and the shorts for tomorrow.'

Laurel nodded and cleared her throat.

'Right, I will. I'll just be a minute.' She gathered the clothes and hurried up the stairs. There was a clatter from above, from what Nate assumed was the bathroom as she knocked over bottles in her hurry to get her overnight things ready.

'I'll be two minutes,' she cried.

'Don't rush, it's okay,' he cried back, tucking his hands in his pockets.

'I don't want to be late.' She popped her head around the door.

'It's okay. Alex will be late and so will Lucia. They're always late,' he said.

'That's fine for them, but I don't like being late,' she huffed. She shut the door and reemerged after a moment or so, rolling her carry-on suitcase behind her. 'Okay, I'm ready.'

Her face was flushed with exertion.

'Okay, let's go.'

He moved up the stairs to reach for her case and she let him take it, ushering him out the door, and onto the street.

He led her around the corner to the car.

'Wow, is this yours?' she asked, dragging her fingertips across the bonnet.

'I've hired it, but I've got one at home,' he said opening the door for her before putting her case in the boot. She looked at him with that eyebrow up questioningly as he made himself comfortable in the driver's seat.

'I like cars.' He shrugged.

'I'm not really one for cars,' she said. 'But I like this one.'

'Shall I put the top up or keep it down?'

'Down.' She looked at him like he'd just given her candyfloss. 'I've never been in a convertible before.'

'Down it is.'

He smiled, pulling off.

CHAPTER FIFTEEN

LAUREL

Being driven around with the top down was really fun. The wind whipped around her, but not so much that it was uncomfortable, and not so much that her hair became ridiculous.

'Tell me about your friends. What should I expect?' she asked, thankful for this time for a briefing.

Nate's eyes crinkled as he smiled.

'Jess will gush, she loves people. She'll ask you ten thousand questions. Paul will have eyes only for his girlfriend, Angeline. It's the first time we're meeting her.' Nate glanced at her. 'Owen is friendly, and, well, you know Alex.'

Was that a bit of distaste showing in the way Nate pinched his mouth?

'And Lucia?'

'Lucia is…' he hesitated. 'She's Lucia. She's the star of the show,' he said wearily. 'We'll have a good time though.'

'Yeah, it's going to be so nice not being in Lower Houghton. You were right. I do need to get away once in a while.' Laurel relaxed back against the headrest. 'Thanks for bringing me with you.'

'No worries,' Nate said, shooting her a smile. 'Just to warn you…'

Laurel groaned. How much more was he going to warn her about?

'Benji, Jess and Owen's boy, is a bundle of energy. Also, Jess and Owen are absolutely loaded.'

'Loaded?'

'Do you remember Owen from uni?'

She shook her head. She only remembered him, Alex and Lucia. The rest of them were just vague blobs.

'Well, Owen was working as a junior in a financial advisor's office. A new client came in with an idea, and Owen got in on the ground floor with it. Made millions.'

Laurel's eyebrows shot up her forehead.

'Millions?' Good lord.

'Well, two or three, but that's still a plural. It was right place, right time,' Nate said.

That was more than she would ever see in her life, probably more than her entire family would see in their entire lifetimes, all put together. 'Jess did alright as well. She works as an executive producer on some kind of daytime TV program.'

'Christ.'

Laurel was suddenly extremely aware of her very nice, but decidedly high street, dress she and Rebecca had painstakingly chosen last night. She fretted over her hair in the little mirror in the sun visor. The roads were getting smaller now. They were nearly there.

Nate glanced at her. 'Don't worry. They're just normal people.'

Mmm hmm. Normal people who have millions of pounds.

'I've got a bottle of wine in my handbag. It was only a tenner. Can you stop so I can get them something better?'

'Laurel, no.' Nate was firm. 'Stop stressing.'

She looked at his profile as he drove and blew out a breath.

'Okay fine, but remember, I'm just a farm girl.'

'Laurel Fletcher, you are so much more than "just a farm girl",' he said, eyes fixed firmly on the road.

Laurel felt that blush creep across her chest, and she looked at her hand clasped tightly in her lap, unable to stop a little smile spreading over her lips. She looked at him.

Nate indicated left and turned into the driveway marked 'Fairy Hollow Farm'. Laurel's face crumpled with laughter.

'It's a farm? You've brought me to a farm?'

'Okay, okay, I get it,' he said, the car rumbling slowly down the gravelled drive. The house hadn't come into view yet. 'But they only bought the farmhouse and an acre or two. They've got some sheep, a couple of cows and a couple of ponies for Benji. He's eight and wants to be a farmer when he grows up.'

'Must be nice to have the money to be able to indulge him,' she said wistfully, thinking what she would do with millions of pounds and how many holidays she could send Jack, Rebecca and the kids on. Hell, she'd buy them a holiday home with a pool somewhere hot, by the sea. She'd buy them two, three.

'It's not about money though, is it? It's about giving kids a stable and loving home,' he said, bristling a little.

'Yes, you're right, it's exactly that.'

He pulled the car to a stop next to a battered VW Polo, some kind of dusty four-by-four and a family sedan. 'Paul's already here, that's his Polo,' Nate said. 'Alex isn't here yet, and I don't know how Lucia is supposed to be getting here.'

He grinned at her. 'Come on.'

Laurel stepped out of the car and looked at the farmhouse. Huge didn't cover it. It was obviously renovated and extended, sympathetic to the original structure and the pond in the front garden area was well kept and luscious. She sidled her way around the side of the car, eyes taking in as much of the smallholding as she could. She'd like to see the animals, see what it was like to be a non-commercial farmer, just doing it for fun.

Nate lugged her hastily packed case out of the boot and set it down next to his own on the gravel. She extended the handle, but Nate took it off her.

'I'll take it,' he said, strolling across the driveway.

She trailed after him. 'This is huge, Nate. Look at it!'

'I've been here before, Laurel.'

She grabbed his arm, and he stopped and faced her.

'Are you sure it's okay for me to be here? I mean, I don't really fit in with,' she gestured around, 'all this.'

'Laurel, don't be ridiculous. You'll be absolutely fine,' he put his hand on her arm reassuringly, and she relaxed a little. 'We're here to have a good time, so stop overthinking everything, okay?'

'Okay, but if I give you the signal, you have to come and rescue me.'

He looked confused. 'What signal?'

She nudged him lightly on the shoulder. 'Oh, for god's sake, Nate. You'll *know* okay?'

'Alright,' he laughed. 'Seriously, stop stressing. We're here to have fun.'

Laurel took a breath. He looked so handsome, but this was not a date, regardless of whether he called her beautiful or not. Certainly not an overnight date. NOT A DATE.

NATE

He kind of got why she was worried, but she seriously had absolutely nothing to stress out about. She was beautiful, accomplished and his friends were just normal people.

'Nate! I thought I heard a car,' Jess called, gravel crunching under her little feet as she hurried over to them. 'And you must be Laurel. I haven't heard anything about you!' She threw her arms around Laurel in a hug.

'Oh,' Laurel exclaimed, surprised but returned the hug. 'Hello.'

'Did you get here okay?' Jess asked, sparing a cursory smile for Nate as she linked her arm with Laurel and led her away from the car.

'Yeah, nice to see you too, Jess,' Nate grumbled, grabbing both cases.

Laurel looked over her shoulder at him with a worried smile, but he just waved her on. Jess would look after her.

'Nate, you're in the room you were in before, drop the bags off and we'll be in the garden,' Jess called.

'And Laurel?'

'Yes, Laurel too!'

Fine. Jess would have sorted something out. He'd made it clear in his email that Laurel was coming as a *friend*, and that they weren't together.

Nate headed through the front door and up the stairs to his guest room, dragging the two cases behind him. The house was large but homey, toy trains scattered in the hallway. He needed to dump these and have a beer. He pushed open the door to his guest room and groaned.

Jess had not sorted anything out. The king size bed stood proud in the middle of the room. No separate bed, no blow-up bed. Not even a blanket so he could sleep on the chaise lounge by the far wall. Jess obviously hadn't got the message that they were just friends. Or she had, and she didn't care. Owen would sort it, and he would be having words with Jess.

Nate was ambushed as soon as he stepped into the hallway.

'Oof,' he gasped, as a plastic sword hit him across the back. 'Who was that?' he growled.

Benji stood behind him, blue mask across his eyes, swords at the ready.

'I'm Leonardo, and I've been waiting for you, Splinter.'

Nate's face dropped in dismay.

'Splinter? I always liked Donny. Can I be Donatello? Daddy can be Splinter.'

'Okay, Uncle Nate. I'll get the stick and the mask.' Benji ran off to his room and reappeared with the mask which Nate dutifully tied around his head.

'Mum said you've brought a girl. Can she be April?'

'You'll have to ask her, Leo.' Nate ruffled the boy's hair. 'Now, let's go get Splinter.'

They stealthily descended the stairs through the house and hid behind the kitchen island. The bifold doors were open, meaning that the entire back of the house faced out into the garden.

Nate adored this house, not just because how Jess had made the indoors flow seamlessly into the outdoors and the kitchen large enough to house an entire family, but because it was thoroughly lived in. Sometimes, people with loads of money had homes where you were afraid to touch anything and nothing was out; no clutter, no nick-nacks, nothing to indicate that actual people lived here.

Not Jess and Owen. There were family photos, trinkets and memories of places they'd visited, books stacked haphazardly, Benji's toys dotted around. It was a happy home.

They edged their way into the back garden, hiding (not incredibly successfully) behind shrubs and bushes, creeping up on Owen. He was at the barbeque with Paul, both of them considering the best way to light the coals. Paul kept throwing glances over to the ladies sat on the garden sofa, a glass of rosé in each of their hands.

Laurel looked happy, she was smiling with Jess as the brown-haired woman, Angeline he presumed, told them some story about Paul on their dig.

'Ready?' He looked at Benji, who nodded excitedly, adjusting his grip on his sword. 'Okay, one, two, three!'

They exploded from behind the shrubs with a yell, and Nate picked up Benji under one arm and ran him the ten steps to a surprised Owen and Paul, shouting incoherently.

'Ha, we've got you now, Splinter,' Benji shouted, aiming a precise blow to Owen's arse as Nate put him down.

Owen clutched his bum and fell to the grass, groaning.

'Leo! Donny! I can't believe you've caught me,' he said, 'but I won't let you get me next time.'

He grabbed Benji and dragged him down to the ground, tickling him relentlessly.

There were amused laughs from behind him, and he lifted his hand to Laurel, a grin plastered on his face. Owen was a good father and he adored Benji. That much was evident. Paul was laughing and pulled a can of beer from the cooler at his feet to give to Nate.

'Thanks, man,' he said, hugging him with one arm. 'Good to see you.'

'You too, how you doing? Good drive?' Paul's smile was wide and genuine, his rich brown skin glowing from time spent in the French sun.

Nate nodded. 'Yeah good. You get here okay?'

'Yeah, we got here last week,' Benji shrieked as he got away from Owen, running towards Jess. 'Been staying at my parents. Got here last night.'

'Where are Alex and Lucia?' Nate asked, wanting to be prepared.

Owen stood and clapped Nate on the shoulder.

'Hey man, Alex is running late, obviously, and I don't know about Lucia. She's a rule unto herself.'

'Need some help with that?' Nate indicated the barbeque and the pile of coals stacked haphazardly in the middle.

Owen handed him the firelighters and the matches wordlessly. 'I cannot take you seriously with that mask on.'

'Uh, I prefer it if you address me as Donny, or Donatello,' he said. 'Either way, once this is lit, I want to meet Angeline, Paul.'

'And we both want to meet *your* girl.' Owen grinned. 'Although I'm not sure we'll get much of a look in. Jess has been beside herself since you emailed.'

Nate glared at his friend. 'Look, I'm going to say this once. Laurel and I are not together. She needed a break, so I brought her here. As a friend. We're friends. That's it.'

'Okay, okay! Sorry, man!' Paul held his hands up in mock surrender. 'She's attractive though.'

'I know what she looks like, thank you,' he snapped, glaring at his friend.

Paul and Owen exchanged knowing looks and crowed with laughter.

'I think it's time I got some new friends, you bastards,' he grumbled. 'Actually, while we're at it, do you have another room for her?'

Owen just grinned. 'Nah, sorry, all rooms are taken.'

'Really? All of them?' he gestured behind him to the massive farmhouse.

'Yep,' Owen took a swig of his beer.

Paul sniggered behind his hand, earning another glare from Nate.

'An airbed? A blanket? Anything.'

Owen clapped him on the shoulder. 'Don't worry man. I'll make sure you're sorted.'

Nate nodded and shuffled the coals around in the barbeque, trying to make it so they were in a little pile and pushed a few firelighters in. Yeah, he was sure Owen would make sure he was 'sorted'. Mmm hmm.

He looked over to check on Laurel. Benji was demonstrating some of his Teenage Mutant Ninja Turtles moves to Laurel (rapt), Angeline (confused) and Jess (indulgent). He smiled.

LAUREL

Benji was just the cutest. He was tall and gangly for his age, with Jess' dark hair and Owen's full lips, and he was the most amazing Leonardo Laurel had ever seen.

'I'm going to be a ninja, Laurel,' he said, for the third time.

'Benji, darling, why don't you have some TV time for a bit?' Jess suggested, and his eyes lit up. 'You've got thirty minutes, okay?'

He scampered off, leaving one of his plastic swords lying in the grass.

'He's adorable,' Angeline said.

She was exotic in that pale and interesting way, with light brown hair that fell most of the way down her back, milky skin and clear blue eyes. The way she looked at Paul as well, Laurel could tell that they were absolutely smitten with each other.

Laurel glanced over at Nate at the barbeque and laughed out loud, pointing at him when Jess and Angeline both looked at her quizzically. The other two women burst out laughing as well, and all three men looked at them before heading over.

'What's so funny?' Owen asked, perching on the arm of Jess' rattan chair. Her garden furniture was a beautiful dark grey woven set, with cushions covered in green and pink mandalas. It was like they were in an incredibly beautiful Grecian story.

Paul kissed Angeline full on the mouth, like he couldn't let his lips be away from hers for any longer. Nate sat next to Laurel on the low sofa, and she burst out laughing again.

'What?' He frowned at her.

'I just—' She tried to catch her breath. 'I cannot take you seriously with that mask on.'

The purple mask was little more than a piece of fabric with eye holes cut into it, tied around his face, but him wearing it and chatting away normally to Owen and Paul was the most hilarious thing.

Nate touched his face, seemingly surprised that he was actually still one of the Teenage Mutant Ninja Turtles. He smiled sheepishly and tugged it off over his head.

'When a kid hands you a Teenage Mutant Ninja Turtle mask, you put it on.' He shrugged.

She laughed. 'Your hair, it's all…'

Nate smoothed it down, extremely badly.

'No, it's not—'

He attempted to smooth the other side down, frowning.

'Oh, for god's sake,' she said, exasperated, and reached up to flatten a stray lock of hair that he'd missed.

Laurel did not miss the meaningful look that passed between Jess and Owen, and fought to keep a blush down. Did Nate's friends think they were together? Was she being too obvious? She should have kept her hands to herself and let him look stupid. She didn't want to put Nate in an awkward situation, and certainly didn't want his friends to see something between them that wasn't there. He had made it perfectly clear that she was there as his friend, and that was that.

She shuffled away from him, putting a little space between them, and straightened the skirt of her dress over her legs. Jess was wearing a pair of cut off denim shorts with a white lacy top and whilst Laurel could tell they weren't Primark, they were certainly not designer. In fact, nothing about Jess or Owen, or their house, was pretentious, they were just normal people with a lot of money. The barbeque was a battered old thing that had seen better days, and the house was big but homely.

They'd obviously spent money on Benji, making sure he had the best they could afford – the house was filled with toys, and they had bought him a farm for crying out loud, but who wouldn't? If Laurel had money, and a child, then she'd spend every penny making sure that child was happy. There was a hint of spoiled-ness about the boy, but surely, wasn't every only child that little bit spoiled? They didn't get hand-me-downs, they didn't have to share, and all their parents' attention was on them. Although, it must be lonely to grow up without any siblings.

Yeah, she'd spent a lot of her childhood mothering Robin, but they'd had some really good times. Days spent swimming in the lake and picnics with Jack, until he got too old and started helping on the farm. Pirates, cowboys, spacemen. Whatever Robin wanted. As much as she moaned about her brothers, she loved them, and she loved their childhood.

'You alright?' Nate asked quietly, snapping her back to

the present. Owen telling some ridiculously convoluted story that was only funny to the four of them who had been at uni together.

'Yeah, good.' She nodded.

'You want another?' he indicated her nearly empty wine glass.

'Yes, Owen, grab another bottle, would you?' Jess said, elbowing Owen off the arm of her chair.

'Whatever your command, my love.' He bowed away from her. 'Guys? Another beer?'

'I'll help,' Nate said, leaving Laurel on the sofa. Paul reluctantly followed.

Jess watched her friends head into the house.

'He's completely smitten,' she said.

Laurel grinned at Angeline. 'He is, and you two are so cute together.'

'No, I meant Nate.'

Laurel spluttered on her wine. 'Uh, no, no, I don't think so. We're friends.'

'I've known Nate a long time, and he doesn't bring just anyone to meet us.' Jess smiled.

'I don't, we're not,' Laurel took a breath. 'I needed a break, and Nate suggested I come here. Seriously, we're just friends.'

'Okay,' Jess said, knowingly.

What could she say to that? Jess wouldn't believe her anyway.

They were quiet for a moment, and Laurel fiddled with the stem of her empty wine glass. Eventually, Angeline broke the awkward silence.

'Paul told me about who would be here today. Are you expecting Alex and Lucia, is it?'

Jess nodded, draining the dregs of her wine. 'Yeah, both of them are always late. Alex because he's a lazy shit, and Lucia because she floats through life being beautiful and successful.'

Laurel and Angeline shared a look. Weren't Jess and Lucia supposed to be friends?

'Don't get me wrong,' Jess said. 'I adore Lucia. I do, but she is always late. She'll be the first to admit it.'

'The only thing I remember about Lucia from uni is that her and Nate were this golden couple,' Laurel said. Okay, she was prying a little.

'I don't remember you from then,' Jess said, tilting her head and frowning.

'No, I'm a couple of years younger.' Laurel coughed, a little embarrassed.

'Yeah, well they were, but after uni it wasn't the same. Uni's like this surreal bubble, and university relationships don't last after university unless you both want the same things, both change to accommodate the real world,' Jess said, with surprising insight.

Laurel gazed at her. She was right. University was a surreal, kind of out-of-body experience. You live with random people, don't have the pressures of the real world, have somewhere to go home to, are still a dependent, really.

Her friendship with Rebecca had survived, but there was no one else she kept in touch with from uni. People frittered away, finding new lives, new friends. It was nice that this little group had kept in touch, and she guessed it was Jess who was the driving force behind that.

The men returned with the drinks and they slipped into easy conversation.

It all became a little less easy about half an hour later when a soft, feminine voice floated to them, followed by a douche-y male voice.

'Hola, hola! We're here!'

'Get the party started!'

As if summoned, Lucia appeared, followed by Alex.

CHAPTER SIXTEEN

NATE

Laurel had been laughing so hard at Paul's story that she couldn't catch her breath, and Nate had grabbed her glass from her hand. This was exactly why he had invited her, so she could relax, have fun.

But she stiffened ever so slightly at the sound of Alex's voice.

Jess squealed and jumped up to embrace Lucia.

'Lu! You could have come earlier you know.' It was a gentle jibe at the fact that she was so desperately late. Way past acceptably late.

'Oh, I know darling girl, but I just got waylaid,' Lucia said, returning her hug with gusto.

'This is from the both of us,' Alex said, reaching around Lucia to hand a bottle of wine to Owen, a smirk on his face, trying to indicate exactly why they were late. Probably because Lucia couldn't possibly bring herself to be on time for anything because the world revolved around her, rather than Alex getting his leg over.

'Paul, my man, how are you?' Alex cried, pumping Paul's hand vigorously. 'And this must be the beautiful Angeline.' He reached for her hand and planted a kiss on the back of it. 'Enchanté,' he said, with the worst possible French accent.

Nate tried not to roll his eyes.

'Angeline,' Lucia gushed, bending over and hugging her

on the sofa. 'So nice to finally meet you, Paul has said so much about you.'

Laurel put her glass on the low table to the side of the sofa in readiness for hand shaking or hugging.

'Oh, sorry, Nate, didn't see you there. How are you, old man?' Alex asked disinterestedly.

Nate stood up and stuck out his hand, making a show of being the bigger person here. The last time they'd spoken it had been tense, to say the least.

'I'm good thanks, Alex, you?'

'Yeah, you know.' Alex shook Nate's hand lazily. 'Laurel,' he said by way of greeting, running his eyes over her dirtily. Nate's jaw clenched.

'Do you want a drink, guys?' Owen asked.

'Yes, go on then,' Alex said, settling himself in a chair, one ankle crossed over his knee.

Lucia turned to face him and a small seductive smile crossed her face. Christ, she wasn't going to make this easy, was she?

'Nate,' she said breathily. 'It's been way too long.'

She hugged him, turning her face into his neck and pressing her body against him. Nate patted her awkwardly on the back. What was she doing? She never hugged him like this, usually it was a brief squeeze and then she'd move on as if she had something better to do.

'Lucia, hi,' he said, extricating himself. 'How are you?'

He was polite and gave her a tight, if slightly confused, smile.

'Really good thanks, so nice to be back in England for a little bit.' She flipped her curls over her shoulder and looked at Laurel as if she'd only just noticed her. 'Oh, you're new.'

You're new? What was that?

'Hi, I'm Laurel.'

If there was one thing about Laurel, it's that she was a people pleaser, but he knew she was nervous, especially with Lucia's frosty greeting.

'Hello.' Lucia draped herself on the arm of Alex's chair, his arm resting lazily around her hips, a teasing smirk playing on his face. 'I'm Lucia, Nate and I go way back.'

Nate sat down a little closer than was absolutely necessary to Laurel, a buffer because his ex-girlfriend was being really weird.

'Yes, I remember, I went to university with you. I was a couple of years below you,' Laurel said.

'I don't remember you at all,' Lucia said, accepting a glass of wine from Owen. 'What did you do? Archaeology? Are you an archaeologist now?' Taking a sip, Lucia's eyes widened in mock realisation. 'Oh, no, no, no! Alex said you work on a farm!'

Alex snorted into his drink.

'Yes,' Laurel said easily, but he could feel the tension building. 'I do.'

'That's interesting,' Owen said, leaning forward, oblivious to the snideness coming from the other end of the little coffee table. 'Sheep, cows, pigs? Or do you grow crops?'

Laurel smiled at him in relief. 'All of the above.'

'But it's not just that,' Nate jumped in. 'It's a massive business with a cafe and farm shop, a conference centre, a lake, they do weddings, Pick Your Own, and of course that's where I'm digging. Laurel runs all of that.'

She looked up at him, unreadable.

'Thank you, Nate,' she said pointedly. What? 'Yes, Little Willow Farm isn't just a working farm anymore.'

'But regardless, everything still stinks of shit,' Alex said, guffawing like he was hilarious.

'Alex,' Nate warned.

'You get used it, being around it all the time. You get that, don't you, Alex?' Laurel said blithely.

It was silent for just a second too long. Jess laughed, breaking the awkward tension. Lucia flicked through her phone. Paul stared wide-eyed between Laurel and Alex, whose face was thunderous, but Nate couldn't help but smile.

'I hate to bring up work, but I just wanted to say thank you for endorsing Little Willow Farm, Alex. We very much appreciate it.'

Good on Laurel, holding out the olive branch. Hopefully Alex would be big enough to accept it.

'Yeah, well,' he took a swig of his beer. 'It wasn't a given, you nearly didn't. I mean, it's not an ideal site, is it? It's not an ideal anything really.'

Nate rolled his eyes. Couldn't Alex keep himself in check? Paul frowned at Nate, clearly sensing the change in their relationship. He shook his head slightly in the universal signal for 'I'll tell you later'.

'You've found bones, I presume?' Lucia piped up. Laurel opened her mouth to say something, but Lucia carried on. 'When I was in Cambodia…' she started but Nate tuned out.

He'd heard all of Lucia's stories before, and they all ended the same way - her finding something amazing/mothering a lost child/saving a village from water drought/having to perform an emergency arm amputation so someone doesn't get trampled by wildebeest or something equally ridiculous. Angeline was enthralled.

Benji bounded up to them and Owen pulled him onto his knee, whispering something in his ear.

'Laurel, Daddy says that you're a farmer. Do you want to see my cows?' Benji asked, jumping up.

Owen looked sheepish.

'I didn't say she was a farmer, Benji. I said she ran a farm,' he said, rubbing the back of his neck. But Laurel just laughed.

'Of course I do, Benji. Lead the way.'

She let the boy take her hand and lead her away across the garden.

Nate was going to have a few brief words with Alex and Lucia.

LAUREL

Laurel's mind was absolutely all over the place as she walked across the garden, hand in hand with Benji as he led her excitedly towards what he called 'the cow house'.

There was Lucia, with her glossy chestnut Latina curls and beautiful, dark, soulful eyes. How could she get away with wearing what essentially looked like a hemp sack? Somehow, she pulled it off, swishing in to give Nate the weirdly intimate hug, punctuated with the clanging of bangles and anklets. Perhaps she still had a thing for him?

The thing that was the most annoying, however, was the fact that Lucia had the tiniest, silver septum piercing. It didn't make her look like a bull with a ring through her nose. No, it accentuated her golden skin and her ridiculously full, rosy lips. She probably got it from somewhere like Addis Ababa in a special ceremony or something.

It was extremely unprofessional to talk about work in a social setting, but she had wanted to thank Alex and hopefully make it good so they could enjoy the weekend. But those snide comments about her working on a farm and smelling like shit? What was he, twelve?

Laurel had been all prepared to let that go for the sake of the weekend, especially after the 'you're not just a farm girl' discussion she and Nate had in the car earlier. But no, Nate had to go and jump in and be a saviour, going on about everything there was at Little Willow Farm. Well, she didn't need a saviour, and by doing so he damn well proved that status did matter to him. That he felt embarrassed by her being just a farm girl.

Perhaps it was good that she found this out now so she could take a step back, nurse her broken heart and move on.

Perhaps she was overreacting.

'We've got four cows and three of them are in the field, and one of them is pregnant in the cow house. Mr Stapleton says it's a big one,' Benji said knowingly.

'Mr Stapleton?' Laurel snapped her attention back to the boy.

'Yeah, he helps us with the animals.'

Benji tugged at her hand, urging her to go faster.

'Benji, Laurel, wait for me,' Nate called from behind her. He was jogging through the garden to them, stupid salt and pepper hair flapping beautifully in the breeze. When he got to them, he touched her elbow lightly. 'You okay?'

'Mmm hmm.' No, she was not. She was annoyed with him.

'Look, I'm sorry about Alex and Lucia, they're just—' He pulled a hand through his hair. 'I don't know what they are, but I'm beginning to see them, Alex especially, in a new and very unflattering light.'

What did he expect her to say to that?

'Right,' she murmured.

He frowned at her.

'What's the matter? Are you okay?' Nate waited.

'Hey Benji, why don't you run ahead to see if Mr Stapleton is there?' she said to the boy, who pouted but ran off.

Laurel turned back to Nate.

'I don't need you, or Jack, or my father, or anyone else for that matter, to defend me,' she started. 'I don't need a saviour.'

'A saviour? What are you talking about?'

Really? Was he that stupid?

'You had to jump in to tell your high-flying friends that I wasn't just a farm girl, so I wouldn't embarrass you, yeah?' she hissed.

His face screwed up like newspaper.

'That's not it at all, Laurel. Not at all. I would never be embarrassed by you,' he said earnestly. 'You've accomplished so many amazing things. I just wanted people to know that,' Nate shook his head and looked around, as if searching for divine inspiration. 'I was embarrassed at how Alex and Lucia were treating you, acting like they were malicious, jealous teenagers. Pathetic.' He shook his head. 'But embarrassed? By you? No. Never.'

He looked back at her, holding her gaze defiantly. She assessed him warily.

'Right, well I need to go and see Benji in the cow house.' She took a few steps away from him, before turning back, 'Thanks for bringing me here, Nate.'

As she walked up to the cow house, she tugged her phone out of her bag and googled how far the local train station was. Christ, that would be an expensive taxi ride.

'Laurel, don't be like this!' Nate jogged after her. 'I have absolutely had enough of Alex acting like a fucking twat all the time. I'm not letting him get away with it anymore, and I'm sorry you got caught in the crossfire just now.'

Laurel crossed her arms over her chest and raised her eyebrows at him.

'I just think it's amazing what you've built at Little Willow Farm and wanted to tell my friends. You won't blow your own trumpet, so I wanted to do it for you.'

Laurel watched Nate colour slightly. He was impressed by her? Perhaps what Jess had said was right, and Nate had brought her to meet his friends because he, what, liked her? But he had made it clear that this was a friends thing.

What was she supposed to say?

'Uncle Nate, Laurel, come on!' Benji cried.

Nate looked over her shoulder and pasted a smile on his face.

'Coming, mate,' he said and his eyes fell back on hers. 'Look, if you don't want to be here, I'll take you home. Or if you don't want me to, I'll organise something else for you. I just thought you could do with a break.'

Nate took off to Benji, leaving her standing in the ridiculously large garden.

Well, now she felt like a shitbag. She'd had a go at him, and all he was trying to do was help. That's what friends do, wasn't it? He was there for her through the George Hibbert fiasco, a quiet, solid presence that she knew she could turn to. If only her heart would stop clenching every time their skin brushed. Having Nate Daley as a friend was better than not having him at all, she supposed. She followed him quickly across the garden.

'Nate,' she called, and he turned, waiting for her to catch up. 'I'm sorry, alright? Sorry. Alex just puts me on edge.'

'Yeah, I get that,' Nate said. 'He's a dick.'

'I want to stay. I'm having a good time,' she said.

The worry on his face smoothed into a slight smile.

'Good,' he said, after a long moment. Nate slung an arm across her shoulders. 'Come on, let's go and see this pregnant cow.'

Laurel's stupid heart clenched again.

NATE

Laurel was so prickly sometimes. Couldn't she just accept his help? He hadn't lied; Laurel had built an amazing business, and quite frankly, Alex was a dick and needed putting in his place. Whatever. They were past it now and were standing in the farmhouse, with Stapleton, the farmer.

The others had joined them, and Owen was explaining how he had bought the farmhouse and some land. Even Alex was there, turning his nose up at the smell and Lucia was telling them about how she had bonded with a sacred Indian cow.

'Laurel here runs a farm,' Owen said and Laurel smiled at Stapleton.

'Hard work,' the old man told her, obviously dismissing her as a farmer, but Nate kept his mouth shut. He had learned his lesson there. 'Cattle?' Stapleton asked, and she nodded. 'How many head have you got?'

'Little over fifteen hundred,' she said.

His eyebrows raised into his grey hair. 'Oh, big farm then?'

'Little Willow is the biggest in the south,' she said proudly.

'We're arable as well, and diversified into different revenue streams.'

He looked confused. 'I thought Fletcher's Farm was the biggest in the south? I haven't heard of that one.'

'Well…' Was that embarrassment flushing up her neck? Embarrassment for commercialising her farm? 'We rebranded to a more family friendly name.'

'Are you Bill Fletcher's girl? I met him once at a show. Nice man,' Stapleton said.

Laurel broke into a grin.

'I am Bill Fletcher's girl, yes. Nice to meet you, Mr Stapleton.' She held out her hand and the old farmer shook it heartily.

'John, please,' he said. 'We had to parcel the land and sell it off. My kids didn't want anything to do with farming. Can't say I blame them. It's a tough business, so much paperwork and not much help anymore. Your dad has done the right thing, with all that diversification.'

She snorted.

'Oh, I had to fight tooth and nail. If Dad and my brother Jack had their way, the farm would be dying now,' Laurel hesitated. 'They don't like it. I'm not sure I like it, but the bottom line is that we need it.'

Stapleton nodded wisely.

'Laurel, come and see the pregnant cow.' Benji tugged at her hand, and she followed the boy into one of the side pens.

'The rest of the herd is over with our neighbouring farm now, but this young man here wanted to keep a few, so I sold his dad my favourites.' Stapleton ruffled Benji's hair. 'This is Penelope.'

'I call her Bessie the Cow,' Benji whispered loudly, and Stapleton smiled sadly.

Laurel ran her hand down the side of the cow.

'She's ready.'

'Won't be until tomorrow afternoon,' Stapleton said gruffly, obviously not liking the perceived challenge.

'Gosh, it's big,' she said. 'Do you have a history of calves this big in this herd?'

'No, this is unusual.' He ran a loving hand across the cow's neck.

As they were crowded around the pregnant cow in the cow house, Benji started saying about how he had renamed Stapleton's favourite cows, and Nate realised that this entire situation must be incredibly sad for Stapleton. To come in to work every day to his farm that he had to sell off because he couldn't make it work, to see the house that he probably brought up his children in turned into something else, his favourite animals having their names changed.

It must have been heartbreaking for him.

'Come on, you,' Jess said, grabbing for Benji's arm. 'Time for bed.'

It had gotten darker since they'd been in the cow house and after saying their goodbyes to Stapleton, who wandered off across the fields to wherever he now lived, they headed back to the seating area. The barbeque had long since been forgotten (as it always was) and Owen put the meat in the oven, making sure that everyone had wine or beer.

Jess reappeared sometime later with food, and flicked on the festoon lighting that encircled the seating area.

'Oh, these lights remind me of when I was working on the Bakoni Ruins of Machadodorp in Mpumalanga,' said Lucia, 'That's in South Africa,' she added for Laurel's benefit. 'We stayed at the Incwala Lodge, and they were so good to us.'

'Oh, yes?' Laurel said, and Lucia launched into some ridiculous story.

She droned on, but Nate tuned her out again. He pulled his phone out to see if his mother or Anwar had tried to get hold of him.

'I'm sorry. Am I boring you?' Lucia snapped, forcing his attention back to her.

'Lucia,' he sighed, 'we've heard it all before. How you helped the good people of Incwara Lodge with their irrigation system, the terraces that you helped excavate in lower Zimbabwe.'

There was a heavy silence in the garden as Lucia just looked at him, that ridiculous nose ring glinting in the festoon light.

'I didn't know you felt that way, Nate. That I'm boring everyone, boring my friends, boring you,' she said tightly.

'That's not what I meant,' he said, tilting his head.

'No, I think we all know what you meant, that you're too good for your old friends, now you've got a...' she assessed Laurel, 'shiny new plaything.'

'What the fuck are you talking about, Lucia?' He lent forwards, towards her.

'Alex told me what you did, Nate. Punching him? Really? Choosing some bit of skirt over your best friend?' Lucia flicked her eyes to Laurel in disdain.

Nate took a deep breath. 'Alex made some unsavoury comments. I asked him to stop and he didn't.'

'Oh, I'm sure Alex was just joking,' Lucia said, putting her hand on Alex's leg, like it would make him jealous or something. 'Weren't you, Alex?'

'Of course I was, Lu. I'm an enlightened man.' Alex's face erupted into a smug smile. 'Nate just doesn't understand comedy anymore.'

'Don't fucking start, Alex,' Owen said.

Jess rolled her eyes and Paul whispered something to Angeline. It had taken so long for him to see Alex for what he actually was, Nate was a little embarrassed. And now Lucia was the only one left who had it in her to defend him.

'Fuck off, Owen,' Alex said under his breath.

'What was that, Alex?' Jess snapped. 'Because if you told my husband to fuck off in his own house, you can leave. Right now.'

'Come on, I think things have all got a bit heated,' Lucia said. 'What about another drink, and we can all relax.'

Nate looked at Jess for guidance. It was her house, after all.

Jess narrowed her eyes at Alex. 'Alright, but no more shit from you.'

Laurel stood, brushing her skirt down. 'I'm going to leave you guys to it, head up to bed.'

'Laurel.' Nate tugged on her hand to sit. 'Stay.'

'No, it's okay.' She gave him a reassuring smile. 'I'll see you guys in the morning.'

'I'll show you up,' Jess said, glaring hard at Lucia.

Nate watched the swish of Laurel's skirt in the yellow glow of the lights as she went into the house with Jess, who was no doubt apologising for whatever the hell was going on.

'You've changed, Nate,' Lucia said bitterly, when Laurel and Jess had disappeared. 'As soon as there's a bit of skirt in your eye line, you change everything about who, and what you are. Alex can see it, I can see it, we can all see it.'

Paul coughed politely and shared a look with Nate that said 'what the actual fuck is she going on about'.

'Changed? What the fuck?' He spread his arms wide

'Nah, man. I saw it first hand,' Alex said, swigging from his bottle. 'You're not the same.'

'You know what? Perhaps I have changed, and that's alright,' Nate said. 'I've grown up, I've got different values, I want different things. In case you haven't noticed, we're not twenty-five anymore, and, unlike some, I'm not behaving like it.' He snapped his mouth shut and sat back in the garden sofa.

'What the fuck are you trying to say, Nathanial?' Alex drawled from his position next to Lucia.

'That it might be time for you to grow the fuck up, Alexander.'

Nate downed his drink. 'Sorry, Owen,' he said and headed into the house.

CHAPTER SEVENTEEN

LAUREL

Laurel did *not* want to get involved in whatever that was. They were Nate's friends. He could deal with that. With friends like that, who needed enemies? Why did Jess and Owen even keep Alex and Lucia around? All it seemed they did was cause drama. Jess had fallen over herself apologising for her guest and almost pleading with her not to take it to heart. Lucia was used to being the centre of the world, and here was Laurel, all beautiful and kind and successful, with Nate. Laurel had protested that they were just friends, but Jess just waved that away. A rather tipsy Jess left her at her door, Laurel reassuring her that she was okay, that it was fine, she absolutely did not care what Lucia thought. Which was mostly the truth.

Besides, she was slightly tipsy herself, and bed was calling. Laurel kicked off her shoes and grabbed her case.

Wait.

Why were there two cases sat nicely against the door? Whose was that one? Surely, surely, her and Nate weren't sharing a room with only one bed? Ah, there was a blanket and a couple of pillows on the chaise lounge so one of them would have to sleep there. Although it was very small.

Regardless, she was going to have to take her makeup off and get changed. Oh god. She had grabbed the first thing that had come to hand; the wine-coloured satin cami and short set Rebecca had got her. Well, that was that then. Laurel was tiddly enough that she wasn't even that shy about him seeing her in those short shorts and lacy top.

Laurel pulled her phone out and called Rebecca.

'Oh my god, why are you calling me? You should be having fun, Laurel.' Rebecca didn't even say 'hi'.

'I am. I've just come up to bed and wanted to talk to you,' she said, flopping onto the bed. 'I'm on a farm. Nate's friends live on a farm.'

'Uh, what do you mean? Up to bed?'

'Rebecca, you won't believe this. He didn't tell me it was an overnight thing.' She dropped her voice to a whisper. 'We're in a room with only one frigging bed.'

'You couldn't write that shit.' Rebecca cackled down the phone. 'You should one hundred percent jump him!'

'Uh no,' Laurel said, flopping back on the bed. 'Did you and Jack have date night tonight?'

'Aah, look at you sister-in-law, away with a handsome man and worried about your best friend.' Rebecca was enjoying this way too much. 'To answer your question, we did.'

'And?'

Jack had better have got his act together and realised that Rebecca was the best thing to ever happen to him, and that he needed to treat her better.

'We've booked a holiday.' Laurel could hear Rebecca smiling down the phone.

Laurel sat straight up, shocked. 'You have not! Where? When?'

'October half term, a week in Spain. It was even Jack's suggestion.'

That was amazing news. After years and years of only Rebecca going away because Jack was insistent that he couldn't leave the farm, he'd finally realised that they needed a break. They needed family time, all together. He needed to be Jack the father, Jack the husband, not Jack the farm manager. He also needed to relax.

'No frigging way. That's amazing, Rebecca, I'm so happy for you.'

'Yeah, I know. He's really listened. We're even going away for a weekend as well, just the two of us. He's going to book it. It'll be a surprise.'

'No way. Where is your husband and what have you done to him?' This was not the Jack she knew. It was a new and improved Jack, and Laurel was fully there for it.

Rebecca's voice quietened. 'After Nate opened his eyes a little bit, pointed him in the right direction, I think Jack got a bit scared I would take the kids and leave him,' she said quietly. 'I wouldn't. I mean of course I wouldn't. But it worried him.'

She had never thought Rebecca would leave her brother, but now it had been said, Laurel could fully see it. Jack, inattentive and taking her for granted, would have been oblivious.

'If you ever did need to do that for you and the kids, I would support you, yeah? I wouldn't be judgmental.' Laurel followed up quickly. 'Don't get me wrong, I would be forever trying to get you and Jack back together, but I would be there for you.'

What sounded suspiciously like a teary sob came down the phone. 'You're the best best-friend-slash-sister-in-law anyone could ever wish for.'

'I love you too, Rebecca.' Laurel smiled.

'Enough of that. You are staying in a room with only. One. Bed. Please tell me you took the sexy pjs?'

Laurel groaned. 'It was the first thing that came to hand. I was in a rush!'

'Laurel, I need you to do something for me,' Rebecca said. 'I need you to put on your big girl pants and get some sexy times on the go with Nate Daley.'

Laurel blew out a harsh breath. 'Rebecca, I don't think he—'

'No. Stop there. I've seen the way he looks at you, with

his greedy eyes. He's desperate for your smile all the time, hanging on your every word. He's taken you to meet his friends, overnight. Be brave, my girl.' Rebecca clapped her hands. 'Also, you really need to get laid.'

Laurel snorted a laugh. Rebecca was right.

'But what if he doesn't—'

'He does, Laurel.'

'But if he—'

'Laurel,' she said. 'He *does*.'

She pinched the bridge of her nose and didn't say anything. He'd told her she was beautiful. They'd had *moments*. The long looks at her mouth, the way his eyes tripped across her collarbone, his strong hands in her hair.

And she was just tipsy enough to ignore the fact that it was a bad, bad idea. She could have sex with Nate, once, and it would be fine. They would just carry on like normal. There wouldn't be any awkwardness, her heart wouldn't become dangerously close to breaking. It would be fine. Fine.

Rebecca was right. She really needed to get laid.

'Now, go and put on that sexy satin set. I'll talk to you tomorrow.'

The door to the room opened and closed whilst she was sorting herself out in the en-suite.

'Laurel?' Nate called, knocking gently on the door.

'Two minutes,' she said back, finishing off rubbing in the moisturiser on her face. She counted to sixty, twice, to ensure that it was two minutes and she didn't look like an eager puppy dog waiting for Nate to arrive.

When she opened the door, Nate was sat on the edge of the tiny chaise lounge that he'd made up as a bed, elbows resting on his knees, head bowed. His pyjama bottoms sat low on his hips and there was a light dusting of hair over his bare chest. Laurel definitely did not stare.

'Laurel, I've got to apologise,' Nate said, raising his eyes to meet hers. He blinked a couple of times at her, his jaw slack. 'You look…'

'Yes?' she asked, raising an eyebrow at him and certainly, most definitely, keeping her eyes on his face. He shook his head a little, as if clearing it, and started again.

'Fuck,' he breathed, his eyes darting over her chest, her legs and back up to her face. He swallowed.

Come on, Laurel.

The cream carpet was plush under her feet as she took three slow steps towards him. He sat up straighter as she nudged his knees apart with her legs, coming to a stop between them. Nate was flushed and pink as he looked up at her, lips parted. His fingers slid against the softness behind her knees, and it was electric. Dragging her fingers against the stubble of his jaw, she gently urged him to standing. There was a sliver of air between them, and a deep breath would have her hardened nipples brushing his bare chest through the satin of her top. Nate's hands tightened around her waist, and he wet his lip.

Taking the smallest step closer, Laurel pressed her hips against him and a strangled groan came from his throat. She ran her fingers across his chest and explored his collarbone, feeling how his breathing caught and juddered under her touch. Hardness grew against the bottom of her stomach and she bit her lip, looking up at him coyly. His eyes had darkened, watching her explore him with heated desire. A warm hand slipped underneath her top and pushed firmly against her back, pressing her to him.

She couldn't tear her eyes away from his mouth.

'You should probably kiss me, Dr Daley,' she breathed.

She heard a strangled *god yes* before his mouth crashed against hers

It was hard and fast, his lips moving against hers, his tongue probing against her lips. She opened her lips and whimpered as his tongue pressed softly into her mouth. The kiss became deeper, more breathless, and she reached up on her toes to wind her arms around his neck, desperate to get closer to him. A strong hand slid down her leg and hitched under her knee, bringing her leg up around his waist. The friction against her thin shorts wasn't enough and she squirmed against him. His teeth nipped at her lip before he angled her head so he could slide his cheek across hers and run his nose down her neck, breathing her in. A moan came from her throat.

'I've wanted to kiss you here for so long,' he murmured against her throat.

In between hot breaths, she managed to force out a whispered, 'Have you?'

'So long.' His hand was splayed across her ribs and grazed the underside of her breast with long, teasing strokes. Her back arched, wanting more, wanting *anything*, needing friction. He smiled against her neck and planted kisses on the length of her jaw, finding her lips again.

'Fuck,' he said under his breath, and she smiled as his cock twitched in his thin pyjamas. She stood in front of him, a deep breath and her nipples would be brushing against him.

'Laurel,' he whispered, dark eyes fixated on her lips.

Laurel placed her hands on him gently, let them glide up his chest, curl over his shoulders, up the back of his neck and into his hair. She pressed her body against his, his erection straining against her lower abdomen. His fingertips trailed her back, sensuously over her rear, slipping just under the hem of top, bringing her closer to him.

She pushed her lips to his, her tongue seeking entrance to his mouth, gladly given with a low groan from the back of his throat. It was urgent, hot, and she couldn't get close enough to him.

Nate dragged his teeth across her bottom lip and turned her suddenly, pressing her back to his chest, his arm wound around her. His lips roamed her neck, one hand firmly holding her in place on her hip, the other splaying across her ribs, grazing the underside of her breast. Her back arched against him, trying to tell him that she wanted his hand, his fingers, anything, on her tender nipples. She wove one arm around the back of his neck and tilted her head to allow him better access.

Nate dragged his fingers, agonisingly slowly, across the

bud of her breast, and her breath caught in her throat as he pinched it, just the right side of pain.

'Nate.' She cried.

'Mmm,' he murmured, rolling her nipple resolutely between his fingers. The other hand slid to her rear, stroking and squeezing, pulling her hard against him.

'How do you want me first?' he asked roughly, teeth nipping at her ear lobe, and her core clenched. Hard. 'Fingers, tongue, cock?'

Laurel couldn't help the whimpering.

'Everything,' she rasped out. She would explode as soon as he touched her. She was so wet and ready for him. Her legs trembled in anticipation.

'Good girl,' he whispered, pinching her nipple harder, making her jerk against him.

Good girl? God yes.

What was he doing to her? She was melting, hot and desperate, her hips rolling against his abdomen, his cock straining against her. Jagged breaths escaped his throat and she was desperate, greedy for his touch. She would beg if she had to. She needed him to touch her.

He was sliding the strap of her cami off her shoulder when he froze at the knock at the door.

'What the fuck,' Nate mumbled.

'Laurel? Nate? Are you awake?' came a muffled Jess.

This had got to be a joke. They were so close, not quite, but nearly in the middle of sex.

'No, fuck off, we're busy,' Nate called harshly, hands unmoving on her.

'I'm really sorry, but it's important,' Jess said through the door.

He sighed heavily and kissed her neck one more time.

'I'm sorry, baby,' he whispered against her skin and stalked over to the door, yanking it open abruptly. 'What?'

'Oh god, I'm sorry, I—' Jess started, not knowing where to look, because quite frankly, it was patently obvious what they had been doing. Nate's thin pyjamas did not leave much to the imagination.

'Shit,' he said under his breath and hid his lower half behind the door.

Laurel grabbed Nate's zip up hoodie that was thrown over a chair and slid her arms through it, trying to calm her racing heart and bite down on her disappointment.

'What's the matter?' Laurel asked, opening the door wider and giving Jess a tight smile. There was nothing she could do about her swollen, just-kissed lips and not-quite-sated glaze to her eyes.

Jess was wringing her hands together.

'It's Bessie the Cow, she's got a baby cow's leg sticking out of her and Alex and Owen are talking about pulling it out,' she said desperately, as Laurel rushed past her. 'Alex said not to get you, that he'd watched a YouTube video,' she called, but Laurel was already down the stairs, through the house and out of the back door.

What the fuck did these city boys think they knew about birthing heifers? They could seriously damage her, maybe even kill her and the calf. A fucking YouTube video?

The grass was dewy and cold against her bare feet and Nate was calling her name behind her, but she couldn't slow down, couldn't stop, not until she skidded to a halt outside the door of the stables.

Alex was giggling drunkenly, videoing the poor cow with one calf leg sticking out of her. Owen was holding the birthing chains like they were some kind of poisonous snake. Lucia was lounging against one of the stable doors, her foot propped elegantly on a little stool, looking cool, calm and fucking collected, a glass of wine in her delicate fingers.

'What the fuck do you think you're doing?' Laurel snarled.

Owen dropped the birthing chains with a clatter.

NATE

By the time he'd pulled on a hoodie, run outside and reached Laurel, she was pulling on wellies. Owen was unfocused, a little shaky and red eyed, the alcohol clearly tiring him out.

'Why the fuck have you got her, Jess? We had it under control,' Alex spat.

Owen snapped to.

'Don't speak to my wife like that,' he said, pointing a wavering finger at Alex. Even Lucia was standing up straight, watching Alex and Owen, wide-eyed.

Laurel swooped to pick up some chains from the floor and stroked her hand down the side of the cow, murmuring softly. True enough, there was a leg sticking out of its back end.

'Have you phoned the vet?' she said.

'No, and Stapleton didn't answer,' Owen said, like a scolded schoolchild.

'Fucking Stapleton. This is his actual job,' Alex chugged on his beer and slung an arm over Lucia's shoulders, who rolled her eyes. Huh, so much for that liaison.

'Mr Stapleton is over seventy, and no, it is not his actual job to be on call twenty-four-seven,' Laurel snapped. 'Bring me the phone and the vet's number.'

Owen scurried as fast as he could.

Jess found Nate some of Owen's too small wellies and he forced his feet into them.

'What can I do?' he asked, standing not so close that the cow could kick him if she wanted to, but close enough.

'Nothing, yet,' Laurel said, pressing her small hands to the swollen side of the cow.

Owen emerged from the office and held out a portable phone to Laurel.

'Here you are, it's ringing,' he said, chastised. Laurel wedged it under her chin, looking at the cow's backside and the leg sticking out of it.

'We could have done it. I don't see what the big deal is,' Alex muttered to Lucia.

Nate whirled on him. 'If you don't have anything supportive or helpful to say, keep your fucking mouth shut.'

He was done with Alex and his shit. Absolutely done. He'd had his lips on Laurel, her leg around his waist. She had wanted him, and Alex had fucking ruined it.

Alex pushed off the wall and strutted closer to him, puffing up his chest. 'So now I can't even exercise my right to free speech?'

'Don't be a dick, Alex,' Nate said, shaking his head, but not taking a step backwards.

Jess pushed her hands through her hair and stepped between them, her back to Nate's chest.

'Guys, come on. We're all tired and drunk,' she said. 'Let's not get into it tonight, yeah?'

Alex sneered at Jess, fucking sneered, at one of his oldest friends and Nate wondered what had gone wrong in Alex's life to mean that he was like this. How had he gone from carefree and lovable, to bitter and spiteful? Or had he always been like this, and Nate had just turned a blind eye? Alex's vitriol was mostly directed towards Laurel. Was there more to the story about Alex and her in university than Nate knew about? He'd ask, but now was not the time.

'Whatever, man,' Alex said, sauntering back to Lucia.

She narrowed her eyes at Nate and leaned into Alex's side, tilting her head and cocking her eyebrow defiantly. If that was supposed to make him jealous or chastised, or whatever, it really wasn't working. He put his hand on Jess's shoulder and turned her to face the cow, their backs on Alex and Lucia.

'What's wrong with him?' Jess whispered.

'Fuck knows,' he whispered back, training his eyes on Laurel. Owen hovered with a pair of long, clear, plastic gloves and a plastic apron.

'Yes, the old Stapleton Farm,' Laurel was saying to the vet. 'Yes, I'm Bill Fletcher's daughter.'

Bill Fletcher was famous in farming, obviously.

'Not for an awfully long time,' she said, her voice climbing higher. 'But you'll come as soon as you can?' Laurel nodded. 'Okay. Thank you.'

She handed the phone back to Owen who pushed it into his back pocket. Nate held his breath as he looked at Laurel, waiting for her to say something.

'We're going to have to deliver this calf.' She visibly swallowed. 'Owen, I need ropes, I need those gloves, I need those chains. I need you guys to back up,' she said, ushering him backwards.

The cow mooed louder, obviously distressed. Whether it was because she was actually giving birth or because there were loads of people watching, Nate wasn't sure.

Owen produced some rope and Laurel quickly made up an impressive looking harness to tether the cow to a support on each side to keep her still.

She unzipped his hoodie and threw it at him, before pulling on the arm-length plastic gloves Owen had brought. He wished she'd put a bra on under that tiny scrap of satin before she'd rushed out of the room because he could feel Alex's dirty leer behind him. Nate turned his head and glared at him, silently warning Alex that he would kill him if he uttered one word about Laurel's breasts.

He passed the hoodie to Jess and stepped closer to Laurel.

'Can I help?' he asked quietly.

'Not yet.' Her eyes were on the leg sticking out of the cow. 'But I'll need you to help pull in a bit.'

Pull? Pull what?

'Oh, okay,' he said. She looked up at him with a tight smile.

'It's been a long time since I've done this,' she said, very quietly. 'And the last time it wasn't a massive calf, or half as difficult as this.'

'You can do it, it's all good. You've got this,' he said,

because quite frankly, Laurel Fletcher could do anything she put her mind to.

'Okay,' she said, more to herself than him. After pulling on the gloves, she braced one hand against the cow's arse.

Laurel gripped the hoof protruding out of the cow's behind and pushed it gently back inside, her arm disappearing inside with it. Nate tried to keep his face neutral, to ignore the sucking sounds of the cow's insides, and general disgust coming from behind him.

'Okay, I can feel the other hoof and head. Head is the right way.' Laurel shuffled to rearrange herself and her arm disappeared further into the cow. 'Okay, I've got both hooves now.'

Nate nodded, even though she wasn't really talking to him. 'Good, that's good.'

Her arm quivered as she pulled, and there, with a sucking noise, her hand came out, clutching two wet, slimy hooves. She pulled until they were both free of the cow and then rested her hands on her knees, out of breath.

'Right,' she said, brushing her hair out of her face and leaving a smear of cow juice across her forehead. 'This calf is really big. Owen, do you have a winch for the chains?'

Eyes swivelled to Owen who shrugged his shoulders, wide eyes trained on the rear end of the cow.

'Owen,' Laurel snapped his attention to her. 'Do you have a handle? Where did you find the chains? Bring me anything that was with them.'

She looked up at Nate as Owen stumbled off, rolling her eyes in exasperation.

'Oh for god's sake, I'll go,' Jess muttered, following her husband into the office.

'What's next?' he asked her.

'Doesn't it just flop out now? Give it a tug and it'll be done?' Alex called. Laurel ignored him.

'She needs some help because the calf is so big. I'll use the chains, but you'll have to help me okay?'

He wasn't going to have to stick his hand up the cows vagina was he? Because he would, for her, but he really didn't want to. Like, at all.

'I won't be able to pull it on my own, so you'll need to pull as well, okay?' Laurel said.

'Yes,' he said, nodding. Pulling was fine, he could pull stuff.

'I've got this, but that's all that was in the box marked "chains",' Jess said, holding up a curved metal hook.

'Brilliant, thanks,' Laurel said.

She wrapped the chains just above the ankles (is that what cows have?) of the calf sticking out of the cow and hooked it together tightly. 'Here you go.' She handed Nate the end of the chain, fitted with a handle.

'You'll have to tell me when,' he said, suddenly nervous. What if he couldn't get the calf out? What if it went wrong?

Laurel winched the little hook onto the middle of the chain and looked up at him with a determined smile.

'It's coming out one way or another, Nate,' she said. 'Pull when I tell you to.'

Her forearm tensed as she pulled on her handle, leaning backwards to get more weight behind it. No movement, but the cow made some urgent, low noises.

'Pull,' she ground out and he shifted his weight and pulled, gently at first. 'Harder than that, Nate,' she urged, and he leaned backwards, arms tense. There was a slight slithering sound and the legs of the calf pulled further out, followed by a nose and a mouth.

'Stop!'

Laurel swiped at the calf's face with one hand, wiping amniotic fluid out of its nose and mouth.

'Again.'

Laurel pulled and Nate followed suit, watching as the head popped out completely. Its eyes were closed and ears stuck back to his head, covered in slime, but it was amazing.

He pulled, straining on the chain, wondering belatedly if it hurt the poor calf's legs. They continued like this for some minutes, starting and stopping, letting the cow do some of the work, trying not to damage her. Well, at least that's what he assumed was happening.

Laurel didn't say a lot more other than 'pull' and 'stop' and whispering sweet nothings to the mother.

The baby slithered out some more, shoulders now showing and Laurel dropped her hook completely.

'Pull it downwards,' she said, pointing to the ground. 'That's it,' she said when he crouched down.

Was it going to flop out onto the floor? Surely that would hurt?

The calf's chest was out now, and Laurel was pushing and turning it down towards the ground.

'Turn your end too,' she commanded. Alright.

With one last pull, the calf flopped out onto the damp hay of the stables and Nate fell backwards onto his arse, also onto the damp hay of the stables.

Laurel was on the calf quickly, making sure its face was clear of all gunk and rubbing it vigorously on the chest. She grabbed its legs and started working them back and forth, making sure that everything was moving, before dragging it around by its forelegs to the head of the cow. She bent its front legs and laid the head gently on it, and then deftly removed the makeshift harness around the cow's head.

Mum started to lick the baby, and Laurel stood back, hands on hips, satisfied smile on her face.

Nate couldn't stop the smile spreading across his face as he sat there, watching the newborn calf. Helping Laurel made him feel so much more alive than he had felt in a long time.

LAUREL

The birth had gone well. The heifer was licking the calf, the limbs all worked fine and besides it being the biggest goddamn calf Laurel had ever seen, mum and baby were doing well. She peeled the gloves off and held her hand out to Owen for the phone. The vet answered in three rings.

'It's Laurel Fletcher at the old Stapleton Farm,' she said, unable to keep the smile out of her voice.

'That sounds like a positive birth,' the vet said, distressed horse noises in the background.

'Yes, everything went well, thank you,' Laurel frowned as one of the horses on the vet's end of the line kicked something viciously. 'I'll let you go. You sound busy.'

'Mum is licking? Joints movable?' The vet ignored Laurel's attempts to go.

'Yes, to both,' she said, very aware that she was standing in someone else's stables with cow amniotic fluid all over her, bits of hay stuck to her knees, and she was not wearing a bra.

'Okay, I'll come in tomorrow. Oh, today, thanks Laurel. Stapleton is lucky you were there,' the vet said and the line went dead. She handed the phone back to Owen.

Laurel stood in the middle of the stables, unsure what she should do next, except cross her arms over her chest so people couldn't see her nipples poking through the thin satin. It was the middle of the night, and she was cold.

There was a beat of silence.

'Well, I think we've got a lot to learn,' Jess said, putting her arm around a shell-shocked Owen.

Damn right they did.

How can you have animals if you can't care for them properly? Laurel did her best to keep her face still, because all eyes were still on her and she did not want Nate's friends to hate her with her raised eyebrows and judgmental looks.

'Perhaps you can help us, Laurel?' Jess asked hopefully. 'Put us in touch with someone who can train us? Tell us where to go? What to do?'

Laurel nodded.

'That, I can do,' she said, heading for the door to the

stables, thinking sarcastically that just perhaps Mr Stapleton might be the place to start.

'Is that it? Do we have to do anything else?' Owen asked, a little distraught at the idea of leaving the newborn calf with its mother. What did he think Penelope would do? Eat her own calf?

Laurel held in the eye roll and pasted a thin smile on her face.

'No, mother is licking, the joints are working. We can leave them to it now.'

'Is that what you were doing? Testing the joints?' he asked, timidly.

'Yeah.' She was tired and covered in goo, and this was not a conversation for now. 'I'll tell you about it tomorrow.'

Nate put his arm around her shoulders and edged her towards the door. He seemed eager to leave the stables, and honestly, she was as well. She'd had enough of Alex's leering glances and Lucia's marked indifference for one night. Besides, who knows what type of judgment or disgust would be lurking there as she stood, in all her glory, having just pulled a calf from a cow, and in the process, proved that yes, she was just a farm girl. A covered-in-cow-juice farm girl.

'I wouldn't get too close to her, Nate,' Alex said loudly, a smile hidden in his voice. 'She stinks of cow shit.'

Lucia smothered a laugh. Come on now, guys. Be better than this. Couldn't he think of anything more original to say? How pathetic.

Nate tensed his arm around her shoulder and she could feel his anger rising. Laurel leaned into him and shook her head softly. Alex wasn't worth it. Not one little bit. They carried on into the darkness of the garden and back to the house. Behind them, Owen had broken out of his shock and his voice rang out.

'Alex, you are a petty, ridiculous little man, aren't you? And you're no better, Lucia.'

'What the fuck do you mean by that?' Alex shouted.

'I'm sorry about him,' he said quietly to Laurel.

'Don't worry. It's not your fault. He's obviously a wanker,' she said. 'I just want to have a shower. I am covered in cow gunk.'

Nate snorted a laugh.

'Don't worry about it. Hey…' He stopped and looked at her. She was a little hazy around the edges, hair jagged and tousled, but she was beautiful with the moonlight shining just right across her cheekbones. 'You were brilliant just then. Absolutely brilliant.'

Her shoulders raised in a little shrug.

'It was nothing. Anyone would have done it.'

'No, Laurel,' he said, gripping the tops of her arms. 'Not anyone. You.'

'Okay, not anyone.' What was she supposed to say to that? 'Thank you.'

'But,' he grimaced slightly, 'you do have, um, cow juice on your face.'

On. Her. Face.

'Okay, I really need to shower,' she said, breaking out of his grip and hurrying back into the house.

Nate followed her up the stairs. 'I do as well. This stuff gets everywhere.'

'Um, you don't have anything I could wear, do you? My pyjamas are a bit icky.' Of course, she hadn't brought any spare sleeping clothes, because who would have guessed that Nate was bringing her to a farm where she'd have to birth a cow. Absolutely no one.

He grinned and dug a shirt from his case.

The shower was warm (not scalding) and she soaped everywhere, and washed her hair. Twice.

Jack would have been proud. It had been years since she'd been hands on (in) a cow giving birth, especially not a complicated birth of a massive calf like that one. The smile stilled on her face.

Had she been a bit strong with Jess and Owen? A bit too

angry with them for not knowing what to do? No. She was in the right, and if you're going to own animals, then you have to learn how to look after them. At least after tonight, it seemed that Jess and Owen were open to learning.

She dried herself, and pulled on Nate's shirt, undoing an extra button. Towel drying her hair, she scrunched it to give it a messy, wet look. It wasn't quite sexy underwear, but yes, this would work. Once Nate was done, they could pick up where they'd left off.

CHAPTER EIGHTEEN

NATE

If he'd thought the wine-coloured pyjamas were sexy, there was nothing that could have prepared him for wet-haired Laurel wearing nothing but his shirt. His cock had stiffened just at the sight of her.

Now, he stood in the shower, scouring his body free from cow gunk.

God, Laurel was impressive. She was passionate, knowledgeable, commanding and absolutely beautiful. She cared so much about everything and was, quite frankly, amazing. There was no other word for it, and the worst thing was that she didn't know it.

He'd brought her here as a favour because she needed to relax, and they were friends, right? That's what friends did.

What friends didn't do was kiss and stroke and nip at swollen lips. He couldn't stop thinking about the way her mouth had tasted, and how she had reacted to him, urging him to touch her with moans and sharp breaths. God, he wanted her.

But it was more than that.

A little thought at the back of his mind niggled at him. If he were truthful with himself, he'd brought her here to meet his friends for another reason, hadn't he? She'd shared so much of her life and he wanted to show her a little bit of his.

The hot water pulsed down on his shoulders as he investigated his feelings even further, slowly brushing away the layer of dirt obscuring the find underneath. Laurel well and truly triggered his defensive instinct. Whether it was George Hibbert, her knob of a brother Robin, or his longest friend, it didn't matter. But, why?

There was something more, something not quite enough to touch. He'd have to dig deeper, otherwise this confusion would linger and that was the last thing he needed. Nate was a clear-headed archaeologist, not a little lost lamb.

Laurel hadn't needed his help with the BAS endorsement. She was fully capable of dealing with it herself. But he didn't want her to have to deal with it by herself. She should have help, someone standing beside her to share the burden, to support her, to make her happy.

It should be him standing beside her, holding her hand.

What was it Jack had said about the way he looked at Laurel? The not-so-veiled comments Jess had made? Christ, even Anwar had made some snide little remarks that he'd waved off.

Laurel Fletcher had hidden herself within him, and he hadn't even realised it had happened.

He was in love with her, and that was a deep, hard, irrefutably evidenced find.

Just like every other discovery he had made since he'd met her, he wanted to share this with Laurel. Wanted to tell her about this amazing find that he'd just uncovered, so deep down it had taken an awfully long time to find.

Nate would have to talk to her, have to tell her. It was bursting out of his chest, trying to claw its way to her. He would lay his find at her feet and hope and hope and hope that she felt the same way.

What if she didn't? He couldn't think like that. He had to believe there was something there and all he had to do was blow the dust away and find it. Because otherwise, he would have the agony of working with her, being around her and knowing that she would forever be unattainable, she would forever not need him, not want him. Would he risk that? He would have to. He couldn't know this, feel this, and not tell her.

Also, they were too old for shit like hiding feelings, tiptoeing around each other, not being able to communicate effectively. They could be grown ups about this.

Nate closed the door to the en-suite softly behind him. Laurel had turned off the main light, and the bedside table gave a soft yellow glow over her where she lay in the bed.

Sleeping.

So much for his speech.

He snapped off the bedside light, pulled the duvet back and climbed in, trying not to wake her. She was looking forward to a lie in and he wasn't about to maul her in her sleep. Her eyes flickered and she rolled over to him, hooking a leg around his and an arm across his waist, cheek against his chest.

Well, there were worse ways to sleep than with the woman you loved sprawled across you.

It was heaven. It was hell.

Christ, her feet were cold though.

He was awake before her because, quite frankly, he was uncomfortable. Laurel must have been desperately tired, because she hadn't moved all night and he didn't want to disturb her. If she needed the sleep, she needed the sleep.

Alex better not show his face this morning, or, if he did, he'd better be so bloody apologetic that Nate might find it appropriate not to cut him out of his life forever. Because last night he had been a complete and utter wanker, and Lucia hadn't been much better either.

Laurel stirred against his chest and rubbed a hand across her eyes.

'Oh,' she said, her throat rusty with sleep. She shot upright, unwinding herself from him and shuffled back to her side of the bed, taking all the warmth with her.

'Nate, I'm so sorry. I didn't realise I had actually limpeted myself to you.' She put her face in her hands. 'I'm so embarrassed.'

His shirt collar crumpled around her neck, her hair gloriously messy around her face.

'Don't worry about it, Laurel,' he said. Nate sat up, scooting backwards so he was resting against the headboard, adjusting his morning glory so he hoped it wasn't evident, and crossed his ankles.

'I suppose we should get ready,' she said.

Before she could turn to swing her legs out of the bed, he caught her warm hand in his.

'Laurel,' he said, but his voice came out a whisper. He cleared his throat. 'Laurel, I need to talk to you.'

'Okay,' she shifted on the bed to give him her full attention. He looked down to his hand holding hers. This had been so much easier when he was thinking about it in the bathroom last night.

'I'm a stupid, stupid man, Laurel. I didn't see it, I didn't see—'

'Uncle Nate, Uncle Nate! Laurel!'

What the hell was that little cock blocker doing? He loved Benji, but not right now, no please, not right now.

'Uncle NATE, Mummy said I could jump on you at ten o'clock, and it's ten o'clock in three, two, one.'

Laurel laughed and pulled her hand away from his as the door burst open and Benji hurled himself at the bed. He managed to cup his crown jewels as the entire weight of an eight-year-old boy landed on his stomach.

'Morning Benji,' he groaned. 'How are you so heavy?'

'It's because I eat all of my vegetables,' Benji said proudly. 'It's ten o'clock and mummy said I could come and get you because Bessie the Cow had a baby last night, and I want to go and see it, but mummy said that I had to wait for you, Laurel.'

Nate couldn't bring himself to be mad with Benji, because he was so excited.

'Laurel, why are you wearing one of Uncle Nate's shirts? Don't you have any pyjamas?'

She laughed.

'I know Bessie the Cow had a calf last night, because me and Uncle Nate helped her. It was super late, so I was wearing my pyjamas and they got really dirty.'

'You helped?' Benji looked at her wide-eyed. 'And you helped too?'

'I did,' Nate said, shuffling to get more comfortable. 'But Laurel did most of the work.'

'Can we go and see her, can we go and see? I want to see the baby cow,' Benji said, bouncing.

'Yeah, okay, okay, but stop jumping up and down on my peanuts please, Benji,' Nate said, and Benji threw back his head and howled with laughter.

'Peanuts! You call your boy bits peanuts!'

Laurel was laughing now as well, they were a tableau of joy. Looking at her, his heart clenched, because this is what he wanted. Laurel, comfortable, laughing and happy, with him.

'Go on,' she said to Benji. 'Me and Uncle Nate will get dressed then we'll go and see Bessie the Cow. You'll have to choose what to call the calf.'

'I get to name her?' Benji asked.

Laurel frowned at him. 'Bessie the Cow is your cow, isn't she?'

The boy nodded thoughtfully.

'Then you get to name her baby.'

'I get to name a baby,' Benji whispered. 'I'll wait outside and think. It's got to be a good name.'

'Go on then,' Nate said, pushing him onto the floor.

Benji ran outside.

'Shut the door!' Nate called.

'What were you going to say?' Laurel said.

He smiled ruefully. 'Nothing that can't wait.'

LAUREL

Laurel had just about gotten over her embarrassment of practically suctioning herself to Nate all night. She'd slept with her head on his chest, and it had been the best sleep of her entire life. He'd been kind about it, but he'd also been shy and nervous and wanting to talk to her about something. It would be letting her down gently, telling her that whilst she had decided that the best place to sleep was his chest, that he had been a stupid, stupid man because he could *finally* see that she was desperate for him, but he just didn't want her in the same way.

The hot, passionate kisses last night, the feel of his skin on hers, had just been the wine talking. The only one bed. The proximity. But that talk could wait, or never happen at all. She did not want to go through the same thing as she did ten years ago. Not again.

But everything was normal as they were sitting having coffee after visiting the stables. Normal, normal, normal. If she kept saying it, if she kept believing it, it would be true.

Mother and baby were doing well. The calf was walking and suckling. Joints were good, eyes were good. Laurel was happy, as was the vet with her assessment. Nate's eyes found hers more often, or was she just more aware because she knew how his face looked when it was soft from sleep.

Benji, the gorgeous boy that he was, had decided to call the calf Penny and John Stapleton, who had arrived early to find his favourite cow birthed and happy, had nearly cried.

Jess and Owen had requested the old farmer let them take some of the burden and help more. Or at least learn the basics. Stapleton was gruff, but relieved. Benji was adamant that he was going to get up at five every morning to feed Penny. They'd see how long that lasted.

'Are you sure you have to go now? You can't stay for lunch?' Jess was saying in Laurel's ear as she hugged her.

'No, we've got to get back,' Laurel said apologetically.

'It's been so nice meeting you though. Thank you so much for having us.'

'It's been lovely, and I'm really sorry about…' Jess trailed off. 'You know.'

'Yeah, don't worry about it.' Laurel smiled.

They'd not seen Alex or Lucia this morning, who were either still asleep (although with the noise that Benji made, unlikely), or hiding (way more likely after the bollocking Jess said she gave Alex last night).

'Don't leave it so long next time.' Owen clapped Nate on the back. 'Lovely to meet you,' he said, giving Laurel a kiss on the cheek.

'Laurel, will you make sure that Uncle Nate visits more please?' Benji asked earnestly.

She squatted down so she was at eye level with the boy.

'I'll tell you what, how about you come and visit Uncle Nate at my farm? We've got lots and lots of animals for you to help out with.'

'Do you mean it?' Benji's eyes lit up. 'Do you have cows like Bessie and Penny?'

'We have hundreds and hundreds of cows just like Bessie and Penny, and of course I mean it. I'll get mummy's phone number from Uncle Nate and I'll organise it, because,' she looked around theatrically before whispering, 'Uncle Nate is rubbish.'

'He is rubbish,' Benji said, throwing his arms around her neck.

'Right, come on Benji. Let Laurel go please, pal,' Nate said, prying the boy off her for a hug of his own.

'Where are Paul and Angeline?' Laurel asked Jess. It was about eleven. Had they already left?

'Oh, I wouldn't bother them. Paul is a notoriously long sleeper and we don't expect to see him for another half hour or so,' she said, wrapping an arm around Owen's waist. 'Thank you so much for coming.' Jess glanced over Laurel's shoulder at Nate swinging Benji around in a monster hug. 'He's happy.'

Okay. That was a weird thing for her to say.

'I'll get your number. I'm holding you to a visit.' Jess pointed at her.

'Of course. Any time,' Laurel replied.

They made quick work of getting into the car and setting off, Benji running down the drive after them, racing the convertible.

'So?' Nate said, turning onto the main road.

She cut her eyes to him. Here it was. The let's-just-be-friends, the it's-not-you-it's-me, the I-just-don't-think-of-you-like-that.

'So… what?'

'So, was it as bad as you were thinking, meeting my friends?' He gave her a quick smile before returning his eyes to the road.

Laurel's shoulders relaxed.

'I didn't think it was going to be bad! I really liked them all. Well, except Alex. Obviously,' she grumbled, turning her hands over in her lap. And Lucia, but she wasn't about to bring up the ex-girlfriend.

His jaw clenched.

'Yeah, he's a prick. I'm requesting a new liaison at the society. I can't work with him anymore.'

'Nate, don't do that for me.' She would feel desperately awful if he threw away years and years of friendship over her. Even if Alex was a prick.

His lips quirked in a tight smile at the road.

'I'm not. I should have cut him loose a long, long time ago. He's just not…' Nate hesitated. She reached over and patted his hand resting on the gear stick.

'I know,' she said.

They used to be kind of interchangeable at university, but Alex and Nate were so different now. Nate had grown up, moved on, become a rounded human being. Alex, however, was still acting like a twenty-two year old and it was more than a little pathetic.

Laurel leaned her head back and closed her eyes. A

convertible was so much better than her own battered car. Or a tractor. She was thankful that she had brought a long-sleeved top even though the heated seats were lovely. A car like this, she could really get used to.

It was a few minutes before Nate asked if she was sleeping. 'No, why?'

He cleared his throat and turned to look at her dark eyes, 'Are you busy when we get back? I need to talk to you, and I don't think the car is the best place.'

Laurel sighed. Nate was determined to have this conversation, and she had about twenty-three minutes to prepare herself.

'Sure.' She tried to sound light and bouncy, but her heart was lead. 'Where do you want to go?'

'Wherever you feel comfortable.'

Oh great. Just great.

She got to choose where she would have the memory of Nate Daley rejecting her, again. Well, not her flat. She wouldn't have that tainted by him, and not the farm because she didn't want everyone else to watch her heart break. Top of the hill? No, that was her and Rebecca's place. It would have to be the pub. The Dog & Gun was close enough to her flat so she could make a quick getaway via little Sainsbury's for heartbreak snacks. There was also fortification at the pub. A large glass of white wine would be enough to soften any blow.

'The Dog & Gun.'

He frowned but nodded.

The silence was tense for the rest of the way home.

NATE

The Dog & Gun. He was hoping she'd choose somewhere more secluded, somewhere a bit more private for him to bare his soul to her. As it was, the pub would be full of Sunday lunchers, afternoon drinkers, students. Oh god, the students.

But it was her choice. She had to be comfortable, and if that's what she wanted, then that's what he would do.

'Hey, can you take me home first? I'll take my bag up and meet you at the pub?'

'Sure, I'll get you a drink.' She'd have to come then, if he was getting her a drink.

'Celebration prosecco?' She laughed, but it was brittle and tight.

'Do you want celebration prosecco?'

'God no, it tastes like warm cat's piss. I will have the largest glass of sauvingon blanc they can muster. A pint, a tankard, a Viking horn. Anything.'

Thank god she didn't want celebration prosecco, because she was right, it did taste like warm cat's piss. He'd buy a bottle of Lanson from little Sainsburys if they had any, just in case. Just in case.

Nate sat on the wall outside The Dog & Gun with a treacly pint of ale and the sharp burn of the shot of vodka he'd downed at the bar in his throat for the longest ten minutes of his life. Laurel's largest glass of wine was getting warm. Eventually, he spotted her coming down the road and moved to the edge of the forecourt with their drinks to greet her, just like he had before. He forced himself to look away. She wasn't his to stare at. Not yet.

'That mine?' she asked, when she was close enough.

'Yeah, all yours. There's a Viking horn with your name on it behind the bar.'

She smiled as she took the drink from his hand, but it didn't reach her eyes. Laurel took two big gulps and wiped her mouth with the back of her hand.

'Okay, I'm ready.' She looked up at him. 'Nate, the floor is yours.'

'Let's sit.'

He could delay this. He could just not say anything.

This was a lot harder than it was last night in the bathroom. A lot harder. This time, he actually had a real live Laurel to talk to.

Nate broke the tense silence when they'd found a seat by the wall.

'Laurel, I am stupid. I am a flat earther. I am King John, too reliant on complicated military strategy that always failed.'

She snorted and a smile flashed across her mouth. He took her hand, clenched into a tight fist on her lap, and smoothed his thumb across her knuckles.

'I found something yesterday. I want to tell you about it because I want to tell you about everything I find.' Nate took a breath. Christ, this was hard.

'Okay.'

There was a frown on her face and she glanced between his thumb stroking across her knuckles, and his face. He was red, blushing, desperate.

'I took you to meet my friends and it wasn't because I'm altruistic and you needed to relax, although that was a part of it. I know your family, your passion, your life, and I want you to know me. I want that, because I want you. I want your smile in my pocket, I want your smell on my clothes, I want your hand in mine. I want to give you everything, every part of me. Laurel, I'm freefalling here.'

Nate hadn't taken his eyes off hers, because he couldn't. Her lips parted and she was sucking in air like breathing wasn't a natural physical occurrence. She was flushed and beautiful, and gaping at him, floundering.

'You don't have to say anything.' Although he wished she would.

Couldn't she see him dying on a low wall in the middle of a tiny English village?

'You tell me that…' Her voice was hoarse, and her throat bobbed in a swallow. 'You tell me that here?'

Nate frowned; she'd chosen the place where she'd feel most comfortable.

'Come with me.'

Laurel grabbed his hand and took off, at pace, up the road to her flat. She fumbled with the key as he stood beside her, until she finally unlocked the front door to the street. She ran up the stairs and unlocked the door there, and he followed. What was happening?

He took in her flat. This wasn't Little Willow Farm Laurel, this was all black wood and silver highlights, industrial and futuristic. It was so *Laurel*, to fit herself into what she thought people wanted from her, what people needed. She wasn't the cute, sweet little farm girl with shabby chic, rustic, mismatched chairs. She was cool and granite, sleek and amazing. Her TV was screwed to the wall, with books stacked on floating shelves either side. The black curtains twitched lightly in the breeze from the open window. A hallway led off from the main room, down to where he presumed her bedroom was.

'Say it again,' she demanded. 'Please.'

The last was a whisper.

'It's been ever since you rushed me out of the cafe and let me into your office, let me into your life.' Nate stepped forward, once, twice. Laurel's breath hitched. 'It's more than wanting to share every little moment of every day with you. You're under my skin, Laurel, and I wouldn't want you anywhere else.'

Nate watched her as she weighed everything in her mind. He could see it play out on her face. The confusion, a flash of sadness, then fear, cold and bright.

'Can I kiss you?' He was desperate to.

She looked up at him with those drowning bronze eyes and nodded.

His heart thudded in his chest as he moved forward, letting his fingers glide across her jaw, his thumb across her bottom lip. Laurel's eyes fluttered closed as she waited for him to touch his lips to hers, but he wanted to savour it, to memorise her face, to remember this moment as the beginning of everything.

Her lips were raspberry pink, plump and ready as he slipped his hand into the hair at the back of her neck, tilting her head back. Her hands slid up his chest, gripping his shirt tightly in her fists. His breath was a puff of joy against her lips, because she was holding back, she was waiting for him. Perhaps she had always been waiting for him.

'Nate, please,' she breathed, and he couldn't wait any more.

His lips touched hers, gently, softly, so he could remember that she tasted of wine and sherbet. The tender, soft pressure of his lips on hers. She wrapped her arms around his neck and pulled him to her. Then, it was desperate, wet mouths against each other, as if they could never be close enough. It was beautiful, open-mouthed kisses across her jaw and she gasped when his tongue touched the softness just behind her ear.

He'd bared his soul to Laurel Fletcher, and here she was, letting him kiss her, running her hands across his chest, through his hair, pulling him close as if she couldn't get enough of him. He nipped at her bottom lip and she groaned as he made his way down the column of her neck, dropping wet kisses in the hollow of her collarbone.

'Yes,' she breathed, and his heart hammered a blacksmith beat in his chest at her acceptance.

LAUREL

At this exact moment in time, Doctor Nate Daley was nipping the skin at the base of her throat, drawing soft mewling noises out of her that she had never ever made before. He wanted her, all of her. He was falling, *freefalling*. She had already fallen. She'd fallen the moment he'd pulled her up from a cow dung covered yard. No, scratch that, it was happening again. She was falling again.

Nate kissed up her neck, tasting her, marking her skin with his lips, his tongue, his teeth. His large hands splayed across her ribs, restrained, but barely so.

'Laurel,' he breathed as his mouth came back to hers. He spoke her name reverently, as if in prayer.

Her shaky fingers worked at his shirt buttons as she greedily searched for his skin, slipping it over his shoulders. She pulled back from him, and she was ogling, she knew she was, but she couldn't stop. Her hands explored his broadness, dragging a nail across his tender nipple that caused a beautiful groan. Her fingers trailed through the dusting of dark hair that started across his chest and trailed down in a tantalizing line to the top of his trousers. She pulled at the waistband, easing the button through the small hole.

Nate's large hands circled her wrists to stop her. Oh god, had she gone too far? Had she misread this whole situation?

'Laurel, if you don't feel—' A harsh swallow. 'The same way, then I can't. I can't... know you and not have you. I can't.'

Laurel's hands cradled his face. He was beautiful, vulnerable, looking at her with worried eyes. Desperate.

'Yes,' she breathed, even though he hadn't asked a question. 'I want all of you, Nate.'

That was all he needed, because he lifted her against him, hands under her thighs and she wrapped her legs around his waist as he strode with her down the little hallway towards her bedroom. They didn't get far because he stopped, pressed her back against the wall and let her legs slip down to the floor. Her shirt was between them so he worked at the buttons, his thighs pressed against her and oh god, she wanted him.

The shirt was discarded and he kissed greedily down her neck, pressing her against the wall, trailing his tongue over the swell of her breasts. Nate reached behind her, fiddling and pulling at her bra hook and she reached behind to help him.

The bra dropped to the floor, her nipples hard and wanting, desperate for him to kiss them, lick them, bite them. He looked at her, as she had him, exploring her chest with his fingers, swirling around each sensitive – oh god, so sensitive – nipple, muttering things like 'perfect' and 'oh god' and indecipherable words meant just for him.

His mouth followed his fingers and with every nip and suck, Laurel's hips bucked and breathy gasps came from her lips. He rolled her other nipple between his fingers and she cried out, raking her fingers across his scalp. He slid a hand over her stomach, reaching the button of her shorts. Buttons, apparently, he could undo, and as soon as he did, his fingers were gently pushing at the outside of her wet lacy underwear.

God, she was wet.

Laurel shimmied her hips and pushed her shorts and knickers down, opening her legs wider so he could have better access to her. He bit down on her nipple as he slid a finger inside, then another, and she groaned deeply. But when his thumb pressed lightly on her clit, she cried out and flung her head back against the wall, gasping for air. Nate trailed his tongue down her stomach, keeping his fingers working in and out slowly, and his thumb rhythmically circling those nerves, until he reached his knees. He undid his trousers to release his hard (and huge) cock (how was that ever going to fit inside her?), and looked up at Laurel as if asking for permission.

Oh god, yes. Yes.

Stroking his cock with the same rhythm as his fingers moving inside of her, he leaned forward.

First it was a long lick from where his fingers still curled inside her, pressing against somewhere she'd tried to find, but never had before, up to where his thumb had been. He was rewarded with a loud groan and her bunching his hair in her fist. Concentrating on that bundle of nerves, he sucked and licked, kissed and stroked. Murmurs of 'so good' and 'mmm' reached her, but she couldn't process it, the pressure was building inside her and all she could do was grip his hair tightly and breathe, breathe, breathe.

Her legs began to tremble and he pressed into her more and more, devouring her. He was so greedy.

'Nate, Nate,' she breathed. 'Stop, stop.'

He looked up at her sharply, stopping everything.

'What's wrong? What did I do wrong?'

'Nothing.' Her throat bobbed in a long swallow as she regained her composure, trying to pull herself together. 'If you don't stop, I'm going to come.'

A smile spread across his face.

'Baby, that's the idea.'

Nate adjusted himself on his knees and went back to work.

'This is for you,' he breathed against her wetness. 'I want to feel you come undone... on my fingers... on my tongue... I want to taste your pleasure.' He licked her languidly every few words and with a gentle scrape of his teeth, her legs quivered and shook. She couldn't keep herself up. She was buckling. Nate let go of his cock to wrap his arm around her, keeping her upright. His fingers curled inside of her, and he flicked his tongue over her clit once, twice, then sucked.

Laurel cried out as she shattered around him, legs shaking and core clenching, fingers pulling at his hair.

His tongue was relentless in working her through her orgasm until she wilted, spent and sated.

Nate kissed just below her belly button and gently took his fingers out of her. She was gasping for breath, but he wasn't finished yet. Hoisting up his trousers, he stood and scooped her up, one arm under those shaky knees and another around her back.

'What are you doing?' she whispered, voice raspy from her orgasm.

He kicked open the door to the bedroom.

'I'm taking you to bed, baby,' he said, laying her gently on the duvet cover.

Laurel fiddled in the bedside table while he got rid of his

trousers and pants. With her hair splayed across the pillow she was a goddess, satisfied, relaxed, and completely his.

'What are you looking at? Get over here,' she said, voice dripping honey, condom between her fingers. Kneeling next to her, with his cock pointing proudly upwards, she explored, her fingers working up and down, around the smooth head, stroking from base to tip. He trembled at her touch and she smiled at the amazement that she could make him shudder like that.

'Laurel,' he ground out. 'I can't wait anymore. I want you.'

She ripped the wrapper and knelt up to kiss him hard on the mouth. She rolled the condom down his length, then squeezed his balls lightly in her hands. He moved over her and settled gently between her legs.

'I'll be slow… I want to remember… savour everything.'

She guided him to her entrance, canting her hips up to meet his and he pressed in, holding himself up on his elbows, moving steadily, slowly. God, yes. This was everything, she was full and needing, and pulled his lips down to hers, desperate for him. He skimmed a hand down her side, over her hip and hooked her leg over his back as he picked up pace.

'I can't… hold back,' he said into the crook of her neck.

'Then don't,' Laurel nipped at his neck, scratching her nails lightly down his back.

He rolled them slightly and bent his knee, angling her so he could sink into her deeper. Then he was faster and harder, saying her name over and over in breathy murmurs until he stilled, shook and shattered into a million pieces against her.

CHAPTER NINETEEN

LAUREL

Lying in bed at 6pm on a Sunday evening with the most gorgeous man, tired, satisfied and comfortable, was obviously the very best Sunday that Laurel could have hoped for.

The first time she had come was, well, it was nothing short of amazing. She'd never had a guy go down on her while she was standing up before and never, ever, had that type of soul-destroying orgasm before.

Nate could do that all he wanted.

And when they'd had sex the second time, her on top and him using his fingers on her clit, her nipples. Yep, they could do that again.

Then on her knees in the shower, the brutal passion of his hands in her hair.

That could also be done again.

'I'm hungry. Are you hungry?' Nate asked, tracing lines across her back with his fingers.

'I could eat.'

Damn straight she could, and she reached up to kiss him. He kissed her like he could gain all his sustenance from her lips and tongue, but she could hear hunger rumbling in his stomach.

'Okay, I get it,' she said. 'Shall I cook?'

He screwed up his face. 'Shall we order something?'

'What are you saying about my cooking? You've never

even had my cooking!' She smacked him playfully on the shoulder.

'What I'm saying is…' He rolled on top of her and pinned both of her hands to the pillow. 'I can't do this if you're cooking,' he said, tickling her ribs.

'Okay, okay,' she said, breathless from laughing. 'Okay, okay, Chinese or pizza? That's the choice.'

He tilted his head in thought.

'Pizza, but not with pineapple.'

'Urgh, I'm not a heathen,' she said, pushing him off her and rummaging in one of her drawers for a pair of knickers and an oversized t-shirt.

'Where are you going?' he whined as she headed for the bedroom door.

'If you want something to eat, Dr Daley, I have to find my phone and order it.'

Quite frankly, him sitting naked in her bed, hair tousled from her fingers, with a sloppy, satisfied smile quirked on his face, nearly made her think screw it and head back to bed with him. But then his stomach rumbled again.

'We didn't have lunch, did we?'

'No, I think we were a bit,' he grinned deviously, 'distracted.'

Distracted indeed.

Laurel's phone had spilled out of her bag across the table when she'd thrown it, desperate to hear Nate's words again. His phone was on the table too, flashing.

'Nate, you've got messages and stuff,' she called and heard movement from the bedroom.

She'd order the pizza first, then check her own messages, no doubt from Rebecca pleading for an update on Laurel's social engagements.

Arms snaked around her waist, and lips found her neck.

'If you want pizza, let me order,' she said, but tilted her head so he could get better access to her sensitive pulse.

'Okay, fine,' he grumbled and snatched his phone from the

table, plonking himself down on the sofa. She could get used to having men wearing only pants sitting on her sofa with their feet up on the ottoman. No, scratch that. One man.

God, his thighs were sexy.

Laurel finished ordering the pizza and sat next to him, checking her messages. Nate pulled her legs over his and rested his hand on her bare thigh.

Rebecca

So? How did it go?

Are you back yet?

When are you getting back? Are you alive?

Don't tell me, it went so well that you're now having SEXY TIMES.

Robin

What the fuck did the cleaners do with my Playstation? I can't find it.

Rebecca

YOU ARE HAVING SEX OOOOOOOOH

Robin

Found it.

Jack

Please text Rebecca back, she's driving me mad.

Rebecca

Text me back when you finish licking the chest of the gorgeous doctor.

To: Rebecca

I'm back and no, you can't have details.

To: Robin

Don't be a dick.

Robin

Fuck you :)

Rebecca

YOU CAN'T LEAVE ME HANGING LIKE THIS.

Before she had a chance to text back, her phone vibrated in a call. Uh, no thanks Rebecca. Not now.

Rebecca

Oh my god. He's still there isn't he, that's why you're not answering my call! I'm so excited for you!!! Call me later xxx

'What are you smirking for?' she asked, poking a smiling Nate with her toes.

'I've got messages from Jess saying how much she loved you and telling me not to fuck it up.' He glanced at her before continuing. 'And I've got a badly worded message from Benji, on Owen's phone, saying that you're his new favourite, not me.'

He pulled the blanket off the arm of the sofa and covered them both with it.

Ah, what a sweetie Benji was.

'I'm sorry if inviting them to the farm was the wrong thing to do, I just got kind of caught up in the moment,' she said, nervously.

What was she thinking? That's right, she *hadn't* been thinking, because if she had, she would have thought things like 'don't be so ridiculous' or 'head first' or 'why, in the name of all that is holy, would you invite Nate's friends to your farm?'.

'It was exactly the right thing to do. Benji will absolutely love it. Jess is thrilled,' he said, leaning his head back on the sofa, and her panic subsided a little. 'Is it okay with you? You know you can cancel, right? You don't have to do anything you're not comfortable with.'

'Not at all, I just didn't want to overstep, you know...' she trailed off, looking around her front room that fit the two of them in so snugly.

Nate cupped the back of her neck and kissed her firmly.

'I love the fact that you want my friends to visit us.'

There it was. Us.

'Us' was good. This is what she wanted, and the reassurance that this is what he wanted too made a small smile pull at her lips. This was happiness.

'Is that...' she started, but suddenly found the weave in the blanket over them very interesting. 'Is that what you want? An us?'

Because if he didn't, how would she live without kissing him again? How would she survive having to work with him every day and not being able to slide her arms around his neck? Take him home at the end of the day, back to the flat that held them both so nicely.

'I thought I'd been—' He shifted on the sofa and cupped her face, stroking her cheek with the calloused pad of his thumb. 'In case of any misunderstandings, ever again.' He leaned his forehead against hers, eyes drooping closed. 'I want everything, Laurel. I want everything with you.'

'Okay,' she whispered, leaning her face into his hand.

'Okay,' he whispered back.

Us.

NATE

The next three weeks passed in a haze of organising the funding meeting, pulling more and more gold and bones out of the earth and, of course, Laurel. He couldn't keep his hands off her, and they quite simply couldn't work in the same office anymore, not since Sylvie interrupted them, ahem, 'working' on the conference table. Nate worked on the kitchen table in Robin's house and when Laurel left, she took him with her back to her flat.

There was long, warm, tantalising sex on the living room sofa, in bed, in the shower, and fast, passionate sex bent over the kitchen table. Sometimes they didn't even make it to the flat. Good job the front door that led to the street was sturdy.

Except, of course, for the four days when Laurel got her period. She had said he didn't have to stay, but how could he not? Not when she was in pain and bloated and tired and needed looking after. He cooked her rice pudding (not as good as her mother's, apparently), pasta carbonara and brought ice cream and sorbet ('I just want cold things!'). He made sure the hot water bottle was always hot and the sofa blanket was warm.

It was home. It was perfect.

The one blight on his pretty pink horizon was the funding meeting. He hated that kind of stuff, hated being wheeled in front of donors, on display.

Also, Alex would be there. He would have to be. It was generally accepted that the British Archaeological Society would give a speech commending the finds and the prospective finds, and he knew a lot of organisations gave heavy weighting to what the BAS had to say. If the site got a bad report from Alex, it probably didn't matter what he said, what he had found, people weren't going to throw money at him if the BAS weren't fully on board. So, Alex had to be enthusiastic, not just go through the motions.

Nate sat at Laurel's dining table, frowning at his emails.

'Have you heard from him?' she asked, wrapping her arms around his neck and planting a kiss on his cheek.

'Not yet, I have to send him at least two more chasers before he deigns to reply,' he replied.

'Wine?' she asked, as she wandered into the kitchen.

'Yes please.' He could do with a glass of wine after the day he'd had.

Handing him a glass of red, she curled up on the sofa and beckoned him over.

'Tell me.' She sipped her wine, her oversized jumper falling off her shoulder.

'Alex won't reply to my messages. I'm going to have to go to his boss because it's getting ridiculous. I thought we were past this when he'd confirmed BAS endorsement, but—' He sighed.

'Hmm,' she said, incredibly diplomatically.

'I know, I know, it's work and I've got to separate work from friendship, but I...' he trailed off.

It was more than that. Threatening to shop Alex to his boss for being a dick was one thing. Actually doing it was another.

'Okay, if he hasn't replied by tomorrow, midday, I'll call his boss and request another liaison. Send the paper trail of me trying to get hold of him.'

'Okay,' Laurel said, obviously relieved.

It wasn't just him personally that Alex was affecting, it was his job, his students, his site, and by extension, Little Willow and his relationship with Laurel.

'Thanks again,' he said, sliding a hand up her thigh. 'For helping with the organisation, for sorting the cafe to do the catering, for letting us use the Conference Centre.'

'Of course, it's no problem.'

'Uh,' he started. 'You will be there, won't you? For the funding meeting?'

He wanted her there, he wanted her beside him, not just to show her how much he thought of Little Willow, but because he needed her there for support, for grounding. Because they were a team.

'Of course I will,' she said. 'I wouldn't miss you in action.'

His heart lifted.

'Dad will be there, and Jack and Robin, all there to support the farm and, of course, you, Dr Daley.'

Nate had firmly cemented his place as Jack's friend, as well as Laurel's boyfriend. Even Robin had accepted him as a new but irrefutable part of Fletcher life.

'I'm going to go for a drink with Rebecca in a bit. Do you want to come?' she asked.

God, no. He did not need to be that clingy boyfriend.

'No, I'm going to work on my speech some more for next week.' Perhaps it was a hint to go home? To Robin's house. 'I can go. It's no problem,' he said with a smile, hoping that it didn't come over as needy or say 'please don't make me go back to that house with those horrible students'.

'Go?' She looked hurt. 'Do you want to go?'

'No, I don't want to go, I'm just giving you the option,' he said, his little finger stroking the inside of her thigh, just before the seam of her underwear under her skirt.

'Well, I don't want you to go.' She took a sip of her wine. 'There are things I want to do to you when I get home, Dr Daley.'

Her eyes skimmed over his lips and he grinned.

'Alright then. I'll be here when you get home.'

Possibly naked. Probably naked. Okay, who was he kidding? Definitely naked.

Laurel left him to get changed and he scrolled through his messages again, reading the thread he shared with Owen.

Owen

Have you heard from Alex? He left without saying goodbye. Rude bastard.

No, and I don't expect to. Did Lucia say goodbye? Apologise for being a dick?

Owen

After you guys left, she spent the morning crying at Jess. You know how she gets — dramatic.

Jess wouldn't put up with any shit. Lucia had had the choice to make friends with Laurel, she had the choice to not be an absolute dick, and she had emphatically made that choice. The toxic manipulation of her tears may have worked on him, and Jess for that matter, when they were in uni, but it hadn't taken long to figure out that when Lucia was in the wrong, the sprinklers turned on. She just feels so guilty, she's having such a tough time, she's sorry, she didn't mean to, it's just so hard being her at the moment, blah blah blah.

He texted Owen now.

Anything from Alex or Lucia? And send me a picture of my favourite ninja turtle.

Owen

Nothing. What a pair of dicks. I don't think we'll be seeing them again any time soon. They've got a lot of ground to make up.

Imagine not even saying goodbye to people who have fed and watered you, put you up, who you were incredibly, unbelievably rude to and who were supposed to be your oldest and best friends.

There then followed fourteen selfies of Benji pulling various funny faces.

Nate sent back pictures of him making the same faces, but he had to own it. Benji was way cuter than him.

LAUREL

'Look how gorgeous he is,' she said to Rebecca, showing her a picture that Nate had sent her of Benji pulling a silly face.

'If you keep showing me pictures of someone else's child, I'm going to revoke your status as "best auntie",' Rebecca said. Okay, she knew a warning when she heard it. But Benji was really cute.

'Okay, sorry. Lila and Micah are obviously my faves, always will be,' she said apologetically. 'How's life? How's my brother? I feel like I haven't seen you!'

'That's because you've been too busy shagging Nate, Laurel,' Rebecca said airily. 'And I don't blame you one little bit.'

'You're still not getting details,' she said, laughing.

'Jack's good. Nate is a good influence on him because he's still pulling his weight. I expected it to fade away after a couple of weeks, but he's going strong,' she said, then added, 'I think he had absolutely no idea how much I actually did.'

'I fully agree. It probably didn't even register in his tiny little man brain,' Laurel said, waving at Robin who had just come in with his gaggle of boys. Rebecca followed her gaze, then lent over the table conspiratorially. 'What's happened to Robin as well? He seems to be going out less and actually doing stuff around the farm,' she said quietly. 'The pig pen actually got re-felted last week.'

'Jack thinks there's a girl,' Rebecca said knowingly.

Laurel rolled her eyes, because there was always a girl.

'No, a girl that he really likes, not just a shag.' Rebecca topped up both of their glasses and put the screw top back on the empty bottle.

She assessed her sister-in-law.

'Really?' she asked, skeptically.

'Really.' Rebecca was adamant.

'That would mean it would be someone on the farm. Do you think it's one of the students?' Laurel mused. 'Oh god, not the one with the eyelashes and no bra. Can you imagine her at Sunday lunch? Dad wouldn't know where to look.'

Rebecca snorted on her wine, choking down a laugh.

'I bet her name is something like Rain, or Hemp, or Serendipity,' she said.

Laurel's face dropped. 'It had better not be Sylvie.'

'Why not?' Rebecca frowned.

'Uh, because if he shags her and then breaks her heart then it will be the most awkward thing ever, and she'll leave, and I don't want her to leave.'

She couldn't leave, what would Laurel do without her? Sylvie kept everything running smoothly, and she was already seeing the benefit of that business course thing Sylvie was on.

'But Sylvie's a nice girl,' Rebecca said, sipping her wine. 'She'd keep him on the straight and narrow, wouldn't she?'

Her eyebrow raised of its own accord.

'If she gets her heart broken by her boss's little brother, it's not going to go down well.'

'You've literally invented workplace romances, so you can't kibosh it.' Rebecca leaned back in her chair. 'Besides, I heard what you and Nate were doing on your conference table the other week.'

No. Fucking. Way.

Colour shot up her face and Rebecca threw her head back and cackled loudly.

'Oh my god! It is true! I said to Jack that no, not my Laurel, she wouldn't do something like that.'

Laurel buried her face in her hands.

'Oh my god, Jack knows?'

'Jack knows, Robin knows, your dad doesn't know, but pretty much everyone on the entire farm knows.' Rebecca said through bursts of laughter. 'Don't worry, I think it's great, you deserve some happiness.'

'Does Nate know that everyone knows?'

Forget how good Sylvie was at her job, Robin could go out with her, smash her heart into a million pieces, whatever.

'Probably, him and Jack are besties now, it's so weird,' Rebecca said. 'But weird in a good way, Jack needs a forward thinking, progressive friend to drag him out of the nineteenth century.'

'I'm going to kill Sylvie,' Laurel said, fanning her red face.

Rebecca laughed again.

'Yeah, best of luck with that.'

'I'm obviously not going to kill Sylvie,' she said, pouting.

Subject change, anything to get away from Sylvie walking in on her and Nate on the conference table.

'Are you coming to the funding meeting presentation thing?'

It would be so nice to have Rebecca there, a bit of support for Jack. It was their farm, and making the funding meeting a success would result in all kinds of untold benefits. Besides, Rebecca could schmooze with the best of them.

'It's in the middle of the day, Laurel,' Rebecca's lips pursed. 'I can't just leave work whenever I feel like it.'

'Of course. I'm sorry,' Laurel said. 'I shouldn't have asked.'

She kicked herself mentally. This had been a longstanding argument between her and Jack. Rebecca couldn't just up and leave in the middle of the day, couldn't just drop everything. Rebecca had her own high-flying career, and it was unfair for Laurel to have asked.

Rebecca's face softened. 'But I will come after I finish. Will it go on that long?'

'It should do. There's a drinks reception after the talk and stuff, so yeah,' Laurel said, making a mental note to check on the preparations for the buffet and drinks with the cafe.

'Alright then, I'll be there, probably with the children. Perhaps I'll see if the nanny can stay a bit longer and watch them. We'll see.' Rebecca sipped her wine.

Another bottle later, and they were both quietly sozzled, and a smidge slurry.

'Robin,' Laurel called. 'Are you going back to the farm or are you being naughty and staying out?' She giggled, because Drunk Laurel was funny.

'I'm going back,' he said, draining his pint. 'You coming?' he asked Rebecca.

'Yes, Robin Fletcher, Sir. I am definitely coming.' Rebecca stood and flung her jacket on. 'Come on, Laurel Fletcher. We'll walk you home.'

Rebecca linked her arm with Laurel's and marched her out of the pub door, not checking to see whether Robin was following or not.

'So, I think you and the good doctor are great and I like him for you,' Rebecca was saying as they meandered down the high street. 'But I will kill him if he makes you cry, okay? Or certainly give him a stern talking to.'

Now, that was surely a fate worse than death.

It had gotten colder, and Laurel pulled her coat around her, not having quite drunk enough wine for a suitable beer jacket.

'Well good, because I like him too,' Laurel said tartly.

'Oh my god, can you talk about something else? It's sickening,' Robin muttered behind them.

'Ooh, Robin. I have to say…' Laurel turned and pinned her brother with wavering eyes. 'If you break my Sylvie's heart, I will smother you in your sleep. Okay?'

Robin rolled his eyes and pulled out his phone to type a message.

'No, I mean it,' Laurel continued. 'I love you, obviously, but I adore Sylvie, and if you're going to be nice to her then that's fine, but if you're going to break her heart then I may have to burn you.' She squelched down on a hiccup.

Robin finished his text and put his phone in his pocket.

'Sylvie?' he huffed. 'Who even said I like Sylvie?'

Laurel shrugged theatrically, and Rebecca stifled a laugh.

'I'm just saying, you know, just in case.'

'Oh look,' Robin deadpanned, pointing over her shoulder. 'It's Nate.'

'Nate!' she cried, dragging a giggling Rebecca over to her front door, where Nate had magically appeared. He exchanged a look with Robin. 'Look, Rebecca, it's my boyfriend!'

'It is your boyfriend!' Rebecca squealed.

'Okay, she's your problem now,' Robin said, and gave Laurel a light shove into Nate's arms.

He smelled so good.

'I'll just sleep here, on your chest,' Laurel said, snuggling against him.

'Okay, good,' Nate said, smiling.

Okay. Good.

CHAPTER TWENTY

NATE

Nate was sweating under his shirt collar.

'Relax, Nate, you're doing well,' Laurel whispered to him as they moved from one group of academics to another.

'Are you sure? Is it going alright?' he asked anxiously. No matter how many of these he did, his heart still beat hard against his chest, and his voice seemed sluggish and strange.

Laurel nodded. 'It's going perfectly, okay?'

'Okay.'

Having Laurel on his arm whilst talking with funders, industry professionals and university members was incredibly calming. She was convivial, friendly and engaging, the perfect partner in selling both the site and her farm.

Alex, however, had studiously kept as far away as he could, mingling with people at a very precise ninety-degree angle from him and Laurel, wearing a mismatched blue jacket with crumpled black trousers. Didn't he even own an iron?

'I knew you and Nathanial here would find something brilliant, Lauren,' Professor Rowlands was saying.

'Professor, thank you, but it really was all Nate and his team,' she said, squeezing his arm gently.

'Well, I think you make a very good team together,' the old Professor said warmly.

'Alright, Ivor, we'll be moving on now, before you try and steal my girlfriend,' he said, giving him a wink.

'Yes, yes, off you go. Mingle. Don't forget to speak to the Chair of the University. Make sure she knows how important this site is,' Ivor said sagely, before wandering off to the tea and coffee table, manned by one of the cafe's immaculately dressed staff.

'You should go and speak to them,' Laurel said, but he really didn't want to let go of her. She was his safety blanket here in this annoying academic-slash-corporate world.

'Nate, I need to go and make sure Robin isn't hitting on anyone inappropriate.'

'Alright, but if I give you the look, you need to come and rescue me,' he said, giving her a brief kiss.

'You don't need rescuing, Dr Daley. This is all you,' she said, and his chest swelled at her belief in him.

Laurel wandered off into the melee to look for Robin, and Nate took stock before heading into battle. Alex was still pointedly at a right angle from him, across the large conference room, near the table with all of Nate's publications.

To obtain funding, you had to put on a show, and people bought into the person rather than the site. If that person (or persons) had a very well-received, famous even, paper that had led to television appearances, that had possibly altered the collective thought of how, say, the Picts were perceived, then it did well to have that spread out everywhere. Nate had managed to rein that in to one table by the coffee and tea area, with the backdrop picture of the stylus and the dig site, rather than the backdrop picture of him and Alex sitting on the breakfast TV sofa Jess had organised.

There were his lesser-known papers as well, his PhD dissertation, his journal articles, his body of work. Yeah, he was proud of his work, his passion, but he didn't want to flaunt it. The archaeology on the Little Willow site should speak for itself. He shouldn't need to drag all his previous stuff out to sell the new dig.

'Dr Daley, lovely to see you,' the Chair of the University intoned as he reached the little group where she was holding court. 'I am looking forward to your talk later. Well, in about ten minutes.'

'Thank you.'

'Dr Daley will be presenting with his British Archaeological Liaison, Alexander Woollard, who is another one of our graduates. It's so good to see our graduates out there, making a difference in the archaeological world,' she went on.

There were brief introductions and Nate plastered a smile on his face that he knew was brittle and tight, but he hoped would do. He played the role as well as he could, answering their questions appropriately, talking up the university and the site, and trying to catch Laurel's eye across the room without being too obvious about it. She would be much better at this. He could hear the tinkle of her laugh as she moved Robin towards Jack and Bill, away from a blushing Sylvie and the shabbily dressed archaeology students.

'Ah, and here is our other eminent graduate, Alex,' the Chair called. 'Do join us.'

There was a hesitancy about Alex as he caught Nate's eye and he glanced longingly at the publications table. He sauntered over to them.

'Alex, how are you?' Nate said, extending his hand.

He hadn't spoken to Alex, except via terse and difficult work emails, since that ill-fated weekend barbeque at Jess and Owen's, but there was no way Alex was going to drag him down to his level.

'Good,' Alex said, shaking his hand firmly, before turning to ask questions of the Chair and be introduced to the other members of the little group he had infiltrated.

Nate knew full well when he was being sidelined and frankly, he didn't care one little bit. If that's what Alex needed to do to make himself feel better, then that was absolutely fine. Nate was secure enough to not give a shit. His work, the site and the finds stood for themselves, and no matter how much Alex tried to make it about him, he was just a liaison. He didn't pull anything out of the earth. Actually, he hadn't done an awful lot. Alex was just the personification of the British Archaeological Society and yes, the backing of the Society pretty much guaranteed funding, but it could have been anyone. It just happened to be Alex.

Nate was listening to Alex drone on about the Society's work and how invested he had been in the Little Willow dig site, when a hiss of feedback cut him off.

Laurel stood on the raised platform that served as a stage, a projector screen behind her and the table with his notes and laptop to her side.

'Hello, and welcome to Little Willow Farm. I'm Laurel Fletcher, and this is our family's farm.' She beamed at the congregation. 'It's nearly time to welcome Dr Nate Daley and Alex Woollard to the stage to present the finds here at Little Willow, so please do take your seats.'

There was a bustle of movement as people meandered to the folding chairs put out before the stage. Laurel waited until people were settled before she continued.

'I'd just like to let you know that there will be a buffet and drinks after the presentation, made on site with our local produce grown and farmed here at Little Willow. If you have any questions about the farm itself, please do have a chat with me, Robin, Jack or Bill over there.' She pointed to the sheepish Fletcher men. Bill stood straight and stoic. Robin and Jack both shuffled nervously by their father's side. Alex snorted and Nate shot him a warning glare.

Laurel caught his eye and gave him an encouraging smile.

'Ladies and gentlemen, if you could put your hands together for Dr Nate Daley and Alex Woollard.'

Nate steeled himself and strode to the stage to tepid, academic applause, putting his coffee cup next to his laptop and accepting the microphone from Laurel. Alex followed shortly behind, taking some battered cards out of the inside pocket of his jacket. Laurel gave Nate a quick wink as she headed down the steps and to the back of the room.

He touched his laptop to bring it to life and checked that the title slide of his presentation was showing behind him.

'Hello, everyone, and thank you to Laurel and the Fletcher family for welcoming us to their farm.' There was scattered applause. 'You're all here to see what we've found here at Little Willow, so let's get to it.'

LAUREL

Nate was a brilliant speaker. He was clear, concise and perfectly paced. She knew he would be from the practice runs of his presentation, but it came across so much better in a well-fitted, dark suit (with a waistcoat that was causing her to melt into a small puddle), on a stage, over a microphone. He was damned sexy, with hints of grey at his temples and short stubble across his jawline. Flashes came from the photographer the University had hired, and she reminded herself to get a few of the pictures for advertising. Nate was calm and collected, and there was not a hint of nerves as he caught her eye. He winked with a sly smile that was meant just for her, but in full view of everyone.

There was applause as he finished his presentation. Yes, he may hate it, but if his reception was anything to go by, then people were going to be showering Nate with money. Provided Alex didn't fuck it up.

Alex went next, the crumpled record cards he'd been shuffling during Nate's speech awkward in his hands as he tried to use the mic. If Laurel had had any sympathy left for him at all, she would have been embarrassed at the car crash of his public speaking. Sure, it wasn't everyone's cup of tea and yeah, it was okay to be nervous. But Alex was badly prepared and badly presented. He obviously hadn't been through his speech more than once, and that one time had been on stage, just now. Compared to Nate's consummate performance, he was woefully inadequate. At least he had said the important words of 'the BAS see the potential here and fully endorse this site'.

What. A. Relief.

The bumbling and badly toned jokes didn't last very long and there was a small spatter of applause before Nate opened the floor for questions.

A raven-haired lady put her hand up. She was an academic.

'Dr Daley, Mr Woollard, are we to expect another groundbreaking collaborative paper from the two of you?'

Nate laughed slightly. 'Perhaps, Andrea. We haven't discussed it.'

He and Alex hadn't discussed it, because Alex hadn't been answering his emails. Nate had told Laurel there was no way he was collaborating academically with Alex ever again. Never.

'But the Pictish stylus paper was such a decisive change in how we look at the Picts, perhaps there is something on this site that you could use to change the thinking around Anglo-Saxons?'

Laurel rolled her eyes. For god's sake, Andrea, just drop it.

'I'm sure there are extremely interesting finds here and with further and better interpretation, I believe we will be able to add something individual and new to the existing body of work,' Nate said, shutting her down, flicking his eyes to other members of the audience with their hands half-raised.

Laurel glanced at the publications table. She should probably read Nate and Alex's paper on the Pictish stylus she found, see what it was that made it so special. Be a supportive and interested girlfriend.

She headed over to the table quietly and scanned the publication extracts, all neatly stapled in the corners before she found the one entitled 'Refocusing Pictish Interpretations, Alex Woollard and Nate Daley'. Alex coughed loudly over his mic, but she ignored him and started reading, the questions continuing in the background.

There are scant historical artifacts that influence our interpretation of the Picts. In fact, the majority of our knowledge comes from heavily biased, negative Roman sources. But what if the Romans were wrong? What if the Romans didn't understand Pictish society and let their prejudices of the tattooed, Viking-esque peoples prevent them from seeing any 'modern' development?

Huh, that seemed slightly familiar. From what she could remember from university, it didn't seem as formal or dry as other academic papers.

The discovery of the stylus at Hadrian's wall can illuminate the Picts in a different, more advanced light, an illumination that the Romans likely chose to ignore. The way in which the Romans invaded and conquered did not include the desire to learn from different cultures, but to dominate and assimilate. Thus, our commonly held idea that the Picts were 'uneducated heathens' likely comes from the Romans' desire for uniformity and eradication of indigenous culture.

Something picked in the back of Laurel's mind. Hadn't the paper that she'd left in Nate's pigeonhole all those years ago started similarly? Possibly, but more than one person can have the same idea. Didn't she have all her university work saved in a long-forgotten file in her Dropbox? She'd check. Another cough from Alex over the mic. He really was awful at public speaking.

It took a while, but she finally found the paper, buried at the end of the 'Uni Junk' folder. It took a while to load, but there it was, entitled 'Refocusing the Picts, Laurel Fletcher'. She scanned her eyes across the first paragraph, then frowned and read through it more carefully again.

It was the same.

Exactly. The. Same.

Laurel blinked a couple of times and refocused on both essays. There wasn't a single word of difference between the two introductions. The whole premise of Nate's superhero paper was based on her essay. The entire introduction had been lifted from her essay. The essay that she had written as an undergraduate. She'd been so proud when she'd written it, so nervous putting it in Nate's pigeonhole with a note asking him to meet her for a drink to discuss her ideas. Instead of having a constructive discussion and giving her feedback, he had sent Alex to humiliate her and then committed the cardinal academic sin.

He'd stolen her work. Stolen the work of an undergraduate and passed it off as his own.

It was a coup that a Masters student had come up with such a comprehensive essay, but an undergraduate? Unheard of.

Laurel flicked the pages of Nate's essay to the end to check the conclusion and compared it with hers. It was completely different, with better observations and more cohesive arguments. But the introduction was the thing that got people reading, that hooked people.

Angry tears pricked at the back of her eyes.

Dr Nathanial Daley's public popularity had waned after the initial rush of interest with his Pictish papers, and she scanned his other, drier, more academic papers. Not at all as engaging as her not-quite-academic introduction.

Laurel looked up at Nate on stage, mic in hand, answering another question with a secure, self-assured smile. How could she have been so stupid? Of course he wanted to forget about what happened ten years ago, because he had built his success on the paper he had stolen from her.

A fat tear smeared across the printed page of Nate's academic writing.

Feedback crackled over the speaker and she lifted her eyes to Alex, sweating profusely. He coughed again, put the mic down on the table and sidled off the stage, motioning at his throat.

Oh, hell no.

Alex was heading for her. There was absolutely no way she wanted to talk to fucking Alex now. Or ever again.

She could just imagine them now, laughing over how best

to humiliate her. Yes, make her feel ugly, disgusting, pathetic, so she would hate them so much, be so destroyed, that she wouldn't even bother to read the groundbreaking paper they'd written. Well, *they* should have included Laurel. Alex and Nate, *Nate*, had cut her out of it altogether. Stolen her work and published it as their own.

What was all this to Nate now? Just another ploy to get the Little Willow Farm dig site up and running? Another coup for the brilliant doctor's career? How could she have been so stupid?

Laurel fled the conference hall, pushing past Robin and Jack by the door.

'Laurel, what's going on,' Jack hissed, but she ignored him and burst out into the cold autumn afternoon.

The door closed behind her again, and it was Alex who had followed her out.

'Leaving your own reception, are you?' he asked derisively.

'What do you care?'

Alex took two large steps towards her, and he was quick for a big guy. She would not step back even though he was crowding her.

'Read my paper, have you?' he asked, smugly.

'You and Nate stole my work, then you decimated me, destroyed me in that student union bar, so I wouldn't ever come after you. You two are fucking horrendous human beings,' she ground out, desperately trying to keep her tears in. 'You're the worst kind of academics. You're *thieves* without any original ideas.'

'I was sparing you. Telling you the truth. Giving you some much needed advice, Laurel.' Alex gripped the top of her arm tightly. 'And now I'll give you some more.' His voice had dropped, low and dangerous.

'Get your fucking hands off me.' She tried to rip her arm away from him, but he was too strong.

'You need to listen to this,' he whispered, ruddy face way too close to hers. 'Because you seem to think that you've got some kind of power here. You don't. You're worthless here, you understand? You are nothing to Nate, you just keep his bed warm at night until he moves onto the next, better girl.'

'You don't know what you're talking about,' Laurel said, but her voice was small.

'Yes, I do. I know him better than he knows himself. He still thinks of you as that pathetic, scared little girl playing dress up in your ridiculous black dress, trying to steal him away from his girlfriend, who, by the way, is much more of a woman than you will ever be,' he spat.

'Fuck you, Alex.' Her voice wobbled unsteadily.

He snorted and leaned closer. 'You're not scared, are you Laurel?'

Laurel opened her mouth and then closed it again, because she was confused and hurt and desperately sad. And yes, she was scared, because Alex was enormous and angry, his grip a vice on her arm.

'Get your hands off my sister,' Jack said from behind Alex, voice like iron, and she had never, ever, been so glad to hear her big brother.

NATE

Nate cut the questions short when Alex jumped off the stage and rushed outside after Laurel. Whatever that conversation was going to be, 'good' was not an outcome he expected.

Sylvie had taken the stage in lieu of Laurel and directed the audience to the buffet and drinks area, which was good, because that meant he had a clear run outside. He glanced around, but Jack and Robin were nowhere to be seen either.

His stomach dropped. This wasn't good.

Nate burst outside, taking in the Fletcher boys flanking Laurel, her face tear-streaked and shattered. He moved to her, but she shrank away from him into Jack's side. What? He frowned, then looked to his old friend.

'What the hell is going on?' he asked, warily. 'Alex, what have you done?'

Alex's shirt was hanging out, blood dripping through his fingers clutching at his nose.

'I haven't done anything! That fucking farm boy punched me!' Alex spat blood on the ground.

Nate looked at Robin, who shook his head and pointed to Jack.

Jack? Why had Jack punched Alex? Laurel was at Jack's side, his arm slung over her shoulder.

'What's happened?' Nate asked, reaching for her.

She flinched away from him and pulled out her phone, tapping viciously at it.

'All I know, is if that bastard puts his hands on my sister again, a broken nose will be the least of his problems,' Jack said, voice steely.

Nate's anger burst to the surface.

'You did *what?*'

'Come on, I didn't do anything. This has all been blown out of proportion.' Alex spread his hands wide in appeasement. 'I was just having a little chat with Laurel here.'

Nate looked at her, and his smartwatch vibrated.

'Yeah, we were having a chat,' Laurel said, voice thin.

He took a step towards her, but she flinched away again. His stomach clenched.

'Can you please tell me what's happened?' he asked gently, holding up his hands as he would do to a scared animal.

'I'll tell you what's happened,' Laurel said in a quiet, dangerous voice he had never heard before.

'Uh oh,' Robin said under his breath.

'No wonder you wanted to forget about what happened ten years ago, Nate,' she started, stepping away from Jack, her hands clenched at her sides. 'Because you stole my work, and sent your best friend here,' Laurel shot a dirty look at Alex, 'to tell me what a waste of space you thought I was. An ugly, pathetic loser who had no business writing a paper, and what the hell was I doing trying to get between you and your golden girlfriend, Lucia, because you wouldn't look twice at someone like me. That frankly I was arrogant and you couldn't ever speak to me. That you were so embarrassed for me.'

Tears were flowing freely down her face, dripping off her chin onto the gravel floor.

'Laurel, I don't know what you're talking about.'

'Then you published *my* paper. You stole my work, Nate. You and your best friend here. Then you have the gall to come to my home and ask me to forgive you? To worm your way into my life? Fuck, you're cold.'

'Laurel, I don't—' He stepped towards her, but stopped as Robin stepped forward too. Nate knew a warning when he saw one. Was this what had happened ten years ago? Did Alex really say those things? 'Stole your paper?'

'Really? You don't know anything about it?' she asked, but the sarcasm was heavy. 'You don't remember sending your best friend to eviscerate me? You must have blocked out receiving my paper because it was too embarrassing, yeah?'

'What paper? Laurel, I swear to you, I never saw your paper,' he said, racking his brain, because surely he would remember something like that.

'Well, you've got a chance to revisit those memories, because I've just sent you a copy of it, and it would appear that the introduction to your 'breakthrough paper' was actually lifted word for word from the essay that this pathetic, arrogant, embarrassing undergraduate wrote.'

He looked at Alex.

'What did you do?' he whispered.

There was a flit of hesitancy across Laurel's face as they all looked at Alex, wiping blood on the sleeve of his jacket.

'Oh, mate, I didn't do anything you didn't know about. Come on, Nate,' he said.

'Laurel, I didn't—' he started, but she interrupted him.

'You asked me to forget about it, to start afresh, and it was all because you wanted to keep your dirty little plagiarism a secret,' she said and fresh tears sprung to her eyes. 'Was everything a lie?'

'No, Laurel, that's—' he said, reaching for her, but she held up her hands.

'I can't be around you,' she whispered.

'Rebecca's home. You can go to her,' Jack said.

Laurel walked away as quickly as she could. Nate started to go after her, but Robin caught his arm.

'Nah, mate,' he said, eyes flashing with anger.

Robin exchanged a quick confirmatory glance with Jack before pulling his arm back and punching Nate hard in the face. Christ, it was as if he had been hit like a tractor. He crumpled to one knee as pain exploded across his face, clamping his hand over his cheek where Robin had solidly landed his fist.

'I told you if you hurt my sister, we would smash your face in,' Jack said blithely. 'And the two of you have pissed her right off.'

'Alex, what the fuck?' Nate shouted, getting back to his feet as quickly as he could. Somehow, this was all his fault, Nate knew it in his stomach.

'Nate, come on, man. It's not my fault she took it the wrong way,' Alex huffed.

'Took *what* the wrong way? What about a stolen paper?' Nate asked, stalking forward towards his old friend.

'I don't know what she's talking about,' Alex lied, and lied badly.

Nate gave a brittle laugh. 'Don't give me that shit.'

Alex looked around, but there was no one to help him. Jack and Robin were watching intently, wondering whether either of them needed a further punching.

'Look, I didn't do anything you wouldn't have done,' Alex said.

Nate frowned at him and barked out a harsh laugh.

'I'm not sure that's true, Alex.'

'Come on, mate,' he said, easy camaraderie barely masking his distress. 'I didn't say anything you didn't think anyway.'

'How the fuck would you know?' Nate shouted, all semblance of calm completely disappearing. 'I had absolutely no fucking idea that she'd written a paper, that you said those vile things and completely destroyed her.'

Alex sighed dramatically. 'Alright, alright. I walked past her and saw that something had been left in your pigeonhole, so I took a look.' He shrugged nonchalantly. 'She'd even written a note on it asking you to meet her for a drink.' Alex snorted. 'Yeah right,' he said under his breath.

What the actual fuck?

So, Alex was a thief, a plagiariser, a goddamned awful human being, and moreover, Nate was implicated as well.

'Let me get this straight.' Nate pushed a hand through his hair. 'You saw something in my pigeonhole, read it, stole it, met Laurel, berated her, and then fed me her paper bit by bit as your own personal ideas?'

Alex finally started to look nervous and he licked his lips, eyes glancing to the hardened Fletcher boys. They were taking it all in. Nate would not want to be in Alex's shoes if Robin and Jack decided to avenge Laurel further. Robin was a barely tethered Doberman.

'I wouldn't put it exactly like that,' Alex said, wringing his hands.

'How would you put it,' Jack paused for a second, 'mate?'

Alex threw an incredulous look at Jack as if he wondered how Jack even dared talk to him.

'I'm not sure that you would understand.'

Robin's neck strained as he held himself back, but Jack just laughed. Threw back his head and belly laughed.

'I think the only one who doesn't understand things here is you,' he said, eyes crinkling from mirth. 'You see this boy here?' He flicked his thumb over his shoulder at Robin, who gave Alex a feral grin. 'I'm the only thing stopping him from ripping your face off, so I suggest that you get the fuck off of my farm, and never *ever* go near my sister again.'

Nate vowed to never get on the wrong side of Jack, because Alex looked as if he was about to piss his pants. He shot a pleading look over to Nate, but Nate just shook his head.

There was no way he was going to help Alex out of this shit storm, or any other shit storm, ever again.

CHAPTER TWENTY-ONE

LAUREL

'I can't believe I've been so stupid,' Laurel whispered into her hands. 'So stupid.'

'Let me get this straight,' Rebecca said, pacing by the long side of the table. The kids were watching the TV in the front room. 'Nate Daley, the archaeologist, and Alex Woollard, the British Archaeological Society liaison for said Nate Daley, stole your essay when you were in university, published it and became famous as a result?'

'That's right,' she said bitterly. Her head was starting to hurt.

'And what happened then?' Rebecca said, more gently this time.

'What do you mean? I didn't know that they'd stolen it, I thought Nate had just chucked it or something, after...' she trailed off. 'Then I came home from uni and that was the end of it. I put archaeology behind me, remember? I didn't think of it again until I saw their paper today. Well, the first page of my paper.' She rubbed shaky hands over her face. 'I'm so stupid.'

'You're not stupid, not at all,' Rebecca said, sitting next to her. 'Tell me, what did you mean when you said "or something, after..."?'

Sometimes it sucked having a solicitor as a best friend, because she was intent on dragging every little detail out.

'Alex humiliated me because Nate told him to.'

It was a whisper because she couldn't seem to make her voice any louder.

'What?' Rebecca said coldly. 'Alex Woollard did what?'

Laurel looked at Rebecca with wet eyes and told her everything. Told her how she had left the essay in Nate's pigeonhole, how she had left a note on it asking him for a drink to discuss it. She talked about Alex and Nate arriving, laughing with Lucia and others at the bar. Laurel repeated every word that Alex had said to her, burned into her memory forever.

Some wounds, no matter how old, are still raw when you pick at them, and this was like taking a sledgehammer to her rebuilt confidence.

'And then Nate turned up here,' Rebecca was saying.

'He turned up here and he was so charming, and he didn't say anything about it, he just wanted to put it behind us, he wanted us to be *us*, and I…' She stifled a sob. 'I fell for it all.'

'Oh Laurel.'

'I wanted to,' she carried on, throat burning. 'I wanted to believe him, but he lied. He stole my work and passed it off as his own. Can you imagine what my life would have been like if he hadn't betrayed me?'

'Laurel, you can't think like that,' Rebecca said gently. 'You would have still come back here, you would have, because this is your home, this is your life.'

'But it didn't have to be,' Laurel said forcefully. 'Can you imagine if my paper had been published by me, the person who actually wrote it? As an *undergraduate*? It would have changed everything.'

'You would have still wanted to come home and help the farm. You can tell yourself that you wouldn't, but I know you, Laurel Fletcher, and you would.' Rebecca took a breath. 'But that's not the real issue here, is it?'

As much as she hated to admit it, Rebecca was right. Laurel could never have let her family farm go under, not her mother's home, their family home, her home. Regardless of how many opportunities could have presented themselves, how many doors may have opened, she would never have walked through them. Laurel had been needed here, and she would never have turned her back on her family.

Laurel shook her head. No, it wasn't the real issue at all.

'I trusted him. He made me fall in love with him, and look, he's just like everyone else,' Laurel said bitterly, tears flowing freely down her blotchy face. 'He's a liar, a betrayer, a selfish manipulator. Everything he said about wanting a future with me, introducing me to his friends.' Laurel shook her head again. 'I believed him.'

'Laurel,' Rebecca said, as fresh sobs wrenched from Laurel's chest. 'Shh, shh, come here.'

Laurel lay her head on Rebecca's shoulder. Something inside her was breaking, cracking, wilting and dying.

Rebecca shifted and picked up her phone that was vibrating on the table. Laurel didn't let go of her.

'Jack? Are you with him?' she asked. 'No. Absolutely not.'

There was a pause.

'I'll stop you there, Jack,' Rebecca said, using her curt solicitor voice. 'I don't give a flying fuck whether Nate Daley has grown chicken feet and a teat that produces orange juice. There is no way he is coming in this house.'

God, she loved Rebecca.

'Tell him to go to his own house, the pub, his precious hole in the ground, drown in the lake. I. Don't. Give. A. Shit.' There was a pause where Jack obviously debated whether to relay that to Nate or not. 'Mmm hmm, when are you coming home? I need to take Laurel back to hers. I'll be there a while.'

Another pause.

'Okay, love you too,' she said before putting the phone back on the table.

They sat for a long time, Rebecca stroking her hair and rocking her gently, as she would rock one of the kids.

'Jack will be back soon, then I'll take you home in your car. You don't want to be here.'

Laurel nodded, exhausted and eminently grateful that Rebecca knew her so well.

But did she want to be at home? She'd been sleeping in one of Nate's t-shirts (a threadbare blue Time Team Archaeologist one), his papers were spread across her dining table, his running trainers by the door. Her bedroom smelled of him.

But she could sanitise it, get rid of him from her flat. Rebecca would help.

And then, maybe it would be better.

NATE

Nate did the only thing he could think of. He worked. He was first at the site, he was last to leave, and it didn't stop there. Sleep was evading him, so he catalogued everything, described everything in minute detail. When he finally fell, utterly exhausted, into bed, he had three or four hours of fitful dozing before he repeated the whole groundhog day again. He was dying inside, and Laurel wouldn't talk to him. She didn't believe him.

He had to work to get the anger out. To fill his mind with something else. Anger at Alex, mainly, but also angry at Laurel. How could she not even give him the chance to explain himself? She obviously believed Alex's bullshit story and he had done the worst thing an academic could do. Plagiarism was punishable by death. Well, not exactly, but you wouldn't work again in a historical academic environment. Ever.

It was career ending, and Alex had put them both in this position. There was no saving Alex from himself this time, and Nate had to hope he had enough academic clout to distance himself from this entire debacle. It was going to come out sooner or later. Surely, *surely*, someone would have overheard, and academics were notorious gossips, especially about something as juicy as this. He had to get in front of it, had to minimise damage for himself and for the dig site. But how? Whatever he did, he had to do it soon. It had been nearly a week.

Ivor wasn't going to be much help. He could go to the Chair of the University, but was that overkill? He could throw Alex under the bus, but quite frankly, he had already done that to himself.

And Laurel wouldn't talk to him.

It was such a mess, and he couldn't work it out by himself. He needed her arms around him, her reassuring smile, her sharp mind. She obviously didn't need him because if she had done, she wouldn't have had Sylvie reply to his emails (both personal and business). She would have replied to his text asking to let him explain, his voicemail saying it wasn't true, that he *didn't* know what Alex had done.

Nate's throat tightened again as he checked his phone (just in case) for the fourteenth time in half an hour. He put it back in his pocket and dragged his hands over his face. Nothing.

'Dr Daley! Nate! You need to see this!'

Nate turned to see Anwar, who was waving wildly at him from trench one.

'It's a bone, Dr Daley. I think it's a jawbone, I can see teeth.'

'Good, Anwar.' Nate jumped down into the trench and bent to examine what Anwar had found. Nate's heart beat steadily as he assessed it. 'Yes, and see here? That's the zygomatic bone.' Nate brushed away soft dirt just above. 'Which one is that?'

'The bottom outside corner bone of the eye socket.' Anwar was hopeful.

'Good, and what should we find next to it?' Nate murmured, soft strokes of his soft brush pushing at the earth.

'The maxilla along the bottom and the frontal along the top.'

'Male or female?'

'Too early to tell. We'll need to get to the supraorbital margin first.'

'Gut?'

'Male. I think it's a warrior burial.'

Nate thought so too, the jaw was square and it felt *bulky*, much more so than a female skull. 'Why?'

'We found a shield boss, it's at the top of a mound... I don't know, I've just got a feeling.' Anwar flicked his fingers against his thighs quickly.

'Female warrior?' Nate pushed.

Anwar sucked in a breath. If it was, which Nate was pretty sure it wasn't, it would change history. Anglo-Saxon female warriors were usually high status (for example, Aethelflaed of Mercia) and therefore buried with a lot more fanfare than this soul here. There was that burial in Norfolk of a woman with a sword-like instrument which was without doubt not high status, but that was Viking. This was Anglo-Saxon in the heart of the Kingdom of Wessex, so it was unlikely.

'That would be amazing. Do you think it is?'

'I don't know, Anwar. You'll have to find out.' He knew it wasn't, but he needed to let Anwar discover so for himself.

The student gaped at him. 'Me? Don't you want to... you want me to do it?'

'You found it, didn't you?' Nate smiled benevolently. As much as he wanted to greedily uncover the bones, he was here to teach and to mentor. 'You know your way around a skull. Just be careful and call me if you're uncertain about anything. *Anything,* Anwar.'

Anwar nodded, his eyes locked on the jawbone and eye socket jutting out of the earth.

Nate climbed out of the trench and left Anwar excitedly pointing out the bones to the undergrads. He pulled out his phone and scrolled to Laurel, hesitating before he pressed the green call button. But she deserved to know, didn't she? She had a *right* to know. It was her land, after all, and this was a massively significant find. It would mean at least another year of dig work, and another two, perhaps three, years of research analysis. Apart from the gold and other bits found, these bones would provide a central focal point for any visitor attraction. But more than that, he wanted to share the find with her. He wanted her excitement, her happiness.

He pressed call, and waited as the phone rang once, twice, heart in his mouth.

'This is Laurel Fletcher. I'm sorry I've missed your call, please leave…'

Nate heart sagged. He left her a voicemail:

'Hey, it's Nate. I wanted to tell you that we've found a skull in trench one, it's probably male and I would go as far as to say this could be quite a significant burial site.' He swallowed. 'I just wanted to tell you. I can show you, if you like?'

Was that too much? Well, he'd said it now.

'Okay, bye.'

Nate stared at the phone, hoping Laurel would ring back. But she wouldn't. She hadn't returned any of his other messages.

The discovery of this skull meant that there would be more scrutiny on this dig, more interest. He had to do something about the whole plagiarism thing. Something like that could ruin this dig, and he was not going to let that happen. Not to his students, and certainly not to Laurel.

He would fix this. But how?

LAUREL

Laurel saved the voicemail message after she'd listened to it, just like she'd saved the last two. She read his texts again and again. The ones where he had said he didn't know that Alex had lied to him, that he would never have done what he was accused of doing. Every email was forwarded to Sylvie to deal with. Laurel had read them, of course. Nate sent dig site updates at the end of every day, a commentary on his professional life.

He'd sent one explanatory email after the disaster of the BAS endorsement conference, asking her to talk to him, let him explain, that he hadn't known *anything*, that he would never ever deal with Alex again.

She missed him.

But how could he not have known? Had he been stupid enough to think that Alex had an interest in developing the historiography of the Picts? He had obviously known. And he had stood there, laughing with Lucia, whilst Alex... well. She wasn't going to think about that again.

The conference had been a success, that is, until it had all imploded.

Little Willow had put on a good show. The cafe had excelled itself with the local produce and Sylvie had been the most amazing deputy she could ever wish for. After the buffet, she'd walked the entire conference up to the site, roped Anwar into giving a little talk about the trenches, and promised them more wine back at the conference centre. The English Heritage officer had been impressed, and Sylvie had formed a lovely relationship with her.

Sylvie's damage control deserved more than a bottle of cheap wine, and Laurel made a note on the pad on her desk to talk to Barbara, the accountant, about a pay rise.

Even though it was in the university's hands now, the advertising and promotion opportunities from the conference had been immense.

Laurel waited until six, until she knew that the students would have put down their tools for the day, and the site would be clear and quiet. She really wanted to see the skull. This was a success of all the work she had put into this dig, and she wanted to be part of it. Although, she wanted to be a part of it on her own terms, without a certain archaeologist whose fireworks and earth smell she wanted wrapped around her.

The last time she'd been up to the dig was when she'd done the first walking routes with the academics before the presentations. Sylvie had ended up taking over the last few. She had stepped into the large void left by Laurel and had been absolutely fantastic. She definitely needed a pay rise.

There was going to be one hell of a thunderstorm soon. She could feel it, as the sun settled over the fields, making the dig site shiny and golden. Laurel trudged her way up the slope to trench one and slid unceremoniously into the hole in the earth. It must be there, under the rectangular tarpaulin pinned to the ground in the top left of the trench. Careful not to disturb anything, Laurel picked her way through the trench and knelt in the earth. Her hands trembled as she unpinned two corners and peeled back the tarpaulin.

There it was, sitting proud against the earth; jawbone, cheekbone, eye socket, the curve of the top of the skull. She didn't know much about facial bone structure (bones hadn't really been her thing because she liked shiny things), but if Nate said it was male, it was male.

Laurel rocked back on her heels and closed her eyes against the dying sunlight. A weight lifted from her. This had English Heritage written all over it, and this find, this *person,* would bring in so many visitors to Little Willow Farm, visitors who would need somewhere to park, somewhere to eat, and perhaps a walk around the lake, exclaiming 'Oh look, what a lovely place for a wedding/conference/birthday party!' This was everything.

'Oh, hey.'

Laurel's eyes snapped open and a weight reappeared like a stone in the pit of her stomach. She pulled the tarp back over the skull, hurriedly pinning it back into place.

'I thought everyone had gone,' she muttered. Because she wouldn't have come if she knew he was going to be here.

'Yeah, no. I was just finishing up,' Nate said, indicating the shiny new dig tent that the university had sprung for now they'd had BAS endorsement. He hopped down into the trench. 'I can show you if you like?'

'I've seen it.'

There was a moment of silence between them, and it was not comfortable. Not in the slightest. She pushed herself to her feet and headed back the way she'd came, away from his pleading face. Away from him.

'Laurel, please stay. Please talk to me.'

She couldn't stay, she couldn't talk to him. She was too angry, and being too angry led her to make rash decisions. Like calling Ivor Rowlands at the university to tell him that his prize pupil was a lying, thieving, plagiarist. Like calling the British Archaeological Society and getting Nate and Alex disbarred or disavowed, or whatever it was. Excluded. Ruined. Like her.

'I don't want to.' She didn't look up at him as she sat on the edge of the trench and swung her legs up.

'Stay? Or talk to me?'

There was a slight accusative tone to his voice that Laurel didn't like one little bit. 'Both.'

'It hurts, you know.'

Laurel finally looked at him and raised her eyebrow sceptically. What? How had she hurt him? He didn't have an archaeological career stolen, one that he'd never even known about.

'That you don't trust me. That you won't even give me the chance to explain, to convince you,' Nate said. He didn't try to move towards her, didn't try to touch her and for that she was grateful.

'To convince me that Alex acted on his own accord? We both know that Alex Woollard couldn't tie his own shoelaces without guidance, Nate,' she scoffed.

'Laurel, please.'

Nate's voice broke and she watched his throat work into a long, heavy swallow. She couldn't let him talk to her. If she did, he would use his pretty, perfect mouth to manipulate the situation, to control it just as he had ten years ago.

'Nate, *no*.'

Laurel pushed herself to her feet and forced them forward. She needed to put some space between them, otherwise she would be tempted to scream and shout and cry and kiss and that wouldn't do well for anybody, especially her.

CHAPTER TWENTY-TWO

NATE

Nate tried a different tack. He explained everything ad nauseam, to Jack and Rebecca.

Rebecca had been so harsh in her cross examination, picking into every single detail. 'You knew *nothing* of Alex's words to Laurel?… You really thought he was coming up with those ideas *himself?*… And Laurel is supposed to still fancy you?'

Yes, he admitted he has been a stupid, stupid man on more than one occasion, and he'd had that spelled out to him by Rebecca excruciatingly clearly.

Jack was sick of hearing the story. He could repeat it word for word.

But even Jack and Rebecca could not get Laurel to talk to Nate. She had an escort to and from her car, refused to let him into her office, refused to see him and apparently shut down every conversation in which Nate's name was brought up.

It was the truth. He didn't know about any of it.

It was Alex who had stolen Laurel's paper out of Nate's pigeonhole. Alex who had plagiarised it, copied it word for fucking word. Alex who had sat opposite Laurel in the student union bar and told her that she was wasting her time with both archaeology and Nate. It was Alex who had told her she was pathetic, less than nothing, destroyed her self-esteem, laughed at her, all because he didn't have the brains to come up with anything original himself. All because he was *jealous* of her work.

He remembered seeing Alex sitting across from a young Laurel in a black strappy dress, drink on the table. Remembered her leaving. Remembered Alex saying 'you've got to let them down gently when they chase you'. Remembered *laughing* with Alex about it.

Nate felt slimy and icky every time he thought about it.

Then there was the paper itself. Yes, the introduction had been good, epic even for an academic paper. It had entered a brave new world of engaging language, enticing non-academics to read further, getting people excited. It had got him excited anyway. But the rest of Alex's (Laurel's?) essay had needed work, needed honing, needed further exploration and a widening of scope. The conclusion had needed work, needed expansion and tightening. Nate had written and rewritten and edited and revised and rewritten the essay over and over.

But he had never touched that introduction.

'Dr Daley.' A soft voice interrupted his staring into space thinking about nothing. 'Do you want a cup of tea or anything?' The girl with the spider eyelashes asked him. It seems it's Dr Daley again now. Good.

'No thanks,' he replied, with a tight smile.

He hated living in Robin's house, with these students.

He wanted Laurel's warm sofa, the smell of her shampoo in the morning, coffee from her cafetiere, her arms around him.

But she didn't want to talk to him, and he couldn't blame her. Actually, screw that, he could blame her. If Laurel actually cared about him, she would at least give him the opportunity to explain. Explain that it was all Alex, that he had never known she'd written anything, never known what Alex had said to her that fateful day in the university pub.

He understood why she was acting like she was, but if only she would let him explain.

Nate was sunken and hollow. He'd invested everything into this relationship with Laurel, and it was falling apart around him.

Then things started to happen.

The Chair of the Ethics Committee from the university called, expressing their 'extreme discomfort' at such allegations being levied against one of their most prestigious and celebrated staff members. The Ethics Committee representative made it eminently clear that his job was on the line. The career that he had worked so hard for, for so long, was at danger of becoming lost in the smoke, and all because of Alex. Nate accepted the emergency ethics meeting set for next week.

The second was a stroppy text from Lucia.

Lucia

> What the fuck, Nate? You're getting your friends fired now? You're a bastard, you know that. I can't believe you.

He ignored it.

Then, Owen called. He'd heard from Alex that there had been an argument, that Nate had been 'unreasonable' and 'wouldn't listen' and 'was making a huge mistake'.

'Is that what he said? That I got him fired?' Nate shouted down the phone. He was full of rage.

'Yeah, well, he's suspended because of something you did. They're having a disciplinary meeting to look into it. Something about ethical violation?' Owen sighed. 'What the fuck did you do?'

'What did *I* do? Why do you immediately think that it was my fault? Didn't you think that Alex phoning you was his clumsy-ass attempt to get out ahead of it?' Nate snapped. 'He's the one who has put my relationship, not to mention my entire career, in danger, without me even knowing about it!'

'But what is it?' Owen said, shuffling the phone. He could hear two sets of breaths. Jess was there as well.

'You want to know what he did?' Nate took one of the student's cans of Fosters from the fridge and snapped it open. 'I'll tell you.'

They were appalled. There was no other word for it.

'But how do the BAS know?' Jess asked, distorted down the phone.

'It all happened at the fucking funding meeting, Jess,' Nate said, running a hand through his hair. 'You know what academics are like, massive gossips. It must have spread like wildfire.'

There was silence at the end of the phone.

'What?' he prompted them.

'So, really, Alex didn't contribute anything to that paper, did he? There was Laurel's introduction, and then you did the grunt work in polishing her ideas, as presented by Alex.' Jess put it succinctly.

'Not just polishing,' he commented.

'Well, there we are then, you essentially collaborated with Laurel, not Alex,' Jess said. 'How did none of us see that Alex wasn't clever enough to come up with those imaginative ideas? Anyway,' she hesitated, 'what has Laurel said?'

Nate deflated.

'She won't talk to me. She thinks I was involved. She thinks I knew.'

The hole in his chest ached.

'She's hurting, she's feeling betrayed, she's struggling with all of this. I know I would be.' There was silence at the end of the line, before Jess said, 'Nate, do you love her?'

Did he love her? Could he not think without knowing she was alright? Was he crawling out of his skin not being able to talk to her, to touch her, to kiss her? He'd loved her since the moment he had picked her up out of the cow dung in the car park.

'Yes,' he said, hoarsely.

'I'm glad you've admitted that to yourself because we could all see it,' Jess said.

But saying it out loud, admitting it to his friends, he felt vulnerable. It scared him more than he wanted to admit. Laurel didn't want anything to do with him, and it was just going to make his chest ache more.

'So, if you love her, which you do, then what are you going to do about it?' Jess was tough. He rubbed his eyes, his chin quivering slightly.

'Jess,' he whispered. 'She doesn't want to see me.'

'Right, if I have to come there, I will.'

No thanks, Jess.

'I saw how she looked at you. I talked with her. She loves you just as much as you love her, and at the moment she's hurting and it's easier to ignore you.'

He could only wish that was true, that Laurel loved him back.

'So, are you going to sit around moping in your ratty jogging bottoms?' Jess asked.

He picked at his ratty jogging bottoms, self-consciously.

'Or are you going to do something? Are you going to prove to her that you are the man she thinks you are?'

'Jess, I don't know.' He didn't want to push Laurel.

But Jess carried on.

'A grand gesture, Nate, that's what you need. A grand gesture. Let me help.'

He didn't have anything to lose at this point.

'Okay.'

LAUREL

There was no makeup in the world that could make her look human. Laurel tried, but the dark rings under her eyes just wouldn't be covered up. Her skin was pallid and drawn, and because she had mainly eaten mini sausages and chocolate for the past week, oily and bumpy. But life went on, and there were emails to answer, there were people to cultivate.

The easiest way to cope, Laurel had found, was to not think about it. To keep extremely busy, to wear out her body and mind until the point of exhaustion so she didn't have to lie awake thinking of him.

Laurel was finishing off an email to the vet querying how much the medication had cost for pig mastitis, because surely that invoice was way too high, when her door opened.

'Sylvie, I'm busy,' she mumbled without looking up.

'Uh no. No, no, no,' Rebecca said tartly, heels clicking on the floor as she strode into the room. 'This is not how your life is going to be, thank you.'

'Rebecca, why aren't you at work?' Initial relief was quickly replaced by anxiety. 'Are the kids alright? Why are you home?'

'Yes, they're fine, the nanny has them,' Rebecca said, checking her phone. 'I'm here for you.'

'Me? Why? What's happened?'

'Oh good lord, Laurel. You are a mess. A big fat mess, and I, as your best-friend-slash-sister-in-law, am not going to allow this anymore.'

Rebecca was pristine in her wide leg trousers and silk shirt, hair beautifully waved, the epitome of a successful businesswoman.

'Rebecca, I just want to finish these emails, then I'm going home,' she said, face dropping.

'No.'

'What do you mean, no?' Laurel asked, her tiredness forcing her to snap.

'I mean, no.' Rebecca pursed her lips and hardened her face. 'Come on, there's something you need to see.'

'Whatever it is, I'm sure Sylvie can—' Laurel started, turning back to her computer.

'I know what Sylvie can do, she is amazing, and you don't pay her enough.' Rebecca checked her phone again. If there was somewhere else she wanted to be, then she could just leave. That would be fine.

'But this isn't about Sylvie. This is about you.'

Laurel sighed. Rebecca meant well, they all did. Jack had tried talking to her about Nate, and even Robin attempted to work him into conversation. She shut those down quickly. There was no point in torturing herself. A clean break, that's what it required. Another week, she would start to feel better and then she could talk about it. Maybe.

'What?' she asked, not bothering to hide her frustration.

'Come on, it's nearly time,' Rebecca said, looking at her phone again and waving at Laurel to stand up.

'Rebecca, I'm warning you. I don't want to see—' she didn't finish her sentence.

'I know, I know,' Rebecca tilted her head to the side. 'But you'll have to talk to him sooner or later.'

'Later will be fine.' Laurel grabbed her phone and shoved it in her pocket. 'What do you want to show me?'

Rebecca grinned and her eyes sparkled.

'Come on. Follow me.'

It would help if Rebecca didn't strut off like a viper was chasing her. Laurel cursed under her breath as she rushed to keep up. But Rebecca only made it down the corridor to Sylvie's office, into which she disappeared with a grin.

What the bastard-hell was going on? If it was some kind of surprise party, some kind of thing to cheer her up, that was not something she could deal with today.

Not. At. All.

'Guys, what's going on?' Laurel rounded the door timidly.

She didn't put it past Rebecca to think that it would be best for her to see Nate, perhaps hiding in Sylvie's office, wilting forgiveness-begging flowers in hand, stupid crooked smile, all contrite and apologetic. That, sweet Rebecca, would not go down well.

'Shh, it's starting,' Rebecca said, motioning her to come in and sit down.

Sylvie's computer screen had been turned around and the four chairs in the office set in front, like a cinema showing. Robin was lazing on one chair, arm across the back of Sylvie's chair who was perched uncertainly next to him, paperwork on her lap. Rebecca was next, and she patted the hard seat of the chair next to her for Laurel, eyes glued to the screen.

'What's starting? What are we watching?' Laurel said, but was quickly shushed by all three of them.

It was an afternoon talk show with a roving reporter talking animatedly into the camera.

Wait. That looked like the lake at Little Willow, and was that her woodland just behind it?

'Is that here?' Laurel asked. When had this happened?

'Yes!' Sylvie said excitedly. 'They came a couple of days ago, I wanted it to be a surprise for you. You're not mad, are you?' Sylvie suddenly looked anxious, bless her.

'No, not at all. That's amazing Sylvie. You've got us on TV. Really, really good job,' Laurel said. Definite pay rise.

'It wasn't me,' the girl mumbled.

'But it's not just luscious fields, peaceful cows and a delightful little cafe here. There's something a lot more interesting going on here as well,' the reporter on screen was saying, 'and we have Dr Nathanial Daley here to explain.'

'No.'

Laurel started to stand, but Rebecca grabbed her arm and forced her to sit down.

'Yes,' she said forcefully. 'If you're not going to listen to me, the least you can do is sit here for five minutes.'

'I hate you,' Laurel said, not meaning it.

Rebecca shrugged. 'Whatever, sister-in-law.'

'Yes, that's right, Katie. The Anglo-Saxon burial in this field is an exciting and captivating find,' on-screen-Nate said. His voice was brittle but calm as he talked about the various finds that had been pulled out of the ground.

'But something else has caused quite a stir in the archaeological world recently, hasn't it?' Reporter Katie was serious and Nate nodded gravely.

'You may remember that Dr Daley was a guest on our show ten years ago, with his ground-breaking interpretation of a Pictish writing implement that could indicate that the Picts were a lot more educated than we gave them credit for.' Laurel clenched her teeth and rolled her eyes. 'Can you tell us what's happened?'

Nate looked at the camera.

'It's recently come to light that the paper that was published under mine and someone else's name plagiarised an undergraduate's work.'

'Tell us why this is a big deal, Dr Daley,' Reporter Katie carried on, drawing the story out of him.

'This undergraduate had her work stolen and has never received credit for her ideas or work. Actually, I've been in touch with the publishers who are issuing a statement and removing the paper from publication. I hope that I will be able to collaborate with her to hone and shape this paper the way she originally envisaged it.'

The publishers were retracting it? Was he saying he didn't know about it? Surely he wouldn't be spouting this unless he was one hundred percent sure that it wouldn't be proved otherwise. He wants to work together on rewriting the paper?

This was a lot of information for Laurel to take in.

Sylvie reached across Rebecca and shoved the paperwork she had been holding into Laurel's hands. It was the front cover of the extract of the Pictish stylus paper with her name there, in bright, bold letters, just underneath Nate's.

Not Alex's. Hers.

A Post-it note scrawled in Nate's handwriting was stuck haphazardly across the title:

It's not settled yet, but this is what I'm pushing for. I honestly didn't know. I would never have let him. N

'But there's more, isn't there, Dr Daley?'

Laurel's attention snapped back to the TV screen, where reporter Katie's face was plastered with a smug grin.

'Yes, Katie, there is.' Nate took a breath. 'I'm going away to give the author some space because, understandably, this has been a big shock to her. But when I'm back I hope she forgives me, because…' He looked straight at the camera, directly at her. 'I am in love with her, and I can't live without her.'

Laurel stood and the mocked up paper fluttered to the ground.

The world fell away.

'Where is he?'

NATE

The taxi had been late because it was hammering down. Yes, the British rain had well and truly found its way to Little Houghton and the back roads were slippery and pot-holed, and half of them were built on peat so they shifted uncertainly every time there was a downpour. He should be at the train station by now, it would be leaving in five minutes. Well, there was always the next one. Jess and Owen wouldn't mind if he was late.

Giving Laurel some space would be the best thing. Little Willow was her home and he had to let her work through this herself. Nate had thought of going to Paul in the south of France, but what if she wanted him? What if she needed him? It would take a day to get back to her, rather than a couple of hours on the train.

Nate's eyes were rusty from lack of sleep and his beard was too long.

He checked his phone again. Nothing.

Surely Laurel would have seen it by now? Rebecca and Sylvie had promised. They'd promised.

Perhaps his grand gesture was too much, too intimate to be splashed all over daytime television. Although, he silently thanked Jess, once again, for her insistence that her afternoon chat show cover this 'human interest' story.

Fucking human interest.

Nate scrubbed a hand over his face and groaned. He was so damned tired.

'You alright, mate?' the driver asked, looking at him through the rear-view mirror.

'Yeah,' Nate sighed. 'Shit, watch out!' he cried, because

there was a big green tractor bursting through a gap in the hedgerow, straight onto the road in front of them.

'Shit!' the driver shouted, slamming on the brakes.

Nate was thrown against his seatbelt as the car skidded, his phone flying from his hand.

'You okay?' The driver turned to check that Nate wasn't injured.

'Yeah.' He nodded.

Who the hell was that? Why were they driving that tractor like a maniac in the pouring rain?

'Oi! What are you doing?' The driver had the window down and obviously had the same thought as Nate had.

It was raining so hard, he could only make out two splodges in the cab of the tractor, but then one climbed down. One with a black dress on and long brown hair.

Nate launched himself out of the car because it was Laurel, standing there in the middle of the road, in the pouring rain.

His Laurel.

'Where are you going?' she called over the hammering of the rain on the tractor and the car. Why wasn't she wearing a coat, a hood? She would catch her death being out here in just that flimsy cotton dress.

'I'm going to Jess and Owen's to give you some space,' he said, his voice hoarse.

She was beautiful. Tired and exhausted. But beautiful.

He took a cautious step forward, not caring that he hadn't done up the zip of his jacket, and the front of his shirt was saturated.

'Are you coming back?' she asked.

He made a mirthless laugh.

'I don't want to pressure you, Laurel.'

It was her turn to take a step forward, into a puddle, but she didn't seem to notice.

'You didn't know,' she said. It wasn't a question. It was a revelation.

'I didn't know.' He gave a tight smile.

'I'm sorry, Nate, I should have listened to you, I should

have let you explain. I was just so hurt, so upset. I thought you'd betrayed me. I didn't,' she stuttered, 'I couldn't.'

He was a few steps in front of her, but he couldn't close that gap, wrap his arms around her and bury his face in her hair. No, he had to wait for her. He'd laid himself bare on television. It was up to her now.

'Did you mean it?' There was barely concealed hope in her eyes, and his chest bloomed with heat.

'Yes,' he rasped. 'I meant it. I'm in love with you, Laurel Fletcher.'

Laurel's throat bobbed in a swallow, and the tears on her cheeks mingled with the rain still falling hard from the sky.

She took a deep breath.

'If you need to go, then go.'

Nate drooped. This was it, where his heart was pressed into nothing and was overtaken by the void in his chest.

'But come back, because I love you, Nate Daley.'

Nate looked at her blankly. She wanted him to come back? Because she loved him? She loved him, like he loved her.

A crooked, nearly desperate smile blossomed on her face. She was waiting for him, but all he could do was stand there, watching the rain fall on her.

Laurel Fletcher raised her hand and held it out to him, raindrops dripping off her fingers.

Nate's face split into a grin and he strode forward, grabbing her hand and letting her pull him to her.

'I'm so sorry I didn't talk to you, I'm sorry,' she was muttering, but he didn't care. Laurel was crying, and he pushed the soaked tendrils of hair out of her face and wiped her cheeks.

'Can you kiss her so we can all get back inside, please?' Robin shouted from the cab of the tractor, bundled up against the weather.

Nate cupped her face and did just that, crushing his lips to hers as she wound her arms around his neck.

It was them, together.

Laurel and Nate, Nate and Laurel.

CHAPTER TWENTY-THREE

EPILOGUE - 10 MONTHS LATER

LAUREL

Laurel stood in the conference centre at Little Willow Farm, tightly gripping Nate's elbow.

'What if they don't like me?' she asked, pulling at her slightly too tight dress to adjust it. Again.

'They will love you, Laurel,' Nate whispered, trying to loosen the grip she had on his arm.

But what if they didn't? What if they laughed at them, laughed at her? She only had a degree. She wasn't a doctor like Nate, and she had never, ever published anything. Let alone something with so much media interest.

Jess had been right: human interest sells. The media had been all over them both since the day his declaration of love had been aired, wanting an update, wanting a happily ever after. It was a classic take of girl fancies boy, boy's friend steals her work and publishes it with said friend as his own, boy meets girl ten years later, falls in love, boy's friend's duplicity is discovered, girl feels betrayed, and boy announces his love on national television.

But apparently, people were invested and that was good, because Little Willow had never been as busy as it was now. Ever.

The conference centre was booked months in advance, they were full every weekend throughout the spring and summer for weddings. The cafe was expanding into home delivery veg boxes, meat boxes, and even some restaurant supply. The Pick Your Own was still closed, but reviving.

Sylvie headed up on stage, absolutely rocking the tight midi skirt and heeled boots that she had taken to wearing with her new job as Deputy Manager. Laurel hadn't the time so much anymore, not since Nate had persuaded her, not that it took much persuasion, to take a Masters in archaeology part-time. Of course, so she could still have oversight of the farm.

Giving more responsibility to Sylvie had been a steep learning curve for Laurel. Letting go of some of her need to be in control of everything was hard. But Sylvie was amazing. Here were cameras on her, and an awful lot more people here than when Nate and Alex had presented the Anglo-Saxon finds at Little Willow, but Sylvie's voice didn't waver once. Pride bloomed in her chest.

'So, without any further ado, I would like to introduce Dr Nate Daley and Laurel Fletcher.'

There was applause as Nate led Laurel up to the stage.

'Come on, they're waiting for us,' he said, smiling down at her.

Laurel reached up onto her toes and kissed him.

'No surprises, like the last time you were on TV?' she murmured.

Nate breathed out a laugh.

'No surprises,' he assured her.

'Okay, let's go,' she said, slipping her hand into his and tugging him up the steps to the stage.

Laurel accepted the microphone from Sylvie, and Nate grabbed the spare one from the table.

'Thank you all for coming today. I'm Dr Nate Daley,' he said.

'And I'm Laurel Fletcher.' She let him take the lead.

'She is, but one day, I'm hoping she'll be Laurel Daley,' Nate said. The audience tittered.

Laurel's eyes widened and her mouth dropped open. Nate shot her a smug wink. She rubbed her belly gently.

No surprises, indeed.

ACKNOWLEDGEMENTS

I love reading authors acknowledgements and was so excited to write my own, and then I had to actually sit down and write them. I'd heard that acknowledgements were the hardest things to write, but I didn't believe it. How hard can they be? Answer, very hard.

There are so many people to thank, so many people who have helped make this book a reality. Firstly, thank you to all at Kate Nash Literary Agency, but especially my Super Agent, Saskia, who took a chance on me as a debut author, championed my story and held my hand throughout the entire process (still holding my hand, literally right now whilst typing this).

A massive thank you to Olivia at Serendipity and everyone at Legend Press for putting up with my 'non high maintenance'-ness. Thanks for loving *Carbon Dating* as much as me, and making my little author dreams a reality. A big thanks to Bailey Designs Books for creating the cover of my heart!

I need to thank Emilie Tumulty, my best across the pond writing friend, for reading every single draft, laughing and crying with me and being there with me every step of the way. We're doing it baby!! GOOD.

Thanks to Karen and Alex, who have been so supportive (except when taking the piss, and calling me Penelope Tulips). Ann and Vicki – you ladies keep me in fits of laughter with those voice notes. I don't know what I'd do without you mofos!

Thanks to Kit for coming up with the most ridiculous titles, and to Owen and Pauly for letting me nick your names.

Thank you to my force of nature best friend, my biggest cheerleader, and all round spectacular human being, Gemma, who has been excited to read everything I've written over the last ten years. Thanks for letting me be part of your life.

Of course, thanks to Mum and Dad for always buying me books and encouraging me to do whatever I want. Thanks to my sisters, Lizzi and Catherine, who are always so excited for me, whatever I do.

Thanks to Luke and Lauren – I hope I can keep on making you proud, and no, you can't read it until you're older. Thanks to Dave, my Hero Husband (no, I don't want feedback), who stands next to me in whatever random stuff I choose to do. Your support is everything, and I love you.

And to you, Dear Reader, who has taken the time to read my little story. I hope you love Nate and Laurel as much as I do. See you next time!